PRAISE FOR
A SOLDIER'S
SECRET

★ "A female Civil War soldier is brought alive for readers. . . .
Moss convincingly but never gratuitously portrays the gore,
horror and boredom of war. An intimate look at a soldier's life
from a compelling, historical perspective."

—*Kirkus Reviews*, starred review

★ "A captivating piece of YA historical fiction."

—*Publishers Weekly*, starred review

"Moss combines fiction with biography in this compelling
account. . . . Many battles are graphically described, and the
novel is crammed with atmosphere and detail."

—*Bay Area News Group*

"Whether a valiant soldier or angel of mercy, Sarah is a brave
and loyal historical figure, well deserving of readers' attention."

—*School Library Journal*

"Moss' novel offers a fascinating, first-person portrait."

—*Booklist*

"The novel is well-written, vividly capturing the drama of
Edmonds' story as well as larger wartime realities."

—*Library Media Connection*

AMULET BOOKS
NEW YORK

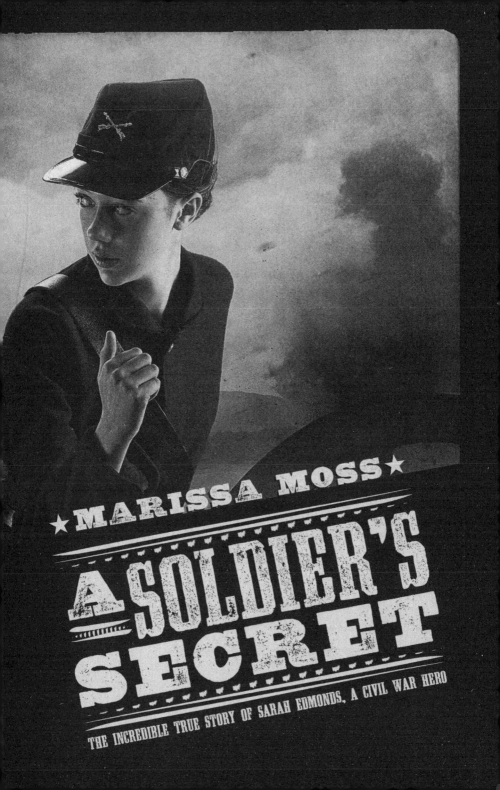

★MARISSA MOSS★

A SOLDIER'S SECRET

THE INCREDIBLE TRUE STORY OF SARAH EDMONDS, A CIVIL WAR HERO

The Library of Congress has catalogued the hardcover edition of this book as follows:

Library of Congress Cataloging-in-Publication Data
Moss, Marissa.
A soldier's secret : the incredible true story of Sarah Edmonds, a Civil War hero / by Marissa Moss.
p. cm.
Summary: Nineteen-year-old Sarah masquerades as a man during the Civil War, serving as a nurse on the battlefield and a spy for the Union Army, escaping from the Confederates, and falling in love with one of her fellow soldiers. Based on the life of Sarah Emma Edmonds.
Includes bibliographical references.
ISBN 978-1-4197-0427-7 (alk. paper)
1. Edmonds, S. Emma E. (Sarah Emma Evelyn), 1841–1898—Juvenile fiction. 2. United States—History—Civil War, 1861–1865—Women—Juvenile fiction. [1. Edmonds, S. Emma E. (Sarah Emma Evelyn), 1841–1898—Fiction. 2. United States—History—Civil War, 1861–1865—Women—Fiction. 3. Impersonation—Fiction.] I. Title.
PZ7.M8535So 2012
[Fic]—dc23
2012008319

ISBN for this edition: 978-1-4197-1032-2

THE ART OF BOOKS SINCE 1949
115 West 18th Street
New York, NY 10011
www.abramsbooks.com

{ FOR ELIAS, MY SOLDIER, MAY YOU COME HOME SAFELY.

CONTENTS

THE WAR BEGINS

"JUST A MINUTE THERE." THE RECRUITER STOPS ME AS I lean over to dip the pen in ink. "You can't enlist."

I freeze. Can he tell? I'm wearing a shirt, vest, and trousers as usual, my curly hair cut short except for a lock that insists on falling over my forehead. I brush it away nervously and meet the man's eyes. I've been passing for nearly three years now, but every new encounter still brings with it the same fear. I take nothing for granted. The key thing, I remind myself, is not to reveal anything, to act as normal as possible.

"I beg your pardon," I say as if I haven't heard him clearly. I keep my voice calm and low, pushing down the panic that's bubbling up inside me.

"I know you love your country," the man says kindly, "but you need to grow up a bit before you join the army." He looks at my peachy cheeks, free of any sign of a whisker. "We aren't taking sixteen-year-olds."

"But . . ." I start to protest, relieved and frustrated at once.

"By the time you're old enough, son, this war will be over. Now go on home." The recruiter takes the pen and passes it to the unshaven farmer behind me. Sure, he has plenty of stubble, whiskers to spare.

My ears burn red with shame. I'm nineteen, plenty old enough, but with my soft skin and large brown eyes, I look more boy than man. There's no way for me to prove my age, no way to show my mettle. I want to argue—even if I were sixteen, I should be able to enlist. After all, three years ago, when I really was that age, I got my first real job, the kind that pays every week, the kind that earns good money.

I'd been doing odd jobs, chopping kindling, harvesting hay, nothing regular, going from town to town, when I ended up in Hartford, Connecticut. I admired the handsome main square with whitewashed buildings and maple trees all around it, all ordered and comfortable-looking. I walked around the courthouse, the school, the dry-goods store, wondering what kind of job I could find, when a sign in a window caught my eye. The neatly lettered placard advertised for a traveling book salesman. That sounded like mighty fine work to me—getting to read all the books I wanted, roaming around to sell them, never staying in any one place for long. What could be better? I didn't wait but strode right in and introduced myself to the stout, jowly man with thick pork-chop sideburns behind the counter.

"I'm Frank Thompson," I said, extending my hand, "the salesman you need." I looked him in the eye, man to man, the way I'd taught myself.

The pork-chop man took my hand, chuckling. "Well," he drawled, "you sure have the confidence of a salesman." And that was how I met my new boss, Mr. A. M. Hurlburt, of W. S. Williams & Co., Booksellers. He hired me on the spot, asking me to supper that night with his family to seal the deal.

I was surprised how comfortable I felt sitting at that table, surrounded by Mr. and Mrs. Hurlburt and their six children. The youngest was a small babe, the oldest a freckle-faced twelve-year-old. They shared jokes and sto-ries, asked my opinion of everything from politics to player pianos. I'd never been treated that way—like a promising young man, someone with energy and wit whose company they enjoyed. I didn't know what to talk about, so I found myself describing the personalities of horses and cows. I knew animals much better than people then. At first, I felt foolish, but the five boys, ages four, six, eight, ten, and twelve—they must have scheduled their births to have them so neatly arranged—laughed and begged for more.

"That's horses, but how about mules?" asked the eight-year-old. "What kind of character do they have?"

I glanced at Mr. Hurlburt. Had he had enough of this foolishness? He smiled at me and nodded.

"Go on, now, Frank, don't keep the boys waiting."

I dabbed at my mouth with my napkin. Maybe I was good at this, telling stories. At least to young folk. "Well, then," I began, "there's the flirtatious mule, the one with small feet, a nicely trimmed tail, and perked-up ears. You know the kind—he tosses his head, skips, and prances, thinks himself a pony, he does. He would practically stand on his head if you flattered him enough."

Sam, the towheaded twelve-year-old, giggled, "I know that mule—that's Mr. Harper's!"

"Then there's the hysterical mule." I was warming up, saying things off the top of my head, giddy at being listened to. "That one is melodramatic, bucking and rearing, kicking out viciously until the harness is taken off, then shaking his head smugly since he's gotten his way. This mule is best avoided if you don't want a big bite taken out of your arm."

"Oho!" said Peter, the ten-year-old. "We know that kind, too. The preacher has a mule just like that!"

"Finally, there's the woe-is-me mule." I paused to swallow a mouthful of potato. "He's the thinnest, smallest, weakest creature you've ever seen. His whole appearance, from his drooping ears to his bedraggled tail, is a picture of meek misery. He wants you to feel guilty for putting even the weight of a pat of butter on his swaying back."

"That's the mule Pa's going to give you to take on the road, selling books!" Sam guffawed. "That's Joe-Joe, isn't it, Pa?"

Mr. Hurlburt cleared his throat. "I have no intention of

foisting poor Joe-Joe on Frank. He needs a horse for this job, not a mule. If you tell stories like these to your customers, I'm sure you'll make a lot of sales. Just make sure you're describing the books, not animals."

I blushed, looking down at my plate. "Of course, sir, I'll do my best."

And I did. Having grown up with only the Bible to read, I wolfed down the stock of books Mr. Hurlburt sold until I could describe each story so enthusiastically to my customers, I rarely missed a sale. In fact, I don't mind boasting that I was the best salesman the company had had in its thirty years in business, and I wore the fine suits and hats to prove it. Now I could even afford to drive my own horse and buggy—which made me a dashing figure to the young ladies. I swear the way to a girl's heart is through a fellow's purse. I could see how my clothes and buggy impressed them. What did they care if I couldn't grow a thick mustache or prickly beard?

I loved my job, traveling from Connecticut to Ohio, from Nova Scotia to New York, enjoying the changing landscapes, the new faces, so different from my life before, when I was pretty much stuck on the farm with an annual outing to the river for laundry day. My childhood had been closed in, confined, with animals for my best friends. Now I met lots of folk, and whenever I was back in Hartford, I had supper with the Hurlburts. I was part of a bigger world.

I admit I was nervous at the first house I called on,

worried that the woman who opened the door would see through my disguise. But she didn't. Instead, the farmer's wife thanked me for calling on her. She said I was "a charming young man" and bought a subscription to an adventure serial. Just like that. Each door I knocked on, it was the same thing. No one blinked an eye. I presented myself as Frank Thompson, bookseller, and that's how folk saw me. And the more I read, the more I learned from the books I carried, the better I did at selling. I loved the frontier-pioneer stories best, and often I'd end my sales call with the whole family circled around me, drinking in my descriptions of sagebrush deserts with towering orange mesas or amazing but true histories of settlers clashing with Indians. The better I told the story, the more books I'd sell. It got so I could tell how much folk would order by how hard they listened.

I'd read more books and traveled more widely in the last three years than the previous sixteen, ending up in Flint, Michigan, when my boss offered me a new territory. The West! That was where the best stories happened—I wanted to travel all the way to Texas! I thought I'd get there selling books. Then something happened that changed my mind. And my life.

It's the spring of 1861, and President Abraham Lincoln has called for 75,000 volunteers to fight in the new Union army and return the seceding Southern states to the Union. Large posters paper the walls of towns calling on us to prove our PATRIOTISM AND LOVE OF COUNTRY, and DEFEND OUR

NOBLE UNION. When I see those words, I don't hesitate. I join the long line of men snaking around the Flint courthouse, caught up in the shared frenzy of patriotism. I jostle elbows with farmers, mill workers, and clerks, some young, some not, all eager to give back to our country. Women and children bustle along the line, encouraging us. One old missus hands out fresh-baked biscuits, "to fuel us for the fight ahead," she says. Another passes out handkerchiefs she's made from a bedsheet, eager to contribute to the cause. I've never seen anything like it, this coming together of people into a charged-up community, all part of something big and important, a moment in history. I don't know how long the war between the states will last, but I want to help for however long it takes. How many times does a person get the opportunity to be part of history? For most, the chance never comes. I'm not going to miss mine.

When the recruiter sends me away that day, it's the first time I don't measure up as a man—just when it matters most. I would trade all the church socials with young ladies, all the box picnics with giggling girls, for that stranger's respect. I'm used to being taken at my word, and to be labeled a wet-behind-the-ears boy is plain insulting. Worse, it's keeping me from playing the role I'm meant to have. I had a giddy taste of doing something that really matters during that hour in line when the townsfolk cheered us on. And now I'm rejected, unworthy of the biscuit I've eaten, undeserving of the handkerchief tucked in my pocket.

When the first group of men leaves for Fort Wayne, Indiana, for the basic training that will turn farmers into soldiers, I join the crowd of well-wishers seeing them off. I cheer with everyone else, but watching the women wave their handkerchiefs in farewell, I'm disgusted with myself. I don't want to be like them, stuck at home, while the men take the risks and fight the battles. I want to be one of those marching away, not one of those sniffling a teary good-bye.

A month later, another chance comes. The first recruits signed up for a three-month commitment, but they've barely started basic training when the federal government realizes it needs more men, ones who can freely give at least three years of their time. The patriotic posters go up again, this time offering $600 for the first two years of service. That's more money than most folk make, a tradesman's salary, so I expect an even bigger crowd this time. Maybe among so many I won't stand out as much. I haven't miraculously grown whiskers, but I line up once again outside the court-house anyway.

This time the recruiter barely glances up. "Another boy," he mutters, shaking his head. He's probably already signed up a dozen gangly teenagers—the youngest I saw in line can't have been more than fourteen. All he cares about is whether I can read and write. The way he stares at my soft hands, the recruiter can see I'm educated. No farm boy has palms free from calluses, no mill worker has fingernails so clean.

"Yessir." I nod. "I can read and write. And I'm not afraid of blood. I want to work as a nurse."

"You'll see plenty of blood, all right," the recruiter says, sighing. "We need field nurses. It's not a popular job. Not many fellers have the stomach for it." He looks like he's wondering if I will, with my soft, coddled skin. Every country boy has seen his share of slaughtered cows and pigs, but he takes me for a prissy city boy who doesn't know what blood and guts are. "You'll find out soon enough if you can take it," the recruiter says as he hands me the pen.

I sign my name with a flourish, grinning. I've done it—I'm Private Frank Thompson in Company F, Second Michigan Volunteer Infantry of the Army of the Potomac.

The recruiter shakes my hand, wincing at my firm grip. "Welcome to the army, son," he says. "You just passed the physical."

2

YOU'RE IN THE ARMY NOW

I CAN'T STOP GRINNING AS I JOIN THE LINE TO THE
supply tent set up behind the courthouse. I collect a uniform,
a blanket, boots, a canteen, a rifle, and a Bible. Opening the
pages, I read the inscription: "My men, put your trust in the
Lord, and keep your powder dry." I like that kind of advice,
spiritual and practical at once, but I don't need it to feel
inspired. The air crackles with excitement. Men laugh and
joke about how we'll send the Southern Rebels home before
supper. We swap stories and wild rumors, pausing only long
enough to take the oath of service. It's my first day in the
Army of the Potomac, and I feel completely at home. Much
as I loved being a traveling salesman, it's been a lonely life.
I like breaking bread with hundreds of people, sharing a
common purpose, having constant company.

Then I see the tent I've been assigned to, and next to
it my tentmate. I have to share a tent, sleep with someone
else in the same tight space? Where am I going to change

my clothes? How can I hide what has to be hidden? And why didn't I think of all this before I enlisted? I was swept up in the excitement, worried only about getting past the recruiter, not about what came next. Now, meeting my tent-mate, I panic. I'm sure he can see right through me and is laughing at my stupidity.

Still, I make an effort to seem calm, normal, natural. "Frank Thompson," I squeak, introducing myself. "Seems like we're assigned this here tent."

The gangly blond engulfs my hand with his enormous paw and shakes it. "Damon Stewart. It's a pleasure to make your acquaintance. I'm sure we'll get to know each other real well, eating, sleeping, and drilling together. And sending those Rebs home with their tails between their legs!"

I nod, licking my dry lips, pulling my hand free from his knuckly grasp. I hope we don't get to know each other too well, but how much distance does a narrow tent allow? I swallow the lump in my throat. I'll figure out a way to pass. I have to.

For the first few months as a soldier, I work as hard figuring out how to stay clear of prying eyes as I do practicing drills. Since we all wash clothes only every few weeks, I can keep my bandaged breasts hidden under the shirt I always wear, changing only in the darkness of night when Damon is at the latrine. Myself, I huddle behind trees and shrubs to do my business instead of joining the line of soldiers pissing into the designated ditch. Each day that passes bolsters my confidence that I can do this. Damon treats me like his new best friend. No one else glances at me twice. I'm just another young, wiry recruit, one of thousands.

Washington has been transformed into an enormous garrison. One hundred thousand soldiers are camped in the city. Stacks of rifles crowd the rotunda of the Capitol Building and the lobby of the White House. Tents surround the unfinished Washington Monument and line the grounds of the White House. Soldiers march in drills, bugling and

GRAND REVIEW OF THE UNION ARMY, WASHINGTON, D.C.

drumming past once-sleepy neighborhoods. Senators push their way through ranks of soldiers to get into the Capitol. Once they shoulder their way in, they find recruits napping on their cushioned seats. The business of government grinds to a halt while the business of war takes over the city.

I've seen a fair number of towns in my travels, but nothing as big and elegant as this city, even bloated as it is now by endless rows of tents. The broad boulevards are as wide as rivers, lined by dignified trees set at regular intervals like sentries. The expansive distances and the cold marble buildings are intimidating, grander than anything in Flint. But it's the sight of the army that fills me with the most pride. I'm part of a grand adventure, no question about it.

And I want to play as big a part as possible. To my relief, no one questions my abilities as a soldier. I'm a better shot and horseman than the city boys, as good as the country ones. The only thing that sets me apart is my eagerness for hard work. Well, it's partly a need to work, partly a need to avoid the constant company of my fellow recruits. I like doing drills or eating meals in large groups. I even like cleaning rifles or patching clothes with other soldiers. But I hate the gambling and drinking. I hate the loud, rough talk, the fights over nothing, the lewd stories and jokes.

Which is how it seems to me most of the men spend their evenings. Even Damon, sweet as he is, can't resist a card game, and he has an impressive collection of bawdy stories he loves to share.

"Come on, Frank," he begs me. "You should see the special stereopticon this one soldier has. If you pay him a penny, you'll see scenes like you ain't never laid eyes on—I mean, curves, real curves! Bared for all to see!"

I feel my checks go hot and pink. "I'm really not interested, Damon. Besides, I have work to do. I'm helping out in the hospital tents." I hurry off to my refuge, going from bed to bed in the tents that house the many sick recruits. It isn't a quiet or restful retreat, but there's an order to the patients, to their care, that makes me feel I belong there. And there's no drinking, no salacious stories, no gambling, nothing to make me blush or cringe unless you count diarrhea and hairy bottoms that need wiping.

Not a single battle has been fought and there aren't any war wounds yet, but every bed is occupied. Men suffering from typhoid, cholera, dehydration, and sunstroke fill the wards. The army has no general hospitals, and most nurses are recovering patients themselves. I figure all I need is a strong stomach, like the recruiter said when he signed me on. If I can stand the stench and the gore, I'll do fine.

Anyway, I doubt I'll get the chance to become an experienced nurse. Like everyone else, I'm sure the war will be over quickly—after one battle, two at the most. Damon brags that he'll be home before the corn ripens on his farm.

"Tell me about your home," I ask him one afternoon after drills. It's a clear summer day, and some of the fellows have decided to go down to the Potomac River for a swim. I beg off, saying I don't know how, but it's pleasant sitting on the bank, watching the men splash around. I admire their lean, muscular bodies. Damon's lying on his stomach next to me, his white buttocks facing up like poached eggs. He's sleepy from exertion and sun, but he turns his face on his arm to answer me.

I'm asking partly out of curiosity and partly because I've learned that the best way to avoid questions is to ask them. Besides, I like to imagine what my life could have been if I'd been born someone else. And I like Damon. He's sweet and simple, with a broad, earnest face and a stubborn blond cowlick that make him look younger than his twenty-one years. He's docile and hardworking and honest. Of all the soldiers I could have shared a tent with, I'm lucky to have him for a partner despite his fondness for ribald jokes. Even those are quaint compared to the kinds of stories I hear other soldiers tell. Being around Damon makes me feel older and wiser, not boyish at all compared to his country innocence. And he's not the type to get suspicious, to notice things. He accepts me. More than that, he likes me.

"It's just a regular farm," says Damon, squinting up at me. "I'll tell you what's special about home—the girl I got waiting for me. As soon as I'm back, we're getting hitched. I can't hardly wait."

I try to smile. I know I should say something crude, tease Damon about his wedding night or something, but marriage isn't a joke to me. So I change the subject. "When do you think we'll head out? We've been sitting here for months. If you've got an army, aren't you going to use it?"

Damon nods. "Don't worry, we'll see battle soon enough. After all, you can't take a group of yahoos and turn them into disciplined soldiers overnight! But I think we're close to ready. And I've heard rumors . . ."

I prick up my ears. "What rumors?"

He lowers his voice, though there's no one around for miles but fellow soldiers. "I hear we're heading for Centreville, someplace between Washington and Manassas Junction, nearby in Virginia. The Confederate army is camped near there, just waiting for us." Damon chews on a piece of grass thoughtfully. "It'll be the first battle in this war. I'm guessing it'll be the last. I just hope I get a chance to see some action. I don't want all this training to be for nothing!"

I lie back on the grassy slope, my hands tucked behind my head. I try to imagine what a battle would be like, but I can't. I've seen bucks fight, their antlers clashing with heavy thuds, and dogs tear apart a raccoon in a chorus of growls and snarls. Once I even saw a mountain lion bring down a sheep. But those aren't anything like thousands of men facing each other with cannon and rifles.

"Frank, are you awake? Did you hear what I said?" Damon's voice cuts through my thoughts.

"Yeah, yeah," I murmur. "I heard you. I'm just thinking, wondering what it'll be like."

"No point in that," Damon says. "We'll find out soon enough."

For once the rumor turns out to be true. The next day we're told we'll be heading out for Centreville, just as Damon predicted. That night I'm as excited as everyone else, eager to get moving, to do something, anything but sit around in camp and drill, drill, drill.

Tuesday, July 16, 1861, dawns bright and hot as regiment after regiment marches westward. Only, the yahoos haven't been turned into soldiers after all. At least, they don't act like a disciplined force. Men break ranks to pick blackberries or rest under trees. Some of them decide their ammunition is too heavy to lug, so they dump it by the side of the road. Others toss their canteens. I'm as green as everyone else, but I know better than to throw away anything that might come in handy. I might have soft skin like a city slicker, but growing up in the country taught me plenty. When I see the cartridges and canteens by the roadside, I'm plumb disgusted by the stupidity of those recruits and scoop them up, adding them to my own pack. Damon laughs at me for shouldering the extra weight, but I can't help it— Ma raised me not to waste a crumb.

Senators and townsfolk ride by in buggies with picnic lunches as if the battle will be an amusing spectacle. I don't know what the fighting will be like, but I doubt it's going to make for good entertainment. I don't understand why nobody seems to be taking the coming clash seriously. This isn't a berry-picking expedition, a stroll in the country, or a Fourth of July picnic. So why is everybody acting like it is?

A tall, skinny soldier from Flint walks alongside me. His name is Miles Tyler, and I've seen him at the post office in town, collecting his mail.

"I ain't got a good feeling about this, I sure ain't," Miles says. "What's everyone so blamed happy for?"

I'm relieved that at least one other person shares my fears. "I know we'll crush the Rebels. I know that. But can it really be so easy? Months and months of drilling and only a day of actual fighting?"

Miles wipes the sweat off his forehead. "It's hotter 'n hell here. You'd think that'd be enough to take the cheer out of folks, but no, they're frolicking in the fields like lambs. I don't get it. They take some kind of happy tonic or summat?"

Maybe it's the excitement of being on the move at last, the optimism of a quick defeat of the enemy, but spirits stay high—except for Miles's and mine. We worry and grumble together. "There's nothing to fret about!" Damon insists after the day's march has ended and we're hunkering around the fire for supper. "Unless you're worried we won't find the Rebs, hiding as they are. They're not eager to fight us—the closer we get, the farther back they scramble. Can't blame the sorry cowards!"

Damon turns out to be right again. After two days' marching and camping out, we close in on Centreville, only

STONE CHURCH AT CENTREVILLE, VA., USED AS A HOSPITAL FOR UNION TROOPS.

to learn that the Confederate troops have fallen back to the southwest of a high-banked stream called Bull Run. That means another night camping in preparation for battle the following day. But this time we'll finally face them. The Rebs aren't retreating anymore. They're waiting for us.

There's a different feeling in camp that night. This time we know we'll engage the enemy in the morning. No more berry picking, no more picnics. The air is charged with nervous excitement. I'm edgy but relieved. At least everyone's taking the coming fight seriously now, so seriously that three different soldiers ask me if they can have their canteens and shot back. Even Damon's not so brash anymore. He looks miserable as he writes in his diary.

I help set up the stone church at Centreville as a hospital to handle the wounded, unfolding row after row of cots,
piling up cloth for bandages, fetching water to clean wounds
with. It's mindless work and I want to exhaust myself so I'll
be able to sleep. Coming back into camp, I pass soldiers
cleaning their rifles or writing letters home. I join a young
boy with barely any beard leading a group huddled together
in prayer. I mouth the words, sing the hymns, but I don't feel
any safer, any closer to God. We're all trying to keep busy, to
fend off our fear. A thick blanket of somberness lies over the
camp. Maybe the yahoos are soldiers after all.

{3

BATTLEFIELD JITTERS

I TRY TO SLEEP, BUT MY THOUGHTS WON'T LET ME. AM I a soldier? Can I do this? Can I kill other men? Here I am, crammed into a camp with tens of thousands of men, about to fight tens of thousands of other men. The war seemed distant when we were training in Washington, but suddenly it's all too close. I'm terrified I won't measure up. I don't think I'm a coward, but you never really know that kind of thing about yourself until you're forced to face the truth.

I've been pretending for so long, maybe I'm lying to myself now, imagining that I have guts, that I'm like everyone else. The truth is, I don't know anybody like me. It's hard even now to admit what I've done.

Growing up on a farm in New Brunswick, Canada, I learned to handle a gun and a horse, working hard to please Pa. Edward, my sickly, weak brother, disappointed him, so I tried to do everything Edward couldn't. My two older sisters were married, living away from home with their angry, brutish husbands, which left just me and Edward to help out Pa. Of course, Ma was there too, but her chores were women's work—milking the cows, tending the vegetables, cleaning, and cooking. When Edward was feeling poorly, he'd stay with Ma, hoeing the weeds from between the peas, churning butter, fetching water from the well. I'd be out hunting or plowing or breaking in the new colt while he was planting potatoes.

I thought that would make Pa respect me, and maybe it did, but not enough to show it. He wasn't much for praise, so I didn't expect that, just a grudging acknowledgment that I did my work well, that I contributed to the homestead. Now that I think back on it, I can see that he relied on me, enough so that he didn't hit me the way he did Ma and Edward. All Ma had to do was put a slightly burned biscuit on his plate to get a slap across the face. And poor Edward, he could be sitting at the table, innocent as you please, and if Pa had banged the plow on a rock or if a horse had thrown a shoe, that was enough to earn my brother a clout on the ears.

"You useless son of a bitch," Pa growled in a typical outburst that came out of nowhere. "Eating my food! Wearing my clothes! Doing nothing but piddling women's work! What kind of a son are you?"

I watched, horrified, as silent tears ran down Edward's cheeks, and I swore to myself that I would never be as weak as him, that I would never let anyone treat me that way.

Ma rushed to Edward's defense. "He can't help it," she cried. "He does the best he can." Which earned her a rough slap across her chapped cheeks.

"Don't you sass me, woman! You're both a pair of useless ninnies!" A few more punches landed on both Ma and Edward until Pa had enough. He sat down and shoveled in his supper while Ma and Edward sniveled. Me, I tried to eat without looking at anyone, but my throat tightened up. I was suffocating in that house.

The only time I felt free was on my horse, Trig. I'd broken him myself, and we understood each other so well, I barely used the reins when we thundered through the woods, leaping over fallen logs, clearing streams in a soaring bound. He was all taut muscle, fierce and lean and fast. When I was astride him, I felt powerful, like nothing could touch me—not Edward's tears, not Ma's cringing, not Pa's bullying. I was part of a different world with Trig, a big, open place with vast skies and adventure in all directions, not the closed-in farmhouse where the air was sour with misery.

The evening after I turned fourteen, I was rubbing down Trig after a long day in the saddle shooting pheasants and partridges. The barn was peaceful with the sounds of hooves shuffling through straw, hay being chomped, a low snort every now and then. The light through the wide-open door was raking and low, sending shadows stretching into the corners. It was the hour of day I liked best, when chores were finished, my muscles sore and tired with the pleasure of work. I was alone with my best friend. I brushed Trig's gray dappled coat and whispered into his neck how much I loved him. He cocked his ear back listening, and I had to laugh at how attentive he was. No one on that farm knew me except him. No one trusted me the way he did. He would jump a ten-foot fence if I asked him to, sure that I knew what I was doing. And I trusted him.

Pa sauntered into the barn, breaking the magical spell of the place, smiling with liquor. "Ah, good, you're prettying him up, I see."

I hated Pa when he was in that kind of mood, one of boozy fake friendliness. He came close enough so that I could smell the whiskey on his breath as he patted Trig on the withers.

I pulled back, mistrustful. That was something Pa never did—he never touched anyone or anything with affection. There was a reason for his gesture, and I had a feeling it meant something awful.

"Yes, he's a fine horse. A fine horse," Pa announced, rocking back on his heels. "Worth a pretty penny, he is."

"Not that we would ever sell him of course," I said.

"Whyever not?" Pa chuckled, an ugly rasp. "Of course I would sell him—for the right price." He reached into his pocket and pulled out a wad of bills. "And this is the right price. Can you believe what stupid Old Man Ludham paid for a horse?"

"I can't believe you sold him! He's my horse—mine! You

didn't even ask me!" I choked back angry tears. "You'll give the money back. You have to!"

Pa's eyes hardened into chips of coal. "He's my horse! Everything on this farm is mine, you included." He hauled back his fist. I dodged the blow, catching it on my shoulder instead of my face. "Think you're so high and mighty, do you? Think you got any say around here!" I tried to run past him, but Pa's a big man and I was only fourteen. He grabbed me by the neck and started to choke me. I kicked at him, flailed wildly with my arms, but I was no match for his weight and muscle. He held me down with one hand and with the other hit me so hard, I could hear my nose crack. The fight drained out of me then, and I lay there in the dirty straw, blood streaming out of my nose while I watched Pa put a halter on Trig and lead him out of the barn.

"Say good-bye to your precious horse then," he sneered.

I squeezed my eyes shut tight and stayed that way until I couldn't hear footsteps or hoofbeats anymore. I swore I'd never let him hit me again. If I couldn't get big, at least I'd get strong and do whatever it took so that nobody ever had that kind of power over me. When I opened my eyes, the barn was filled with dark shadows. The sun had gone down and a chill crept into my bones. But I was damned if I'd set foot in Pa's house, eat at his table, sleep in his bed. Instead, I climbed into the hayloft, curled up with the cats, and spent the night in the barn. I slept there for three months, until the snows came and it got too cold even for me. But the house was never my home after that. I was biding my time, waiting until I was old enough to escape. I didn't say another word to Pa, either. He'd broken more than my nose that evening. He'd broken any bit of family feeling I'd had—any connection there had been between us was destroyed. I'd lost Trig, and I felt all alone in the world.

Shame rushes through me, thinking of how I didn't fight back then, how I let Pa stomp on me. Will I have the guts to fight back now? Sure, I'm older, bigger, stronger, but am I brave? I look over at Damon, asleep beside me. I don't want to let him down, to let myself down. I clench my fists so tightly, the fingernails dig into my palms. Tomorrow's my chance to prove myself, to make up for years of cowering in front of Pa. I have to fight the Rebels the way I never dared fight him. After all, I remind myself, releasing my fists, now I have a gun. You don't need muscle to be daring with a rifle. I'm a good shot, and that's all that matters. Tomorrow I'll prove myself to be a real man.

{4}
THE BATTLE
OF BULL RUN

THE SKY LOOMS CHILL AND DARK, NO LONGER NIGHT but not yet day, when the order comes for our regiment to join General Samuel P. Heintzelman's Third Division. There's no time left to wonder what battle will be like. Every muscle in my body tenses, and every sound seems magnified to my anxious ears. The tramp of thousands of feet, the creaking of the artillery wheels, the wind rustling the grasses, the croaking of frogs, all rumble loudly in the summer stillness. Column after column of blue uniforms weaves ahead of me, snaking along the green hills, through the valley hazy with morning dew. One division heads south toward Manassas, while the two other divisions, including ours, swing north to head off the Confederates near the stone bridge crossing Bull Run.

The thundering roar of our cannon stuns me, echoing all the way to the soles of my feet. I've never heard anything so terrible, so full of doom. Damon, standing next to me, grabs

CONFEDERATE FORTIFICATIONS, MANASSAS, VA., FOR THE FIRST BATTLE OF BULL RUN.

my arm. I flinch as always when someone tries to touch me. For a second I worry he'll think I'm a coward. The truth is, I might be.

"That's our boys! We hit 'em before they even fired a shot! I knew it!" He grins, pointing toward the Confederate forces looming behind earthworks built up from the steep shore on the other side of the stream. Shooting up at an enemy doesn't look like an easy prospect to me. I know from hunting that you want to be above your prey, not the other way around. My stomach twists with sour fear. This isn't going to be the easy victory everyone predicted. It's going to get ugly, and soon.

A sharp whistle screeches overhead, and before I can duck or react, a shell explodes behind me. After that, I'm not a soldier—I'm a nurse. I don't think about what I'm supposed to do. I just race to the center of the explosion, where a man lies broken in a pool of his own blood. I recognize the battered face of the young recruit who led the prayer service the night before.

"Don't die on me," I beg. "I'm getting you back to the hospital." I cradle his head in my lap, but it's too late. His blue eyes stare lifeless in their sockets. I set his head back down gently on the ground and close his eyelids. It's the least I can do. The Battle of Bull Run has just begun and I've already seen my first death. But it doesn't feel real— nothing feels real. I'm caught in a strange dream world where nothing makes sense.

The battle is a swirl of chaos: color and movement and the sharp crack of guns. I can't plan what to do. I can't think at all. I can only react. My mind shuts off and my body takes over. Whenever a man falls, I rush to his side. Often there's nothing I can do—I can't even allow myself the luxury of closing the corpse's eyes like I did for that first soldier. I need to save precious minutes for the living, for the times when I can drag soldiers to stretchers, help carry them away from the field, bandage them as best I can, then race to aid another fallen comrade. Running from body to body, I notice the sun filtering through the leaves casting lacy shadows. Deep-blue wildflowers carpet the ground. How strange, I think, that such a pretty place should be splattered with blood, torn up by shells. The blue of the petals, the red of the men's gaping wounds, all have a dreamlike intensity. I want to scream and wake up, but I can't. Instead, I simply become eyes, ears, hands, feet: a machine to help the wounded.

It's the first time the Army of the Potomac has seen battle, and it's a grisly sight for all of us. I see one recruit running away from the battle, screaming in terror. I see another hide behind a tree, shaking, eyes wide yet unseeing. I watch Damon pass the dead and dying and stop to vomit, sickened by the brutal wounds, the mangled bodies. Me, I don't pause, I don't think. I do my work. The strange image of Ma snapping the neck of a chicken comes to me, how calm and collected her face was as she twisted the life out of the bird. Now it's men having their bodies broken, but I feel the same iciness creep into me as when I watched the chickens die. I push down the bile rising in my throat and focus on the task at hand—not preparing a meal, but getting the wounded to safety.

The dead and maimed pile up, like sheaves of wheat. It's a bloody and abundant harvest, more and more bodies being added to those already writhing in pain or motionless in death. Still, we seem to be winning, and by the afternoon, the Confederate army falls back and renewed confidence surges through our troops as they rush forward, howling with rage and fierce energy.

I've been waiting for a break like this to get needed supplies and borrow a horse from a doctor to ride to Centreville, seven miles away, for brandy to clean wounds and ease the soldiers' pain and for more cloth to tear into bandages. It's the first time there's been a lull long enough for me to think about what's happened, what battle is actually like. I'm relieved that I didn't turn tail as so many others have, but have done my duty as nurse as well as the next man. I haven't even thought about needing to disguise myself. In fact, I haven't thought about myself at all. It seems strange to be grateful for something as horrible as a battle, but in an odd way I am—it's the first time I've been part of something so enormous and horrific, I don't matter at all. The only thing that counts is doing the job, helping the wounded, killing the enemy.

As I spur the horse on, I watch two Union batteries push forward, set to clear out the remaining Rebel stragglers. Riding away from the dead and dying, I am overcome by a rush of energy—the battle is almost over and we've actually won. We . . . *I* am part of this victory, and an unfamiliar sense of pride surges through me.

Except that's the moment Confederate reinforcements arrive. They cut down our blue vanguard in a rain of shots, shells, and cannon fire. The men scream like avenging furies, and the shrill Rebel yell, a mix between a fox-hunt call and a banshee shriek, makes the skin crawl on everyone who hears it. *"Ya-yoo-yoo-yoo, ya-yoo-yoo-yoo!"* screeches out of thousands of throats, terrifying our troops. I can't leave, now that the Rebels are mowing down our soldiers. It's a terrifying sight, a complete rout, but not the one we had expected. Panicked, men and officers throw down their arms and flee. The supply trains, artillery, dead, and wounded are left to the field while everyone who can retreats, rushing to get as far from the enemy as possible.

I don't understand what's happening. I can't find my regiment. Just moments ago, I was so sure of myself—now I'm mired in confusion. As I head for the battlefield, all I see are troops running away from it. I'm swept away with them in a current of panic, turning back in the direction I came from.

"Where are we going?" I call to a foot soldier next to me. "What are the orders?"

The soldier stares up at me, glassy-eyed. Then he turns away, without a word, and keeps on running.

"You, there!" I try someone else, a burly man with a gash on his forehead. "Where are the generals? What are the orders?"

"Retreat!" he shrieks. "Retreat!"

I'm not sure where I'm supposed to retreat to, but I don't want to join the mass panic, the crazed mob rushing from the field. I'm still a nurse, so I ride to the place where I know I'm needed, back to Centreville, where hundreds lie in agony, waiting for some kind of doctoring. I hear the church-turned-hospital before I see it—groans and moans and screams of pain. As I come nearer, I see the full horror of what war means. The churchyard stinks of death. Bodies are piled up like so much firewood. Next to them, heaps of amputated arms and legs make a grisly sight.

I tie up my horse and head inside among the living, where it's even uglier. There's no trace of the neat rows of cots I arranged the night before. There's simply a mass of bodies, some on beds, some on the floor, some writhing and moaning, some as still as death. I've never seen such suffering—men whose bodies are crushed and mangled, wild with pain; others who lie smothered in hopelessness and panic and blood. And there's nothing I can do for them except press a cool cloth to their feverish faces or dribble some water down a parched throat.

"You, there, nurse!" a doctor yells at me. "Help me with this man. Hold him down now. I've got to cut off his leg."

I lean forward, putting all my weight into my arms as I hold down the slender man, his face white with pain. I look into his eyes, willing myself not to see the doctor take the saw and start hacking right above the knee. The soldier howls an ungodly sound that pierces deep into my gut. Then he faints, mercifully unaware of the dreadful sound of blade on flesh and bone.

Once again, I shut off my thoughts and feelings. I'm a water bearer, a wound washer, someone to hold down a heaving chest and thrashing arms while a surgeon amputates yet another leg. I'm an ear to listen to last prayers, a

AMPUTATION BEING PERFORMED IN A HOSPITAL TENT, GETTYSBURG, PA.

kind face to smile and reassure young men crazed with the fear of death.

One soldier, his head swathed in a bandage, wheezes at me. "Please tell my mother I love her. And cut off a lock of my hair to give her. Please." I write down his name and address with trembling fingers and fold a lock of his clipped hair into the paper. I want to be a nurse, but I feel like an angel of death, taking down last requests from the bloody mouths of the dying. It's the only solace I can give.

The sun is setting and a drenching rain has started when the regimental chaplain rides up, his horse lathered in sweat.

"Everyone leave!" He cups his hands and bellows through them. "The Union army is gone, back behind the Potomac River. Centreville is surrounded by the Confederates!"

The army has abandoned us, left the wounded to be taken as prisoners? I hurry outside, searching for any sign of a blue uniform in the fading light. My horse has been taken in the panic, so I walk down the road a ways to see what's going on.

It's true, the army is gone. But there are wounded men who still need me. I turn back to the church. Only what about the Rebel army? They're closing in—I feel it in my gut. Where are they?

The answer gallops up as I melt into the shadows by the side of the road. A group of gray-uniformed horsemen appears.

I crawl behind a bush and wait, my heart pounding noisily. I'm sure the Rebel soldiers can hear my panicked gasps, so I hold my breath as they pass by. I stay frozen in my hiding place beside the road until my muscles are stiff. When it seems safe, I shake out my legs and rush back to the makeshift hospital.

The church is dark when I get there. The chaplain has left with the doctors and other nurses. The wounded men lie groaning with thirst and despair. They know they will be taken prisoner and there's nothing they can do about it. Anyone who could walk or ride is already gone. Those who are left are too maimed or weak to move. I go from cot to cot, offering water, the only thing I have left to give. I can't leave them. I won't.

"You have to go," one soldier rasps. "We're dying anyway."

"Go!" seconds another. "You can't help us once the Rebels get here."

It's Miles, the soldier I marched next to on the way to Bull Run. He lies with two bandaged stumps where his legs used to be. I take his hand and shake my head. "I can't abandon you."

"The doctor didn't want to leave, but he did. We told him to," Miles insists. "He worked like the devil to save us, but he couldn't, you see. He couldn't and you can't, either. So go, please go. The Rebels are coming. It won't be long." He drops his head back, exhausted by the effort of so many words.

I blink away tears. He's right. There's nothing more I can do for any of them. I'm failing them, failing myself. Miserable, I set out canteens within the reach of any man who still has arms to hold one and turn toward the door when a voice calls me back. A young officer from Massachusetts holds out a gold locket.

"Open it, please," he gasps. "I can't."

I flip the locket open, revealing a sepia daguerreotype of a woman holding a small baby. "You have a beautiful family," I soothe, handing it back to him.

He nods and presses the picture to his lips, tears streaming from his tightly closed eyes.

"Tell them I'll always love them. Tell them . . ." His voice drifts off weakly as he shoves the picture back at me and closes his eyes.

"I will, I promise." Is he still alive to hear me? There's no time to check for a pulse on the still, pale body. I write down his name on a scrap of paper and tuck the locket away as the clatter of hooves echoes from the road. If I'm going to leave, it has to be now.

I slip into the darkness, away from the main road. As I climb fences and zigzag across fields, I remember playing hide-and-seek with my brother and sisters in the woods around the farm. I tell myself it's only a game, like then, an innocent, easy game. I try to push the ugly images of the day out of my head, the horrors of what men can do to each other, and think about nothing but moving one foot in front of another.

{5

BACK IN WASHINGTON

IT'S MIDDAY, THE SUN BRIGHT AND HOT OVERHEAD, BY the time I limp into the capital, two days later, my feet sore with blisters, my clothes drenched in sweat. I stand for a moment, wavering, taking in the neat rows of tents. Relief washes over me—I'm back where I belong. But I can't stop thinking of those left behind, either dead now or prisoners. Beyond the tents, the Confederate flag flaps in the breeze over Munson's Hill, a reminder of how close the enemy is. The Rebel army, fueled by their victory at Bull Run, seems poised to attack Washington. I try to push it down, but the despair of defeat wells up inside me as I stand there, too tired and dispirited to take another step.

"Frank! We thought you were dead! Oh, it's good to see you." Damon runs up to me and claps me on the back. "I thought for sure you were a goner."

I force a smile but my cheeks feel wooden. "It's good to see you, too, Damon. It wasn't as quick as we thought, was it?"

Damon laughs uneasily. "Nope, sure wasn't. I learned me a lesson but good. Still, we're both breathing, with all our arms and legs, so there's reason to be thankful." He folds his arm protectively around me. "You look like you just came from hell. Let me show you where our tent is and you can rest up. I'll bring you some pea soup and bread."

Normally I avoid any touch, but it's a comfort to let myself be led through the rows of tents, and I lean into Damon's shoulder until he stops in front of one, lifts up the flap, and helps me inside. I sink onto my cot, feel the weight of my exhaustion cover me, and I sleep.

I wake up late the next day, my head throbbing, every muscle in my body stiff and aching. I blink, trying to remember where I am, what has happened. Then I see Damon is in the tent with me, his forehead wrinkled in worry.

"Good to see you awake, Frank. You were fit for the hospital yourself when you got in. Here," he says, offering a plate of bully beef. "It's not hot no more, but I expect that don't matter much to you."

It's strange—after so many years holding myself apart from people, isolated by my secret, a rush of affection for Damon overwhelms me. I can't recall the last time anyone has been this kind and gentle with me. I remember Ma's cool palm pressing on my forehead whenever I was sick with fever, and tears well into my eyes.

"Thank you, Damon—you take good care of me," I murmur.

Damon's cheeks turn pink. "You'd do the same for me! We're in this together, Frank."

While I bolt down the food, Damon catches me up on the news. The battle was every bit as disastrous as I feared. Now with the Rebels camped just southwest of Arlington, Washington is girding for a fight in the capital itself. There have been minor skirmishes between the pickets—advance guards for each camp—but nothing worse so far. Everyone's nerves are on edge, waiting for the blast of Confederate cannon, the rush of gray uniforms, or the eerie Rebel yell.

I feel queasy. I never for a second thought the Union could actually lose the war. Could it all be over so quickly, with the South triumphant?

And I haven't even shot at the Rebels, my rifle slung uselessly over my shoulder the whole time. I was so busy working as a nurse at Bull Run, I forgot to be a soldier. Now I chew my lip, angry at myself for not doing my share, for not helping to defeat the enemy. I abandoned the wounded in the church and I didn't kill a single Confederate. I want another chance—now.

"We should attack them first, before they come at us," I growl.

Damon grins. "That's the spirit! Too bad you're not a general. Privates don't get to tell the army what to do. We're supposed to sit tight and drill and drill and drill, so that when we do fight again, we'll win."

I nod, but I'm not good at waiting, and practicing drills

isn't enough to keep me busy. Guilt gnaws at me. I told the army I'm a soldier, but maybe I'm not one after all. I hear Pa's voice in my head, calling me useless, a ninny like my brother. I see Ma's eyes full of disappointment. And I imagine Edward curled up in the corner, trying to ward off Pa's blows. I didn't help him then and I'm not helping anyone now.

Working with the doctors is the only time I feel useful. When my official rounds are over, I go from hospital to hospital, checking to make sure everyone I know even remotely is all right, giving myself a second nursing shift. I'm touched by how the soldiers visit their wounded friends, how much they care for each other. The men may be crude or coarse, but they're brave and loyal in a way I'm not. These men love each other, would die for each other. There's nobody I care enough about to feel that way, nobody I would sacrifice myself for, nobody who feels that way about me.

I spend a day at the post office, packing up and sending out the keepsakes and letters the dying soldiers entrusted to me. I open the gold locket one last time before wrapping it in a cloth scrap and tucking it in an envelope. Before I seal it up, I add a note:

Dear Mrs. Robertson,

I was given the good grace to be with your husband before he succumbed to wounds received during the Battle of Bull Run. He was a valiant soldier, fearless and strong, who gave his most precious gift, his life, to preserve the Union of this great Nation. Before passing, your husband asked to see your likeness one last time and pressed the sweet image to his lips for a final precious kiss. He asked me to tell you that he loves you and your child forever, in spirit if not in body. May his memory be a blessing to you and may his sacrifice not have been in vain.

Yours truly,
Frank Thompson,
private, 2nd Michigan

I write many letters like this, to wives, sisters, mothers, and fathers. As often as I do it, the task never gets easier. Each time, I imagine the grief of the reader, the depth of the loss. But I'm also lifted by the love the dying man had for his family. It's an honor to be the messenger of such devotion. It's as close as I come to being part of a family.

And what if I died? Who would notify my parents? Nobody knows my real name. Nobody knows who my people are. Does it really matter? Would they weep for me or consider me a traitor they're well rid of? Either way, I'm surprised to realize I don't care. I shed that family the way a snake slips out of its skin.

Instead, I think about other families as I carry out the last wishes of dying soldiers. I track down kin and send off watches, lockets, hair clippings, rings, an array of personal treasures that will tumble out of the opened envelopes, telling the recipients, even before they began reading, that the news is not good, that this is a farewell letter.

When I get a package back from a stranger, my fingers tremble to open it. I never get mail. No one who knows me has any idea how to find me. Unfolding the letter, I read that it's from a grieving mother. She's sent me the socks she knitted for her now-dead son. I finger them, feeling the love that was woven into each stitch. When I put them on, my feet feel warm, caressed. I've never treasured anything as much as those socks.

A month has passed since the Battle of Bull Run, and the hospitals are as crowded as ever. The rushed retreat from the battlefield, through rain and mud, sent as many soldiers to sickbeds as the fighting itself. The doctors are both good and terrible. Some are gentle and patient, like

Dr. Caruthers, while others are brusque and cold, like Dr. Garner, who looks like a butcher carving up a side of beef instead of a surgeon removing an arm. Skill comes down to speed—being able to saw off a leg in less than thirty seconds. Then once the limb is gone, the real danger begins. The wounds often ooze green pus—a good sign according to the doctors—or turn black, a definite bad sign. Either way, the more the wound festers, whatever the color, the quicker the patient dies. The mercury balm we put on the cuts doesn't seem to help. Nothing does. It's pure chance who survives and who doesn't.

And the chances aren't good. For every man who dies in battle, two die from disease. If bullets don't kill them, then dysentery, typhoid, cholera, pneumonia, scurvy, or diphtheria do the job. But I refuse to give up hope for any of them and do my best to cheer up the patients, catching fresh eel in the nearby river for one old man when he asks for it, bartering for roasted chicken for another soldier when he tells me that's what he's craving. There's so little I can do for the gaping wounds and endless diarrhea, when there's something I can actually offer, I'm quick to do it. And maybe that's the best cure, offering hope and a familiar taste from home, like the fish a beloved wife used to cook or a mother's hoecake recipe.

So I offer sympathy and whatever treats I've been sent by the families grateful to hear their dead soldiers' last wishes. Since that first package of socks, I've received brandy, cakes, soap. Today it's a pie. Usually I share only with the patients, but this afternoon I'm touched by the sight of a dark-haired soldier holding the bandaged hand of his wounded friend so gently that he seems a nursemaid with a child.

"Would the two of you like some cherry pie?" I ask.

The visitor looks up, his eyes black with sadness. "Are you taking good care of my friend here?" he asks in turn. "Is he getting out of here soon?"

"Now, now, Jerome, you're not being polite. This is Frank Thompson, the best nurse around. He takes very good care of me. See, he even brings me pie—what could be better than that?" The wounded man winks at me. "Don't mind Jerome. He's tetchy when his friends get hurt. You'll never meet a more loyal soul."

"Oh, I don't mind him at all," I say. "I'd like to think I'd be the same way." I put a dish of pie in the patient's good hand, then give one to his friend. "I'm pleased to meet you, Jerome."

"I'm sorry, I didn't mean to be rude. I just hate hospitals." The visitor stands up and offers me his hand. "Jerome Robbins from Matherton, Michigan."

I take his hand and shake it. "Sounds like we're from the same neck of the woods. I'm from Flint."

Somehow that starts a conversation that lasts long into the night, from standing in line for supper to past moonrise. Jerome's a year older than me, a college student with a quiet, gentle manner. Despite his hatred of hospitals, he's been assigned to start nursing next week and he's dreading it.

"I don't know how you stand it, Frank, how you don't go crazy with nightmares," he confides. "I mean, you can't help these poor fellows anyway. Don't you just want to scream sometimes, it's all so ugly and unfair?"

I shake my head. "I don't think about it like that. Maybe I can't bring back a leg once it's been cut off, and I can't cure typhoid, but I can ease the pain a little, even if it's only the comfort of sending a last message home." How can I explain that, to me, nursing is better than shooting at the enemy? It sounds cowardly. But I feel a strange kinship with these broken men. They bring me as much comfort as I give them.

Jerome reaches over and rests his hand on my arm. "You're a good man, Frank. I wish I were more like you."

Something happens when he touches me, something I don't understand. I pull back, startled. My skin tingles where his fingers rested, and my stomach clenches. At first, I think it's because he called me a good man, a rare compliment. I blush to think that I look and act the part so well that I could be a model for someone.

I shift on the log we're sitting on, brushing away the sensation. I try to look at Jerome again, but I can't meet his eyes, so instead I stare at a spot above his left ear and say, "Don't worry, I'll help you out until you get used to the routine. I'll teach you to be a good nurse."

That night in the tent, I lie awake, trying to figure out what has happened. I've never met anyone like Jerome before, someone I can talk to so easily, someone who understands and appreciates me, an educated, literate man. That's it, I think, that's why I feel this way—Jerome is my first real friend. Damon's a buddy, a pal, but Jerome is someone I can open my heart to, tell the things I really care about. I haven't had a confidant since Trig was sold. And I've never had anyone who speaks to me like that. I sigh and close my eyes, warm and happy in a way I've never been before. I have a friend.

{6} FRIENDSHIP

FOR THE NEXT MONTH, JEROME AND I WORK LONG shifts at the hospital together, then take walks in the moonlight to clear our heads. We talk about everything—or almost everything: our childhoods, fears, and dreams for the future. I'm surprised by how much I confide. I tell him about Pa selling Trig. I even tell him I've run away. But I leave out the most important details. Those are things I can't tell anyone.

So this is the story I don't tell Jerome: After Pa sold Trig, I promised myself I'd leave, but I didn't. I couldn't. Two years passed and I was sixteen, more than old enough to set out on my own. Still, I clung to the security of the farm, to a life I knew, ugly as it was. I told myself I needed to stay to protect Ma and Edward, but I couldn't really help them. They would have peace only when Pa died or got so old he couldn't bully anyone anymore, like a miserable toothless dog.

If I had been able to stand up to Pa, maybe things would have been different. But I couldn't save Trig from being sold, and two years later I couldn't change Pa's mind about selling me.

He didn't call it selling, but it amounted to the same thing. When Pa told me I was getting married, it felt like he'd hit me in the stomach. I knew Pa wasn't giving me a choice. And it wasn't a joke. Pa never told jokes. We were at the supper table, and the first clue that something wasn't right came when Pa looked at me and smiled. I didn't notice at first because I kept my eyes on my plate as usual, but somehow the air felt thicker, the silence more charged than usual. I looked up to see both Ma and Edward staring at Pa, their faces tight with fear. So I followed their gaze and saw that it was me Pa was focused on, me he was grinning at with an evil, black-gummed smirk. The piece of ham I'd been chewing turned into gristle, and I forced myself to swallow it. I set down my knife and fork and met Pa's eyes, trying to look firm and brave, though inside I was quaking.

"Sarah," he bellowed, "I've got some wonderful news for you, I do."

I didn't say anything. If I didn't ask, he wouldn't tell me. Whatever it was wouldn't happen. I could stop it all just by staying quiet. Even as I told myself that, I knew it wasn't true. But my tongue was so heavy and wooden, I couldn't say anything even if I'd wanted to.

"Well, don't you want to know what your hardworking Pa has done for you? Don't you want to know the wonderful gift he's found for you?" His eyes hardened, drilling into me.

Minutes passed with me still silent and Pa's face blackening with rage.

"Well?" he roared. "You ungrateful brat!"

I nodded quickly, numbly. Best get it over with. There was no way to stop Pa, not once he'd started.

"That's more like it, you little bitch! Here's what I've done, and you'd best be on your knees with gratitude. I've found you a husband!" Pa paused, letting the news sink in.

"A husband!" he repeated. "Never thought I'd see the day! What man would want someone like you—a scrawny tomboy with nothing of a woman to her at all? I thought you'd live and die an ugly spinster, but no, miracles happen, I tell you."

Ma and Edward looked relieved at the news, but I was more horrified than ever. A husband? That meant a man who beat you, who yelled at you, who treated you like a cow, there for milking, branding, and breeding.

"Who?" I squeaked.

Pa's evil grin returned, wider and nastier than ever. "Now that's the best part—it's Old Man Ludham, the same one as bought your darling Trig! You'll be back with your horse, so what could be better? And he's offering me the field between our lands in exchange for your knobby little hand in marriage." Pa slapped the table, satisfied. "Never thought I'd get good land for the likes of you! I told you miracles happen."

Old Man Ludham! The man was so old, his face looked like a dried apple, and he had only a few teeth left in his mouth. And he was the brute who'd taken Trig from me. Wasn't that enough? Did he have to take me, too?

"But . . ." I began.

Pa stood up so fast, his chair hit the floor. Before I could think, he'd hauled off and punched my jaw so hard, a yellow-purple bruise bloomed there for a week.

"Haven't you learned not to sass me, young lady? You do as I say! You're getting married in a week whether you like it or not."

I cowered then, as I did whenever Pa had a fit of his ugly temper, hating myself for not fighting back. I was taller than the time he had beaten me in the stable, lean and muscular, but he still had a good eighty pounds on me and fists like hammers. What could I do? Ma took her husband's kicks and punches as something women were meant to endure— like the pain of childbirth. I'd never wanted to be like my mother, and I'd seen what had become of my sisters after they got married. Anyway, I'd always assumed I'd have a different fate—I was too boyish for a husband, so I'd take over the farm when Pa grew too old. Normally, that would have been my brother's role, but Pa thought Edward couldn't plant a single acre, much less tend a whole farm. We had an understanding, Pa and I, or so I thought. I'd fill the role of son for him and he'd grant me the farm. Of course my brother would stay on, but I'd be taking care of him rather than having some man provide for me. I thought I was an exception, the daughter who would be allowed to live like a son. Now I realized my whole childhood had been a lie, a promise Pa had no intention of keeping.

Four days ticked by and I still couldn't grasp the horrifying news. After clearing the dinner table, the house silent around me, I looked into the mirror hanging in the parlor, the one my mother was so proud to own. My eyes stared back at me, fierce and intelligent. Was this the face of a mild, obedient servant, of a docile, hardworking wife? I didn't know if I was pretty or not and I didn't care. I just knew I wanted more from life than being harnessed as a mule by a grouchy old man. I'd already had years of that with Pa. I wasn't going to trade one master for another. It was time to leave, like I'd promised myself so long ago. Hiding in the loft wouldn't be enough this time—I had to get far away, to start a new life.

The house was empty. Everyone was in the barn or the fields, where I should have been as well. I listened to the loud ticking of the grandfather clock, another of Ma's prized possessions—one that had actually been my grandfather's, so I used to joke to myself that it was my grandfather's grandfather clock. I knew I should be plowing the back field, outside in the glaring sun, not inside the cool, darkened, hushed house. It was only a few days until the wedding, and Ma and Pa were determined to get as much work out of me as possible before I started in planting Old Man Ludham's acres.

I didn't know whether to cry or scream, despair or fight. Next week I'd be in a different farmhouse, one with strange smells and sounds, no comforting ticks from the grandfather clock, no familiar whiffs of Ma's canned peaches or her homemade soap. I'd sleep in a strange bed with a strange man, my nose full of his leathery sweat. I didn't know what to do, how to escape, but I wasn't going to allow myself to be led tamely away, as Trig had.

I stared into the mirror, wishing I could disappear. I didn't plan the next step—it simply happened, as if my body knew what to do before my mind did. My hands took Ma's sewing scissors and with a steady *snip-snip* chopped off my long curls. I tried to keep from trembling as I put on my brother's shirt and pants. I'd worn his pants to hunt in before, but this felt different, as if I was changing more than clothes—I was changing skins. Now only my shoes gave me away, but they were so worn and old, they could scarcely be called dainty or ladylike. The nape of my neck felt lighter without my heavy hair coiled against it. My legs felt free without a long skirt to hem in my stride. It was strange— I felt stronger, braver, dressed as a man. I could do this. I could make my life my own.

Wadding up my dress, apron, and shorn hair into a ball, I slipped out of the house, my lungs tight with fear. I could see Pa's silhouette in the far north field behind the plow. My brother had to be nearby, hidden behind the slope of the land. I could hear the steady whack of the hoe as Ma worked in the kitchen garden with her back to me. Now, this moment, was my chance. I ran quickly into the woods, clutching the wadded-up clothes to my chest. Once in the shadow of the trees, I kept on going, not daring to look back. I ran flat out, snagging my pants on brambles, pushing aside branches that clawed at my face, until I couldn't see the farmhouse, couldn't see the barn, couldn't see anything because the trees grew so thick together that their branches blocked the sky. The heavy silence between the trees was broken only by birds calling, insects humming. I stood still a moment, bent over with my hands on my knees to catch my breath. I waited until the blood had stopped pounding in my ears. Then I buried the remnants of who I'd been, entombing Sarah Emma Edmonds under a decaying log. As I patted pine needles onto the mound covering my clothes and hair, I felt like a new person. I wasn't afraid anymore. A bubble of happiness rose from deep inside me. I shed a lifetime of misery, years of feeling like a failure, of cowering and fear. I wouldn't have to marry Old Man Ludham. I wouldn't have to marry anyone now. No man was ever going to beat me or treat me like a servant again. I was free.

Now I needed to pick out a new name, something that fit the person I was becoming, the person I could be as a man. I wanted something firm and strong, something with an honest heft to it. Frank, I said to myself, letting the word fill my mouth, settle in my throat. That was a good name, a competent name. Frank Thompson, a name that wouldn't stick out in a crowd, just a regular fellow's name. I chanted my new name as I strode farther and farther away from home. I didn't know where I'd spend the night or what I'd eat, if anything, but I knew I'd never been so happy. I felt more at ease in my brother's clothes than I ever had wearing a dress. I could go wherever and do whatever I wanted.

For a young woman alone, everything would have been difficult—traveling, working, finding shelter. But as a man I could do anything. I could hop rides on carts, chop firewood for a meal, sleep in a barn and feel completely safe. And I did, for miles and miles, feeling stronger with each step. I crossed the border from Canada into the United States, trading bridal finery for trousers, trading soft "Sarah" for strong "Frank," trading countries even, without a single regret. Once I discovered the exhilaration of taking big strides unhindered by heavy skirts, even after I was far from Pa's reach, I couldn't put a dress back on.

I know it's illegal to masquerade as a man. The law condemns it as "an infringement on the Rights and Privileges of the lords of creation." In plain English, men hold a natural position of superiority and women should stay in their place. I may have been breaking the law, but I've never felt more right about anything. I'm as capable as any man and deserve the same respect and liberty. Since they aren't granted to me as a woman, then I'll take them as a man. I've tasted freedom and I'm not giving it up. Why should I? Isn't this what Pa had said I could do all my life—fish and hunt and ride as hard as any man?

I've been telling myself that nobody will ever suspect I'm a woman. I'm tough and wiry, like a boy, lean and muscular. Besides, women don't dress like men, they can't act like men, and they definitely won't fight like men. Folks think a dog is as likely to put on pants and shoot a gun as a woman is. But now, living in close quarters with thousands of men, I've put myself in a position where I can easily be found out. What if I get shot in a battle and a doctor tears open my shirt? What if I slip one day, talking to Jerome, and say something that gives me away?

It's odd for me, this comfort and closeness, this kind of sharing. I've never had a friend like Jerome, and it scares me that I'm not as vigilant with him as I should be. I worry that he can tell I'm hiding something. The more time we spend together, the more troubled each of us grows, for our own different reasons.

Jerome doesn't know what it is, he can't put his finger on it, but I can tell he thinks there's something odd about me. We'll be thick in a conversation when suddenly he'll hesitate, stare at me strangely, then continue in a faltering way until he relaxes into our friendship again. It makes me newly wary and I put on my best manly show, spitting and grunting, scratching at my crotch the way Damon constantly does. He can't possibly suspect a woman of such behavior. The cruder I am, the safer I feel. I imagine him talking to the other soldiers, telling them that I'm an excellent nurse, a disciplined soldier, a smart man with a good sense of humor, but there's some mystery to me, as if I'm hiding a secret. Maybe he thinks that my father is a criminal or that my mother is a slave and I'm a black man passing for white. No matter what Jerome might guess, I'm careful he'll never stumble onto the truth. Even if it means hiking for half a mile before I relieve myself or sleeping in the same clothes for an extra week.

Once he caught me tucking my bloody menstrual cloth into a pile of filthy bandages, but I mumbled something about how we need more clean wrappings, the wounded men go through them so quickly. I'm grateful the hospital provides the perfect place to stash the evidence of my monthlies. It's another reason I like nursing—it makes my disguise easier even under Jerome's watchful eye.

For me, even though Jerome isn't hiding anything, he's still a complete mystery. I've never had this kind of friendship, never heard anyone describe his life, his family, with so much detail. I feel I know them too—his doting, hardworking mother, his rigorously demanding father whose penchant for practical jokes offsets his high standards, his flibbertigibbet sister, consumed with a social whirl of parties and dances, and his grandfather, a gentle, warm soul whose hobby is watchmaking. I've been welcomed into the smallest detail of Jerome's history, and still I don't understand what he sees in me, what I mean to him. I know his moods, grow expert at deciphering his frowns and smiles, recognize the whiteness around his mouth and eyes as signs of exhaustion, not illness. But I can't read his heart.

Even worse, I'm confused by my own. At first, I think that the excitement that bubbles inside me whenever I see him, the longing that seizes me when he's absent, the way I savor the smell of his skin and the tone of his voice, all that is friendship. Except it isn't. I don't want to, but I begin to dream about Jerome in ways that are distinctly romantic. In fact, in my dreams I'm dressed like a woman and he's holding my hand, kissing my cheeks. He's courting me. Which is totally ridiculous, since as far as Jerome knows, I'm a man. And as far as I know, I'll never love a man. I'd have to be a woman for that, and I can't imagine taking on that limited role ever again. I want to be Frank Thompson for the rest of my life, not ever go back to being Sarah Emma Edmonds.

Still, despite all my efforts to quash any hint of femininity, I can't avoid a new nickname given by one of the soldiers in the regiment. During one marching drill Carl Cox noticed how small my boots are. I'm average height for a man, five feet six inches, but I still have the feet of a woman, the smallest in the army. I try to distract attention from that by marching with manly vigor, squaring my broad shoulders, and glaring with what I hope is male intensity. Still, after the drill, Carl called me "our woman." As in "Our woman has some fancy footwork." Once Carl said it, the name spread like wildfire, and now everyone's calling me "our woman" or "our little woman." I hope it's more because they miss their womenfolk than that they truly think I resemble one. Surely they would never call me that to my face if they really suspect I'm a woman, would they? Still, when Jerome repeats it, I can't stop myself from blushing. I want to sink into the ground, to vanish in a cloud. But I force myself to face him and search for a way to explain my embarrassment.

"I suppose I shouldn't mind being called a woman, so long as no one doubts my bravery," I try. "It's the price I pay for having small feet."

Jerome grins. "If that's all that's small, there's no need to worry. But if there's another feature that's less than ample . . ." Here he stares pointedly at my crotch.

I turn a deeper shade of red. "I assure you," I lie, "I'm more than man enough there."

Jerome claps my shoulder. "An unproven man, I'll wager, but you're young yet—you'll have your chance, I'm sure."

The conversation is getting worse and worse. Even the tips of my ears feel like they're burning crimson. There's nothing I can say to prove myself. Instead, I mumble a hurried "I must be off" and race away, sure I've made an absolute fool of myself. I hope I seem just an idiot virgin and not a woman.

That night Jerome has the kindness to apologize. "I'm sorry," he says as he lines up behind me for supper rations. "I couldn't resist poking fun. No hard feelings, are there?"

"Of course not." I sigh, relieved. For now my fictional manhood is intact. But I'm more vigilant than ever when relieving myself and take great care when changing my clothes. I even report to the quartermaster that I've been given small boots by mistake. They're too tight and I need a bigger size. I don't ask for ones that are much larger, just a little, enough to make me more convincing, I hope. I stuff the toes with bandages. It means blisters and calluses after long marches, but that's better than the agony of embarrassment.

The summer is drawing to a close and the Union army has more than tripled in size since the Battle of Bull Run. But still we stay in camp, drilling and waiting. The Confederates don't attack, either, and it seems like both camps wait to see who will decide first that it's too expensive to house and feed a sitting army. I've been impatient for action before, but now I'm used to the routine of making the hospital rounds. And having Jerome nearby makes all the difference. I don't want anything to change.

Every morning I worry we'll get the order to march out. When the noon hour passes with no news, I whisper a prayer of thanks for another day with my good friend. And Jerome seems just as attached to me. He tells me that he's written about me in his diary, describing his wonderful new comrade, a person of honor and integrity, intelligence and humor.

"You see how highly I regard you," Jerome says. "You make me laugh—that's the best gift a friend can offer!"

No one has ever said that about me before. Of course at home there was never the friendly chatter that I now hear every night around the campfire. We weren't a family of talkers. Supper was a silent affair unless Pa was in one of his moods. Then he would be loud, angry, insulting, lashing out with his words or fists or both. Funny to think that the one I talked to most wasn't a person at all, but a horse, Trig. When I lost him as a confidant, I lost my voice as well. I simply didn't talk. The first and last time I can remember making anyone laugh was at that long-ago supper at the Hurlburts' home, when the children found my descriptions of mules hilarious. Then, I thought that I could at least entertain young folk, but here's Jerome, a grown man, and he likes the way I talk.

Around Jerome I practically babble, as if all the words that have been pent up for so long are rushing madly for release. Now that I know he likes my sense of humor, I try to be my wittiest, honing amusing stories and descriptions in my head for hours so that when I see him again, I can carelessly let fall some brilliant bit of fancy. If he laughs, or even smiles, I'm richly rewarded for my efforts.

But I want him to see me as more than funny, as more than a best friend. I'm not sure exactly what I want. All I know is that the more time we spend together, the closer we become, the more restless and unhappy I feel. It doesn't make sense, but there it is. Then things get distinctly worse.

Jerome starts telling me his most intimate feelings, particularly those regarding a certain young lady back home named Anna Corey, who, according to Jerome, is the perfection of womanhood—virtuous, noble, good, kind, and, of course, beautiful, with warm brown eyes, creamy skin, and flowing chestnut tresses. Everything I'm not and never could be, even if I do decide to put on petticoats again.

My stomach twists in knots when Jerome describes his dream of holding Anna's delicate hand. Every time he receives a letter from Miss Corey, he rushes to read it to his best friend, unaware of how my mouth tightens whenever I see the telltale purple ink on the lilac-scented paper.

I can't help imagining what it would be like if Jerome thought of me the way he feels about Anna. Why can't he see me that way? I wonder, except of course he can't. Even if he knew I'm really a woman, I couldn't measure up to Anna's refined feminine charms. I'm too rough and crude for that, a miserable failure of a lady.

Usually I'm so worn out with the long days of drilling and nursing, the effort of keeping my male mask firmly in place, that I sleep soundly. Lately I've been tossing and turning at night, my dreams a mix of images—me, Jerome, Anna, all trading faces, places, and names until I'm not sure who's who anymore.

"What's going on with you these days?" Damon asks. "You're grinding your teeth in your sleep and muttering things. Have you had bad news from home?"

"No, nothing like that," I say, rubbing my bleary eyes. I'm certainly not going to tell him the truth. Instead, I offer him something that sounds plausible. "I guess I'm just anxious that it's already October, the weather is changing, and we're still sitting here, no closer to winning this blamed war than ever."

Damon nods. "Yep, you're right about that. And here I thought I'd be home with the corn harvest! Now it looks like I'll be lucky to make next year's crop. I just hope my pretty girl will wait for me. It seems like every day I hear about another feller who got a 'Sorry, Sweetheart' letter."

I sit up, suddenly wide-awake. "What's that? What's a 'Sorry, Sweetheart' letter?"

"Guess you wouldn't know that, since you don't got no sweetheart," Damon teases. "It's what I call a letter the lady writes to tell her gentleman she's marrying someone else. Seems like a lot of gals don't have much patience. If their feller's gone too long, they just find themselves a new one." Damon drops his lighthearted tone and stares sadly at his boot tips. "I sure hope that don't happen to me."

"Oh, Damon, of course it won't," I reassure him. "Where would she find someone as good as you, who loves her so well?"

Damon looks up, searching my eyes for any hint of

hollow insincerity. "You really think so? I mean, I do love her. No one could love Polly like I do."

"And she knows that," I soothe. "She's no fool."

Damon grins. "You're right—I just have to have faith."

Me, too, I think. I have to have faith. A strange hope surges through me. Maybe Anna Corey will write Jerome a "Sorry, Sweetheart" letter. All I have to do is wait until Little Miss Perfect crushes his heart, and then I can come along and heal it.

This morning I feel lighter, easier than I have in a long time. I trade riddles and jokes with the patients and hum as I change bandages. Even the putrid smell of festering sores or the sight of maggots in wounds doesn't upset me. All day I'm aware of Jerome's presence. He keeps trying to catch my eye, to snatch a quick conversation, but the doctors keep us busy and we don't have five minutes to exchange words. I know something's on my friend's mind that he's eager to tell to me, but I'm in no hurry. I savor the proof that he needs me so much, that I'm his closest confidant as he is mine.

At the end of our shift, Jerome rushes up as I put away the liniments and elixirs.

"I've been bursting all day with this news! I couldn't wait to tell you!" His eyes sparkle with excitement, and I can't help noticing how handsome he looks. Handsome? I've never thought that about anybody. What does it mean that I'm applying that word to Jerome? Nothing good, I fear. I can't allow myself to feel womanly around him. I fret that my own nature will reveal what I so carefully try to hide. If only I knew what my nature really is so I could control it better.

"Well, can you wait a minute more?" I ask, lowering my voice to sound especially manly. "I'm about finished here, and we'll have more privacy if we go outside."

Jerome nods, hopping from one foot to the other like a little boy in his anticipation. What is making him so happy? He certainly hasn't gotten the "Sorry, Sweetheart" letter that I'm praying for, but maybe that will come tomorrow. I'm actually glad it hasn't arrived today to spoil whatever good news he's enjoying.

Finally, the supplies are neatly organized. I lead Jerome to the big oak that has become our refuge after our shifts.

"So what is it?" I ask. "What's your good news?"

"The best news possible!" Jerome crows. "I asked Anna Corey to marry me and she said yes! She said yes!" He reaches into his pocket and takes out the distinctive stationery. He unfolds the letter with trembling fingers, releasing a waft of sweet perfume. "Here's what she says: 'My darling, I know you may be gone a long time, but however long it is, I will wait for you. My heart is yours and yours alone.' Did you hear that? She loves me and she doesn't care how long I'm stuck in this army!"

I sit there frozen, my back stiff against the tree bark. It feels like a giant fist has reached into my chest and crushed my heart. "No," I blurt out. "No, you can't. You can't marry her."

"What do you mean I can't?" Jerome looks at me. "Well, not now, but when I get home."

"No, never!" My voice rings hollow with anguish.

"Frank, what's wrong with you? You're not talking sense." Jerome frowns, puzzled. "I thought you'd be delighted, that you'd help me plan the wedding and you'd be my best man."

"I can't be your best man!" I wail. I'm caught in a nightmare, one where demons claw at my entrails.

"Why not? What is going on here?" Jerome presses. "This has to do with your secret, doesn't it? Listen, Frank, I don't care if your mother was a slave—you're white to me. And you're going to be my best man."

"My mother was a slave?" I roll my eyes—he *has* thought that, just like I've suspected. "That's not it! The reason I can't be your best man is because . . . because . . ." I hesitate, my heart pounding furiously, my breath caught in my throat. I don't want to say it, I wrestle with myself, but the words burst out by themselves, stronger than my will. "Because . . . I'm a woman!" As soon as the admission leaves my mouth, it feels as if all the air has been pushed out of me. I'm left flattened and empty. And then relief washes over me, tremendous relief. After four long years, I've shared my secret. And the earth hasn't swallowed me up. The skies haven't split in two, pouring down hellfire. I lift up my chin and face Jerome. "I'm a woman," I repeat. I want to project femininity, to speak with a gentle, sweet voice, but I sound awkward, unconvinced myself.

Jerome pulls back and stares. He doesn't say anything for a long minute, just gapes in shock. Then he blinks his eyes and shakes his head. "All this time, you . . ." he mumbles. "No, it can't be. You can't be . . ." As the truth sinks in, his surprise turns into rage. "Why are you telling me this? I don't want to know! You're ruining everything!"

I reach out and grab Jerome's hand. There's no way but forward now that I've revealed the truth. "I'm telling you because I have to. Because I love you and you can't marry Anna Corey." Suddenly everything is perfectly clear. We'll finish serving our terms in the army; then I'll turn back into Sarah and marry Jerome, and we'll live happily ever after.

Jerome looks horrified. "I can't marry you! You're like a brother to me! I don't even believe you're really a woman. You're just saying that because you don't want me to marry Anna. Why, I have no idea."

"No," I insist. "It's true." I want to tell Jerome everything. How I cut off my hair and put on my brother's clothes, how I chose the name Frank Thompson, how I lived and worked as a traveling bookseller, how I thought I'd never put on a dress again, but then I met Jerome and something shifted inside me. But all I can tell him is that I love him as a woman, even if I'm living as a man.

I wait for him to answer, every inch of me edgy and tense. This feels more dangerous than any battle.

Jerome tries to cover the disgust in his voice. "You're unnatural. This is unnatural. I can't be your friend any-more."

"No!" I wail. It's like a kick in the stomach, the realization I've risked everything for nothing. Jerome can't see me as a woman, can't fall in love with me. I'll always be a man to him, a fellow nurse and soldier. I've done too many unla-dylike things in front of him. I've held down men twice my weight as the surgeon sawed off an arm or a leg. I've seen and touched every part of a man's body that could be shot at or stabbed by a bayonet. I've cleaned up blood and guts and hacked-off limbs. I've seen horrors no lady could look upon without fainting. I close my eyes and cry. No wonder I seem unnatural to him. I seem unnatural to myself. What woman does those things?

"Please," I whisper. "Can we still be friends? I shouldn't have told you, I'm sorry. Let's just go back to how we were before. I'm Frank Thompson, not Sarah."

"I don't know," Jerome says gruffly. "I need time to think."

I nod. I need time to think as well. Waves of emotions sweep through me—hurt, anger, and most of all fear. I've never been so confused, so unsure of myself. I've allowed myself to be vulnerable, opened myself up to someone, and what's come of it? Cold betrayal. Trig has been my only true friend. Only a horse could accept someone as unnatural as me.

Jerome doesn't love me. Now he doesn't even want to be my friend. What if he decides to be my enemy? What if he tells somebody about my real identity? Would I go to prison? Should I sneak out, disappear as Frank Thompson, and take on a new name and a new story before I get caught? I want to serve in the army, to help fight for the Union, but now staying means taking the chance of being discovered. Why did I ever trust a man? I'm completely at Jerome's mercy. He doesn't need to beat me to ruin my life. All he has to do is speak. I've never felt so powerless.

DESERTION

WE'VE ALL HEARD RUMORS OF SOLDIERS SNEAKING out of camp, hoping to walk home to their families, but desertion is punishable by death. As often as not, the runaways are caught, given a quick trial, then shot by a firing squad. I figure it will be easier for me to escape than for most since I can rely on the convincing disguise of a woman, something a man wouldn't be able to pull off. That is, if I can make it out of camp. Crossing the pickets will be the hard part. After that, all I have to do is find a dress to trade for my uniform and I'll be fine.

It's a clear, crisp autumn night, the harvest moon bathing all of Washington in a silver glow, casting purple shadows on the ground. I wait until Damon's breathing deepens, then slip out of the tent. I walk as quietly as possible but can't help feeling terribly obvious in the bright moonlight. How could a picket not see me? I wish there were trees to hide among, but I have to pass a guard before getting to the woods. I thread my way, crouching low, through the rows of tents. Snores erupt from one tent so loudly, I wonder how anyone within a two-tent distance can sleep. Suddenly to my left, a hand reaches out of a tent to pull the flap open. I duck down behind another tent before the soldier who crawls out can see me. I wait, holding my breath, while he gets up and heads toward the ditch used as a latrine by the entire regiment. When his shape melts into the night, I turn in the opposite direction and continue my stealthy escape.

Containing over 200,000 soldiers, the camp stretches for miles. I've gone a good distance despite the bright moonlight when out of the corner of my eye I see something move. I turn around and my stomach plummets. A sentry strides toward me, a rifle cocked on his shoulder. There's no point in running. The soldier sees me for sure, and making a break for it would only gain me a bullet in my back. So I stand there, waiting for him to reach me, trying to think of a good reason for a midnight walk. Too bad I'm not heading in the direction of the latrine, the most obvious excuse.

"Hello, there, soldier!" the guard calls out. "What's your name and regiment?"

"Private Frank Thompson, Company F, Second Michigan Volunteer Infantry, sir!" I salute.

"Any reason you're not in bed with the rest of your regiment?" The soldier eyes me carefully, as if looking for signs of desertion. Good thing I haven't taken a knapsack with me. That would really look suspicious.

"Couldn't sleep, sir. I thought a walk might calm me down." I keep my tone steady and even.

"Calm you down from what? Feeling nervous about something?" the soldier prods.

"Not nervous, sir, just sad—and mad." I hesitate. "You see, I got a 'Sorry, Sweetheart' letter today. I thought Anna would wait for me, but she's marrying someone else." I stare at the ground sorrowfully, imagining what a jilted lover would look like and trying to shift my face into exactly that look. Actually, I have been jilted—by Jerome. I remember how he spurned me and then I'm not acting anymore. My face is hollow with hurt, darkened with anger. I look up and lock eyes with the soldier. "I'm here, doing my duty, and this is how she treats me!"

The soldier sighs and claps me on the back. "You're not the only one. Women! You just can't trust them, not a single one of them, I tell you. Look, I have something that will make you feel better." He pulls a flask out of his hip pocket. "A couple of swallows and you'll forget all about what's-her-name, I promise you. You'll have someone new in no time, a handsome lad like you."

Handsome? I'm handsome? I've never considered myself beautiful, but maybe I'm a better-looking man than woman. Maybe that's why Jerome rejected me, because my face will never have a woman's soft sweetness. I've seen women like that, with mannish chins and horsey jaws, beetling brows and sharp, jutting noses. Is that the kind of woman I am? I hate the thought, and my mouth turns sour with disgust. I'm ugly, and here I am, planning on turning myself back into one of those women with faces like shovels.

I take the flask and drink. The liquid burns going down and makes my eyes water. I have to force myself not to sputter it back out.

"Thank you," I gasp, returning the flask. The soldier takes a long pull, then returns it to me.

"One more," he offers, "for the road."

"For the road," I repeat, tipping back the whiskey. This time I manage to swallow better. The burning becomes a steady warmth, all the way to my toes. I never understood before why men take to drink. It seems like such a wasteful habit. But now I can appreciate it. I want more of that feeling like nothing matters. Who cares if I have a horse's ass for a face? Who cares if instead of an ample bosom, anthills barely break the flat silhouette of my chest? Who cares if I'm an utter failure at being one of the masters of creation and an even greater failure at being the fairer sex? I take another long drink.

"Whoa, there, buddy. That's enough. Think you can sleep now?" asks the guard, pocketing the flask.

I grin, suddenly cheerful. "I think that's about all I *can* do!" I start to walk back to the tent, but my legs feel rubbery and weak, my head thick and cottony. I plop down on the ground, still smiling, every ounce of worry drained out of me. Who cares if I can't walk? I'm fine right where I am.

"Come on, now, you can't sleep here. You'll catch a chill. I'll help you back to your tent." The soldier pulls me up, slips an arm around me, and half carries me in the direction my wavering finger points. He huffs and puffs as I collapse against him. I relish being nestled close to him, held safe in his strong arms. If only Jerome would touch me the same way.

"You're a nice fellow," I say. "You know that? You're nice to me." I pucker my lips, filled with a sudden urge to kiss a total stranger.

"Sure I am," the soldier grunts. "But I'm not your sweetheart." He lifts the flap of the tent and shoves me in. "Don't worry—you'll get yourself a new girl. Now sleep!"

"Good night!" I call back. I crawl under the blanket, and soon my own snores join Damon's.

In the morning I wake up with a throbbing head and a dry mouth. When I remember what happened the night before, I'm even queasier. Did I almost kiss that soldier? Did I really cling to him like some fainting Southern belle? Some escape! I'm stuck here, waiting for my ex-friend to turn me in.

I want this day to be normal, just another day in camp, so I show up at the hospital as usual and start my rounds, forcing myself to concentrate on the patients through the fog of my aching head. When I see Jerome, my stomach flutters and my breathing quickens. Am I in love with him or simply afraid of him? And what does he feel for me? All I know is that he pointedly ignores me, turning his back whenever we come close.

As the day wears on, the headache subsides and I'm myself again. If nobody has arrested me yet, then Jerome hasn't revealed my secret. And if he hasn't already done that, doesn't that mean he never intends to? The next day passes and the one after that and the one after that, and still we work together, speaking only when necessary, avoiding each other as much as possible.

Until Jerome breaks the silence. "Listen, here, Frank," he says one frigid November morning, "let's forget the whole fuss. I can't even remember what we fought about now. Can we shake hands and go back to being friends?" He holds out his hand shyly.

He can't remember? It's hard to believe, but I search his face and see that he desperately wants to be friends. If that means pretending I'm a man and that he's never had an inkling otherwise, so be it. A wave of relief passes through me. He'll keep my secret. He won't betray me. Gratitude swells into sympathy for him. Jerome does love me, the only way he can, as a brother. I manage a smile and take his hand.

"I want nothing more," I lie.

At first, our conversations are stiff and awkward, but

gradually we fall back into the old ease and warmth. The only difference is that now Jerome never mentions Miss Anna Corey. And he's careful never to touch me. No slaps on the back, no pats on the arm. That handshake is the last time we touch.

By January, Jerome seems to have forgotten the whole incident. He treats me like his best friend, plain and simple. But I haven't forgotten. And it isn't any easier for me to be so close to a man I love who doesn't love me back. The long hours together in the hospital only make me love him more. He's such a kind, gentle nurse, such an intelligent, sensitive companion. I want to hate him for rejecting me, but I can't. Instead, I hate myself for being so unwomanly. I'm lucky he still values me as a friend, and that has to be enough.

But it's not. I know Jerome won't change. I know I can't, and my heart will only bruise more and more over time. Worse yet, being around him confuses me, makes it hard for me to act naturally like a man. I feel a new urge to soften my voice and manners, to wake up the girl slumbering deep inside me, so I do the sensible, safe thing. I ask the commander, Colonel Orlando Poe, to reassign me.

I expect to be moved to a different hospital, but Colonel Poe needs something other than a nurse. He needs a regimental postmaster, a risky job since the mail is often ambushed by Rebel soldiers on the long, lonely routes from camp to camp, inside and outside Washington. I don't hesitate for a second. I'll have my own horse, plenty of fresh air, and a break from the bleak suffering in the hospital. Best of all, I'll spend the whole day away from Jerome. Once again I'll feel sure of myself as a young man, an eager soldier for the Union. If I can't have confidence in myself as a woman for Jerome to love, it's the next best thing.

8

TOWARD RICHMOND

THE MEN IN THE HOSPITAL DEPENDED ON ME FOR FRESH dressings and doses of brandy, but now all the soldiers in the regiment rely on me for something much more vital—news from home. No one is more important to the average recruit, no figure more widely recognized, than the postmaster. I like being appreciated for my reliability, but more than that, I'm proud of my reputation. Damon tells me I'm famous for my good nature, ready wit, and warm curiosity. He boasts to everyone that we're tentmates, that he knows me best, and I don't correct him. It's like when Jerome read me his journal entry describing how witty I am—a mirror is being held up to me, showing me a different image of myself. I'm not an awkward, silent tomboy, or a lonely traveling book salesman, or a cowardly soldier, or a mule-faced woman trying to pass as a man. I'm Frank Thompson, regimental postmaster.

GENERAL POST OFFICE, ARMY OF THE POTOMAC, CULPEPER, VA.

In just a few weeks I have many friends. Delivering mail, I get to know everybody. I ask after soldiers' parents, sisters, brothers, and wives by name. I know who writes a lot of letters and who receives them. I even know which men are writing to two different women, each one thinking she alone is her fellow's sweetheart. Whole stories are crammed into each thin envelope, and I feel I'm a part of the drama simply by delivering those envelopes. Yes, I miss the close relationship with Jerome, but I've learned my lesson. I'll never let myself get that close to another soldier again. The light, easy friendships I develop all over the regiment may not be deep, but they're warm and caring and, best of all, safe.

When my heart is full and I need someone to listen, I console myself with my new best friend, my horse. Flag is a sorrel gelding, steady and dependable. He doesn't have Trig's grace or speed, but he's good-natured, the equine equivalent to Damon. We spend long days together, riding to retrieve and deliver mail—hours when I pour out my worries, fears, and hopes, when I practice jokes and witty descriptions, when I belt out songs and describe my latest dreams. If we have to sleep by the road, Flag is both wind-break and pillow, a warm body for me to press against. True,

he can't talk to me, but the way he nips at my collar and rubs his head against my shoulder, he makes it clear that I'm his best friend, too.

I pass on rumors as well as letters, and by March 1862 the camp simmers with them. General George McClellan announces the end of the long months of drilling and waiting—it's finally time to march out. He praises us for being highly prepared and

MAJOR GENERAL GEORGE MCCLELLAN.

assures us that the Confederate army is no match for our strength. He talks on and on about the glory of the Union and its defenders. But though his speech is long on rousing patriotism, it's short on details. He doesn't lay out a battle plan or even say where we're headed. With nothing specific to go on, we all speculate. Some guess we'll head back to Manassas, an idea nobody likes. Others suggest we'll go to Richmond by way of Fredericksburg. Damon starts a betting pool, turning all the guesses into cash.

"This is more exciting than the horse races," he tells me. "Want to put fifty cents down on Manassas?"

"I wouldn't put anything down on Manassas! The last time was bad enough," I say. "I'd rather any way but that one."

No one predicts we'll march to the wharf in Alexandria and board ships to go down the Virginia coast to Fort Monroe at the end of the narrow Virginia Peninsula. Bounded on the north by the York River and on the south by the James River, the peninsula is Southern territory except for the very tip, where the Chesapeake Bay meets the Atlantic Ocean. That's where Fort Monroe sits, cut off from the Union army by land, accessible only by water. The plan is to march up the peninsula through Yorktown and Williamsburg to Richmond, using the York River to keep supply lines open. Since the bulk of the Confederate army is massed on the other side of Richmond, toward Washington, the hope is that Richmond can be taken before most of the Rebel troops realize what's happening.

It's a daring and difficult plan, starting with the enormity of moving so many men by sea. It takes over three weeks and more than 400 ships to ferry 150,000 soldiers, 300 pieces of artillery, 3,600 wagons, 700 ambulances, 2,500 head of cattle, and 25,000 horses and mules to Fort Monroe. Not to mention smaller weapons, ammunition, food, tents, and hospital supplies.

When our regiment arrives at the port to board a boat, we join a massive crowd both in the water and on the wharf. Sloops jostle next to barges, canal boats edge out steamers, all in a chaotic surge to dock. Once a boat manages to get close enough, the soldiers push their way on, elbowed by those behind them. So many men cram the pier, there's hardly room to budge. I've asked to board with the animals, saying I need to take care of Flag, but my request is denied, so I'm forced to squeeze onto the dock with all the other soldiers. In the mass of bodies, I'm all too close to Jerome. Our arms touch, and if I turn slightly, my nose will be under his jaw. I smell his spicy sweat and feel the muscles of his thigh alongside my leg. I thought that all the months I've kept away from him have created a distance between us, cooled my love into friendly affection. Now, during the long hours waiting to board, I'm drawn to Jerome all over again. I don't mind the wait, I don't mind standing for hours, so long as he's next to me.

"But I can't love him," I scold myself. "And no more talk of being a woman—ever! We're friends, just friends." I chant the phrase over and over in my head as if repetition can make it true. When the crowd in front of us clears and it's our turn to board the already packed steamer, I feel like I'm waking from a long dream. The sun set hours ago, and the men are tired and hungry as they settle on the boat. Jerome falls asleep instantly, but I can't relax. I sit next to him, squeezed shoulder to shoulder, hip to hip, grateful to find enough space to rest, savoring the touch I've avoided for so long. Still, I can't shake off the sadness that fills my throat with a dry ache, and as the dark swallows us, turning shapes into shadows, tears run down my cheeks. I cry because he doesn't love me. I cry because I'm a woman and don't know how to be one. I cry because my life is a lie and nothing will ever be simple for me.

It feels good to let go, to give myself permission to grieve. The tears empty me out, leave me hollow, and exhaustion fills the space they leave. Without thinking, I lean my head on Jerome's shoulder and fall asleep, sitting up like that.

The rocking of the boat wakes me. A sudden storm turns the peaceful crossing into a rough ride, throwing everyone from side to side and lashing us with rain for two days. Many are seasick. Everyone is drenched. I'm afraid my wet shirt clinging to me might reveal the shallow mounds of my breasts, so I keep my jacket buttoned even though it's horribly muggy, my sweat adding even more moisture. The men around me are probably too wretched to notice anyway, but I'm too terrified to risk anything.

"Aren't you stifling in that coat?" Jerome asks. "It's so blasted hot, even with the rain."

I shake my head, clutching my jacket tighter. "I'm fine."

"Nobody's fine in this hellhole!" Jerome snaps.

When the boat finally gets to Fort Monroe, there are so many other ships ahead of us waiting to dock, it's two more days before our turn comes and we can disembark. It's a miserable start to the campaign for everyone, but even worse for me. Being stuck on board is the first time it's difficult to hide my sex. There's no tree to hide behind when I need to relieve myself, only the open air at the boat's rail, where the men either add their spray to the waters below or turn and crouch, dumping a fetid load with a loud splash. There's no choice but to hold my bladder and bowels during the day, drinking as little as possible so I'll need to piss less. No matter how uncomfortable I am, I force myself to wait until it's dark to take my place at the edge of the boat. The new moon, a thin sliver, doesn't cast enough light for anyone to see much if another soldier should happen to decide to relieve himself nearby. Still, the first time I pull down my pants and thrust out my behind into the rain-lashed wind, I can't relax. I'm tense with the fear of being discovered. But as the dark night cloaks me and the sounds of snores and

VIEW OF CAMP AND TROOP TRANSPORT, BELLE PLAIN LANDING, VA.

sleepy muttering waft in the air, I remind myself that I'm as far from being a lady as ever. What young woman would put herself in this position, naked bum hanging over the side of a boat crowded with hundreds of men? It's all the more proof that I'm more boy than girl—always have been and always will be, no matter how much I love Jerome.

We finally touch solid ground only to slog through the sticky Virginia mud in the torrential rain, snuffing out any thought of romance. All I can think of is putting one foot in front of the other. I don't know where Jerome is and I don't care. I lose sight of him as soon as we get off the boat. I can't find Flag either. The ship with all the livestock hasn't docked yet. On the road to set up camp, Damon plods alongside me instead.

"Too bad no one bet we were going to hell," he grunts. "They would have won the pool."

"At least we're off the boat," I offer. "That's something."

"Yeah, it says a lot about the passage that you think *this* is an improvement." Damon's hair is plastered to his head by rain, and he's ankle-deep in mud.

Once camp is set up and we're dry in our tents, the rain keeps us in there. For days the storm continues as fever rages through the camp. Damon and I both fall sick, shivering in the tent for a week. The doctors call it swamp fever, something brought on by the muggy conditions we're living in.

Mostly I sleep, slipping in and out of strange dreams. I see Ma and Pa again, and Old Man Ludham grins at me, claiming me for his bride. He lunges toward me and changes into a soldier whose leg has been blown off.

The first day I leave the tent, the world seems newly sharp and clear, rich in colors, sounds, and scents. Whip-poor-wills and larks call out, rustling through the emerald grasses. Dogwoods and magnolias flower while pillowy clouds scud overhead. I bite into a dry biscuit. Usually chewing hardtack is like chomping on sawdust. This day, nothing has ever tasted as good.

Damon, who recovered a day earlier, grins a welcome.

"Look who's back from the dead." He waves at me to sit next to him on a log as he polishes his rifle.

"Well, you said we'd ended up in hell." I smile back.

"So I did. And I weren't far wrong. Now that the rain's stopped, it's hotter than a furnace. Seems like it either pours on you or broils you up in these parts." He shakes his head. "The South—they can have it, the miserable grunts."

But nothing can spoil my mood. Yes, it's muggy, but I smell the dirt and grass, taste the smoke from cook fires, watch the new leaves flutter on the trees. It feels good to be alive, off the boat, out of the tent, and not wracked with fever anymore. Not aching with love, either. Maybe the fever has burned it out of me. I don't even look around for Jerome. I'm simply happy to be here, in this moment, this place.

"Are we moving out soon?" I ask Damon.

He nods. "A day or two, I think."

The plan is to take control of the York River to establish a clear supply line. The James River is an easier route, but it's guarded by the armored Confederate gunboat *Virginia,* an intimidating sight that General McClellan decides is best to avoid entirely.

"Word is we're to take Yorktown."

Another battle. My stomach tightens. There is something that can ruin my mood after all. This time I won't leave the wounded to be taken prisoner. This time has to be different.

That evening as we sit down to supper, a ripple of excited voices spreads through the camp.

"Nurse!" someone yells. "We need a nurse!"

I set down my plate and run toward the edge of camp, where a group of a dozen or so men straggles toward me. Two of them carry a makeshift stretcher. I recognize Dr. E. J. Bonine, the regimental surgeon. As I get closer, I see that the wounded man is African, and so are the men following the stretcher.

"There's a bullet in his shoulder," the doctor says, setting the stretcher down. "We've got to take it out now. He's lost a lot of blood." I nod, holding the hurt man firmly as the doctor gets out his penknife. It's a scene I've lived through a hundred times before, but never with a black man.

The other Africans start to pray, then sing. At first, I can't follow the words. Then I realize they're thanking the Lord for setting them free, shouting out his glory. Their voices are deep and rich and fill me with a strange sense of hope.

As the surgeon works, he explains what happened.

"I was taking a walk when I saw some men on the other side of a creek about a mile from here. At first, I thought they were Rebel pickets, an advance guard, but when I saw they were black, I knew they had to be escaped slaves. I waved to them to cross over, but they yelled back that they couldn't swim. So I lashed together a couple of logs and one by one pulled them over. They said they'd been forced to work on the Confederate fortifications at the James River, but when they heard a rumor that the Union army had landed, they decided to make a break for it and try to reach us. The Rebels shot at them, killed a man, and wounded another, this one here." He digs out the ball and presses a handkerchief to the wound to stanch the blood. "But he's going to be fine. They all are now."

I nod, pouring brandy on the wound the way I've been taught, then bandaging it up. "Here," I say, lifting up the man's head and giving him some brandy to drink as well. "You need a sip of this and lots of rest. When you wake up, you'll be fine." The man's deep-brown eyes brim with gratitude. I'm touched by the depth of his trust, some-thing I've seen many times in the faces of wounded or sick soldiers. This man, I'm startled to realize, is like all of us. He's just the same. They're all the same, only with darker skin. It's the first time I've been so close to an African, the first time I think about slavery and how cruel it is.

For me, the war has been about saving the Union. Now it's also about something else, something that claws in the pit of my stomach—it's about freeing a whole class of people condemned to being treated like animals. It's about justice.

While their companion sleeps, the other escaped slaves join us for supper. Everyone talks about the contrabands— that's what escaped slaves are called, since they are basically illegal goods—how they haven't waited for the war to end. Instead, they've freed themselves.

I stare at the Africans. Rage rises in my throat at the sight of the welts that crisscross their backs, chests, and legs—scars left behind by an owner's heavy lash. The coming battle has new meaning now. These people deserve to be free. And they've risked their lives so they can be. Why should they be slaves simply because of their skin color? It's the same with women—why should we have such limited lives? Are we really lesser people? Shouldn't we enjoy the same rights as men?

I enlisted in the war to preserve the Union, but now I have another reason to fight: to save people from the tyranny of other people. I can't do it for women, but I can do it for the Africans. And I can do it for myself, so long as I live as a man.

That night we join the newly freed men in songs around the campfire. Tomorrow we'll move on to Yorktown with a new purpose in our step, a new sense of mission and pride. I still fear what lies ahead, but now a sharp edge of eagerness blunts the fear. I think of the countless Africans hobbled by slavery and hone my outrage into righteous anger, ready to face whatever will happen, to get closer to Richmond and freedom for all—men, that is.

THE FIRST SHOT

WITH OUR SENSE OF PURPOSE BOLSTERED BY THE Africans, we set out for Yorktown on the muddiest road we've traveled yet. The mire is so thick and gooey, it takes two days to slog twenty miles. I'm trudging with the rest of the regiment since Flag is hauling equipment. Already, a few weeks after arriving at Fort Monroe, we're short on food. Supply ships haven't arrived yet, so even though we're deep in enemy territory, a handful of soldiers is sent out to forage among the neighboring houses.

Naturally, I volunteer. I'm relieved to have a reason to ride Flag again, to be back with my best friend. "Did you miss me? Did you?" I ask him as I near the corral. Flag trots right up—he knows my voice, and yes, he's clearly missed me. I stroke his soft nose. "I bet your crossing was better than mine. Better company, less seasickness, and you could mess the straw whenever you felt the urge." Flag nibbles at my pocket, searching for a treat. Sometimes I save an apple for him, but it's been days since I've seen any fruit. I'll requisition something for Flag along with supplies for the men.

I hope that collecting food won't be so different from collecting mail, but I know that the people living nearby won't be sympathetic to Union troops. Food won't be offered for sale. I'll have to buy it by force. So I'm surprised by how peaceful the countryside looks as I ride through it. There's no sign of war in the tobacco fields, and when I come to a large plantation house with a broad, welcoming veranda, it seems like something from another time.

After hitching Flag to the iron post by the porch and collecting the baskets slung over the saddle, I knock on the door, keeping my other hand on the holster of my gun, just in case things inside the house aren't as peaceful as they look from the outside.

A tall, regal woman opens the door, her pale skin made even whiter by the contrast with her black widow's weeds. I tell her that I've come to buy whatever food the household can spare. My uniform says the rest. The war has come to the woman's doorstep. Perhaps it's not the first time. I wonder if she is grieving a death from sickness, age, or battle.

The woman forces a brittle smile. "I wouldn't think of depriving hungry soldiers when we are so fortunate. Why don't you wait in the parlor while I gather what I can for y'all."

The smirk behind her smile, the steeliness of her eyes, the rigid way she holds herself all set my nerves on edge. I want to have compassion for the woman's obvious mourning. In another time, another place, I would. Now all I am is suspicious. The woman is a Southerner, an enemy.

"Let me help you," I insist. I follow the black sweeping skirts into the kitchen.

The woman moves vaguely around the pantry, reaching for flour, then putting it back, picking up a side of bacon, then setting it down again.

I clear my throat loudly. "If you please, ma'am. I need to get going. I'll take some eggs and butter, the flour and bacon, perhaps an apple for my horse, and leave you be."

"Oh." The woman faces me, her hands shaking. "I didn't realize you were in such a hurry. I was waiting for the boys to get back and catch you some chickens. They'll make mighty fine eating."

The skin crawls on the back of my neck. So that's what she's up to—stalling for time until the men come home to take care of her unwanted visitor.

"That won't be necessary, ma'am." I spit out the words, scooping the supplies into the baskets I've brought. Something about that kitchen makes me edgy. I want to get out, now. But I'm not stealing—I try to hand the woman a greenback.

She stares at the money as if it's poison. "Oh, I couldn't take that," the widow says. "I wouldn't touch it." She lifts her chin defiantly, and hatred gleams in her eyes.

"As you wish, ma'am." I leave the money on the table

and back my way out of the house, facing the woman's scowl the whole time. She stands on the porch, seething, while I get on Flag and turn to go, every muscle in my back taut from the glare of her eyes.

I can't explain why, but I flinch, ducking my head down toward Flag's mane, just as the shot whizzes over my head. I turn Flag around quickly and raise my own gun as the woman shoots again, this time wide of the mark. I point the muzzle of my seven-shooter squarely at her, panic surging through me as I try to keep my hands steady. Flag seems to understand and stands stock-still. Faced with my gun, the woman drops her own pistol and puts up her hands, her eyes simmering with rage and hate.

Nerves jangling, I take careful aim and fire. The woman screams and falls to the ground, clutching her left hand. The ball pierced clear through her palm, leaving a bloody hole.

It's the first time I've shot anybody, but it won't be the last. Maybe if I really were a man, I'd be ashamed of such ungentlemanly behavior. But I've been attacked and I feel justified using my gun, even if my assailant is a woman. I feel the same icy chill in my veins as during the Battle of Bull Run, the familiar steeliness I used to see in Ma as she wrung a chicken's neck.

I get off Flag, legs still shaking, and pick up the dropped pistol, then unfasten the halter strap to tie it around the woman's right wrist.

"Come on, Flag," I say, patting his broad cheek, reassured by his warm bulk. "We're going home, but we're bringing some company with us." I jump back into the saddle, yanking the woman behind me by the arm as if she's a goat or cow, an unruly creature that needs to be dragged along.

"Your ladyship is coming with me," I bark. Now that I'm not scared, I'm furious.

"Let me go!" the woman shrieks. "Release me now!"

I level my gun at her again. "Any more noise and I'll shut that mouth of yours forever."

The woman nods, her eyes big with fear. She stumbles after Flag, tripping over her skirts and falling several times. Each time, she fumbles her way back to her feet, losing blood and getting weaker with every step.

When she falls for the fifth time, I stop Flag and dismount. True, this woman tried to kill me, but I don't mean to torture her. As the rage drains out of me, I'm sickened by my own cruelty. Is this what being a soldier means? Will I grow flinty and nasty like Pa? Are all men at heart simple brutes, and am I becoming one of them? I shake my head, unsure what to do next. I want to be brave, not vicious. But more than that, I don't want to soften in front of an enemy.

Still, what's the harm in acting like a nurse first, a soldier second? So long as I control the situation, I can provide medical care. Even a foe deserves that, I reason, using a handkerchief to bandage the woman's hand and helping her onto Flag. I brace for a fight, but she's either in too much pain or too weak to do anything more than slump into the saddle. I take the reins and walk alongside her, my heartbeat calming.

"Since we're getting to know each other so well, why don't you tell me your name?" I ask.

"Alice," the woman responds numbly.

"Well, hello, Alice," I say. "Would you mind telling me why you shot at me?" I keep my tone as casual as if I were asking why she prefers bacon to ham.

Alice glares, hatred gleaming behind the pain. "You're a Yankee. You killed my husband."

"I've done nothing of the sort," I snap.

"Maybe not you personally, but your kind. And not just my husband. Yankees killed my father and both of my brothers. I've lost everyone I've ever loved in the last three weeks. They're gone! My life is gone!"

I don't know what to say. I've thought of the woman as an enemy, but now she seems a fragile victim, someone so riven with grief that she's held together only by the intensity of her hate. I can't imagine that much pain.

"I'm so sorry." It's all I can offer.

"Please, don't turn me in," Alice begs. "I shouldn't have shot at you, I know that. But don't make me a prisoner, please. Please, let me go. Please!"

I can't release the woman, but I don't want to jail her, either. The farther we get from the plantation house, the

UNION FIELD HOSPITAL, SAVAGE STATION, VA.

more desperate Alice grows. She wails and pleads, moans and whimpers. I respect Flag more than ever. No matter how much noise she makes, he keeps on going, ignoring her as if I'd set a bushel of potatoes on his back, not a crying wretch.

I wish I could be as stoic, but my hands itch to slap her, anything to make the whining stop. The hysteria in her voice eats at me. Is there someplace else to take Alice? Not a prison, but not the comfort of a Southern home either? I don't know how much I can trust her, but by the time we arrive at camp, I have a plan. I'm ashamed of shooting Alice, of taking her prisoner, ashamed that my fellow soldiers have inflicted so much loss on one simple woman. I decide that the least I can do is take her to the hospital to have her hand properly bandaged and let her stay on as a nurse. Women aren't normally welcome in military hospitals, but these are desperate times, and the doctors need all the help they can get.

I lift Alice off Flag. She stands there frozen while I give him the apple I found in her kitchen. "You've earned it, boy. You have more patience than I'll ever have." I tie the reins loosely to the stake in front of the hospital tent and lead Alice inside. After all her thrashing and pleading, she's strangely docile and quiet as we walk between the rows of cots. I smile and nod at the soldiers I know.

"How are you feeling today, Andy?" I stop to ask a fresh-faced boy with a bandaged stump in place of his left arm.

"Better, Nurse Frank, heaps better, though I guess I won't be much of a hand at playing piano no more."

"From what I hear about how you played, that's something we should all be grateful for," I tease.

"Is that Frank I hear?" a deep voice from the back of the tent bellows. Dr. Bonine strides toward us, wiping his bloody hands on a towel.

"Yes, Doctor, and I'd like you to meet someone." I turn to Alice. "This poor woman had an accident with a gun, and once you've bandaged her, she'd like to help you out if you'll have her. Her name is Alice."

Dr. Bonine takes in Alice's pallor, her widow's weeds,

her despairing eyes. "We don't ordinarily have women work as nurses, but so long as you stay here, in camp, we would be truly grateful for the help."

Alice's mouth trembles. She falls to her knees, wringing her hands like an actress in a melodrama. "Thank you, sir! Thank you, thank you! I won't let you down, sir!"

The doctor and I exchange a look over her bowed head. I don't need to say another word. Her Southern accent has told him the rest of the story.

"You're welcome here, Alice." Dr. Bonine's voice is gentle and soothing. "I hope you'll make a comfortable home with us, basic as things are."

Jerome is another story. "What did you bring that Southern woman here for?" He corners me and pulls me outside so he can berate me without disturbing the patients. "We don't need her. We don't want her. And women don't belong in battlefield hospitals."

My cheeks burn. Is he saying I don't belong here? "You may not need her, but Dr. Bonine does. And what else could I do with her? I couldn't leave her to attack another soldier, and I couldn't put her in a prisoner camp. This seemed like the best solution."

"How about confiscating her gun? That could have worked! Honestly, Frank, what were you thinking?"

I flinch in the face of such rage. Why is Jerome so angry? It doesn't make sense to me.

"I'm sorry, but Dr. Bonine is fine with having Alice at

the hospital, and that's all that matters." I stiffen myself for another outburst. Jerome must really hate me, must hate any hint that I'm a woman. If I want him for a friend, I have to be absolutely manly. I push down the rising softness, the urge to grab his hand and ask him to forgive me, to love me.

"Oh, forget about it!" Jerome snorts, turning away in disgust.

I wish I could. I want to erase the memory of Alice's milky hand raised in surrender and the bloody hole I've torn right through it.

Back on mail duty, Flag and I trudge along the muddy road between Fort Monroe and the camp near Yorktown as the army waits for the siege guns to reach us. While I'm at Fort Monroe waiting for the boat to dock with the mail, I overhear two soldiers talking.

"Did you hear about that ambush on the road to Yorktown last week?" the taller one asks.

"Another one?" His friend frowns.

"Yep, and this time they killed one of the soldiers delivering mail. Some Rebs were waiting round the bend at Painter's Gap. They shot the postmaster—stole his horse and all the mail. Guess they were hoping for some money in those letters."

I know the spot they're talking about, the curve in the road where I always speed up because it feels so isolated and vulnerable. Still, I don't hesitate to do my job, just ride all the faster when I come to that dreaded place. After all, someone has to deliver the mail. Besides, anything is better than being cooped up in camp, surrounded by thousands of men, any one of whom could see through my disguise if I ever let anything slip.

A NEW MISSION

I'M MAKING THE ROUNDS IN THE HOSPITAL TENT IN between mail runs when the regimental chaplain approaches me.

"If you're willing, there's an important job I want to recommend you for. It's dangerous, but I wouldn't ask you if I didn't think you could do it."

More dangerous than riding alone through hostile territory? Riskier than fighting on the battlefield? I wait for the chaplain to explain.

"One of our best spies has been captured and killed." The chaplain presses his long fingers together. "I think you're just the man to replace him. I'd like to give your name to the generals." He pauses, looking intently at me. I wonder if he's having second thoughts because my face looks so young and soft. Still, he's seen me handle the ugliest wounds without flinching, race through gunfire to rescue a wounded soldier, and ride off alone through enemy territory without hesitation. He should have faith in my abilities. The chaplain stares hard, then asks, "Will you do it?"

I don't hesitate. "I'm your man."

The chaplain nods. "I thought you would be. I'll arrange for an interview with the commanding officers."

That night I tell Damon that I've volunteered to be a spy.

"Why'd you do that for?" Damon asks, propping himself up on his elbow as he lies on his bedroll. "As if battle itself weren't dangerous enough for you. Sometimes I just can't figure you out, Frank. You're not like other soldiers."

"Of course, I am," I insist.

"No, you aren't," Damon argues. "You take risks like your life doesn't matter. You wanted to stay with the wounded in Centreville. That was plumb foolish!"

"It's hard to leave people when you're trying to save their lives. You feel you owe them something. Something more than being taken prisoner. That's not taking stupid chances, that's being a nurse."

"Well, the doctor didn't take as much convincing to skedaddle as you did. You know what I think it is, what's different about you?" Damon squints at me.

"What?" I ask, keeping my voice steady. He can't possibly suspect I'm a woman.

"I think it's because you don't have a sweetheart waiting for you. Or parents neither. Heck, you deliver the mail, but the only letters you get are from families thanking you for sending along the last words of a dying soldier. You know, without family, you just don't have as much will to live." Damon is clearly satisfied with his insight.

"That's ridiculous! I don't want to die!" But deep down, I wonder if there might be some truth to what Damon says. I have no ties, no one caring about me, no one I want to live to see again.

"You're wrong, Damon," I say. "I want to be a spy because I think I'd be good at it. I have a knack for disguises like you wouldn't believe." I smile. "And I like adventure. You may think I'm taking stupid risks, but I'm enjoying myself. Being on the battlefield is much worse, and maybe if I do my job as a spy right, we'll do better when the fighting comes."

Damon lies back on his blanket. "Maybe. But I still think a sweetheart would do you good."

I snort, thinking of the women I courted back in Flint to prove myself as a man. The last thing I need now is to work to convince potential sweethearts that I'm manly enough. "Well, then find me one," I tease. "I haven't had much occasion to socialize since I joined the army."

Damon sits up. "I know just what to do! My girl has a cousin. You might like her. Her name is Virginia. I'll write to her about you and maybe the two of you can start corresponding."

That kind of distance is reassuring—anyone can sound like anybody on paper. "Sure," I agree. "But in the meantime, I'm going to be a spy." If I can be both a spy and the postmaster, I might manage to spend most of my time away from camp, away from Jerome. That means less time worrying about being found out. Funny to think that I'm worrying less about being caught as a spy by the enemy than I am about being caught as a woman by my fellow soldiers.

I spend that evening studying weapons, tactics, local geography, and military personnel, intent on giving a strong interview. I'm not sure exactly what a spy should know, but I want to be prepared. Damon watches me bury my nose in the books I've borrowed.

"I've never seen anyone work so hard to get hisself killed," he remarks.

"I'm working hard so I *won't* get killed," I correct him. "You'll see."

The next day, command headquarters calls me in. I square my shoulders and stand ramrod straight as I present myself to General McClellan, Colonel Poe, and an officer I haven't met before.

"Private Frank Thompson, Company F, Second Michigan Volunteer Infantry of the Army of the Potomac." I salute.

"At ease, Private," the general orders. "Take a seat. We have some questions for you."

I sit on the stool across the table from the commanders, looking fierce and determined, the way a spy should.

The three officers take turns questioning me, probing to

see how loyal I am, checking my views on secession and slavery and my motives for becoming a spy. General McClellan keeps pushing to see if I have any Southern connections or sympathies. Too many double agents have been discovered, he warns me, for him to take risks anymore.

It's a good thing I explained my reasons to Damon earlier. Without realizing it, I was preparing for the interview. Now the things I said to him come back to me. I declare myself to be deeply patriotic, with a hunger for adventure that has been sparked by the travels I've made as a bookseller.

"But mostly, sirs, I want to be a spy because I know I'd be good at it. I've always been good at disguises and pretending to be someone I'm not. I can do all kinds of voices." I launch into a litany, from Irish brogue to Southern twang. I deepen the pitch and raise it, going from old man to young girl with my voice alone.

General McClellan nods, satisfied. "All right, young man, I'm impressed. But you need to pass two more tests."

My stomach knots. More tests? What else will I have to do? What other questions do I need to answer? I'm led outside, and Colonel Poe points to a series of paper targets set up at the edge of the camp.

"Take your best shots, son," the colonel instructs. "You don't have to be a sharpshooter, but you need to hit the broad side of a barn."

I relax—this is something I can do. I raise my seven-shooter, take aim at the first target, and as with Alice's palm, send a ball straight through the center. I steady my hand and shoot at the next target and the next and the next. I don't always hit the bull's-eye, but I make the target every time.

"Well done." General McClellan claps me on the back. "Better than a spy needs to be. That leaves the last test, a medical examination."

Medical exam? When I enlisted, the physical was simply a handshake. Will this examination be something more? I can't imagine what it could be, but I don't have much time to think about it either. I'm brought back into headquarters, where we all wait for Dr. Bonine.

I sit stiffly, sweat gathering under my collar as I imagine the doctor discovering that the potential spy is really a woman. Well, I'll have proven my expertise at disguise and infiltration! I try to calm my breathing. I want to be a spy so that I'm less exposed to my fellow soldiers, and here I am, about to expose more than I've ever expected. What have I gotten myself into? Will the doctor make me undress, listen to my heart and lungs, check my lower regions for possible problems? I suppose men must have some kind of difficulties with their private parts that need checking. Really, I don't know anything about men's bodies except what I've seen in the hospital. I can't imagine sitting on a horse with that extra bit in the way. My God, I think, Jerome has that problem, and so does Damon, and Dr. Bonine, and the chaplain, and the officers right in front of me. I can't look at any of them now without wondering which pant leg holds that extra central leg and how does it keep from getting squashed when they sit down?

The general leans forward, possibly squashing his male organ even more. "Don't be nervous, soldier—you've done fine so far. I'm sure you'll pass the last test."

I swallow. Don't think about the pecker, don't think about the pecker, I chant in my head. I'm both grateful I don't have such a cumbersome addition to my anatomy and scared the doctor will discover my lack. "Yes, sir," I say, trying to keep my voice from squeaking with fear.

The doctor walks in and salutes. Then he turns to me and smiles. "I know this soldier, sir. We've worked together at the hospital, and I can attest to his character and courage."

"Yes," the general answers. "I trust his character. And he's a good marksman, too. But what does phrenology tell us about him?"

"Phrenology?" I quaver. I wipe the sweat off my brow and close my legs tight together. Does phrenology have anything to do with the study of peckers? I fervently hope not.

"Phrenology is the study of the head and features and what they tell us about a person's abilities. It's the latest scientific method, and it's proven widely successful. There was a recent murder case that was solved by examining the perpetrator's profile. Criminals, for example, have low foreheads and jutting jaws. It was obvious that the accused man was guilty simply by his bestial forehead." As he talks, the doctor rests his fingers on my skull, pressing around my forehead, temples, and the back of my head.

I stare ahead, trying to breathe normally. Surely nothing on my head reveals that I'm a woman or I would have been found out long ago. I force myself to relax. So long as I keep my clothes on and nothing else is touched, I'll be fine.

"Yes," says the doctor, straightening up. "It's just as I thought. Private Thompson is clearly intelligent. You can see that from his high forehead. He's a person of faith and conviction, as his strong chin reveals. And he's resourceful—his temples show that. In all, the perfect candidate for a spy."

The general stands up, followed by the officers. I stand up too, still keeping my legs close together.

"Private Thompson, you're officially a spy for the Union army now. You should prepare for your first assignment. You'll be going behind enemy lines in three days. Find out all you can about their fortifications, their equipment, their numbers, their intentions. And don't get caught. Spies aren't looked on kindly by the enemy." General McClellan reaches out his hand. I take it and give it a manly shake.

"Yessir, I will sir, find those things out, that is. And I won't get caught. Sir." I'm relieved to clear out the thought of peckers and how they fit under a man's clothes. I need to focus on spying now. Giddy that I've fooled the officers and the doctor, I feel a rush of confidence that I'll fool the Southerners.

For my first mission, I decide to disguise myself as a freed slave. White men, especially Southerners, don't look closely at black men. Slaves are even more invisible than old women. Grateful for my brown eyes, I darken my skin with silver nitrate, put on a minstrel wig and torn clothes, and head off to the Rebel lines just as the sun rises.

In the hush of early-morning birdsong, I crawl along the ground, stopping every time a twig snaps or a branch rustles. The magnolias are in full bloom, pink and waxy, the camellias red amid their broad green leaves, the branches of the plum trees sheathed in a froth of white blossoms. Everything is lush and green and in bloom. It's the season for horses to drop foals, for sheep to lamb, and cows to calve. Having spent so much of my life on a farm, tied to the rhythms of the seasons, I feel strange marking the spring by inching along the carpet of grasses and wildflowers. I'm not setting out to plow a field or coax an anxious cow into the barn to give birth. Instead, I'm an intruder on the land, not part of it.

After I've gone so far I must have passed the sentries, I stand up on nervous legs, looking for the tents of the Confederate camp. Only I don't see any. Could I be hopelessly lost already? I try to guess the right direction from the sun, but I'm not sure which way is east. I stand still, listening, hoping to hear something that will indicate the right way. I've been concentrating for a good ten minutes when I hear voices, Southern drawls, headed toward me. It's a group of slaves bringing breakfast to the Rebel pickets, the men who guard the camp.

"Min' if I join you?" I ask, dabbing at my sweaty forehead with a kerchief. I don't want to melt away my coloring. "I'se lookin' for work."

"We got work aplenty, if that's what you want." A skinny young boy grins at me, offering cornbread and coffee. I wolf it down, nodding my thanks. But after I've helped carry food to the pickets and followed the group back into camp, I'm not sure what to do. The others know exactly where to go and scatter off to their assigned duties. I'm not sure which one to follow, where I will learn the most.

"You there, boy!" a Rebel officer yells. "Who do you belong to? Why are you setting there, gawking?"

"I don' belong to no man," I mumble, keeping my face down. "I'm headin' to Richmond to fin' work."

"As long as there's a Confederate army, y'all belong to SOMEONE!" the officer roars. "There'll be no free slaves so long as our hearts beat strong, and don't you forget it! Now go work on the fortifications if you don't want a whupping."

I nod, relieved the officer isn't taking a closer look. My muscles tense with both fear and anger—fear of being discovered, anger at being treated like a slave. No one has ordered me around like that since I left the farm. It's been four years since Pa yelled at me, but the feeling is so familiar, it could have been yesterday. Just as I did then, I grit my teeth and do as I'm told.

"All the slaves will be free, so long as *my* heart beats strong!" I think, collecting a pickaxe, shovel, and wheelbarrow. I've forgotten about slavery since the rescue of the contraband party. Now I remember again what this war is about. I've been able to free myself by shucking off my skirts and dressing like a man, but how many Africans could pass for white? And who wants to live that kind of lie, always worrying about being discovered? I'm so tired of pretending that putting on a different kind of disguise offers me a strange sense of security, as if now that I'm wearing two masks, people have to see through both of them to discover the real me. It seems like something I could have read about in one of the adventure serials I used to sell—a woman pretending to be a man pretending to be a soldier pretending to be a spy pretending to be a slave. Where is the real person behind all the pretense? I'm not sure anymore, and for right now it doesn't matter. I just have to be the slave/spy combination and shut down the rest of my selves until it's safe to let them out, until I'm alone again or with Flag.

I follow the line of sweating workers pushing gravel-filled wheelbarrows over a narrow plank to build up the earthworks facing the Union army. I'm used to hard work, but by midday my palms are bloody and raw. I'm so exhausted, I almost tip the wheelbarrow twice. Each time, another worker rushes over to help me. I murmur my thanks, touched by the kindness of the other slaves. None of them seems the least bit suspicious of me. None of them are cold or unwelcoming. They're treated like animals, but they laugh and joke with one another. It reminds me of how gentle the soldiers are with their wounded friends, how they comfort and care for them. These people—the slaves and soldiers—are all part of bigger families, while I'm left on the edge. I will never belong to any kind of community. Frank Thompson, yes, but not me, the real me.

I watch a father guide his son as they lay stones onto the earthen wall, and feel a jolt of jealousy. I envy their closeness, the love and respect they clearly have for each other. For a second I feel sorry for myself—I'm nobody's son, nobody's daughter. But I tell myself it doesn't matter. I'm a spy and I have a job to do.

While I dig, wheel, and heap up gravel, I study the layout of the Rebel fortifications. I count guns and note logs that have been painted black and set up to look like cannon from a distance. When night falls, and everyone else sleeps, I take out the paper and pencil I've hidden inside my shoe and write what I remember, listing each piece of artillery and where it's placed.

It feels good to have a specific purpose, a sense of mission. I flip over the paper to sketch the ramparts and mark where each gun stands and where the painted logs have been set to trick the Union troops into thinking we're facing formidable cannons, not tree trunks. Footsteps clomp behind me—someone heading for the latrine? I don't wait to find out but quickly snuff out my candle, fold the plan, and stick it back in its hiding place. Looking up through slitted eyes, I recognize the officer who set me to work that morning. I tuck my chin, trying to disappear, to be nothing but a ragged, bone-tired slave, waiting for sleep to overtake me. The shiny leather boots stride right past.

The next morning, my muscles are stiff and sore and my palms so raw I can't manage the pickaxe. When I see the slender boy with the friendly eyes again filling buckets with water, I get an idea.

"You bringin' water to the troops?" I ask the boy.

"Uh-huh." He nods.

"Would you min' tradin' jobs with me—I ain't got no skin left on my hands and that's the truth. I'll give you thirty cents if'n you switch with me." I hold out some coins.

The boy shakes his head. "I can't use no money, that's for sure. But I'll switch jobs, don't you worry." He peers closely at me. "You lookin' mighty peaked. What happened to yuh face?"

I dab at the streaking color on my forehead, wishing I'd thought to bring silver nitrate with me to refresh my disguise. "It's a condition that comes on me from time to time. Can't do nuthin' 'bout it—it'll jus' pass on its own." I tuck my head down and heave up the heavy buckets. "Thank you for yo' kindness."

I head for a cluster of soldiers, stopping behind a tree to

smear the color more evenly on my face. I hope I still look like a slave, if a light-skinned one now. As I fill canteens, I'm surprised to recognize a peddler, a tall, lanky fellow who comes to the Union camp once a week, selling newspapers and stationery for letters home. He spends a lot of time hanging around headquarters, and now I understand why. The man is still tall and lanky, but he isn't dressed as a peddler anymore. Now he wears a Rebel uniform, and he's busy describing the layout of the Union camp and its defenses.

"Well, I'll be," I mutter, sloshing water on the spy's leg.

"Hey, watch it there, dolt!" the fake peddler yells.

I lower my head. "Sorry, suh, sorry." And I really am sorry, sorry I can't rush back to the Union camp right away and tell the generals the truth. But how can I leave camp safely? It's not easy for a soldier to desert, let alone for a slave to run away, and if I get caught, I'll be shot for sure. Still, I can't risk staying much longer—another day and I'll definitely look white.

I wait until the sun sets before heading toward the pickets, hoping to slip by the sentries the same way I snuck in. If only there were more trees or bushes! Between the two army camps stretches a swell of ground with low shrubs and grasses. The only thing to hide me is the darkness.

I haven't gone far when a voice stops me. "You there," a thickset officer calls.

I turn to face the beefy soldier. "Yessuh," I gulp.

"Take this rifle and head for the picket post by the brambles. The guard was shot. You're his replacement." The soldier hands me a gun. "And don't you even think about shutting those eyes of yours!"

"Nossuh!" I say, trying to keep from smiling. I can't believe the officer is handing over a rifle. Does he think that Africans want to be slaves? Don't the Rebels worry about slave uprisings? I take the gun and picture myself pointing it at the officer's gut and blowing a hole in it. I shake my head. Can't do that. I'll just get myself killed. Best to leave the job to the Union army.

In the moonless night, it's easy for me to take my post and then keep on going. Once I get close to the Union pickets, I curl up on the ground and wait until morning, shivering in the damp chill. Still, it's better than being shot by my own side.

As the sun rises, I take off the wig and wave it at the picket nearby. My hair ruffles cool and free in the morning breeze. "It's Private Frank Thompson," I holler.

"I don't care what yo' name is. Yo' ain't comin' one step closer less'n you got the password." The guard cocks his rifle and squints down the barrel.

"Liberty Bell." I twirl the wig on my finger. The guard gapes but lowers his gun. I must make an odd sight, dressed in rags with splotchy darkened skin and matted hair. I take long, easy strides, tired and hungry but strangely light inside. I've done it—I've carried off my first mission. I really am a spy! And maybe the paper in my shoe will make a difference, help end this war. Being a nurse, I've felt like I'm helping to save lives or at least ease the work of dying, but this work seems even more important.

I pass by the hospital on the way to headquarters to report to the commanders. Jerome sits on a stump outside, taking a break, but I don't stop to talk with him. My assignment isn't over yet, not until I've given the intelligence I've collected. Besides, ever since I started delivering mail, I rarely see Jerome. It's better that way.

"Is that you, Frank?" he asks, standing up and shaking off the dust from his pants. "Where have you been? Your horse was here, so I knew you weren't getting mail. I've been worried sick about you."

"You have?" I'm surprised. Of course Jerome cares for me, as a friend, but it's been a long time since our regular chats.

"Why are you dressed like that? What happened to your skin? What's going on?" Jerome reaches out a finger and rubs at my cheek.

I pull back, my cheek burning from his touch. I shake my head, feeling like a fool, desperate to erase the memory of how his finger felt on my skin. It's spring, the time when young men's thoughts are supposed to turn to love. I'm not a man, but I can't help thinking of Jerome's soft lips, his warm eyes, his handsome, firm hands. And he's a man with absolutely no thoughts of love toward me.

"I have to go to headquarters," I say. "I'll explain everything on the way, if you like." I keep my tone light and friendly. That's what we are—all we are—comrades in arms.

Jerome falls into step beside me and I tell him the whole story. When I'm finished, he looks at me, astonished.

"Now that takes guts." Jerome lets out a long, slow whistle.

"Nah." I can't help it. I feel a blush rise in my cheeks. I look down, hoping he won't notice.

"No, really, Frank, I'm proud of you, proud to know you," Jerome says.

The blush fades as quickly as it came. Just proud? That's all he feels about me? I study his familiar, handsome profile. I wish I didn't love him. I wish his coolness didn't hurt so much. But I do and it does. And I just have to swallow both those truths.

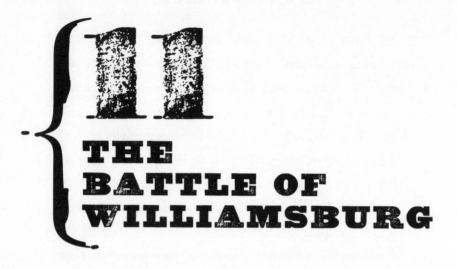

11

THE BATTLE OF WILLIAMSBURG

I REPORT THE PEDDLER AS A SPY, BUT HE SEEMS TO have disappeared. Worse still, my detailed map and list of artillery prove worthless, since before we can use the information, the Confederate army breaks camp and slips away the following night. Their big guns fire at us until morning, when they fall silent and their use as a diversion to allow a quick retreat is revealed. I'm depressed that my mission has turned out to be a waste, but my comrades are exultant. Instead of feeling manipulated or fooled, they're in a celebratory mood—we've taken Yorktown without firing a single shot of our own. But the commanders want more than towns—they want to rout the Rebels, so McClellan sends troops to catch the retreating Confederates before they can reinforce Richmond.

Our regiment, led by Colonel Poe, brings up the rear. It's two o'clock in the afternoon and pouring rain when we catch up to the two clashing armies. Just outside Williamsburg we slog through a thick forest broken up by ditches and swamps, firing at Rebel sharpshooters hidden behind trees, bushes, and fallen logs. They seem to be everywhere and nowhere, impossible for us to see and hit, yet they have no problem finding us with their deadly aim.

I've been marching next to Damon, but in the chaos of the battle I lose track of him, focused only on shooting as many gray uniforms as possible. I aim, shoot, and reload as quickly as I can. My shoulder aches and my fingers are numb, my mind a blank. Before the battle I was worried whether I'd actually shoot anybody, whether I'd do any good as a soldier, but now that the fighting clashes all around me, like the time with Alice, I don't hesitate. I'm a machine, doing what's necessary. It's like Bull Run, when I didn't think about the wounded soldiers, the gruesomeness of their injuries, the gushing rivers of blood. I simply became hands and feet, tools for doing what had to be done.

"You, there, nurse," a slender blond soldier from my regiment yells at me. "Help me retrieve the wounded. I see an officer down yonder."

I sling my rifle over my shoulder and grab the other side of the stretcher, diving into the fiercest part of the fighting. A colonel lies under a barrage of bullets, groaning in agony. Blondie and I heave his weight onto the stretcher and scramble back through a storm of rain and minié balls, searching for the nearest field hospital.

"Dr. Bonine is over there," I bellow, straining to be heard over the boom of cannons. I don't have a free hand to point, so I gesture with my jutting chin and head toward the edge of the battlefield, where a makeshift surgery has been set up.

The shrill Rebel yell echoes in the woods. Shells scream overhead. Gunshots crackle. Men lie crumpled—dying or already dead—but we don't pause. We'll go back later for the others, the ones we can save. Right now we have to get the colonel to safety, to medical care.

I gasp for breath but keep on running while Blondie pants behind me. We come to a pocket of stillness, where Dr. Bonine leans over a growing row of wounded men.

"Doctor," I rasp, "this colonel needs you." We set down the stretcher and unfold a blanket alongside it.

"You take the feet, I'll take the shoulders," Blondie directs. Quickly, we shift the officer onto the blanket, where he lies as still as death.

"I don't see any blood. Where are you hit, sir?" Dr. Bonine asks, probing the inert body carefully. The officer screws his eyes shut and says nothing.

"Are you hit?" the doctor demands. "Are you hit at all?" His voice thunders in anger. "You, sir, are a fake and a coward! Get back to your regiment or I'll report you to the general."

I watch, astounded, as the colonel abruptly sits up, brushes himself off, and strides away. I'm sick to my stomach, thinking of the truly wounded we passed by to rush this fake to safety.

"I'm sorry, Doctor," I say. "Next time I'll make sure the man is really hurt before I put him on a stretcher."

Blondie hangs his head, equally shamefaced. "I'm sorry too, Doctor," he mumbles.

Dr. Bonine claps us both on the shoulder. "You did nothing wrong. That scum should be ashamed to call himself an officer!"

There isn't time to think about the colonel's sneaky trick. The Rebel artillery booms louder and closer than ever. The pace of firing quickens. The battle reaches a fever pitch. Men shoot and are shot at, kill and are killed, in a haze of smoke and blood. I rush back into the tumult of bodies. Hour after hour I carry soldiers off the battlefield to have their legs or arms amputated, their wounds bandaged, their bleeding stanched. Now I'm careful to make sure the men are truly injured, but once I make the mistake of picking up a dead man and carrying a corpse to safety. Or maybe he isn't dead when we start our sprint to the doctor. Maybe he dies as we carry him. My heart feels heavy at the thought. It's best not to think at all, to simply plunge into the minié balls and shells falling as fast as the rain to get to the men who need me.

A cannonball thuds to earth nearby, throwing up mud, branches, blood, and flesh. The soldier who's hit is unrecognizable, reduced to torn bits, a torso, a sleeve, a boot with a foot still in it. I race past the bloody fragments to a man whose leg is crushed from the ankle to the knee. When I come closer, I recognize the captain of our regiment, Captain Morse. It's the first time someone I know has been hit, the first time I feel bile rise up in my throat, and I'm afraid I'll be sick. I swallow the sour taste and try to calm the trembling in my legs.

"Captain! We're here," I say. "We'll get you to safety, don't worry."

"I'm not worried about me," he gasps. "I'm worried about my men. I can't leave them. They need me."

"Not this way, they don't." I lift my commander onto the stretcher as gingerly as I can, but still he grimaces in pain.

"Just cut the leg off and be done with it. I have to get back to my men."

"You will, sir, in good time. Right now we have to get you to the doctor." I pick up one end of the stretcher, nodding at Blondie to do the same. We work well as a team now, having done this same simple act many times over— a mad dash through cross fire, a quick lift of the wounded soldier onto the stretcher, and another mad dash back to the doctor. I try to think of it like that, just another stretcher run. But this time is different. This time I'm carrying a friend, and all the injuries that have seemed so abstract to me are vividly real now.

By the time we set the stretcher down again, the captain

has lost consciousness, a blessing considering the doctor immediately starts sawing at the doomed leg. My own leg quivers as the blade meets bone. And this time I can't stop myself. I lean over and heave, retching up stomach juices. I turn away, tears blurring my eyes. No one should see me like this, weak and panicked and terrified.

Blondie puts his hand on my back. "It'll be fine," he murmurs.

I jerk myself away, ashamed. I don't want comfort—I want to be strong.

The nurse stands there, calm as death. "When you're ready, we should go back in there."

How can he be so indifferent, so unfeeling? I swallow my tears and face his impassive eyes, his careful mouth.

"He could be dying, you know! He's a good man with a wife and three small boys, not just another body!" The rage feels good, surging through me with a rush of power. The trembling in my legs vanishes, and I feel strong enough to hurl boulders.

The nurse nods, steady as ever. "We're in the same regiment. He's my captain, too. I know what kind of man he is, the kind who deserves to be saved. There are more like him lying on the field right now. I want to help them. Do you?"

The anger leaks out of me. He's right. Of course, he's right. "I'm sorry," I mutter. "Let's go."

We each pick up an end of the stretcher and jog back

toward the battle. Neither of us mentions the incident again. I'm grateful for Blondie's discretion, for his compassion. What I've learned about myself isn't as pretty. I snapped, and for those few moments I forgot how to be a soldier or a nurse. I forgot how to be a man.

As the sun sinks below the horizon, I catch sight of a wave of blue uniforms running through the field. Not a patch of blue here and there but a solid mass of men, rifles blazing. Reinforcements at last! A spark of hope cuts through my exhaustion. I join the soldiers as one of them, not a nurse anymore, and fight with a new rush of energy. The fresh soldiers push the battle into our favor, and the Rebels flee.

But there are so many dead, so many casualties, it doesn't feel like much of a victory. As Colonel Poe writes in his journal: "It was an awful battle, awfully conducted, and if it had not been for a handful of Michigan men who threw themselves through the broken ranks of General Hooker's division, the Army of the Potomac would not now be in existence." The Second Michigan, our regiment, actually makes a difference that day, but the win comes at too high a price for us to feel much satisfaction. The regiment loses seventeen men, thirty-eight are wounded, including the captain, and four are missing, their bodies lost in the brambles and woods to be found by vultures and foxes.

General McClellan calls a temporary truce to allow both sides to collect their dead and wounded. As darkness falls and the storm continues, drenching both living and dead, I wade through the bloody mud, shielding my torch from the rain while I search for men to carry to the hospital.

It's a nightmarish sight—the torchlit mouths frozen in grimaces of despair and horror. Even more jarring, shadows flicker on an angelic face calm in repose above a body with a gaping hole torn through it. I slog past corpse after corpse, searching for any sign of life, of movement, of breath. Finally something catches my eye. A man walks toward me, his own torch before him.

"Frank!" the soldier calls out. "You're alive! I didn't see you. I thought . . ." Jerome lowers his torch, lighting his drawn face, his eyes black with sorrow.

My heart lifts, a moment of warmth amid so much ugliness. In all the horror, his familiar voice is a balm to me. I want to rush up to him, to hold him tight, to cover his face with kisses. We're both alive among so much death, and all I want is to feel his arms around me. Instead, I stand stockstill, not trusting myself if I get any closer.

"Jerome, it's good to see you." As if we've met up in the line for supper. As if what has happened, what is happening all around us, is ordinary.

"This is what I imagined Armageddon would be like," Jerome says. "This is my idea of hell." He gestures toward the nearby bodies, arms bent unnaturally, parts of faces, legs, torsos ripped apart by shells.

"Wait!" I cry. "There's someone moving there." I hurry over to a tangle of bodies.

"I see it, too!" Jerome follows me.

Yellow eyes glow in the torch's glare. A raccoon rears up on its hindquarters, baring its teeth.

Fury surges through me. I stoop down, grab a rock, and heave it at the raccoon. "Get away! Go!" I shriek. "You won't eat these men, you ugly critter!" The raccoon turns and bounds away. There are plenty of other places to find fresh meat.

"Come on," Jerome sighs. "Let's head back to the hospital. We're no use here. There's no one left to save."

I nod, exhausted, drained by all the death around me. I trudge heavily, slowly, forcing my hands to stay at my sides. I've never wanted to touch anyone the way I ache to reach my fingers out to Jerome now. But I can't. I have to push the urge down. I try not to look at Jerome. I try to close my ears to his rich, tender voice.

At the edge of the field, corpses lie in long rows, their faces cloaked by handkerchiefs or coats. If they can't have coffins, they can still have some dignity, the coverings seem to say. But to me the anonymity makes the scene even more depressing. Maybe vacant eyes staring into nothing would be worse, but I want these soldiers to be known, to be remembered. I want to care about every single one of them. I bend down and gently lift the corner of one kerchief. The face I look into is young, perhaps sixteen, killed by a ball shot through the temple. The boy looks surprised. I notice he's wearing shoulder straps, that he's already been promoted to sergeant for bravery under fire. I close his eyes and murmur a prayer, like I did so long ago at Bull Run when I saw my first soldier killed. I don't recognize this boy, don't know his name, but at least now I'll remember his face, his valor. He won't be an abstract loss, a number in a ledger, but the person he deserves to be.

"Come," Jerome says softly. "Let's do what we can for the living. They're taking care of the dead." He points to the soldiers digging wide trenches for a mass grave.

I nod numbly.

After a night of steady recovery work, hundreds still remain to be buried. Dead and wounded lie piled together in ravines and rifle pits, covered with mud and gore. In that pitched day of battle, more than two thousand Union soldiers have been killed or wounded, joined by as many Confederates.

For the next two weeks Williamsburg becomes one enormous hospital. Churches, schools, homes—all become wards for the injured. I hardly sleep as I go from bed to bed, trying to keep up the wounded men's strength and spirits. General McClellan has given Confederate doctors permission to treat the injured, so that gray and blue surgeons work side by side caring for gray and blue soldiers. It's a strange sort of truce, a reminder of how close the two sides are, a reminder of how stupidly blind war is.

I'm making the rounds with Dr. Bonine when I recognize a slender black boy, his head swathed in a bandage. It's the slave who traded jobs with me back at Yorktown in the Rebel camp.

"Are the doctors taking good care of you?" I ask.

The boy blinks, surprised by the attention. He nods.

I turn to Dr. Bonine. "I know this boy, and he deserves special treatment. He's helped the Union cause." The boy stares at me with wide eyes.

"I ain't done nuthin'," he protests. "You're mistakin' me for some other body."

"No, I'm not." I pat his hand. "You were generous to me when I asked for a favor. I'm happy to do you one in return. How 'bout I bring you some brandy? It'll help you sleep." I thought I'd never see the boy again, and now I have a chance to actually do something for him.

The boy nods again, mystified. He has no idea that he's ever seen me before, especially not dressed as a slave. And I have no intention of explaining how we first met. All that matters is that the boy gets better, and that when he leaves the hospital he be free, as he always should have been.

The first week after the battle, Jerome and I often eat together. It's easy to fall back into our old friendship. It's a familiar comfort, one we both desperately need. After a day spent cleaning festering wounds and writing down the last wishes of dying men, I crave talking to Jerome, emptying the ugly images out of my head. His familiar face and voice, his gestures and smell, all comfort me, giving me a sense of connection with him. I allow myself to sink into his presence like a warm bath. But it's dangerous to let myself relax too much with him. If I'm not on my guard, my voice will soften or I'll find myself tilting my chin coquettishly, moving closer so that our thighs may touch. I never mean to—it just happens. As if my body has a mind of its own, one that's not listening to me. Horrified, I catch myself mooning over him with big eyes like a ninny or reaching up as if to stroke his cheek. Thank the heavens, so far I've always pulled back before Jerome has noticed anything. I hope he never will.

I'm on nursing rounds in a church I haven't been to before when I find another friend. Tossing with fever, Damon sprawls on a pew, his thigh pierced by a minié ball. The leg is swollen and gray where the bullet has entered. There's been so much confusion after the battle, I haven't noticed that he's been missing. I'm ashamed I haven't thought of him at all.

"Damon," I say, dabbing at his sweaty forehead with a cool, moist rag. "Damon, it's me, Frank. I'm here now. I'll take care of you."

Damon's eyes snap open. "Frank!" he wails. "Frank, don't let them saw off my leg. Don't let them." His hand shoots out and grabs my wrist with feverish force. "Promise me! Promise me! I can't be a cripple! I'd rather die!" His panic surges through his fingers, rippling under my skin. I'm gripped by the urgency of his fear, the agony of his desperation.

"All right, Damon," I soothe, keeping my voice calm. "Don't worry. I won't let anyone touch your leg. Except me. Just let me change the bandage. We'll get you healed, I promise. And you'll keep your leg."

"You promise?" Damon's chest heaves with wracking sobs, and tears run down his eyes into his ears. "Don't leave me, Frank. I'm scared, I'm so scared!"

"Hush, now, you're safe. There's no need to be frightened." I peel Damon's fingers from my wrist and take his hand. I hum a lullaby and stroke his forehead until I can feel the panic drain from his body, feel him slip away into the blankness of sleep. Then I gently unwrap the bloody bandage, revealing a jagged hole white with maggots. I take the brandy bottle that's the universal medicine in every ward and drip it slowly into the wound. Then I wash it clean and put on a fresh bandage. At least it looks better now, though I doubt Damon will be able to keep the leg. Wounds like that normally mean amputation. But I'll do everything I can to prevent that, like I promised. Maybe if I clean and change the bandage every day, that will be enough. Anyway, it's all I know how to do, all I can really offer.

That night I tell Jerome about finding Damon and the promise I've made to him.

"You know he's going to lose the leg," Jerome says. "You've got to be honest with him."

"No, I can't tell him that. And I don't know that it'll be amputated. Maybe it'll heal." I stare at my plate of beans, willing it to be true.

Jerome shrugs. "You're a stubborn one, Frank Thompson, that's for sure. If your pigheadedness can make it happen, then that leg will be fine."

I nod. "Good. It's decided then. Damon keeps his leg."

Maybe it's the constant cleaning, the brandy, the prayers, or simply my stubbornness, like Jerome says, but by the end of the week Damon's leg looks much better. The swelling has gone down and a thick, brown scab covers the hole.

I bring my old tentmate a bowl of porridge the day before we're set to move out again, this time to West Point, near Williamsburg.

"So you think you'll be walking with us or will we be carrying you tomorrow?" I ask, handing Damon his breakfast.

Damon slurps down a generous spoonful. The fever has gone and his color is good. "I'll be walking—you can bet on it. Maybe limping, but still upright." Damon puts down his spoon and looks up. "Thanks to you, Frank. You saved my leg, I know it." His blue eyes brim with tears. "Thanks to you."

I smile and squeeze his hand. "I just wanted to be sure I'd see you dancing at your wedding. Now, come on, eat up. You still need to get your strength back."

I'm not arrogant enough to believe that I cured Damon, but I've helped him, and that's comforting. I can shoot a surrendering woman clean through the hand and still be a good person. I can hold men down while their legs are amputated and still be a caring, kind man. Yes, I think of myself like that, the kind of man I am. Maybe it's simply from the habit of acting like a man so much that even I'm beginning to think of myself that way. Unless I'm around Jerome. Then whatever traces of femininity I've long buried erupt at the most inconvenient times. I actually titter at one of Jerome's jokes—titter like a silly lovesick goose. I try to change the tone midlaugh into a manly chuckle, but I only end up sounding like a panicked turkey. I follow up with a good loud belch. That's sure to erase any notion of me as a woman.

It's a useful trick I've learned. Whenever I'm uneasy about my disguise or worried that someone around me is looking at me more carefully than usual, I spit out a big wad of phlegm, break wind, or belch. Not only do I seem more manly then, I feel more like a fellow. It's strange how acting like something can become convincing in itself if you do it enough.

A good thing, too, since who knows when the next battle will be or how ugly it will get? Whatever happens, I need to be a strong man, determined and fearless. At least, that's the kind of man I want to be, the kind who gets the job done. I was lucky at Williamsburg to race through hours of shooting and shelling without so much as a scratch. I was more numb than scared then. But will my luck hold at West Point? If it doesn't, will I turn soft and womanish—or worse, turn tail?

12
ANOTHER
DISGUISE

IT'S MID-MAY 1862 AND I'VE BEEN IN THE ARMY FOR A
year now. So much for a quick victory! It's strange to think
of how optimistic we were this time last year, how sure
of a quick rout. In our new position we're close enough
to taste the possibility of laying siege to Richmond, but
we know better than to expect a quick finish. We need to
control the railroads running southwest to the city. And
we have to get our artillery over the Chickahominy River.
Both might seem simple, but they're not. Nothing's easy in
this war.

If you ask me, the river is more of a creek, bordered
by wide swamps, something the men and horses can easily
cross but the big guns can't. The bridges have been burned
down by the retreating Confederates, so General McClellan
sets men to building new ones while other regiments push
along the railroad, all the way to the Fair Oaks depot. Our
advance troops are now less than ten miles from Richmond.

MILITARY BRIDGE ACROSS THE CHICKAHOMINY RIVER, VA.

Close but not there yet. Those ten miles may as well be a thousand.

The Second Michigan isn't working on either the rail lines or the bridges. We're sitting in camp, the way we've spent much of the war. Days of intense fighting are interspersed with long stretches of doing nothing, waiting for action. Being stuck in camp is always difficult for me. Not just because it's boring and I feel useless. Not just because it seems like we're doing nothing to help end this war. There's a more practical reason why staying in camp weighs on me. Every time I need to relieve myself, it's like I'm on another spy mission, plunging into enemy territory where my disguise can be discovered. I wish there were more mail to deliver so I could be free of prying eyes.

For Damon, lounging around in camp is welcome news, giving his leg plenty of time to heal. He's walking again, without crutches or a cane. True, he has a limp, and sometimes the ache in his thigh keeps him up at night, but he's lucky, one of the few who have been shot in a leg and haven't lost it to amputation.

"What do you think happens next?" he asks, lying next to me in the tent we've shared for a year now.

"Sounds like we're working to cut off and surround Richmond. I like the idea of a siege much better than another battle." I sit up and face Damon. "How many more clashes before one of us gets killed? I didn't think about dying when I enlisted, but now I think about it all the time." I bite my lip. "Does that make me a coward?" I've never admitted my fear to anyone before, but it just blurts out, lying there like a stinking fish between us.

Damon guffaws. "You'd have to be stupid not to worry about getting killed—or maimed in some awful way. Being brave is knowing what could happen, fearing it but still going ahead and plunging into the fight. You're not one to turn tail. You're about the bravest soldier I know."

Damon thinks I'm brave? A warm buzzing fills my chest at the compliment.

He crosses his arms over his chest and nods. "We'll get through this mess, I promise you. We'll smoke the Rebs out

OFFICERS (*SEATED*) OF THE 114TH PENNSYLVANIA INFANTRY PLAYING CARDS IN CAMP, PETERSBURG, VA.

of Richmond and that'll be the end of it. Maybe I didn't get home by last year's harvest, but I'm making this year's!"

"I believe you, Damon. This year you'll make the harvest!" I want to imagine him home with his sweetheart, both legs intact.

Damon relaxes around camp, playing cards, swapping stories, and writing letters. He has a lot of mail to answer, he gets so much—from his parents, his girl, his sister, even the preacher back home. So when a letter comes for me, something personal, not a thank-you from a family I've notified, he's almost as excited as I am.

"Is it from Virginia? Has she written you like I asked her to?"

"No," I say, opening the envelope. "It's from Mr. Hurlburt, my old boss, the bookseller." I read the few scrawled lines, pleased to hear from someone I actually know, someone I can imagine taking pen to paper, whose voice I can hear as I follow the words. "He hopes I'm doing well and says he'd love to get personal reports of what's happening. He wants to put together a newsletter, to give the folks back home a sense of what their sons, husbands, brothers, and fathers are enduring." I fold up the letter, slip it back into the envelope. "He wants me to write for him. Me, a writer?"

"Why not?" says Damon. "You're everything else— nurse, soldier, spy. I bet you'd be a fine writer, too."

I'm not so sure, but it feels good to have someone to write to, someone interested in hearing what I have to say. I describe the boredom of waiting around camp, the problems with fording the Chickahominy, the battle that might happen but hasn't yet. I don't know if it's good or bad, but I add my "dispatch," as Mr. Hurlburt calls it, to the pile of mail.

Only before riding out on mail duty, I'm ordered to the commander's tent. I know what that means—another spy mission.

"We need you to go behind enemy lines again," Colonel Poe orders. "Find out what their plans are, what their next move is. You leave tomorrow."

"Yessir!"

"And use a new disguise. They may remember the last one."

I wonder who I should pretend to be, but by the time I've ridden to Williamsburg that afternoon to collect the mail, I've come up with a plan. I stop at a dry-goods store and buy an old dress, shoes, a shawl, and a basket filled with thread, scissors, buttons, and other small notions. Sarah Emma Edmonds, now Frank Thompson, is going to turn herself back into a woman, an old Irish peddler this time.

"See, Flag?" I say, showing him my purchases. "I'll be a nice old biddy—what do you think? Will you still like me that way?" Flag pushes his bony head toward my chest, hoping for a treat among the sewing notions. "Of course I didn't forget you," I reassure him, pulling an apple out of my pocket. I pat the blaze on his forehead as he chomps, spraying me with apple juice. "I wonder how you see me. Am I a man to you or a woman? Or simply your friend?"

Flag snorts. To him I'm Giver of Apples, and that's what matters.

When Damon crawls into the tent that evening, he's startled by the sight of an old woman hunched over her sewing, sitting on my bedroll.

"Excuse me, ma'am, but this is a soldiers' tent. Where do you mean to be?" Damon tries to remember his manners, but it's been a long time since he's talked to a woman, and he sounds rusty.

"Well, me sonny boy, this is exactly where I mean to be.

I thought I'd just darn me socks before I'm off, if ye don' mind," I trill in my best Irish burr.

"Um, ma'am, you see, well," Damon stumbles. I can tell he wants to be polite but is worried that his tentmate will stomp in any minute and demand his bed back. "That there bed belongs to my buddy Frank, and he'll be here any second now. So, um, well . . ." He trails off, staring at the ground.

"Now don' ye worry about yer friend, dear. He's not coming back," I soothe.

"He's not coming back?" Damon's head snaps up. "What happened to him? Where is he?"

I whip the shawl off my head. "He's already right here! You don't recognize me? Pretty good disguise, huh?"

Damon snorts in relief. "Frank! Why are you dressed like that? What's going on?"

"I've got some spying to do. So what do you think? Can I pass?"

"You certainly had me fooled!" Damon grins. "But without the shawl, your face ain't womanish enough—or old enough. I know some fellows call you 'our little woman,' but that just shows how much they're missing their sweethearts. It would be too hard to make you look ladyish, but if you look old enough, that won't matter. Some old women look jus' like old men, down to the wiry whiskers sticking out of their chins!" Damon clambers out of the tent and comes back with some charcoal from the cook fire. He daubs circles under my eyes and draws lines around my mouth and across my forehead. "There," he says, sitting back and admiring his handiwork. "You make a fine old hag now. You remind me of Old Woman Forster, two farms down from us. Too bad you don't have an old gray bun, but if you keep your hair hid under the shawl, you'll be the perfect picture of a crone."

"Thanks for the compliment." I smile.

"Now don't you be doing that!" warns Damon.

"What?" I ask.

"Smiling! For one thing, you've got all your teeth. For another, they're not yellow enough to belong to an old hag. Soon as you open your mouth, you're the picture of youth."

Of course he's right. I vow to keep my mouth shut. If I have to talk, I'll pull my lips over my teeth so I'll look like a toothless creature. Pretending to be old is much trickier than pretending to be a man.

"See, Damon, you'd make a good spy yourself. You think of the details, and that's what matters when it comes to disguises—the convincing details. Like my basket of wares. Everything the soldier might need to keep his clothing and looks up, don't you think?"

"You might get some information and make some money while you're at it!" Damon teases. "When do you leave?"

"Tomorrow," I say. "But I wanted to try my disguise out, see if there were any details I needed to fix—like drawing on wrinkles and not showing my teeth."

"Are you going to eat supper like that?" Damon asks.

"Why don't you? You'll see how many people you fool. Come on, I'm starving. Let's go."

I wrap the shawl back over my head and follow Damon to the cook fire. When I see Jerome, I can't resist going up to him.

"My, but aren't ye a handsome lad. Some lass is pining for ye back home, to be sure," I croak. "If I were younger, I'd have ye meself."

Jerome looks startled—panicked even. "That's kind of you to say, ma'am," he finally manages to squeak out.

Damon watches the two of us, a big grin plastered on his face. Having been tricked himself, he finds it even more satisfying to see other men fall for my Irish accent and old-woman manners.

I'm still purring at Jerome, telling him stories about my family back in Kilkenny, about the handsome staff of a husband I had for oh so many years, but the poor dear is dead and buried now, bless his soul, and what is a poor woman to do but make her way in the world as best she can, so here I am with my bits and pieces for sale, and maybe the fine gentleman could use some scissors or buttons, surely some thread?

That's it. Damon can't help it—he bursts out laughing so hard, he almost chokes. I look at him and smile, mouth closed of course, but don't break character.

"Now what could be so amusin', do ye think?" I ask Jerome. "The man is fit to be tied, he is!"

Jerome looks more stupefied than ever. "I don't know,"

he mumbles. He sees something's going on but can't figure out what. Damon decides to have mercy on him.

"That's no peddler," he sputters, pointing at me. "It's Frank in another of his disguises!"

"Frank?" Jerome peers at the wizened face under the shadow of the shawl. "That's you?"

I pull back the shawl. "'Tis, me dear. Though for now ye can call me Bridget Mary, if ye please."

Jerome laughs. "Sure and begorra, you're a fine Bridget, ye are!" he says, trying his own Irish accent. It's so infectious that by the time we go to bed, most of the regiment is speaking with a rolling brogue. If I don't accomplish anything as a spy, at least I've given the men some entertainment.

The next day I tuck the disguise into the basket of peddler's goods and walk out of camp. I'm still wearing my uniform, except for the boots, because I plan on changing clothes later, just in case any Rebels are watching who goes in and out of the Union camp. Of course, tradesmen can sell to either side, but I don't want to take any chance of arousing suspicion—or being asked information about our army. It's easier if I leave a soldier and transform into an old Irishwoman behind a tree or shrub.

Once in the woods, I change into my disguise. I can't shake the memory of five years earlier, when I changed from my girl's clothes into my brother's pants, fled our farmhouse, and buried my dress, shorn hair, and apron under pine needles. Now I'm reversing the trade, wearing a skirt and apron once again and burying my uniform behind a distinctive rock. But this time I don't feel like I'm leaving a part of myself behind. I still feel every inch a soldier. I'm Frank Thompson, a spy for the Army of the Potomac, not Sarah Emma Edmonds. Now the dress is part of an act, not part of who I am. For a moment I wonder if I'll ever really wear skirts again. I can't imagine it. There's no going back now. Unless a miracle happens and Jerome falls in love with me, the real me. He's the only reason I would give up my freedom to reclaim the limited life of a lady. My cheeks burn thinking of it—of living with the man I love as his wife. Then I could hold him and touch him all I wanted, and he wouldn't shrink back. He would love me, too. He would want to be near me. But that will never happen. And maybe it's best that it doesn't.

Pulling the shawl over my head, I take deep breaths. Sweet honeysuckle and pungent rosemary perfume the air. Birds chirp, insects hum, and pink, yellow, and purple wildflowers glisten in the morning dew. The world looks innocent and safe.

After several hours, worried that I'm horribly lost, I come to a farmhouse with a sad, abandoned air. It's not the Rebel camp, but maybe there's food inside—something that matters more to me at the moment. The furniture in the entry hall looms thick with dust, but the kitchen still holds cornmeal, tea, even bacon. The bacon is sizzling in a pan, filling the room with its mouthwatering smell, when

I hear a groan coming from the front of the house. I tiptoe toward the sound. Another moan. Whoever it is, they're in the parlor. Slowly I poke my head in. A man in a gray uniform sprawls on the floor, his skin pale and clammy.

I forget about being a spy and become a nurse again. I kneel beside the man and gently feel his forehead. He burns with fever. His breathing is labored and a deep groan escapes his lips.

I hurry back to the kitchen and moisten a cloth in the bucket of water I've drawn from the well. I lean over the sick soldier, pressing the cool wetness to his forehead.

"There now, laddie," I coo, remembering to use the Irish lilt. "Ye'll be better soon, ye will."

The soldier opens his eyes and stares at me weakly. "Thank you," he rasps.

"Ah, so ye're awake, are ye? And hungry, too, I wager. I'll go cook us up a little somethin' now. Just ye wait here." The soldier nods numbly. As if he could move anyhow. I feel his eyes on me as I scurry out of the room, coming back with hot cornmeal hoecakes, crisp bacon, and fresh water.

The soldier is too weak to sit up, so I cradle his head in my lap, dribbling crumbs and water into his mouth. His name, he whispers, is Captain Allen Hall. He fell ill with typhoid and was still sick when the Union army attacked the Confederates near Cold Harbor. Unable to move quickly, he lost his company when they retreated and found shelter in the farmhouse.

"Hush now," I say. "And sleep. You'll feel better when you wake." Distracted by caring for the dying man, I forget I'm supposed to be an Irishwoman and slip out of my accent.

The soldier's eyes widen and he lifts up his head, his hand reaching for the pistol by his side. "Who are you?" he asks.

I stare at the gun. Is he strong enough to use it?

I could fight or I could lie, and lying seems by far the easiest. "I'm a peddler woman, plain and simple," I say. "I admit I'm not really from Ireland, but you'd be surprised how much quicker you sell things when you speak with a sweet brogue."

The captain drops his head back and smiles thinly. "So that's your secret. Don't worry, it's safe with me."

I know I should be moving on, but I can't abandon a patient, even when he's a Confederate officer. I wonder if I'm a better person for staying with him, less cruel. Or am I less courageous, more weak willed? Being a soldier, seeing battle, has changed me, but I can't figure out how. The only thing I'm sure of is that I respect men now in a way I never did before. I'm surprised by the intense kinship I feel for my fellow soldiers. And the Rebel soldier, enemy though he is, belongs to that brotherhood. Born in different circumstances, he could easily be wearing a blue uniform instead of his gray one.

All through the night I nurse him, feeding him morsels of hoecake and giving him weak tea, soothing his feverish skin with cool compresses. Toward dawn he opens his eyes.

"I want you to do something for me." He fumbles through his pockets and pulls out some folded-up papers and a gold watch. "Please, deliver these to Major McKee of General Richard Ewell's staff. Tell him they're from me."

I take the objects. It's a familiar role, the one of passing on last words and wishes from the dying to their loved ones. "I'll do it, I promise."

"And take this for yourself." He pulls a ring off his finger and fumbles it into my hand. "Keep it in memory of one whose sufferings you've eased." The soldier lies back down and closes his eyes.

"Thank you. I won't forget you," I murmur, unfolding the papers he's given me, turning back into a spy hoping for some intelligence. There's no information, only letters, one to his wife and one to his parents. It's always the same when men die, whether they wear gray or blue. Family is all that really matters in the end.

My eyes well up, but I'm not crying for the dying man, for the wife who will miss him, the parents who will mourn him. I'm crying for myself, alone, without any family to love or be loved by.

The light in the room turns gray, then pink, as the sun rises. I didn't mean to, but I dozed off, and now I wake up with a start. Even without touching him, I can tell the soldier has died while I slept. His open eyes are set in a fixed stare, and a leaden heaviness stiffens his body.

"Don't worry, Captain," I say, closing his eyes, a simple act I've done so many times before, though this is the first time for a Rebel soldier. I fold his arms across his chest and cover him with a blanket. "I'll keep my promise. Your folks will get your letters."

Before leaving, I scour the house for any useful items and find a second basket, which I fill with the soldier's letters and watch, as well as a comb, scissors, and mirror to add to my peddler's wares. I shove in all the pots and pans that can fit, a pair of pillowcases, and a blanket. Then I use a bottle of red ink left in the desk to draw a line around my eyes, making me look even older. Still not satisfied that I'll fool Major McKee, I search through the kitchen again, looking for anything that can change my appearance.

Some mustard looks promising. Ma used to make mustard plasters to draw out pus from wounds, and I try to remember the steps she took to mix up my own strong plaster. The mixture smells something awful when I'm done, but I hold my nose and slather it onto my cheek until the skin blisters, no longer the soft, dewy skin of a youth. The only thing that might give me away now is my pistol, so I bury it behind the house, hoping to retrieve it once my mission is completed.

It's time to go. I take one last look at the dead young man, stooping to snip a curl from his hair to include with the letters. I've seen many men die, but this death strikes me as especially sad—alone, away from his people, with only a complete stranger, an enemy in fact, to offer any comfort. I hope however my life ends, it won't be like that.

Armed with a valid excuse provided by the dead officer, I feel safe following the Richmond road now. I walk directly to the Rebel pickets.

One of the guards, a red-nosed British mercenary, waves at me. "Where've ye been, mother, and where are ye headin'? Have ye seen any Yankees on yer travels?"

I take out a large gingham handkerchief and blow my nose noisily, squeezing my eyes in a great show of sorrow. "I haven't seen hide nor hair of them Yankees, but I did see a fine young officer, a Confederate gen'lman like yerself, who died of the typhoid in a farmhouse down the road a ways. He give me a message for Major McKee, he did, and that's why I'm here, to fulfill a poor man's dyin' wish."

The guard nods. "The major must see ye then, but be quick about it and don't be spendin' the night in camp. One of our spies just came in to report that the Yankees have finished their damn bridges across the Chickahominy. They'll attack us either late today or tonight, and ye don't want to be here for that."

"What about yeself, ye poor boys?" I ask. "What will happen to ye?"

"Don't worry about us, ma'am. Stonewall Jackson is ready for whatever the Union has to offer! There are batteries hidden all around the perimeter—they'll never know what hit 'em. Why, there's one right there." He points to a bush alongside the road. "Fooled ye, didn't it? And it'll fool them, too, fool them to death!"

I want to rush right back to the Union camp and warn General McClellan, but I have to follow through now that I've told my story to the sentry. So I scurry deeper into the Confederate camp, asking after Major McKee. I'm directed to wait by the commander's tent for the major's return.

"Where is he?" I ask a soldier by the tent. "When will he be back?"

"It's not my business to say," the soldier answers curtly.

I shuffle around the tent, never straying too far away so I'll see the major as soon as he returns but trying in the meantime to overhear as many conversations as possible, to learn all I can about troop positions and plans. It's good to be busy, to think about spying. It keeps me from brooding about the dead Southerner and my own lonely life.

Finally, with the sun low overhead and my patience set to burst, the major rides up.

"What do you want?" he asks gruffly, dismounting. "I'm not interested in gewgaws today!"

"Oh, no knickknacks today, sir!" I hand him the watch and letters, then dig in my pocket and pull out the ring. I wouldn't feel right keeping it—the dead man's wife should have it. "I promised to give these to ye, sir. They're from an officer named Allen Hall. I was with the poor man when he died from the typhoid."

The stern major fingers the objects, tears softening his

checks. "He was a good man—the best." He takes out a ten-dollar federal bill and offers it to me. "You're a faithful woman, and I'm deeply grateful to you for this. Here's your reward, and if you take me to his body, I'll give you more."

"Oh, I couldna take your money, sir!" I object.

"You couldn't?" The major is puzzled. "You're a peddler. Why wouldn't you?"

I haven't meant to arouse his suspicions. I need to say something convincing and quick. "Forgive me, sir, but me conscience would niver give me paice in this world or the nixt if I made profit for carryin' the dyin' message of that sweet boy that's dead and gone. I can take ye to the farmhouse, that's for sure, but I ask ye for a horse, as I'm feeling poorly now and me old bones be achin'."

The major nods, tears still streaming down his face. It's horrible, seeing his grief. It's the first time I despise myself for lying, for the betrayal I'm about to commit. I love the thrill and adventure of spying, and I've never felt immoral about it until now. I have to remind myself that the man I'm feeling sorry for won't hesitate to have me executed if he learns who I really am.

A horse is brought for me, and we set out with a small party of cavalry. I lead them to the farmhouse, unsure what to do next. I wait outside on my horse with the men left standing guard, wondering how and when I can get back to the Union camp.

"Do ye think the rumor's true," I ask one of the soldiers, "the Union will attack tonight?"

"I expect so," the guard answers. "We'll show them what for, we will."

I nod. I'm about to suggest that if that's the case, I'd best be heading off, when the soldier saves me the trouble.

"We have to stay here till the major comes out," he says, "but you can ride down the road a bit, thataway, and keep your eyes sharp for Union cavalry. If you see any, you come back here right away and let me know."

"Happy to oblige," I agree, remembering to keep my accent and trying not to sound too relieved. I jog my borrowed horse slowly down the road, then pick up the pace, kicking my mount into a full-out gallop as soon as I've rounded a corner and am out of sight. I ride hard until I get to the Union picket. The sun is beginning to set, but I hope I'm not too late.

"I'm Private Frank Thompson and I've urgent news for General McClellan!" I yell.

The sentry lowers his gun. It's Damon. "Frank! Where'd you get that horse? What happened?"

"I'll tell you later. I've got to talk to the general now!" I kick the horse, lathered and panting from being ridden so hard, but I'm not about to slow down. I gallop straight to headquarters.

Soldiers surround me, surprised by the crazed peddler woman who leaps off her horse like an energetic young man.

I pull off the shawl, wishing I had my uniform back on, but I didn't want to waste time searching for it.

"It's me, Private Frank Thompson," I call out.

Colonel Poe ducks out of the tent. "Frank! Come in— tell me what you learned."

I explain how the Rebels expect an attack tonight. I describe the hidden batteries and troop positions. I give as many details as I can, but somehow I forget to mention the small party of Confederates carrying back a dead body for a decent burial. I know I should tell the colonel about them so he can send out a band of soldiers to attack them, out-numbered and far from camp. But that one last small act of betrayal is beyond me.

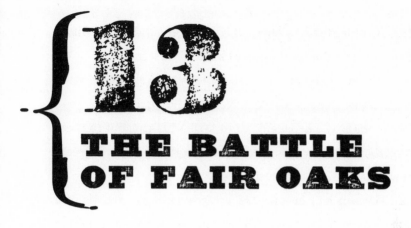

THE BATTLE OF FAIR OAKS

THE NEXT DAY, LATER THAN THE CONFEDERATES EXPECTED, the first of our troops cross the Chickahominy on the newly built bridges and position themselves for battle. Damon and I are among the advance guard, but I have a new job. No longer infantry or nurse, I've been appointed acting orderly for General Philip Kearny, whose regular orderly is too sick to ride. Like postmaster, it's another high-profile, dangerous job. I'll be galloping back and forth along the front lines, delivering messages and gathering information. I'm riding the horse the Confederate major lent me to lead him to the dead captain. I name the bay with the blaze on his nose Rebel. The name fits, not only because he comes from the Rebel camp but because he has a vicious temperament. Normally I don't like to ride with tight reins, but with Rebel there's no choice. If I give him his head, he races off, trying to scrape me off his back by dashing under tree branches. In the chaos of battle, I wish I were riding my old trustworthy friend, but Flag has been assigned to a cavalryman whose horse was shot out from under him in the last battle.

"So you'd better behave," I warn Rebel with gritted teeth as we wade across the river. The horse tosses his head but keeps a steady pace. I hope battle will bring out the best in Rebel, that he's used to fighting and enjoys it. He certainly has a taste for brutishness.

The artillery crosses the bridges while the troops ford the shallow river. Only a few regiments have made it across when a ferocious storm hits, turning the shallow river into a raging wall of water. The wind and waves sweep away one bridge. Another teeters precariously as engineers scramble to reinforce it. They work frantically while rain pelts down and lightning blazes through the sky, coming so close, the thunder is deafening. One bolt slashes into an Alabama regiment, killing four soldiers at once. Seeing that the storm has cut off the arrival of additional troops, the Rebels take advantage of the smaller contingent facing them and attack, adding bullets and shells to the rain and lightning.

"The very heavens are against us!" General Kearny rages, raising his single fist to the darkening sky. The general lost his left arm in the Mexican War but doesn't let its lack slow him down. He's a master at holding the reins in his teeth, swinging his sword in his right hand. Now he bellows at the troops to fight back, to give thunder for thunder, lightning for lightning.

"Frank," he orders, "tell Colonel Poe to move his

regiments to the right. We need to fan out, not be pushed back into the Chickahominy!" Kearny looks worried. We need reinforcements. No matter how hard the men fight, there are too few of us. We were never intended to face the Confederates alone. The rest of the army was supposed to follow, and follow it must.

When I ride back up, the orders to Poe delivered, the general hands me a message scribbled on the back of an envelope. "In the name of God," it reads, "bring your command to our relief if you have to swim in order to get here, or we are lost!"

"Take this," he commands, "and go as fast as that horse can take you. Give it to General McClellan and tell him to send a regiment NOW! Then get back to me immediately and report what he said."

I wheel my horse around, back toward the river. The water is a raging torrent, but I plunge straight into it. There's no question of wading across now. Rebel has to swim to the other side. His hooves finally sink into mud, then sand, then soggy earth. I ride up to the first officer I see, pull up my horse, and hand him the message.

"What answer do I give the general, sir?" I ask.

The commander reads the paper and blanches. "Is it that bad, Private?"

I nod.

"I'll get this to General McClellan right away and Kearny will have his men. Tell him reinforcements are coming."

Now I have to face the swollen river once more. Rebel rears back, unwilling to swim against the strong current again, but I give him no choice. "Damn, Rebel!" I yell, kicking hard, forcing the horse into the tide. "You think I want to do this?"

The water is too wild now for the men to ford safely. All the bridges have been torn away except for one. How many soldiers can one bridge hold?

I look back to see my answer. General Edwin Sumner rushes two divisions across the remaining bridge, shakily held up by only one trestle, the other having already been wrenched away by the floods. As the last soldiers from the artillery battery safely cross to the other side, the trestle gives way and the bridge collapses.

I watch it crumble into the river, terrified that our men will fall in after it, but every single one has made it across. Heart still pounding, I spur Rebel hard, crouching low over his back, until I find General Kearny. "Reinforcements are on their way!" I call over the howling wind.

"Spread the news! Tell them we're whipping the Rebels!" Kearny bellows, galloping along the front lines himself, yelling, "Reinforcements! They're here! We're beating the Rebels!"

I ride off to the other side, repeating the news. I can see the words charge up the troops, and they rush forward with a roar. The Rebels have their howling yell, but we loose a thunderous growl of rage. In the stinging rain and boom of thunder, the voices of the men split the sky with a new force. I'm drenched and cold but feel the surge of power echo from the soldiers back to me. This is what it's like to lead men into battle. I'm part of something much bigger than myself, a single muscle in a tensely coiled body—it's thrilling, terrifying, and immense. I open my mouth and scream louder than ever, "We're beating them! We're crushing the Rebels!" And it's true—in the worst possible conditions, we're actually beating back the Confederates.

Beside General Kearny once more, I wheel in my horse and catch my breath, waiting for more orders. General Oliver Howard rides up, leading his brigades to join Kearny's. This is the good part of war, the part where we strive to do our best and achieve it—where we win!

But battles ebb and flow. Luck changes in an instant from good to bad. I stare as a bullet hits General Howard in the arm, and my frenzied excitement vanishes. My moment of reflected glory as the voice of command is over.

"Permission to attend to the general's wound, sir," I ask Kearny. He nods, and I leap from my horse and rip open Howard's sleeve, pouring water from my canteen on the wound. I hitch my horse to a stump and rummage in the saddlebags for bandages and brandy, ignoring Rebel's rolling eye, flared nostrils, and flattened ears.

"You behave," I mutter, just as the horse turns and savagely bites my arm, nearly tearing a hunk of flesh from it. The pain is sudden, stunning me with its fierce intensity.

But Rebel isn't done. The horse turns and kicks, hitting me squarely in the ribs and sending me flying into the air.

I hit the ground with a thump, the air knocked out of me. My arm throbs, pain slashes through my ribs, and my head and back ache from bearing the brunt of the landing. I grind my teeth to control the splinters of agony shooting up my arm and chest, and force myself to stand on shaky legs. I try to focus on what's happening around me, how the battle is going, but the fierce burning in my arm and side is dizzying.

While I'm on the ground, General Howard rides off to the hospital. He can see I'm no help to him, but Kearny still has a job for me. He doesn't seem to realize that I'm doubled over in torment, or maybe it doesn't matter. The work must be done, so I have to do it.

"Get back on that miserable horse of yours," he orders. "I need you to ride to the old sawmill about a mile and a half from here. Most of our stores are there—tell them to move them farther to the rear. Once the commissary is safe, have all the doctors and nurses report for duty on the field as soldiers. We need every man we can get. The wounded will have to fend for themselves."

Can I pull myself into the saddle? Can I ride like this? I squeeze my eyes to keep from crying, take deep, slow breaths to calm the panic and pain.

Kearny peers at my pallid face. "You can do this, son, can't you?" It isn't really a question. "I'm depending on you."

I look at the general, who is leading us all with his one arm. I can't let him down. I can't let myself down. "Yessir!" I answer. Damned if I'll let myself be defeated by a horse. I glare at Rebel as I swing myself onto his back. I gasp, shocked by how much more my body can suffer. This much pain means my ribs must be cracked. I sit for a minute, catching my breath, pushing down the rising spasms of agony.

"I really named you well, didn't I," I hiss. "You're my worst enemy." I pull roughly on the reins and head to the sawmill, determined to follow orders no matter how much it tortures me. I grit my teeth the whole way, clamping down on the pain as if I can control it through my jaw. I can't, of course, but it does keep me from screaming or moaning, keeps the agony inside me where it belongs.

The sawmill teems with wounded soldiers. Many have crawled from the battlefield to the old building, hoping to find medical care, or at least shelter from further shooting. As soon as I deliver the message, they'll be on their own. No doctors, no nurses, no one to even give them a drop of water. I don't see how I can leave them. I remember the last time I abandoned the wounded, at the stone church in Centreville. I can't do it again. And the general has given me no further orders. He hasn't told me to come back, the way he did when he sent me for reinforcements. I figure I can stay and take care of those who need my help most. If I'm in any shape to give it.

My own injuries seem slight in comparison to the shattered bones and saber gashes all around me. "And I wasn't even hurt in battle," I mutter, ashamed. "What can I tell people? I was maimed by a stupid horse?"

I bind up my arm in a clumsy sling, wrap cloth around my chest to hold my ribs. It's enough to take the sharp edge off the pain, leaving me with a steady, deep ache instead. Now I can set to work with my one good hand. I have no knife or scissors, so I use my teeth to tear open the blood-stiffened clothing covering the men's wounds. I find some brandy and bandages, but not nearly enough for all the moaning soldiers. And I'm not going to make the mistake of going near the saddlebags on my horse again. I've locked the vicious beast in a shed, afraid to even tie him up.

There's nothing to do but find a homestead nearby and get provisions from there. And I'll walk—no more taking chances with Rebel. The sawmill can't be far from farmhouses. I follow the road leading away from the battlefield, and sure enough, it isn't long before I reach a house.

I knock at the door, remembering how the last time I asked for provisions, I was shot at. This time no one will even open the door. I knock again, louder and more insistent.

A face pokes out of the window. "Go away!" a man shouts.

"I mean no harm," I yell. "I need bandages—sheets, pillowcases, anything I can tear into strips."

"Don't got none!" the man barks, shutting the window.

I pull out my pistol, keeping my angry voice level. "I think you do. And I think you'll hand them over right now." I aim the gun at the bucket hanging from the well and squeeze the trigger, plugging a hole through the center of it. "So sorry," I drawl. "Looks like I ruined your bucket. Hate to see what else I might have to shoot."

The man yanks the door open, trembling. "Don't shoot!" he pleads. "You'll have your sheets." His wife pokes her head out next to him. "But you'll have to pay!"

I nod. "I'm no thief."

The woman ducks into the house and returns quickly with two old sheets and three pillowcases. "That'll be five dollars!" she demands.

"They're not even worth one," I say, steely toned. "But I'm a reasonable man. I'll give you two." I move the pistol to the hand in the sling and snatch up the cloth. Then I throw two dollars on the ground. "Next time be nice about it," I advise, "and you won't lose a bucket."

I back away from the house, keeping my pistol trained on the door until I'm far enough away that it seems safe to turn around. Then I hurry back to the mill. More casualties have been carried in, but there are no doctors or nurses. I find two soldiers whose wounds are less serious than the others and ask them to help. One has his arm in a sling, but the other has been stabbed in the leg, so he has two good hands he can use to tear the cloth into strips. Now we have plenty of bandages, but no food. Why didn't I ask for food at the farmhouse? Why, when the stores were moved, wasn't something left behind to feed the wounded? All I can offer is water.

Toward dusk, a man rides up on a fine, strong mare. I recognize him as the chaplain from my regiment and rush to greet him.

"Chaplain May, thank God you're here. We need all the help we can get!"

The chaplain smiles mildly. "Yes, to be sure. But first a man has to eat, doesn't he?"

I nod, my stomach rumbling. "Of course, but there's no food here."

"No need to concern yourself." The chaplain hums and bustles about his saddlebags, pulling out a roast chicken wrapped in a cloth and some biscuits. He sits down to his supper, pauses to say grace, then digs in, ignoring the hungry men around him, not offering me even a bone to gnaw on.

I liked the man before, but now I simmer with rage at his selfish piggishness. The chaplain takes no risks in battle but arrogantly enjoys his nice meal, while the soldiers who've risked everything don't have a crumb. I want to offer him dessert, if he would just go fetch it out of Rebel's saddlebags. It would serve him right to get kicked in the teeth by that nasty horse.

When every scrap of meat has been sucked from the chicken and every crumb of the biscuits devoured, the chaplain sighs and curls up for the contented sleep of the well-fed. I glare at his back, wishing nightmares on him, but it's exhausting to be so resentful and I fall into a broken sleep.

The next morning, the boom of cannon wakes me. I look around, disoriented for a few moments. Then the dull ache throughout my body reminds me where I am. The rain has stopped, and the air is misty and cool. The chaplain and his horse are nowhere to be seen. Good riddance. And it's time for me to go as well. There's nothing more I can do for the men at the mill. I need to report to Kearny, see what I can do as a soldier now.

I force myself to mount Rebel and ride toward Fair Oaks. The horse rolls his eyes constantly, tossing his head angrily as if he's the one who's been bitten and kicked.

"I'm getting rid of you the first chance I get, don't you worry," I mutter between his ears.

The scene on the battlefield is grisly. Thousands of men are strewn in the mud, dead and wounded, while around, among, and beside them the fight rages on. I can't believe I ever considered war noble. All I see now is brutality, as men step over their fallen comrades to shoot at other men. At least we're winning. That is, I think we're winning. I hang back at the edge of the field, feeling useless with my bad arm, searching for General Kearny. I ride close to the river and away from it, but I can't find him in the knots of soldiers, the bloodied stands of trees, or the huddled bulks of cannons.

FAIR OAKS STATION, VA.

By noon the Confederates have been pushed back to
Richmond, but at a very high cost. I hear that more than
five thousand Union soldiers have been killed or wounded,
and nearly six thousand Confederates have suffered the same
fate. As I ride among the dead and dying, my heart aches for
those who have fallen. It's enough to make angels weep to
look upon such carnage. I still haven't seen the general, but
I've found a sense of purpose. I use my horse to carry off the
wounded, keeping a tight hold on the reins so Rebel can't

add to their injuries. One of the soldiers tells me there is supposed to be a better-provisioned hospital set up under a large tree at Fair Oaks station, so we head there. Wildflowers dot the fields with yellows, blues, and purples, while birds chirp in the trees as if all is right in the world. But all around me I see horror after horror, dead men, broken men, men crying over the bodies of brothers, fathers, sons, and friends. I can't make sense of any of it. What is my part in this? Why am I still alive when so many worthy soldiers have fallen?

Once we get to Fair Oaks station, endless rows of men lie spread out beneath a big oak tree, their blood drenching the ground for several acres. The wounded are crowded so closely together, it's nearly impossible to walk between them. Instead, the doctors remove them one by one to dose, bandage, amputate, or bury, as the case requires. Where are the better conditions, what hope is there for the wounded here? I help the two men off my horse, unsure what to do next.

"Doctor!" I call. "These men need help."

"They all do!" a short, dark man, his shirt drenched in sweat, snarls. "Set 'em down and we'll get to them as soon as we can. If they've lived this long, they can survive another wait."

I'm not sure they can, but there's nowhere better to take them. I look around for someone else to help, someone who might be friendlier. A nurse bends over a cluster of patients to the side of the tree. I edge closer, through the tight-packed bodies.

"Excuse me, nurse," I yell. "I know you're busy, but I've brought in some new patients and I'm not sure where best to put them."

"No place is better than another. It's all hell," the nurse answers, turning to face me. It's Jerome! His face is haggard, but when he recognizes me, he pales even more.

"Frank! What happened to you?" he asks.

"Oh, this." I glance at my arm, cheeks burning with embarrassment. "Nothing. It's stupid."

"Let me be the judge of that." Jerome steps over the bodies between us. First he bandages the men I've brought in, leaving them to rest against a log pile. Then he firmly guides me to a stump to sit down on. He unties the sling and carefully unwraps the bloody bandage. Purple and black skin barely cover the gaping, ugly chunk that Rebel's teeth have nearly torn entirely free from the arm. My stomach pitches. I have to look away.

"How did this happen?" Jerome sounds angry. "And what idiot did such a bad job bandaging you?"

"The idiot would be me," I admit. "But in my defense, it's hard to wrap a bandage with only one hand."

"Oh, Frank," Jerome sighs. "You need looking after, you do." Tenderly, he washes the wound with water, then binds it back up, tightly this time, and fashions a new, clean sling. As he sets the arm, his hand grazes my bruised ribs and I wince.

"What? Are you hurt somewhere else?" Jerome asks, worried.

"No, there's nothing!" I push him away. I don't want to show him my cracked ribs, to remind him that I'm actually a woman. He wants to forget what I told him, and that's for the best.

For the rest of the day, I work alongside Jerome, helping to move the most severely maimed soldiers into railcars headed for the pier, where they'll be transferred to hospital ships bound north. The train is a hopeful sign, a promise of a truly better place, where the men will be fed and comforted, if not healed. Not until later do I hear that many die before the end of the train trip, so the soldiers on the other end unload the dead and living together, both festering with maggots.

In the evening, Jerome leads me to a cook fire, sits me down, and fetches a plate of beans and hardtack. I grab the plate, suddenly dizzy with hunger, and start shoveling the food into my mouth.

"Slow down there, Frank," Jerome says. "You don't want to choke to death on beans after facing so many dangers!"

I pause and swallow, trying to remember my manners. "I was starving. Thank you." When I've eaten a few more mouthfuls and the sharp hunger pangs have eased, I relax. "So tell me how the battle was for you. What part were you in?"

Jerome shakes his head. "I heard it, that's all. I was here the whole time, stationed at the hospital. But we were so far away, we didn't get any wounded until the end of the day. Most went to the old sawmill."

"That's where I was," I say. "Well, later, after being on the battlefield, after my evil horse bit me."

"Your horse bit you?" Jerome frowns. "Is that what happened to your arm?"

I nod, shamefaced. "Stupid, huh?" I snort.

"Frank Thompson!" General Kearny's familiar baritone booms out as he nears the cook fire. "I've been looking for you, son."

I jump up, almost spilling the plate of beans. "Yessir!" My cheeks burn red—I'm certain that he's there to call me a coward, a shirker. I spent too long at the sawmill, and I didn't return to find the general the next day. I failed as an orderly.

Instead, Kearny holds out a handsome silver sword. "I have the honor to present this sword to Private Frank Thompson in recognition of his great courage and humanitarian action in the Battle of Fair Oaks. This same sword was knocked from the outstretched arm of a Rebel colonel as he was raising it to strike a fallen Union officer. May you use it valiantly and justly."

I gape. Jerome takes the supper plate from my good hand.

"Sir! Thank you, sir!" Do I really deserve such a

trophy? "I am honored, sir!" I hold the sword with trembling fingers. "She's a beauty, sir," I whisper.

"That she is," Kearny agrees. "And a fitting weapon for you. You were an exemplary orderly under extraordinary conditions."

I look into the general's eyes. The quiet respect I see there warms me. For every idle coward like the chaplain, there are men like the general, men I long to serve well. Thinking of the chaplain, an idea strikes me.

"Sir, I would like to bestow a gift as well, on the chaplain of our regiment, for his . . ." I pause, searching for the right word. "For his service," I falter. "The horse the Confederate officer gave me—I want him to go to Chaplain May. He's earned a horse like Rebel." I really mean it, too.

Kearny nods, the trace of a smile flickering beneath his mustache. "Ah, yes, I know the animal well. A fitting tribute to the chaplain. I'll have it given to him right away. And now you finish your supper, Private. You've earned a good meal tonight. Too bad you have to settle for hardtack."

"Yessir!" I say, sitting down again, turning the sword over in my hand.

"That's a beauty, all right," Jerome says. "And it sounds like you deserve it. So what happened on the battlefield before the stupid horse bit you?"

I set the sword down and take up my supper. I'm filthy and sore, with cracked ribs and a torn-up arm. I've seen the horrors of hell, in battle and in the hospital, but none of that matters right now. I have something to eat and my best friend beside me. If I could lean my head on Jerome's shoulder, if he'd put his arm around me, everything would be perfect. Even without that, as we sit together sharing a meal, I feel a strange warmth in my chest. It's happiness.

{ 14 CHASING TRAINS

THE NEXT FEW DAYS, THE SPRING RAINS RETURN, fiercer than ever, and we hunker down in our tents, welcoming the chance to rest and recover after the hard days of fighting at Fair Oaks. I use the time to write about the battle for Mr. Hurlburt. Mostly I give my own observations, what I saw and did, but I also include rumors. Like the ones I've heard of the high losses the Confederates have suffered, that General Joseph Johnston has been severely wounded, and that now General Bobby Lee is in charge of the Confederate army. He's a tough fighter who inspires fierce loyalty from his troops, but McClellan assures us we'll beat him. All of that goes into the envelope—information and speculation. I haven't heard back from Mr. Hurlburt since I sent my first dispatch, but that's not stopping me.

Between writing and mail runs, I play cards with Damon, and Jerome often joins us in the crowded tent. My arm still throbs where Rebel sank his teeth in, but it's healing. I've bandaged my ribs properly and they're mending, too. I'm almost my old self again, whoever that is.

"Tell us the story about the chaplain and Rebel again," Damon urges, slapping a card down on the crate set up as a table between our bedrolls.

"Just hearing it will warm us up," Jerome adds.

I don't need to be encouraged. It's become one of my favorite stories. "Well," I begin, "the general had Rebel led to Chaplain May, who was mighty touched by the magnificent gift. He circled the horse and boasted to everyone around that Rebel was a splendid animal, worth three hundred dollars at least, a fitting mount for someone of his worth."

"His worth!" Damon hoots. "That Rebel must have liked the praise, because that's when he was gentle as a lamb, wasn't it? Letting Chaplain May pet him, stroke his nose, and feel up and down his legs—as if the chaplain knows how to value a horse!"

"That just shows the horse is a poor judge of character, along with his other faults," Jerome interrupts.

"Until the chaplain turned his back," I remind them. "Rebel must have been biding his time. Now he saw his target, and he landed a solid kick right between the shoulders and sent May flying face-first into the mud. Lucky for him it was a soft landing."

Damon slaps his knee. "This here's my favorite part! That dang horse planted another kick, knocking the poor man down a second time, and then a third! Striking a blow for justice, I'd say."

I laugh. "You should have seen his face. May's cheeks were bright red and looked ready to pop like an angry blister. He yelled for somebody to grab the vile beast and keep the animal off him. I was tempted to take the reins myself, but I didn't want to get too close to Rebel either. Finally a soldier took pity on the chaplain and grabbed the reins dragging on the ground."

"Of course, now Rebel was as mild as milk again and let himself be led away, ain't that so?" Damon's voice is half triumph, half glee. Nothing tickles him so much as tales of comeuppance like this one. "But the chaplain was sputtering and fuming, yelling how he'd sell the cursed creature. Too bad for him that nobody wanted to buy. Everyone in the army knows Rebel's reputation by now. He'll have to find some friendly Virginian to fool into buying the devil. Though folks around these parts know horses."

"And now the chaplain's stuck with him, eh?" Jerome snorts. "Serves the selfish bastard right."

"Too bad he wasn't kicked in the head," Damon says. "Might have knocked some sense into him."

"The good news is I've got Flag back," I add.

"You definitely need a horse you can depend on. How else can you deliver the mail?" Damon sets his cards down, grinning. "That's my game!"

"You win again?" Jerome scoops up the cards and starts

shuffling. "You've got more luck than anyone else I know. And not just in cards. I still can't believe you kept your leg."

"It works pretty good, too. I can march almost as quickly now as I could before I got shot. But then, I only had to contend with a minié ball," Damon teases, "not the teeth of some beast from hell."

"My arm's healing just fine, thank you kindly." I look at Jerome. "After all, I had the best nurse."

"Now that's where I'm going to argue with you," Damon says. "I had the better nurse!"

"Enough now!" Jerome sets down the deck of cards. "I've got to get to the hospital and make rounds. Are you coming?"

"Not today. I have a mail run. See you both in a few days." I pick up the loaded mailbags and duck out of the tent.

"Don't forget to bring me back a present!" Damon calls after me. "Or at least a letter—and not a 'Sorry, Sweetheart' one, either!"

"Can't make any promises," I yell back. "That's between you and your girl!" I've given up hoping for a "Sorry, Sweetheart" letter from Anna to Jerome. It seems like every mail run means picking up two or three of her perfumed letters. Doesn't the woman have anything else to do but write? She certainly lives a life of ease to have so much time for the epistolary arts.

Saddling up Flag and setting the mailbags over his

withers, I'm tempted to pluck out one particular letter, or at least pull it far enough out so that the slightest breeze will free it from the bag and deliver it straight to a mud puddle. Jerome doesn't write near as often as Miss Anna, but his letters are even harder for me to carry. I imagine passionate declarations of love—to her—and it's all I can do to keep from shredding the envelope to bits. I admit not every letter he's written has made it to the post station. Some got caught in briars. One fell into a stream. And one got charred in the fire I'd made to cook my supper on the way to the mail drop. I'm not saying I'm proud of such accidents, but since I let most of his letters go through, I can't deny myself the intense satisfaction of occasional lapses.

The rains have left the Chickahominy high again, which means swimming Flag across. The mail, including Jerome's letter, is safely wrapped in oilskin to protect it, but still I hold the bags over my head as Flag strains his way across. The mail stays dry, but I'm soaked. I ride the rest of the day, drenched and shivering. My teeth chatter so hard, I can't talk to Flag as I usually do. I'm too miserable for much conversation anyway. The fever that has come and gone ever since we landed at Fort Monroe is back again. There's no cure, nothing to do except wait it out. I spend the night by the side of the road, chilled to the bone, shaking so hard I can barely sleep, even with Flag's warm body beside me. Horses, of course, usually sleep on their feet, but Flag is a true friend, and when I first coaxed him to the ground next to me as a sheltering bulwark, he understood right away. My dreams that night are disjointed fragments. First I'm a woman in a frilly dress with pearl earrings, writing on lavender stationery like Anna Corey. Then I'm a man holding a soldier down as the doctor saws off his leg. Abruptly, the dream shifts and I'm in the tent playing cards with Damon and Jerome. They accuse me of cheating, of pulling a fast one on them. I yell that I'm innocent, but as they throw their cards at me, I change into a woman. That's when I wake up feeling out of joint, like I need to pull myself together. It takes me a few minutes to remember who and where I am— Frank Thompson, alias Sarah Emma Edmonds, private and postmaster in the Army of the Potomac. The damp has seeped into my bones, and my body feels stiff and brittle. Without any breakfast I heave myself onto Flag, grateful that as the sun rises higher in the sky, the day grows hot and steamy.

"Strange dreams last night, Flag. I can't figure out who I'm supposed to be. It must be nice to lead a horse's life. You eat, you carry people, you sleep. Not much more to it than that. I suppose some folk live that way—eat, work, sleep. Except they have families, friends, people they care about. Maybe my life is closer to yours than I want to admit." Flag obligingly twitches his ears. I reach forward and pat his neck. "Good fellow, Flag. You listen to me."

By the end of the second day I reach White House Landing, where I deliver the regimental mail and pick up a

new batch for the camp. The chief quartermaster, Colonel
Ingalls, takes one look at my still-feverish face and tells me
to report to the hospital.

"No sir! That won't be necessary. I just have that swamp
fever that half the soldiers fell sick with when we first landed
in Virginia. There's nothing to do but let it pass."

"Maybe you don't need to go to the hospital, but you
don't look well enough to ride."

I start to protest. After all, I've just ridden for two days
and managed fine. The colonel holds up a hand, cutting me
off. "Here's what I suggest. There's a provision train bound
for Fair Oaks leaving this afternoon. I'll get you and your
horse a place on it. And in the meanwhile, I suggest you find
yourself a good, hot meal."

Now that's something I can accept. It would be nice to
sleep on the train, skipping another chill night in the open.
And Flag could use the rest. "Thank you, sir," I say. I know
the best place in town for ham and eggs, and that's where I
head.

It's a holiday. I have a couple of hours with nothing to
do. After filling my stomach, I amble around town, looking into store windows, imagining what I'll do after the
war. Of course, the Union will win, and I could go back to
my old job of bookselling. Only I'm not sure I want to do
that anymore. After all the rootless travel, I want to settle
down. Make someplace a home. And I want to make that
home with Jerome. I can picture myself in an apron, sliding

eggs onto a plate for my husband's breakfast. I can imagine Jerome sitting across from me, eating my cooking with lip-smacking appreciation. I can see the two of us, sitting by the fire on a rainy winter night, me darning socks while Jerome oils his hunting rifle, talking together like an old married couple from one of the stories I used to sell. The images are so clear, a smile curves across my face. I want so much for it to be true.

But of course it can't be. I try to picture another future, but life without Jerome seems hazy and vague to me, impossible to imagine.

There will come a time when the war will be over and we'll all go our separate ways. I tell myself I can always work in a hospital, but without Jerome it would be a cruel reminder of what I'm missing. Besides, I'm a good nurse, but if I can't have Jerome, then I want to work with war veterans, the soldiers I see maimed in battle, the ones I try to patch up as best I can. Those men are my family. I have a deep kinship with them, the only kinship I've really known.

I'm sitting on a bench in the sun, watching the towns-folk go about their business, when suddenly it hits me. I imagine building a big clapboard house with a warm, high-ceilinged kitchen, a place where one-legged men and those missing arms and eyes always feel welcome. I'll run a home for injured veterans, a place where they can live and swap stories, enjoy once again the brotherhood we've had in the army. If I can't make meals for Jerome, at least I can cook for those men.

The vision of the house seems so real, it's as if I've already built the place. I don't decide whether it's something I'll do as a man or a woman, though I suppose it's the kind of thing the "weaker" sex could manage if I choose to stop living a lie. But that's a bigger issue I'm not ready to face yet. Why be a woman if I can't be Jerome's woman? I know I'll have to think about it someday, weigh whether the strain of the deceit is worth the freedom it brings, but now isn't the time. There's no choice about the present.

The sun dips low in the sky. It's time to put Flag on the train and settle in myself. After my holiday, I'm in a rare relaxed mood as I take a seat between a sergeant and another private. I look out the window as the train picks up speed and chugs along. The landscape flies by so fast, it's a blur, and the sensation makes me dizzy. It feels odd to pass by trees and meadows so quickly. Flag may be a slower and bumpier ride, but going on horseback seems more real somehow, like you're part of the land, not hovering slightly above it.

As we reach Tunstall's Station, the shrill whistle of another train interrupts the card game we're playing. Our train quickly switches off to a spur to avoid the approaching train, rushing toward us on the same track. As it clatters past, gunshots and screams erupt from its carriages and the conductor waves frantically at our train, signaling us to follow him.

A LOCOMOTIVE CALLED "FIREFLY" ON A TRESTLE OF THE ORANGE AND ALEXANDRIA RAILROAD. LOCATION UNKNOWN.

I jump up to see better. "What's going on?"

The sergeant next to me shoves his head out the window. "We're going to follow that train. Sounds like there's a fight on board. I bet we'll find Confederates once we stop 'em!"

Now the two trains steam down the track in tandem, one going forward, the other going backward right behind it. At White House Landing, where we started, we grind to a halt. I hear guns fired at dangerously close quarters, watch horrified as men tumble out of windows, either pushed or fleeing. I leap out of the car, rushing toward the troop train and the raucous noise of scuffling, breaking glass, grunts, and yells.

It sounds like a saloon, not a train. The sergeant clambers in before me, throwing punches as soon as he's inside. The fighting is too close to risk pulling a gun, and I'm not sure I can hit anybody with much force. I've never been in a fistfight before. Instead of trying, I thrust past Union soldiers wrestling with Rebels to reach three men who've been wounded.

"Who'd have thought there'd be a battle inside a train," I mutter as I help a man with a wounded leg out of the car. I take off my jacket and use it to stanch the blood, then go back to get another man, this one with a gash in his head. As I clean the bloody wound, a jolt of recognition hits me and I freeze. I know this face. I know this man. He's the spy—the one who sells stationery goods, the one I saw in the Confederate camp by Yorktown when I disguised myself as a freed slave. I don't say anything but finish bandaging the wound with a torn shirt and help the other injured before I report to the provost marshall.

"There's a spy among the wounded passengers," I tell him, explaining how I know the man, how long I've been waiting for his capture.

The marshall sends a guard with me to search the man. Sure enough, we find plans and lists of Union artillery.

"I'm not who you think I am. I'm an honest peddler!" the spy protests.

"What you are is under arrest," the guard barks, jerking the man to his feet and tying his arms behind his back. The spy locks eyes with me, glaring.

"I know you!" he shouts. "I've seen you before!"

I smile. "Of course you have. I'm the kind soul who bandaged your head. Believe me, I won't make that mistake again."

"No, you're lying, I've seen you somewhere else!" the spy rages, but nobody cares. Who would believe him anyway if he remembers me as a slave? It sounds like an even more outlandish story than trying to kidnap an entire train.

A day later than planned, I get back to camp with my fever finally gone. I deliver the mail, along with the juicy adventure story of a failed Rebel train ambush. Turns out it was Confederate General Jeb Stuart's cavalry, two hundred soldiers strong, who were responsible. Before attacking the Union troop train, they burned two schooners loaded with our supplies in the Pamunkey River. I have to admit they had guts.

When I hand Damon his letter and tell him the news, he chuckles.

"Dang, Frank, if you aren't better entertainment than one of those serial stories in the newspaper! Even when you aren't on the battlefield, you're at the center of the action."

I raise my eyebrows. "Is that a blessing or a curse? Anyway, it's something to write about for Mr. Hurlburt."

"And what about Virginia? Are you writing to her?" asks Damon. "That Mr. Hurlburt still hasn't answered you. Why waste time—and words—on him?"

"Well, your Virginia hasn't written to me, either. Seems

like that one letter will be my last. No one else will ever send me anything—nobody I know, I mean."

"Just be patient! She'll write you." Damon's tone is less sure than his words.

"I am being patient." I sigh and smooth out a fresh page of stationery. "But in the meanwhile, I'm writing. A train ambush makes a mighty fine story, don't you think?"

Damon nods. "And if you write it the same way you tell it, folks will be excited to read it."

I don't know about that, but somehow writing these dispatches is much more satisfying than writing in my diary. I guess the difference is the hope that someone else will read my words, that it will matter what I say.

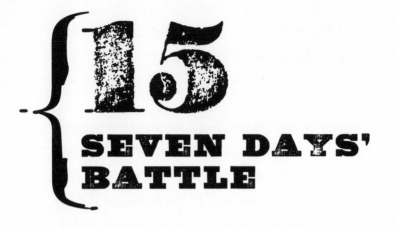

{ 15

SEVEN DAYS' BATTLE

I'M BEGINNING TO LOSE FAITH IN OUR MAIL SERVICE when I finally get a letter back from Mr. Hurlburt. I'm so eager to read what he says, I rip the envelope and the letter both, but I can piece the parts together and make sense of it anyway. He loves my dispatches! He's putting them on the front of his weekly newsletter, and he wants to be able to include one in each issue, so I need to send one a week. He asks if I can do that—and says he'll pay me for my efforts.

Pay me for writing? I would never imagine I could make money from descriptions of army life. When I tell Damon, his face splits into a broad grin.

"Congratulations, Frank! You've got yourself another job!"

"One that isn't dangerous, for a change. And I like to write. If Virginia ever writes to me, she'll find out herself."

Damon looks embarrassed. "I don't know what's got into that girl . . ."

"It's not your fault, Damon. She's probably heard how ugly I am. Why would she want to correspond with me?"

"You're not ugly!" he protests. "And anyhow, it's her patriotic duty to support soldiers in the field."

"I don't need a pity letter. I've got Mr. Hurlburt to write to—and get paid for it!"

I get right to work, describing how, by the end of June, we've pushed so close to Richmond, we can hear the church bells on Sundays. Our blue uniforms greatly outnumber the gray, but in the face of fierce fighting from the Confederates, General McClellan calls for a retreat after the Battle of Gaines' Mill, the third in a week of battles. It doesn't make sense to me—we're winning and yet McClellan insists on retreating. General Lee is losing and still he pushes his thinning regiments forward, intent on driving us off the Virginia Peninsula. In the battle of wills, Lee is the clear victor. I have faith in McClellan, really I do, but I don't understand why he follows our victories with retreats. Sometimes it seems like the only signs of our victories are the Union flags we leave behind as we back away from Lee's army. And that's what I say in my dispatch—not just what's happening, but my worries and fears.

Once again I'm sent to warn the surgeons, nurses, and patients in the nearby hospitals that the army is moving to the James River and that anyone who stays behind will be captured by the Rebels. It's an all-too-familiar errand, but not any easier for that. When I come to the last hospital, Dr.

Evers throws down his saw in disgust. "How can we help the wounded this way? We'll kill them if we move them and the Rebels will kill them if we don't. Damn this war!"

"I know, Doctor," I commiserate. "Doesn't make sense to me, either, but I'm following orders."

"Damn stupid orders!" he curses.

"Damn stupid," I agree. My favorite doctor is Dr. Bonine, but Dr. Evers is a good man, too. He has a bit of a temper, but he genuinely cares about his patients. I'm putting him in an impossible situation, one he's already been in several times before—leaving wounded men to be captured by the enemy.

"There's no hope for the ones who can't walk, but the others can still be saved," I offer.

"How fast do you think a one-legged man can hobble?" the doctor spits. "Did you bring any ambulances with you? Carts? Wagons? Horses? Mules?"

I lower my eyes. Of course I haven't. Just my own horse, Flag.

The surgeon shakes his head. "The bloody waste of it all!"

I hesitate. I'm supposed to report back to Colonel Poe and I might be sent on other missions. I need Flag. But as I look around the clearing where the soldiers lie suffering, bandaged and bloody, I hand Flag's reins to the doctor. "He's only one horse, but he's a good one. You can have men take turns riding him. And you can rig up a stretcher for him to pull. That might help."

Dr. Evers takes the reins. "Thank you, Private. It's a start. Can you help that man over there into the saddle?" He points toward a soldier with a bandaged leg and arm. "We'll start with him and keep going until we reach the James River." A shell explodes in the distance. The Confederates are closing in. "All those who can walk, follow me," the doctor yells. "The strongest help the weakest. Let's get as many as we can to safety."

I try to lift the bandaged man onto Flag, but he's too tall and heavy, especially for my weakened ribs and arm. Sweat pours down my face as I strain to hoist the injured man into the saddle, but it's like lifting a heavy sack of flour over my head. I'm not strong enough.

"Let me give you a hand," a familiar voice says. I wipe the sweat out of my eyes and look up to see Jerome heaving the patient onto Flag.

"Jerome!" I smile. "I'm glad you're here. You can make sure they treat Flag well."

Jerome shakes his head. "I'm not going with them. Someone has to stay with the wounded here."

"But they'll capture you!" My voice is shrill. "You've got to go! You've got to!"

"Maybe they'll capture me. Maybe not. I'll take my chances." Jerome leans over a soldier trembling with fever. He gently wipes the sick man's brow and looks at me. "How can I leave them?"

I bite my lip, miserable. I've left the helpless before, and here I am doing it again. What's the point of being taken prisoner? How does sacrificing yourself help the wounded?

"You can't save them, you know! You'll all be captured. It's a stupid waste." I want to pound my fists on his chest, to make him listen.

"If I can ease their last hours, then to me it's not stupid." Jerome puts his hand on my shoulder. "Look, Frank, I don't mean that you should stay, too. You need to finish your task, report back to the colonel. But this is my task. And I aim to finish it."

My shoulder tingles where he's touched it, and my legs go wobbly. I want to throw my arms around him, to cry on his chest that he has to come with me, that I need him. Instead, all I can do is stare at his handsome face and blink back tears.

Around us, soldiers scramble after the doctor. Those who can walk help those who can't. Nurses bundle up supplies and hand out anything that can be used as a crutch or a cane—sticks, brooms, rifles, whatever comes to hand.

I'm frozen in the midst of the motion eddying around me. I can't leave Jerome. I can't stay. My heart cracks open. "How can I leave you?" I sob.

Jerome is frustratingly calm and patient. "Because that's your duty, just as this is mine. Now go. We'll meet up soon." He unclasps a locket from around his neck and presses it into my palm. "But if we don't, if I don't come back, you know where to send this."

I close my fingers over the locket. "To Anna," I whisper.

Jerome nods. "To Anna."

Ice creeps up my veins, from my ankles to my throat. Anna. Jerome cares about her, only her. Not his best friend, Frank Thompson, and certainly not the woman behind that mask, Sarah Emma Edmonds. I shove the necklace into my pocket.

"Good-bye, then," I croak, "and good luck." I want to hate Jerome then. I try, really I do, but sorrow and longing creep in around the edges. I hate that he's rejected me, that he cares for Anna, but I can't stop loving him.

"Good luck to you, too," Jerome responds, turning back to tend to the men.

There's nothing more to do or say. I trudge back the way I've come, heading toward the sounds of battle rather than away from them. With each step I regret giving away Flag. What difference can one horse make to so many wounded compared to how much he would help me? I've always been too impulsive. Now I'm paying the price for my meaningless gesture. And I haven't helped the person I most wanted to, I haven't helped Jerome.

I finger the locket he gave me. Anna. I spit the name out. A tough skin grows like a scab over my heart. Well, he can have her, for what she's worth. I force the image of Jerome out of my mind and lope down the road.

I pass a pasture on my right and smile. A leggy colt and four mules graze peacefully behind the white split-rail fence.

A barn sits in the front corner of the pasture, the kind of place that might house a bridle, maybe even a saddle. Which animal will make the best mount? My trained eye runs over the colt. He's young but big enough to ride, and certainly faster than any mule. I leap over the fence and duck into the barn, the boom of cannons echoing down the road. I have to hurry or I'll end up cut off behind enemy lines.

The barn holds only a halter, but that's enough. I grab it and rush at the animals, corralling them into a shed alongside the barn. In the close space the colt struggles, throwing back his head, ducking down, snaking away from my hands. Then with one quick movement I slip on the halter and jump on his back, nudging open the shed door with my foot. I don't have any reins, but I sit tightly on the colt, forcing him to obey the pressure of my thighs, urging him up and over the fence and onto the road.

Now that the colt accepts my weight, he gallops steadily toward the thudding shells and cannon. For a moment I'm back in New Brunswick, riding Trig into the countryside beyond the family farm. I grew up breaking horses, and my first taste of freedom came on horseback. I love the speed and strength I get from riding, the sense that I can go anywhere, fly over ravines, soar over fences. On a young, strong horse there are no boundaries, only wild possibilities.

Trees and fields, fences and farms rush by. On the road ahead, a group of men approaches. I squint at them, pulling up the colt for a steadier look. They're wearing blue—yes, they must be an advance guard for our troops! I kick the colt forward, but as I come closer, one of the blue soldiers raises his hand, signaling me to go back. I watch in horror as a gray-uniformed soldier behind him lifts up a rifle and hits the Union soldier on the head with the butt of the gun. The soldier collapses, and another Rebel guard kicks him savagely in the ribs. It's not an advance group, as I'd thought, but prisoners who've been rounded up by the enemy.

I wheel the colt around, racing back the way I came. The Rebels fire after me, minié balls flying past, all wide of the mark. I murmur a prayer of thanks to the bullets for missing and to the brave captive who warned me.

I lean over the colt's mane, urging him to go faster. "I know what to name you," I whisper into his ear. "Lucky, because you've brought me good luck." Flag is a steady, reliable friend, but Lucky is pure wild youth, and on his back I'm younger, more carefree myself. His coiled energy radiates into me, filling me with a strange elation. Riding him, I am protected. Nothing can touch me. No wonder the bullets missed.

The colt snorts as I guide him off the road, across the countryside, circling around past the knot of prisoners, to find the rest of our regiments. Galloping through the fields, jumping fences and ditches, I feel truly myself, as I exist apart from any name, any sex. I'm not Frank Thompson or Sarah Emma Edmonds. I'm me, pure me, someone who loves to take chances, to be free, to be truly alive right now, in this moment. The sensation can't last long, but the memory of it stays with me. Lucky has shown me the part of myself that really matters. It's a quick glimpse, nothing more, but it echoes deep in my bones.

It's dark by the time I join the main column snaking its way through the White Oak Swamp, a murky, gloomy bog that wears the men out. I've left behind the emerald fields for a treacherous morass. Each step means pulling boots out of the sucking mud, trudging through shin-high water. There's no place to rest, no place to sleep. All night, the troops slog through the mire, some men dropping from exhaustion. I pass by one soldier leaning against a cottonwood tree. He's died that way, still holding his rifle, still standing. At least I have the colt to doze on. And it's not my feet that are held by the muck, it's Lucky's. I look up at the stars glittering in the velvet sky. They're coldly beautiful, a relief from the ugliness on the ground. I imagine Jerome seeing the same constellations wheeling overhead, and I hope he's escaped capture.

By dawn the bulk of the army has made it up a slope overlooking the James River. This is Malvern Hill, where McClellan orders us to turn and face the enemy, spent by their own march through the marshes. It seems like an advantageous spot. From the top of the rise, the artillery can pound down on any approaching troops. Our position is so secure that many soldiers allow themselves some badly needed sleep. Myself, I haven't closed my eyes in thirty-six hours. Keyed up though I am about the approaching battle, I can't resist resting for a bit. I don't mean to, but as soon as my head drops onto the bedroll, I fall into a deep sleep, the kind uninterrupted by dreams.

When I wake up, it's the next day, July 1, and the Rebels have already started up the slopes, cannon blazing. I rush to follow Damon to our assigned position, next to the 20th Indiana. We're in a rifle pit, front and center of the action.

Wave after wave of gray soldiers marches up the rise straight into us. Our big guns mow down the Confederates, and still they keep coming. Once they get close enough, those who survive the cannon fire are shot by us, the infantry. It's a complete slaughter. And the most glorious battle I've seen—the concentrated force of gray uniforms streaming up the hill, marching over their fallen comrades, the flash of fire from the enemy guns whose shells fall far short of our lines, the answering roar of our cannon blasting into the Rebel ranks. And then the chance for the infantry to pour our own deadly hail of minié balls onto the Confederates. For once I don't need to rush after the wounded. Instead, I watch the magnificent display of force, proud to be part of such a powerful army. I shoot, reload, and shoot again, aiming carefully at the broad gray chest of a grizzled soldier. I pull the trigger, bracing for the recoil, and watch the man crumple and fall. I'm ashamed to admit it, but it's satisfying to hit the mark, to get it right, even though I know I'm killing somebody's son, brother, father, or husband. But I have to—I'm supposed to. Ours is a noble cause, a just cause. It's the only way to save the Union, to free the slaves, to make this country the great nation it's meant to be.

Damon turns to me, interrupting my thoughts. "This doesn't feel right—it's a massacre, not a battle."

"They'd do the same to us," I grunt. "Better them, I say."

"I guess." Damon sights down his rifle barrel and squeezes off a shot. "But how do you tell the difference between murder and war?"

"Sometimes there isn't any. That's just the way it is. But think of the wounded men we left behind. Think of Jerome. For all we know, they're prisoners now. And I can promise you they won't get the royal treatment. I've seen how the Rebels treat their slaves. I know how coldhearted they are. We have to be just as cold or they'll beat us." I take aim and fire, watching another man collapse.

Damon sighs. "Maybe you're right, but this makes me sick. I'm not proud of this, not one bit. I wish this whole war was over and we could all go home and go back to being farmers. That's honorable work."

I nod, though I consider this honorable work as well. I don't want to admit it to Damon, but I prefer this kind of battle, the kind where the Army of the Potomac is solidly winning, where the Confederates are at our mercy. Of course, I want the war to end too, but I don't mind crushing the Rebel troops in an unfair fight on our way to victory.

There are only a few Union wounded to tend, but the men are hungry and supplies are short. In the late afternoon, during a lull in the fighting, I decide to forage for provisions. From the top of Malvern Hill I spot a farmhouse nestled between the two front lines. It's not in Union territory, but it's not in the center of the action, either, too far to the side to present a real risk. I edge down the hill, ducking behind bushes, crawling behind rocks and high grasses. Then I dart through the unlocked back door and stand up, rubbing my sore back and scanning the kitchen for food.

The cupboards hold a treasure trove. I snatch tins of tea, a ham, flour, eggs, even a wheel of cheese—the kind of food none of us has seen for weeks. I want to shove it all into my mouth, to fill my empty belly. If I had the time, I would cut off a hunk of raw ham and wolf it down, but I stop myself. This food is for everyone. I just have to figure out how to carry it all back. I run into a bedroom and tear the quilt off the bed, wrapping the eggs in pillowcases first, figuring at least a few will survive the trip intact as I load the rest of my haul into a bundle that I knot together. I heave it over my shoulder and stumble into the entry hall just as a shell crashes through the side of the house, throwing me and the quilt onto the floor. I lie there, stunned, as another shell and then another pummels the house. Fire blazes on the roof, and the bedroom the quilt came from has been flattened. My ears ring from the roar of the explosions, but I'm not hurt. I catch my breath and get up on trembling legs, pick up the knotted quilt, and slip out the door. Now I can only crawl slowly, dragging the heavy bundle behind me. I look back at the house and watch aghast as it caves in on itself like a teetering pile of matchsticks.

"Don't think about the shelling," I tell myself. I try to stop the trembling that runs up and down my arms. "Think about all the good food you rescued. Think about how happy the men will be to see it." I scramble up the side of the hill, feeling exposed as I crawl from rock to bush to rock again.

As I clamber closer to the front line, I'm terrified that my own comrades will fire on me. Yes, I told Damon I was heading for the house, but how will he know that the creeping soldier with the big bundle is his buddy, Frank? I sink to the ground, too scared to move, when three soldiers, crouching low, come toward me from the top of the rise. One of them waves, and I recognize Damon's gawky frame and lopsided grin.

"I've been on the lookout for you, Frank," he calls, stretching out his hand to help with the heavy quilt. "What'd ya find?"

"You'll see!" I say, giddy with relief. "We'll have a feast tonight!"

"Then let's get the goods up the hill." Damon lifts up one end of the quilt and I hold the other. Together we hoist the food the rest of the way back behind Union lines, but I don't relax until we're on the other side of the rifle pits.

The two soldiers who came with Damon start a fire,

and an hour later the provisions I secured have become a fragrant supper of crusty bread, fried ham, scrambled eggs with cheese, and hot tea.

As hungry as I am, I don't dive into my meal. Instead, I watch the famished men around me eating and savor a deep wave of satisfaction. I've done this for them, taken care of them in this simple way. It's better than nursing, better than bringing mail. Food is more elemental.

I'm not the only one to think so. The soldier sitting across from me looks up from his steaming plate. He chokes back tears, then starts to speak, seriously, as if he were in church. "That boy, Frank Thompson, risked his life getting this for us. He wouldn't have made it out alive from that burning house if it hadn't been God's will."

"Amen!" the man next to him says.

"Amen!" the circle of men choruses.

"Amen," I murmur. I don't feel like an angel of mercy, but I'm aware a rare gift has been granted to me, the gift of nourishing others. I remember how proud Ma was when she set a good meal on the table for Sunday dinner. I used to think her sense of accomplishment was foolish. It's not hard, after all, to roast a goose or fry up a ham. Now I understand her satisfaction and the value of what she offered. My idea of a home for wounded veterans would be the same kind of thing. I'm more sure than ever that it's what I'm meant to do, the thing that will give my life meaning. I chew on a morsel of ham. Nothing has ever tasted as richly satisfying.

But that pleasure doesn't last long. As the sun dips lower on the horizon, the Confederates make one last push up the hill. Masses of men forge their way across the slope, almost up to the edge of the rifle pits. The whole hill is lit with gun and cannon fire. Damon and I take our places back on the front line, with our guns aimed into a steady assault of gray soldiers. Now the slaughter, so grand before, is sickening. It's too easy, too unfair, like shooting rats when they're frantically clawing up the edges of a bucket. Damon's right—there's nothing honorable in this kind of fight, no matter how glorious the cause.

"Ahead, men, charge!" bellows General Heintzelman, and we leap out of the pits and over the edge of the hill, slashing at the remaining Rebels with bayonets. At least now the fight seems more fair. Still, when it's over, the hillside is covered with gray-uniformed corpses and the wounded. So many men thrash and crawl before collapsing that the field quivers with the dying.

Before I write to Mr. Hurlburt, I collect the horrifying numbers. Fifteen thousand wounded Rebel soldiers are carried into Richmond that week. Lee's army has lost twenty thousand men. Not an inch of ground has been gained by the Confederates. It's an overwhelming defeat. Still, to our surprise, General McClellan doesn't order us forward, toward Richmond. He doesn't press his advantage. Instead, he orders us back to Harrison's Landing on the James River, back through the miserable Chickahominy swamps, back down the Virginia Peninsula, back the way we've come. In seven days of fighting, nearly sixteen thousand Union soldiers are killed, eight thousand are wounded, and six thousand are missing. With such high losses and no ground gained, despite the victories, we feel like we're slinking back in miserable retreat.

I've always admired General McClellan, but now I wonder. What have we been doing? Is there a strategy behind this retreat or simply cowardice? It's a low moment for me. A soldier needs to believe in his command. I don't want to admit it, but I'm not sure I have faith in General McClellan anymore. It's the blackest dispatch I've sent yet, and I wonder if Mr. Hurlburt will actually print it.

Lucky has been requisitioned by Colonel Poe, so I'm on foot in the muck as we retreat this time, trudging alongside Damon. We slog back through the swamp, wondering why we ever bothered.

"What was that all about?" asks Damon. "Will you please explain to me why we didn't jump on Richmond and finish this damn war?"

I shrug, as miserable as my friend. "We're just soldiers. What do we know? I'm sure McClellan has his reasons."

"Be nice if he'd share them with us then," Damon snipes. "Will I be home this harvesttime or not? You tell me!"

"I wish I could." I don't understand any more than Damon does, but I have to at least pretend to have faith in the general. He's a good man, an honorable leader, I don't doubt that. It's his choices that seem terribly wrong.

"Come on, Damon, we must be doing something right or I wouldn't have been able to get all that food out of the farmhouse. And I found Lucky. And I wasn't captured by those Rebels on the road. I have to believe things happen for a reason." I struggle to explain it to myself as much as to Damon.

"Maybe," he agrees. "But we aren't all as lucky as you. I swear, you're like a cat with your nine lives."

"And you're not?" I arch an eyebrow. "This from a man who was shot in the thigh and *didn't* have his leg amputated."

Damon smiles. "You got me there. Maybe you're right. Maybe things happen for a reason."

I clap him on the back. "You'll see. When we get to Harrison's Landing, something really good will happen. Maybe you'll get a nice package in the mail."

Damon looks down at his mud-encrusted boots. "Yeah, maybe someone will send me some new shoes. Maybe I'll get a soft down pillow. Maybe a three-layer cake."

I grin. I've been sent all those things. Families grateful for the final messages I've passed on from their dying sons have been generous, and I always share the riches that come in the mail.

"I'm sure you will, Damon. Or better still, a letter from your sweetheart."

Damon's eyes light up. "You think so? She hasn't written

in a while. Must be busy sewing her sister's trousseau. She's getting married next month, you know."

"That must be it," I agree. "Women's work—who can understand it?"

"It's a mystery, all right, just like women are." Damon pauses. "I still don't understand why Virginia hasn't written to you."

"Don't worry, my feelings aren't hurt. Who has time for romance anyway? It's all I can do to keep my rifle clean and my feet from rotting in my boots."

"You're right—there's no time to think about it when we're in a battle. It's those long stretches between fighting. Then it's all I *can* think about." Damon gapes like a lovesick cow. I blush, thinking how I'm the same way, mooning over romantic dreams of Jerome. When we aren't fighting, all I can do is imagine Jerome touching me, caressing my hands with his, leaning in to kiss me. I can't help hoping that when we reach Harrison's Landing, Jerome will be there, waiting for me.

FINDING OLD FRIENDS

OF COURSE JEROME ISN'T AT HARRISON'S LANDING.
But there is a letter for Damon from Polly and one for me
from her cousin, Virginia. She's actually written to me after
all, and I feel strangely flattered.

Dear Frank,

*I've heard what a brave, handsome soldier you
are, and I hope you won't think it presumptuous
of me to write to you. I want to do what I can for
our great nation, and helping support our troops
is one way I can help. I've enclosed some socks
I've knitted and a picture of myself. Please send
me one of you so I can imagine you as I read*

your letters. If you want to write back to me, as I pray you do.

Sincerely,

Virginia Keyes

"She wrote to you!" Damon beams. "And she sent you a daguerreotype! Let me see if she's grown as pretty as Polly says."

I hand over the small sepia-toned image of a young girl, her hair piled on her head in an attempt to make her look older.

"She's fine enough," I say. "But a bit young. Looks about twelve years old!"

"No, no, she's at least sixteen, plenty old enough to get married." Damon studies the portrait. "I met her once, when she was still in braids. She's all grown now, though I admit she looks a mite strict for someone so young. But what can you tell from a picture? She's softer-looking in person, I'm sure."

"I don't know about that, but I'll write to her. Who knows what will come of it?" Actually, I know that precisely nothing will come of it, but I'll seem more like a man if I have a girl writing to me. And it's always good to get mail, even if the people writing to you aren't really writing to you at all. Frank Thompson is getting letters now, but Sarah Emma Edmonds still hasn't a soul for a friend.

I pen a quick answer to Virginia and fold the requested portrait into the letter. The roving photographer told me I'm a handsome fellow (meaning I'm an ugly woman). Maybe Virginia will be so smitten by my good looks, she'll write me lilac-scented letters like the ones Miss Anna sends to Jerome. I'd like that. I'd like to think that someone, somewhere finds me attractive.

The letter to Virginia is short, but the dispatch I write for Mr. Hurlburt is long. I start by describing the move to Harrison's Landing, something McClellan calls "changing base." He assures us it's not a retreat, even though we're moving in the exact opposite direction necessary to

GENERAL SAMUEL HEINTZELMAN AND STAFF, HARRISON'S LANDING, VA.

confront the Confederates and seize their capital. To make things worse, the Rebels continue to nip at our heels, shooting at the rear guard, even lobbing shells over our heads and into our midst. By the time we arrive at Harrison's Landing, we're sick, exhausted, and demoralized, no matter how many tattered daydreams we cling to.

For the injured it's even worse. Close to a hundred men are stowed in the attic of a big house in the center of town, suffocating in the closed-in heat. The march through the wetlands combined with the scorching sun has seared the boots onto their feet so tight, they have to be cut off. I hate working as a nurse in the cramped, sweltering misery. I've had low moments before, but now I can't shake off the black dread that grips me. This isn't the glorious adventure I imagined that spring day so long ago when I enlisted. I don't feel part of a great historical moment. Instead, I'm stuck in an ugly nightmare, and it seems like dawn will never come.

I set down on paper all the misery, painting a bleak picture of the army. I wonder if this is the kind of slice of life Mr. Hurlburt expected when he asked me to write for his newsletter. He probably wanted inspiring tales of bravery, like the ones in the books I sold for him. Instead, I'm giving him the naked, ugly truth.

It's as if the generals have read my mind when the two armies call a truce to celebrate July Fourth. A holiday? I can't believe it—for one day not only will there be no fighting, there'll actually be an exchange of friendship. For Independence Day the Confederate and Union soldiers are allowed to pick berries together, trade tobacco, coffee, newspapers, gossip, and news. We can act like the neighbors we once were, not mortal enemies who have just spent a week slaughtering each other.

Damon and I walk out together, eager to swap news with the Rebels. I'm curious if they're as miserable as we are. What keeps them fighting? Why do they so desperately want to tear apart the Union?

"Now, you can't talk politics with the Rebs," Damon warns me.

"But that's exactly what I want to do," I argue.

"This is supposed to be a holiday, and you'll turn it into a brawl. Promise me—not a word!" Damon growls.

"Fine," I agree, though really it isn't fine with me at all. Maybe we can talk our way out of this war, convince the Southerners the whole thing has been a big mistake.

"So," I ask as we near a cluster of gray soldiers washing their feet in a creek. "How do you like Harrison's Landing? The folks here treat you well?" I don't mention politics. I think of how I had to pull a gun to get bandages, threaten to shoot a woman to buy provisions. The Southerners have made it clear the Union troops aren't welcome. I wonder if they resent all soldiers as disruptive or only us Northerners.

"Course they treat us well!" declares a slope-shouldered boy who says he's from Louisiana. "They're our folk, ain't they? We're fighting for them, for all of us. Every home is open to us, every woman bakes us pies and knits us socks. After every battle, folks come and help with the wounded, taking them into their homes. Farmers bring provisions to the hospitals. We know how to take care of our own."

"Now that seems like a bit of bragging," Damon says. "I can see them selling you food without being forced to, but giving things away like that . . ."

"You don't understand Southern hospitality!" The boy crosses his arms over his narrow chest. "What would a Yankee know about that? And patriotism! No one beats us for that, especially our women. Our young ladies push their own sweethearts to enlist, and if the fellas refuse, they send them a skirt with a note attached saying that if they won't fight, they should dress like the cowards they are!"

"I believe you," I reassure him. "I've heard stories like that, and I've seen for myself the backbone and pride that your women have. I just wish I could enjoy some of that famous hospitality."

"Humpf!" the boy snorts. "Then give them—give us—the respect we deserve!"

I nod. "I do. I sure respect your general, Bobby Lee. He knows how to fight."

The Louisiana boy flashes a gap-toothed grin. "That he do! You'll see, we'll whup you in the end—and it won't be too long now."

I wonder if he's right. After all, even when we win battles, we lose ground. It doesn't seem like a good strategy for winning a war.

Walking back to camp, Damon munches fistfuls of berries and talks about the Rebel soldiers. "Did you see how raggedy they're dressed? Some have uniforms, but most of them don't. Their shoes look like they're about to fall off their feet. How can we *not* beat an army that looks like that?"

"Because," I say, "they have something that matters more than uniforms or shoes. They've got grit—and a cause they truly believe in. How many of our men can say the same?"

"What do you mean, Frank?" Damon gapes, purple juice running down his chin. "I believe in the Union, I do! And I've got plenty of grit, thank you!"

I slap him on the back. "Yes, you do. So maybe we'll win this war after all." I want to believe it.

After a few days in Harrison's Landing, I'm ordered off nursing duty to deliver mail to soldiers sent to recover in the various hospitals in Washington. It's a relief to leave the steamy hospitals crammed with the sick and wounded. Maybe in the capital I'll get a better sense of how the war is going. Maybe from there it looks like we're winning.

Much has changed in Washington. The vast encampments are gone, but the hospitals are still familiar. I know many of the wounded soldiers who have been evacuated by steamer from the Virginia Peninsula. But I can't find the one I care about most—Jerome. I haven't heard what happened to him and the other soldiers left behind, and nobody I ask throughout the city knows either. I finger Jerome's locket, still hidden in my pocket. I'm not ready to send it to Anna yet, not until I know for sure that he's dead.

I find Dr. Evers and the men he led to safety, however. They're recuperating in Georgetown under the doctor's continued care.

"I'm happy to see you made it out as well," the doctor says. "I can't thank you enough for the use of your horse. He made the difference for many men between living and dying."

I blush, ashamed of how I thought I could have made better use of Flag than the wounded could.

"I wasn't sure I'd see you again," Dr. Evers continues, "so I gave your horse to the quartermaster of General Grover's brigade. I'm sure he'll hand him back to you."

I'm fond of Lucky, but Flag is more than a horse to me. He's my friend. I've missed his nickering for apples, his head shoving against my shoulder, the way his ears cock toward my voice, listening. He knows when to gallop and when to hold up just from the lean of my body. Flag understands me. There isn't anyone else I can say that about.

A strange, tingly excitement grips me as I near Grover's quartermaster. I can't help thinking of the moment when

Pa gave me Trig. Holding the halter of the fine young horse, I felt that same way, like something wonderful was about to happen, like an enormous gift was being granted to me.

But when I talk to the quartermaster, he just shakes his head. "I paid for that horse with good money. He's mine now."

"But Dr. Evers said he gave the horse to you," I protest. "And anyway, he wasn't the doctor's to sell. Flag belongs to me."

"To you or to the army? Either way, the doctor took fifty dollars for him, so he wasn't free. Perhaps that minor detail slipped the good doctor's mind, but I haven't forgotten. The horse is mine and there's nothing more to be said about it." The quartermaster turns to the sheaf of papers on his desk and breaks wind loudly.

I cover my nose from the foul stench, but I'm not about to give up. "You can't take advantage of the chaos of retreat to steal my horse from me. Flag is worth much more than fifty dollars and you know it! It's such a laughable sum, the doctor probably thought you were offering a tip, not recompense."

The quartermaster refuses to look up or answer me. Unless you count the fresh explosion from his nether regions as a response. The army should use him as a secret weapon, sickening the enemy with his fetid fumes.

I stomp off, directly to General Meade's headquarters, gulping in fresh air on my way. To my surprise the general sees me right away and listens patiently as I explain my case. Of course, I don't say anything about Flag being my friend. That would make me look silly. I simply describe the facts of what happened as calmly as I can, leaving out the gaseous incidents. When I'm done, he snorts in disgust.

"Lord, forgive us such idiots! I'm sorry for your troubles, Private." He leans over his crowded desk and quickly scribbles something on a piece of paper. "Take this back to that stubborn quartermaster. I'm ordering him to return your horse without delay. If you have *any* further difficulties with the man, you come back here right away. We'll straighten out the so-and-so."

"Thank you, sir," I say. For every selfish, self-serving man I come across in the army, I meet someone else so noble and bighearted, it washes out the bad taste left by the mean-spirited. I think of all the brave, ordinary soldiers I know—so many, compared to the few like the piggish chaplain, the cowardly colonel who pretended to be wounded, or the greedy quartermaster who refuses to recognize Flag's rightful owner.

Seeing the order, the quartermaster pales, his mustache trembling. Even his rear end behaves. "Well," he sputters, "since it's like that, of course you'll have your horse." He points to the stable down the street, where Flag is in a stall next to an old dappled nag.

Flag tosses his head, nickering when he sees me, as if he's wondering why I've taken this long to fetch him home.

He stamps so much, the horse next to him gets agitated, then the one next to him, until horses are neighing and snorting all along the row of stalls. I can't help grinning. He's as happy to see me as I am to see him.

"Flag, my friend"—I rub the blaze between his eyes— "did you miss me?" He noses my pocket, expecting the usual treat.

"Sorry, boy, I don't have anything for you now, but I'll get you something, don't you worry." I bury my face in Flag's neck, savoring the familiar smell. We've been through so much together. I think of Jerome, my other best friend. His absence is like a hole in my chest, a missing piece of myself. But at least I have Flag again. That's a comfort, an unexpected one.

The next day I'm ordered to appear at regimental headquarters. I brace myself for more arguing over Flag, but it isn't the quartermaster who has demanded to see me. It's the colonel who pretended to be wounded at the Battle of Williamsburg, the one Dr. Bonine ordered back to the field. He's been on furlough since his cowardly behavior but has managed to present himself so well that he's been promoted to brigade commander, all without any achievement in battle whatsoever. He's invented his own past, telling reporters his "story," so it's now widely believed that he was "severely wounded at the battle of Williamsburg while gallantly leading a desperate charge on the enemies' works, and was carried from the field, but no sooner had

the surgeons bound up his wound than the noble and patriotic colonel returned again to his command and led his men
again and again upon the foe, until the day was won, when
he sank upon the ground, exhausted from loss of blood and
fatigue, and was carried the second time by his men from the
field."

The colonel presents the newspaper article describing
his noble exploits to me as if proof that my own memory is
faulty. I read it, my stomach sour with disgust.

"Why show me this?" I ask.

"Because," answers the colonel, "I'm told that you
were one of the men who carried me when I was wounded.
I need you to corroborate the truth of this story, because
the doctor on the field that day, some miscreant named Dr.
Bonine, had the nerve to write to the newspaper that the
whole incident was a pack of lies, that I was never wounded,
not noble, nor patriotic, but a sniveling coward. You saw the
truth! You know how the doctor abused me and called me
vile names!"

I push down the anger boiling inside me and answer
calmly. "If the doctor called you unpleasant names, it was
only because your behavior was despicable. You let me and
the other nurse carry you to safety when you didn't have so
much as a scratch on you!"

The colonel peers at me as if trying to take my measure.
His lips curl in an oily smile, and his tone shifts from outrage to fawning. "Now, Frank, there's no need to make this

situation difficult. You saw what you think you saw. I know what I know. And I know that I can make this handsomely worth your while. All you need to do is sign this document, and you'll find your purse quite a bit heavier than it is now." He slides a paper across his desk.

Not wanting to touch anything fingered by this repulsive man, I lean over the desk and read the short paragraph:

This is to certify that Colonel Burgess has been infamously treated and maliciously slandered by Doctor Bonine, while said colonel was suffering from a wound received at Williamsburg battle. The two undersigned carried him bleeding from the field, and witnessed the cruel treatment and insulting language of Doctor Bonine.

I clamp my lips together, holding in an enraged roar. Bad enough the coward has been promoted, now he's trying to slander someone who truly is brave, noble, and patriotic. I glare at the colonel, who leans smugly back in his chair, sure that money can buy him a valorous past.

Not from me. "There is no way I'll ever put my name to such a lie," I say, seething. "You'd spit in someone's eye and call it honey."

"But I can pay you!" The colonel's voice is shrill.

"No," I say. "You can't." I turn and walk out. I walk

until my fists stop clenching, my breathing relaxes, and the sour taste in my mouth melts away. I reduce the colonel to a funny story and imagine telling Damon about it, acting out the colonel's insulting offer. I wish I had a copy of the bogus newspaper story—we would both have a good laugh over the willingness of reporters to believe whatever anyone tells them. At least I can write what really happened to Mr. Hurlburt. His newsletter can tell the truth, revealing the falsehoods other papers have printed.

As I ride along the Potomac on Flag, I admire the dome that is being constructed for the Capitol. The scaffolding is lit by the setting sun. Washington is a beautiful city, but it cares too much about appearances, about fancy uniforms and family names. I'm eager to leave it, to get back to honest, simple people, my comrades and friends, to get back to the reasons I enlisted in the first place. It's been nearly two years and we're further from winning than ever, but I have to believe our luck will change. There are too many good men fighting for the Army of the Potomac for us to lose. I think about Dr. Bonine and his selfless sacrifices, about Damon's earnest heart, and Jerome's loyalty to his patients. They're all decent people, fighting for the right reason, and I'm honored to be one of them. When I was young, my life was defined by Pa, then by my decision to reject an unwanted marriage and strike out on my own as a man. But now there's a deeper, grander story framing who

I am—it's the story of this war and my place in it, what I've done to help my comrades, from spying to nursing to fighting to foraging for food. When it's all over, I want to be able to lift my head proudly and say I was worthy of serving with my friends, that I knew what an honorable life was and chose to live one.

17

THE LETTER

BACK IN HARRISON'S LANDING, I RETURN TO NURSING duty, where despite my efforts more men die than recover. The mood in the regiment is bleak. It's as if the Confederates have already won and we're simply waiting to get the news.

Rumors fly through the camp about where we'll be heading next.

"I swear," growls Damon, "if I have to march through the Chickahominy swamps one more time, I'm quitting this army and walking home!"

"You're not a deserter," I protest. "You're too loyal for that. Besides, I thought you were growing fond of wet feet and mosquitoes."

Damon snorts. "You can have them both! A man can only take so much. Why don't we just let the South secede? Who wants this land anyway? If you ask me, they can have it, and good riddance!"

Usually I can joke Damon out of his rare foul tempers,

but he's stretched thin. We all are. If humor won't work, maybe reminding ourselves of why we're fighting will.

"We can't leave the Africans as slaves," I argue. "There are too many reasons to win this war to give up on it. You believe in the Union. Our cause is just—you know that!"

"I don't care about the slaves. That's their problem, not mine." Things are worse than I thought if patriotism can't rouse my friend. Damon throws some twigs into the campfire. "I'm sick of sitting here, waiting for nothing."

I sigh. I'm impatient too, but I do a better job of hiding it. I seem to be good at hiding lots of things. Besides, I'm too worried about Jerome to focus much on the prolonged stay at Harrison's Landing. Every day I ask Colonel Poe if there's any news. Each time he shakes his head sadly.

It's become part of my morning ritual. After the morning drills, I head for Colonel Poe's tent and wait until he can see me. Sometimes he simply pokes his head out and frowns before I can even ask. Until the August morning when the colonel greets me with a broad smile.

My heart flips in my chest. "You've heard something? You know what happened to the men?"

"Indeed I do." The colonel gestures to a camp stool. "Have a seat. It's a bit of a story."

As I feared, the Confederates took the hospital the next day, led by Colonel Fitzhugh Lee, General Robert E. Lee's nephew. The colonel could have been vengeful, having just heard that our retreating army had burned his aunt's home in White House Landing to a pile of smoking ashes. Instead, he was the perfect Southern gentleman, considerate of the patients, polite to Jerome and the other nurse who stayed behind. He didn't even take the men prisoner. Instead, he offered to parole them.

I've never heard of parole, but Colonel Poe explains that it's an ancient custom of freeing captured soldiers on the condition that they promise not to take up arms again until they've either been ransomed or exchanged for an enemy prisoner captured by their own army. Earlier in the war, doctors, nurses, and patients who were taken prisoner weren't given that choice. They were simply put in prison, in horrendous conditions. But I have to give the Confederates credit. It was General Stonewall Jackson who considered that practice unethical and started paroling any enemy medical staff taken in battle. Our army followed suit, and by the summer of 1862 such exchanges have become common.

It sounds like an odd situation for the parolees— not prisoners, yet not free to leave either. Jerome and the others were guarded by Jeb Stuart's cavalry—the same group that later ambushed the troop train. Then they were moved to Camp Parole in Annapolis, Maryland, a holding place run by our army where the ex-prisoners would stay until they were traded or ransomed. In some ways it was like being held by one's own side, but naturally the conditions were much better than in an enemy prisoner-of-war camp.

"So Jerome is in Annapolis?" I ask. "I could have seen him when I was in Washington delivering mail?"

"He's only just arrived, but you'll have other chances to see him, I'm sure. And in the meantime . . ." The colonel offers me a folded piece of paper. "He's sent you a letter."

"A letter?" A wide smile blooms on my face. It's the first personal letter I've ever received in my whole life, all twenty years. Not a letter from a stranger, like Virginia's, and not a professional request from a former employer, like Mr. Hurlburt's. But a letter written to me purely out of friendship. And it's from Jerome. I feel a twinge of guilt for all the letters he's written to Miss Anna that I've lost, but it doesn't last long. I'm too excited by the thought of reading my friend's words, of knowing how he's feeling, of what's happening to him, of being invited into his life through the single page I carefully unfold.

I float out of the tent, gripping the letter until I come to a spot behind an oak that offers some privacy.

Dear Frank,

We're all well and were treated quite kindly by our Southern hosts. Now we're in Camp Parole, on Chesapeake Bay. It's a beautiful place and quite comfortable, but I feel guilty to be doing nothing while the rest of you still fight. As parolees, we're not allowed to drill or do any work that could help the Union cause, so we sit around all day, getting soft, reading books, writing letters, or playing cards. There's not much else to do. I've asked the commander here if by taking the parole oath, we've deserted the army (since in fact, that's what we've promised to do), but he assures me that being on parole is a special circumstance and not considered dereliction of duty. That's some comfort, but boredom is hard to contend with. I hope I'm released soon and can rejoin you, wherever the Second Michigan Regiment ends up.

Your loyal friend,
Jerome Robbins

It isn't a romantic message, but the warm friendship, the closeness it shows, means more to me than a syrupy love poem. Besides, what matters most is that, of everyone in the regiment, he's chosen to write to me—to me! And he's telling me honestly how he feels, his guilt and boredom. Who wants flowery sentiment when you can have that kind of friendship? I rush back to my tent to write an answer, enclose some money in case that would be handy, and add the envelope to the stack I'll deliver the next day. I hum happily, mending an old shirt, sitting in front of the tent, when Damon comes by.

"What are you so cheerful about? Have you heard something? Are we finally going to move from here? Or did you get another letter from Virginia? Has she declared her undying affection yet?"

"She's written no such thing! I did get another letter from her, but it's all bland formulas and pleasantries. I don't know that she's actually saying anything at all, though she did talk about the kitchen garden a bit." I bite off the thread and tie a lumpy knot. I never have been much of a hand at sewing. "I don't know how you write to a lady. I can't tell what would be interesting to Virginia. I just write to her the same kind of thing I write to Mr. Hurlburt, and that's probably not a good idea."

"Forget about Virginia, then—you know something!" Damon insists. "I can tell!"

I grin. "Yes, I do! I got a letter from Jerome. He wasn't

taken prisoner. They paroled him instead, so now he's at some camp in Annapolis."

"Paroled? The lucky so-and-so! He's not in a prison camp *and* he doesn't have to fight in this blasted war anymore. Why didn't I think of that?"

I fold up the patched shirt. "He doesn't think he's so lucky. I mean, of course he's relieved not to be a prisoner, but he's frantic from doing so much nothing. He wants to be useful, to help. He's more a nurse than a soldier. I don't think he's ever fought in any battles, just worked with the doctors in the hospitals. He wants to be where he's needed most."

"Well, if you ask me, that's home, with his sweetheart, that little gal of his that's been waiting on him so long. He should just sneak out of that camp and get himself back home." Damon sighs. "That's what I'd do."

I frown. "He's not like you. He doesn't care how long he's apart from Miss Anna. He cares about the wounded soldiers."

"So he says. Every man would rather be with his honey than in a war. That's only natural."

My ears turn red. I don't want to hear another word. "You're wrong," I snap, throwing down my mending and stomping off.

"Oh, no, I'm not!" Damon yells after me. "You're just jealous because you don't have your own girl yet! If Virginia was in love with you, it'd be a different story!"

For two days we don't speak to each other. Our mood fits

with the tense misery that pervades the whole camp. And a couple of weeks later that sour mood swells to anger when General McClellan orders the entire army to leave the Virginia Peninsula, shipping out the way we came. In five months we've given up whatever ground we've taken and lost fifteen thousand men. The utter waste of it all, the complete failure of the campaign, is a terrible omen for how the war will end. Even worse, when the Second Michigan arrives back in Alexandria, we're ordered to march to Manassas, the site of our first terrible defeat at the start of the war. I don't see how things could be worse. We seem cursed to repeat the same mistakes over and over again, and each time, thousands more die.

THE SECOND BATTLE OF BULL RUN

BY THE TIME OUR REGIMENTS REACH MANASSAS, JOIN-
ing the main army led by Major General John Pope,
Stonewall Jackson has already attacked our supply depot
at Manassas Junction. His troops pull up track, plunder our
stores, and torch the station. It's a humiliating incursion,
coming so close to us yet getting away lickety-split without
a single wounded soldier.

The Second Michigan is sent ahead to the front lines,
where we'll bear the brunt of the battle. Everyone in my
regiment except me, that is. Once again I'm a messenger
first, and only once I've finished with that will I join my
regiment in battle. I chafe at not being part of the action,
but I promise myself I'll deliver the messages so fast, I
won't miss much. I beg for the fastest horse. Flag has been
assigned to another orderly, and Dr. Evers has asked to
borrow Lucky. I hope for the bay stallion I've seen in the

corral, the one with the deep chest and fine legs, a horse built to run. Instead, I'm given a mule—a mule!

As good as I am with horses, I'm terrible with the mule. Truth is, I expect him to behave as a horse would, and I take it personally when he doesn't. He can probably tell how much I don't want to be riding him.

To hurry things up, I take a shortcut, riding across country. I usually prefer racing across fields and over fences anyway, but this ride is nothing like that first time with Lucky. Then, I felt like I was flying. Now, nothing I do feels right, but I don't give up, kicking harder, leaning in tighter, spurring that stubborn animal into a gallop. I jump the mule over fences and ditches until I come to a particularly wide ditch that a horse could easily make. I urge the mule over, but the ravine is too much for him. The damn animal rears, pitches me off, then slips down the slope. I'm thrown all the way across the ditch, turning my face in time to see the mule's flank slam into my left leg as he tumbles in after me. I gasp, sucking in air, pain blurring my eyes. Dirt showers onto me as the animal scrambles to his feet. I cover my head, cowering, and try to roll out of the way, but his hind hoof tramples my shin.

I spit out dirt, clear the grit from my eyes, and work to breathe. I'm alive, I tell myself, pushing down the panic and pain flooding through me. I try to think, to plan what to do next, but the agony in my chest and left leg is like a fire, searing and sharp. I feel gingerly along my side and howl as I touch my ribs. I must have cracked them again. I edge myself up onto my elbows and examine the rest of my body. My left foot bends at the ankle in an unnatural way. Other than that, I reassure myself, I'm fine and dandy.

Obviously I can't stay in the ditch all day. I try to push myself upright but can't put any weight on my left leg. "Goddamn it!" I curse, furious with how much it all hurts, how stupid it all is.

Sinking back to the ground, I turn onto all fours and crawl out of the ditch, then grab a tree branch as a lever to haul myself upright. The mule stands next to me, nibbling on some grass, rolling his eye as if to say it's my own fault, no sense in blaming a mule for being a mule. Of course, he isn't bruised or limping.

"It's all your fault, you pigheaded devil," I curse. "But I'm willing to forgive you if you stay there nice and easy and let me get on your bony back."

The mule snorts but doesn't edge away as I hobble close enough to snatch the reins. I grip the saddle and throw my lame leg over, pushing myself onto the mule's back. The movement is excruciating and I sit there a moment, sweat streaming down my face as I catch my breath and wait for the agony to ease up. The pain is so sharp that I'm terrified of actually moving. But I still have messages to deliver. So I grit my teeth and kick the mule with my good leg.

Cannon thud ahead of me, but I can't bear any pace faster than a walk. A trot is agony, a gallop torture. By the time I get to the front, the battle is fierce, with our side clearly losing, but I'm so dizzy and nauseous from pain, I barely notice the chaotic butchery around me. It feels like blood is swirling behind my eyes as well as in front of them. All my focus goes to sitting upright and not collapsing. I manage to deliver the messages; then I do the unthinkable: I report to the hospital.

"Frank!" Dr. Bonine rushes to me when I ride in. "You're white as a sheet! What happened?" The doctor helps me off the mule, but I quickly shake him off, not wanting his hands to linger on me too long.

"I'm fine! No need for concern. I fell off this blasted mule is all. Nothing serious, but I'm in a bit of pain." I will myself to stand as normally as possible. "I can bandage up my own leg if you'll give me some linen and a splint. And maybe some whiskey would help."

"Of course," says the doctor, heading for the supply chest.

I slump down, my left leg straight out in front of me. I can't risk being examined. Granted, my leg seems manly enough, or at least not ladylike, but who knows what the doctor would touch next if I let him set the broken bone. No matter what, I have to convince him to leave me be.

The doctor returns with liniment, cloth strips, a splint, and a canteen of whiskey.

"Thank you, Doctor," I say, taking a quick swallow. "Now go on and tend to the men who really need you. I just have a scratch, a sprain—they have serious wounds."

Dr. Bonine notes the sweat pearling on my forehead, the tight pallor of my face. "Are you sure? Maybe you broke something and don't know it."

"No!" I roar. I compose myself, trying not to sound so desperate. "I mean, it's not bad. I don't want to waste your valuable time."

"I see." The doctor nods. "I'll check on you later, then."

"Thank you." I want to sound casual, cheerful even, but I sound strained, like I've sat on a nest of red ants. "I'll be back at the front lines, but I'll see you when I can."

I wait until the doctor bends over a man with blood streaming from his chest. Slowly I cut back my pants leg to reveal the battered shin. My foot is so swollen, I have to cut off the boot as well. I set the splint, then wrap the bandages around my foot and up my leg all the way to the knee. I'll take care of the ribs later, in the privacy of our tent, once Damon is sound asleep, the way I did the first time. For now I wad up some extra cloth and stuff it into my pocket. I drink another gulp of whiskey, and grabbing my rifle to use as a cane, I wobble to my feet.

Am I in good enough shape to go back to the battle? I'm not sure, but the whiskey certainly helps deaden the pain. I start to limp away when I hear someone call my name.

"Frank! It's me, it's Damon." Two nurses carry him in on a stretcher. This time his arm is bleeding.

With my broken leg, I'm helpless. I can't lift Damon off the stretcher. I can't run and get the doctor. So I do what I can. I lean down and dribble some whiskey into his mouth.

"Frank, stay with me! Don't leave me!" Damon's eyes are wide with fear. "I'm not losing an arm now—don't let them amputate! Curse this war!"

"Hush, now, you're not losing anything. You kept your leg and you'll keep your arm." I stay with him while the doctor digs out the minié ball and bandages the arm.

"He'll live," grunts the doctor. "No amputation, like your friend here promised. And I've got even better news for you, son."

"What?" rasps Damon.

"You're going home. Soon as you feel strong enough. No sense keeping a soldier who can't fire a gun, now is there?" Dr. Bonine winks. He turns to me. "And you look a whole lot better yourself, Frank. Glad to see that."

"Did you hear that?" Damon grips my arm with his good hand. "I'm going home! It's too late for the corn harvest, but I don't care—I'm going home!" Tears trickle down his grimy cheeks.

I'm happy for Damon, truly I am, relieved he'll be far from the battleground. But with Jerome gone and Damon leaving, I'll be lonelier than ever—and limping with cracked ribs and a broken leg. I feel utterly useless and alone.

Even worse, we're reliving that first horrible defeat on this same battlefield. This time our soldiers take the fighting seriously—they don't toss away their ammunition or their canteens. But, just like at the first Battle of Bull Run, society folks from Washington come to visit the battle, eager to witness combat from a safe vantage point. I pass several government clerks, daintily dressed, as I hobble away from the hospital. One flags me down with his handkerchief, as if I were a hansom cab.

"Perhaps you can help us," the clerk says, twirling his hat nervously in his hands. "We want to get on a train back to Washington, but they seem to be crammed with wounded soldiers. No one will answer our questions. How ever are we to get a place? Are we supposed to walk back to Washington?"

"Who invited you here?" I growl. "No one asked you to come, so you can find your own way home. Unless you want to make yourself useful." I offer him my gun. "There's still fighting going on and we could use reinforcements, even ones as lily-livered as you all."

The clerk recoils, his muttonchopped cheeks quivering. "Heavens, no! I'm not a soldier!"

"Then what are you doing here?" I glare. "I'd kick you back to Washington if I could!"

Now the man looks at me as if I'm crazy, and maybe I am. I limp on, but I have to stop so often, I realize there's no point in trying to make it to the battlefield. I'm in no better shape to fight than the cowardly clerk, though at least my spirit is willing. My body, however, is not. I cough up blood and am easily winded, but I don't dare risk a doctor's care. Instead, I find our tent, crawl in, and sleep. The first time I was wounded, it was also from an animal, not from honest battle. I feel clumsy and stupid, allowing a mule to hurt me while men all around me are shot, including Damon. Am I worthy of their company, I wonder groggily before sleep takes over. What kind of soldier am I?

By the time I wake up, pain still thudding through my body, the Battles of Bull Run and Chantilly are over, both heavy losses for the Union, and the Second Michigan is sent back to camp near Washington. I shuffle alongside Damon for the last time. He's set to be discharged as soon as we reach the capital.

"You know, Frank, you could get a medical discharge yourself," he suggests. "You look mighty peaked, and anyone can see you've got a bum leg."

"I just twisted my ankle is all." I force a smile. "It's nothing serious. I'm as fit as ever." I pause. "But dang it all, Damon, I'm going to miss you. And who will my new tentmate be? Someone who snores louder than you, I bet."

"You should have appreciated me more while you had me." Damon grins. "But I expect you'll find a new buddy. James Reid said he'd take my place."

"James?" I consider it. Reid is a strapping, blond lieutenant in the 79th New York Highlanders, a primarily Scottish infantry regiment. He's an educated man, soft-spoken and deliberate. Most important, he doesn't drink or gamble, so the two of us might get along. "What happened to his old tentmate?"

"Died," Damon says.

"Well, I hope he has better luck with me," I snort. "I'm not planning on dying soon."

"You're a tough bird, not the kind to die. I already told James that." Damon rubs his bandaged arm. "You haven't even been shot yet. It's amazing. There you are, in the thick of fighting, weaving in and out on your horse, delivering orders. All around you, men are hit by shells or minié balls. But you must have a guardian angel or something—nothing touches you."

I cringe. I'm ashamed I haven't been wounded. It seems like I'm not really taking risks. "Yeah, instead, I get horses and mules doing me in. Maybe that's just my fate. I remember the preacher telling Ma not to worry about all my wild escapades because 'one who was born to be hanged will never be drowned.'"

"What's that supposed to mean? You're going to be hanged?" Damon shivers. "That's like saying you won't die in battle, but one of these days the Rebs will figure out you're a spy. On one of your missions, you'll be caught and they'll hang you."

"I don't know about that. I've been behind enemy lines three times before the last two battles and managed to get back in one piece. Spying seems safer than fighting."

"When did you do that?" Damon gapes. "I don't remember that."

"I told you I was on mail runs, but really General

Heintzelman sent me to get information on Lee's defenses and strategies. I didn't find out much, and what I learned didn't seem to help at all." I shrug. "Sometimes when I go out spying, I don't end up with anything useful. But when I do . . ."

"Here I thought you'd only spied twice, not five times!" Damon stares at me as if I've grown an extra head. "You sure know how to keep a secret!"

I laugh. "You have no idea!" Maybe that's one valuable thing I offer the Union—my ability to keep secrets and transform myself into an invisible spy, unnoticed by the enemy. Once I disguised myself as a washerwoman, the perfect excuse to go through everyone's pockets. I found some interesting papers that time! When it comes to fighting, I don't do as well. Is it because of my own personal failings or the limitations of being a woman? I'm not sure which is preferable.

Back in Washington, Damon takes one last tour of the capital with me, then boards a train for home.

"You take good care of yourself, Frank!" He hugs me tightly. I want to hug him back, to hold him to me for a little longer, but I wince and pull away, cradling my aching ribs.

"You'll always be my favorite tentmate," I say, blinking fast so I won't cry. "Give my best to Virginia! Tell her I'm waiting for another letter!"

"I'll make sure she writes you as soon as I see her," Damon promises. "And I'll tell her so many stories about you, she's bound to fall in love, just from my descriptions."

I doubt love is so easy, but I'm touched by all of Damon's efforts on my behalf. If only I were really the kind of man a young girl would want. What Virginia really deserves is someone like Damon.

I wave as the train chuffs out of the station. I've said good-bye to soldiers on trains before, always wounded men heading for hospitals. This is the first time I've seen a friend off on a happy voyage, a trip back home. Even though the war is going badly and I'll miss him so much, my heart lifts at the thought of Damon safe on his farm with his girl at his side. I may be alone, but the two people who matter most to me are far from combat now. That's something to be grateful for.

I spend most of the next month nursing my injuries. My new tentmate, James, turns out to be as kind and attentive as Damon promised. I still have to ride for long hours, delivering the mail, but at least when I collapse back in the tent with my foot throbbing, James brings me a plate of hot food and some cool water. More than that, he cheers me up by reading me letters from his wife, telling me stories of home, and singing Scottish ballads. His voice is low and soft, comforting like a blanket. His eyes are a bright cornflower blue, his lips full and sensitive. He's not like Damon at all, but he's someone I can talk to. That takes the edge off the pain of my mending ribs and foot.

August turns into September and still we wait for orders.

There's nothing new for me to put into my dispatches. All I can write about is the sour mood in camp. The soldiers are restless and depressed by the news from the battlefield of Antietam. Although the Union wins, pushing the Rebels out of Maryland, the costs are horrific. More men die that one day than in any other single battle—five thousand killed, twenty thousand wounded. The Second Michigan is still camped outside Alexandria, sitting helplessly by while our comrades are slaughtered. Morale, already low, sinks to even bleaker levels.

But now it's Lee's turn to retreat, and this time the Second Michigan leads the Union advance across the Potomac, back into Virginia. I'm sure that this time we won't leave until we take Richmond.

19
ON THE ROADS OF NORTHERN VIRGINIA

ON THE THIRD DAY OF MARCHING SOUTH, I'M SENT back to deliver messages to General McClellan's headquarters. I ride Flag along the familiar road, passing column after column of the advance guard as it marches toward Richmond. It's an impressive sight—the troops are fit, rested, and eager for battle. I remember how foolish we looked on our way to that first battle, at Bull Run. Now we're a real army, and I swell with pride to be part of it.

I reach McClellan's headquarters around noon and deliver the messages. I'm invited to eat dinner with the troops there but decide I'd rather get back to my regiment as quickly as possible. I don't know why I feel anxious, but I can't shake a sense of dread. I let Flag have a quick drink of water, then get right back on him. But even after I ride for hours, there's no sign of the mass of troops I passed that morning. Where have they all gone? The shadows are long, and it's cold and dark now. The thick dread I felt before is heavier than ever, clogging my throat, pricking my eyes. Flag is the only thing that keeps me steady. I lean over and bury my nose in his mane, breathing in his familiar smell.

It's deep night now. Owls hoot, katydids chirp, and a sliver of moon is all the light I have to guide me. It's foolish to keep on riding, but the back of my neck tingles with nerves, anxious at being alone in enemy territory.

"Well, Flag, what do you suggest?" I ask, needing to hear my voice out loud. "We've been fine sleeping in the open before, but I have a queer feeling about these parts. Something's giving me the willies." I can think of only one reason why we haven't crossed the regiments yet. There must have been some sort of skirmish and they've changed the line of the march. Otherwise we would have met up with them hours ago. Which leaves me no closer to finding them, but I figure we'll have a better chance off the main road since they certainly aren't on it.

I nudge Flag forward across the countryside until we find another road heading south. I sing to keep us both company, and Flag twitches his ears back to listen. When my voice grows hoarse after too many choruses of "Oh, Susanna," I try whistling. When I'm too tired for that, I let the quiet of the night envelop us and pray we'll find our troops soon. I can't explain why the dark silence makes me so edgy— Flag and I have ridden at night many times before—but I can't shake a sharp wariness, a fear that my luck is about to run out.

Stars glitter overhead and still I keep riding, shivering as much from nerves as from the cold. It's only September, but snow falls in thick flurries as we come to a small town. Maybe we can sleep in a barn, I think, but as we near a farmhouse, I spot the ruddy faces and gray uniforms of a small group of Rebel soldiers through the window, lit up in the glow of oil lamps. The scene is cozy and warm, the farmer offering a platter of steaming meat, his wife passing a basket of rolls. My stomach growls, but I suspect I wouldn't be a welcome guest. I guide Flag back across the fields until he decides he's had enough, whether I want to rest or not. He slows his walk, then stops completely, dropping his head.

"Come on, Flag, let's keep going. There's no shelter here." My heels thud into Flag's sides, but he won't budge. "Flag!" I beg.

Flag turns his head back to me and whinnies softly. "Come on, yourself," he seems to say. "I'm tired and it's time to sleep, standing right here if I have to."

"Well, I can't blame you. You're the one who's done all the work today, carrying me for hours and hours. And I'm tired, too." I peer into the night, trying to find something in the blackness that could offer protection from the weather.

Snow drifts around us, but through the flakes I can make out the form of a small building. Going closer, I see it's a woodshed. It's too full of wood for us to get inside, but if we lean against it, we'll have at least one side free of wind and snow. I take off Flag's saddle and blanket.

"Come on, boy," I coax him. "Lie down now, so I can sleep against you. I need you, Flag." I pull down on the reins, urging him to sink to his knees. He understands what I want and hunkers down, even though the snow is several inches deep by then and the cold is numbing. "That's it, Flag." I pat him with frozen fingers. "We'll keep each other warm, won't we?" I curl up beside the welcome heat of his body. As I shiver next to him, he lays his head across my shoulders, a heavy, warm blanket on my chest.

"Thanks, Flag," I murmur. "Good night." I can't remember the last time I've been touched by anyone. Pressed against Flag, listening to his thudding heart, I feel held and loved.

I wake up the next morning with numb fingers and toes, but the dread has disappeared. It's peaceful next to Flag. He's had enough of me, though, and nibbles at my hair, nudging me to get up.

"Good morning," I croak. Everything feels stiff and chilled, including my voice. Flag heaves himself up, shaking off the dusting of snow that has coated him during the night. I throw the blanket and saddle onto his back, then clamber on myself. All around us, the world is white with icy blue shadows. If I were cozy, with a full stomach, I would think it beautiful.

"Come on, Flag, let's find us some breakfast." Down the road we cross a field with stacks of corn. "It's not food for me, but at least you can eat," I offer. Flag looks like he enjoys the corn so much, husks and all, that I can't resist. I tear the husks off an ear and sink my teeth into the frozen kernels. They're too cold for me to tell if they taste good or not. And it doesn't matter—they stop my stomach from growling, and that's all that counts.

I'm standing there, chomping on the corn, when some movement down the road catches my eye. Instantly, I leap back onto Flag, my gun in hand, my muscles tight with nerves. In the pink morning light I make out a small group of blue-clad men on horseback, a party of Union cavalry. The knot in my chest dissolves. Maybe they can direct me to my regiment. Or I could ride with them. All on horseback, we'd keep the same pace.

"Ho, there!" I wave, trotting toward them. "I'm Frank Thompson, Second Michigan, looking for the Army of the Potomac on their way to Richmond."

"Can't say exactly where they are," one of the soldiers answers. "We're searching for a band of Confederate scouts we heard tell are in these parts. Seen any sign of them?"

"As a matter of fact, I have. And I'd be happy to take you to them," I offer, "if only my stomach wasn't so weak from hunger."

The soldier digs into his haversack and takes out a couple of biscuits. "Reckon this'll help?" he asks.

I grab the biscuits and wolf them down, nodding. I'm still chewing as I turn Flag around and head back to the town we passed the night before.

"So where are these Rebs and how many are there?" the soldier asks.

"I saw them last night in a farmhouse not far from here. I can't say exactly how many. Through the window, I could see seven or eight of them. After you get them, will you be heading back to the main army? I could go with you."

The soldier turns to answer but never gets a word out. A minié ball hits him square in the chest, and he falls off his horse. Another shot rings out and another. I whirl Flag around but can't see where to go. Gray uniforms surround us. We've been ambushed. I pull out my gun and aim at a patch of gray. Before I can shoot, there's a loud burst of bullets and Flag jolts back. His head jerks up, eyes rolling white, and I feel the balls hit his body and echo through mine. Blood froths from his nostrils. He bucks, throwing me over his head. I crash to the ground, the gun flying out of my hand. Flag whinnies shrilly, the scream of a dying horse, and falls. He lands on me, his neck thrown across my body. I lie there facedown, trapped and stunned. Warm, sticky blood oozes down the back of my neck and onto my face. I can't tell if it's mine or Flag's. Shots careen around me. A blue-coated soldier hits the ground next to me with a thud. I watch as the blade of a saber rams through his chest, is pulled out and thrust in again. The Reb will finish me off next. I close my eyes and hold my breath. I'm already dead, I tell myself. I'm dead. I'm dead. Seconds pass and there's no more gunfire, no more slashing or stabbing. Just the shuffle of boots, the creaking of saddles, the murmur of Southern accents as the Confederates get back on their horses and ride off. I lie there, tasting dirt and blood, wondering when it will be safe to move. I open my eyes a crack, then quickly shut them as I hear the hooves of a horse returning. The hoofbeats come closer; then the thump of a booted man, dismounting and walking closer. The Rebel soldier grabs hold of my feet and pulls me out from under Flag. He wrenches off my boots, then throws them down in disgust.

"Too small," a voice mutters. "There must be somethin' heah worth the takin'."

I keep my eyes closed without squinching them tightly. I don't breathe as the man rolls me over and rifles through my pockets, taking my watch, Jerome's locket, and a few dollars. As his hands brush against my breasts, I bite the inside of my cheek to keep myself from flinching. He kicks me lazily in the hip, making me swallow a pained gasp. Then he hurls himself back on his horse and is gone.

I scarcely dare to breathe, counting out five long minutes, then ten, then fifteen. I open my eyes slowly. Three men and two horses are sprawled dead in the road, but there's no sign of anyone else. Shakily, I stand up, feeling all over for injuries. My left leg, only just mended from the fall off the mule, seems broken again. But the pain isn't as bad as the first time, and I can limp up the road. There's a big bump on my forehead, and my hands are scraped from the fall, but all the blood on me is Flag's. He's saved my life twice in two days. I look at his still body, three bullet holes in his neck and chest.

"My good, brave Flag," I croon, kneeling down and stroking his nose. "Thank you. For everything. I've never known a better horse, a truer friend." I kiss the blaze between his eyes, finger his silky ears, tears salting my cheeks. All the secrets I've confided to Flag are still in his loyal heart. There's no one else I can be honest with, no one else who knows me so well. Flag never cared whether I was a man or a woman, a coward or a hero.

"Think, Frank." I say the words out loud to give myself courage. "You've got to think what to do next. You can't stay here next to your dead horse." I find my boots and put them back on, grateful for the first time for having small feet, but my fingers fumble nervously. It feels like my hands don't belong to me—none of my body does.

I force myself to stand, not sure where to go except south in the direction of Richmond. I've managed a few stiff paces when once again I hear horses. It's too late to play dead again. And my gun, where's my gun? I look back to where I fell, but the Confederates must have taken it.

I turn to face the horsemen, determined to die on my feet if that's my fate. The men whoop and wave as they come closer. I stiffen, heart pounding, expecting the dreaded Rebel yell. Instead, I hear Northern voices. Relief washes over me, and I see that it's the rest of the group of cavalry, the survivors of the ambush, returned with reinforcements.

They pull up when they get closer. "We're going after those bastards," the commander barks. "And we'll get them this time."

"I'll come with you," I say.

"You look like you've been through enough for one day," the commander observes, eyeing my bloody uniform. "Jimmy here will take you back to camp." He nods toward a short redhead, who jumps off his horse and boosts me onto it.

I nod. "Thank you." Suddenly I can't stop shivering— from cold or grief I can't say. Numbly, I let myself be led to camp. For the first time since I enlisted, I want to go home. I've been in the army for sixteen months, have seen countless men die, have almost died myself a couple of times. And now I've seen one of my best friends killed. I'm bone weary and feel hollowed out, empty. There's no Jerome, no Damon, no Flag, no one waiting to comfort me. In the crowded camp, with men all around, I have never felt so alone.

The next day the small band of cavalry returns to camp, leading the Confederates who ambushed us trussed up as prisoners. Flag is still dead and so are the three soldiers, but the sergeant hands me my watch, my money, and Jerome's locket. I finger the smooth gold oval, then flick open the hinge. Jerome's eyes gaze out at me. At least I still have something to remember him by. I take that as a good omen. Maybe it means Jerome will be returned to me, too, that I won't have to finish my time in the army all by myself.

{20

THE BATTLE OF
FREDERICKSBURG

PRESIDENT LINCOLN, LIKE US, HAS BEEN PATIENT WITH General McClellan's mistakes and defeats, but by November 1862 he's apparently had enough. He unceremoniously dismisses McClellan and puts us under the command of General Ambrose Burnside. To me, to all the men of the Second Michigan, this is a total disaster.

"I'd follow McClellan anywhere, but this Burnside fellow . . ."

"He's not worthy of polishing McClellan's boots, he isn't!"

"The only good thing I've heard about Burnside is that he's got a stylish way of growing the hair along his cheeks in front of his ears—we'll be led by a general known for his facial hair!"

GENERAL AMBROSE BURNSIDE.

Grousing like that makes the rounds at every meal, between drills, in the quiet times when the men have to talk. It doesn't stop when McClellan calls the Army of the Potomac together for the last time to deliver a rousing farewell. He heaps praises on us, noting the risks we've faced, the battles we've won, the strong, coherent army we have at last become.

"'Tis a mistake," James remarks in his soft burr. "McClellan may be slow, but he's sure and steady. He's the man to win this war."

A soldier nearby nods, wiping tears from his eyes. All around us, soldiers are crying. When McClellan urges us to support the new commander, General Burnside, as we have him, a loud chorus of boos erupts. I can't resist jeering along with the others. Of course, I'll obey. I'll serve him to the best of my ability. But I don't have to like him. He'll have to earn my respect and admiration.

At least there's one thing that eases the change of command—at the same time McClellan is dismissed, Colonel Poe is promoted to brigadier general. He's a general I respect. And one who respects me. Poe values my skills and depends on me as a spy, as a postmaster, and in battles as his orderly. I direct all my loyalty toward Poe so that I don't have to think about Burnside.

James has also been promoted, to acting assistant adjutant general to General Poe. Now as well as sharing a tent, we meet almost every day when he passes on the general's orders. His friendship fills the gaping hole left by Jerome and Damon.

Sitting next to him by the evening campfire, I allow myself to relax, to feel at home. The army has been my family for nearly two years, but it's been splintered by the loss of so many fellow soldiers—and my horse, Flag. Somehow the more bloodshed I see, the more sensitive I become. The thick skin I created to protect myself is being worn away with each battle. Now only a paper-thin layer is left, and I'm nearly naked and raw in front of the ugly brutalities of war.

For the first time since Bull Run, I wonder if I'll turn tail like so many other soldiers—if instead of fighting, I'll run away, cower behind a tree or boulder until the killing is over. I wish I could be sure of my own courage. Everyone else seems to think I'm the picture of the daring soldier, but they don't know how much I quake inside.

The army is gearing up for a big battle, and I dread the coming slaughter. Our sentries can look across the Rappahannock and wave to the Rebel pickets, who thumb their noses in return. The water won't divide us for long, however. Burnside has chosen his strategy: to build pontoon bridges across the river, then head straight to Richmond, cutting down the Confederates as they flee.

But will they run? Lee's entire army is massed in Fredericksburg on the other side of the river. To fight them, we will not only have to cross the bridges, exposing ourselves

PONTOON BRIDGE ACROSS THE RAPPAHANNOCK, BATTLE OF FREDERICKSBURG, VA.

to Rebel fire, we'll then have to climb the banks to the city on the ridge above. It will be like the battle of Malvern Hill, only this time we'll be the ones in the suicidal position of trying to storm a hill.

Burnside refuses to hear any objections. The president demands action, and action he'll have! The general insists that Lee will be surprised by our move. We're to build the bridges under cover of night and be across them before dawn, attacking the Confederates as they sleep.

As I listen to General Poe give the orders, the dread I've been feeling for days deepens. It sounds like a suicide mission. How can we possibly get three bridges built and 100,000 men across them before the sun rises?

Like most of the soldiers in camp that night, I can't shake off the black gloom gripping me. I've had too many near misses to expect any more. The next time I'll be shot, hit by a cannonball, run through by a saber. I toss and turn, trying to catch a few hours of sleep, but I'm too anxious to do anything more than close my eyes. On the other side of the tent James sleeps soundly, and I match his slow, deep breathing with my own. If I sound like I'm asleep, maybe I really will be. But of course that doesn't work. I can't shut out the ugly images in my mind's eye—Flag's bloody body, the saber stabbing the soldier next to me, the look of surprise in the officer's eyes when the bullet hits his chest. As the sky blushes pink in the first rays of morning, I still haven't slept, and it's time to report to General Poe.

Thick fog hugs the banks of the river, lifting enough to reveal that the upriver bridge is only half built. The other two are no nearer completion. The fog thins until I can make out on the opposite shore the ridge bristling with hundreds of Confederate guns. The Rebels have been waiting for dawn, and now that they can see, they pour fire on the Union soldiers building the bridges. It's a steady massacre. For every three men working on the pontoons, two are shot. The men keep falling into the water, wounded or dead, but

Burnside demands the bridges be finished. To chase out the sharpshooters, the general orders the cannon to fire heavily on the opposite shore. The town of Fredericksburg is hit, but most of the houses along the bank withstand the barrage, allowing the sharpshooters to keep up their continual fire.

A call goes out for volunteers to cross the river in boats and storm the houses. Three regiments quickly offer to do the job—the 7th Michigan and the 19th and 20th Massachusetts. Even though the soldiers hunker down low in their boats, many are shot. Still, the rest keep going, and enough of them survive to storm the houses, capturing or killing the Rebel sharpshooters. The cost is high, but the bridges are finished.

There's no chance of surprise now. Still, Burnside is convinced that there is no way but forward. The rest of the day is eerily quiet as each side gathers its wounded and dead. We all know the next morning will bring a fierce battle, and a somber mood permeates the camp as soldiers write last letters home or make final entries in their diaries. I pass another bad night, managing only a couple of hours of disjointed sleep. Before dawn I get out my journal, hoping to find relief on the page if I set down a few sentences. Like everyone else, I know I'm likely to die that day. "While I write, the roar of cannon and musketry is almost deafening. This may be my last entry in this journal. God's will be done." Still, I don't regret enlisting, and if it's my time to die, I'm resigned to meet my fate.

I'm grateful for all the army has given me. I know myself better now, my strengths and weaknesses. I'm proud of the soldier, the nurse, the spy, the strong person I've become. I feel deeply connected to the Union brotherhood, to our values of loyalty and selfless hard work. As I write in my journal, I realize that living so closely among men has changed my opinion of them. Yes, some are lazy, greedy, opportunistic, or selfish, but they aren't the dimwitted, quick-tempered beasts I've assumed. I think of Damon, Dr. Bonine, General Poe, Jerome, and my new tentmate, James. They're all men I'm honored to know, fortunate to serve with. They're my real family. I could have been safe at home on a farm with Old Man Ludham, but even facing a gory battle in the morning, there's no place else I'd rather be.

My mind is too full to sleep, so I pick up my pen again, and this time I write to Mr. Hurlburt. It's been a while since my last dispatch, and he's begged me for more. According to him, my part of the newsletter is the most popular. I find that hard to believe, especially when I write much of the same things to Virginia and she responds with more and more caution. Her last letter was particularly distant. If I didn't know better, I'd swear she had a beau, someone close by, in person, taking all her attention. She writes me out of courtesy and duty, nothing else. I've written to Damon about her, told him how she hasn't fallen for me at all like he predicted. But really I don't mind. Her letters have been a distraction more than anything else.

I've barely closed my eyes when I hear the drum banging the wake-up call. It's time to prepare for a battle that seems impossible to win. Today of all days, I'll be wearing a new, fancy uniform, with frills and fringes that don't fit the mood of the army at all.

I'm a general's orderly now, not a colonel's, hence the finer clothes. I'll be taking the same risks, though, riding back and forth along the front lines, delivering messages and orders. I miss Flag's steady company, but I have Lucky. He's young and raw, but bighearted, and maybe his name will keep me safe in the battle to come.

Burnside chooses to make a double-pronged attack. There are two points along Lee's defensive line that he considers vulnerable, though to me Lee's positions seem impregnable. One is Prospect Hill, south of town. The other is directly behind the town's center, Marye's Heights. Both enjoy high vantage points. To reach them, we have to cross open fields that offer little cover from enemy fire. Even worse, a fifteen-foot-wide drainage canal divides the terrain, meaning we have to slog through waist-deep, icy water or slow down into a single-file line to cross the three narrow bridges that span the gap. If any manage to make it across the ditch, there is still the base of the hill, where a stone wall stands. We have to clamber over the wall and climb the hill, all while open to enemy fire.

Burnside admits it will be difficult yet insists it's achievable. He orders General William Franklin to attack Prospect Hill and General Edwin Sumner to take Marye's Heights. Franklin can't believe that the general is ordering an all-out attack. He assumes he's only meant to lead a diversionary group to distract the Rebels from the main fighting, wherever that is to be. He sends one division out but, when they're driven back, makes no more moves, waiting instead for further orders, orders that never come.

Thinking that Franklin has set all his men against the Confederates at Prospect Hill, engaging at least half of Lee's force, Sumner now leads the charge against Marye's Heights. Three brigades lead the first assault, running in an icy rain across the fields. As soon as they're within range of the Rebel guns, the massacre begins. The men fall in waves. The few survivors who make it all the way across the field are killed by lines of Georgia marksmen, hiding on the other side of the stone wall. And still our soldiers keep coming, line after line of them, the living stepping over the dead in a futile, desperate bid to make it to the wall. Soldiers run forward, knowing full well they rush to their own deaths. They watch their comrades die in front of them, but still they follow orders. In the first hour, there are three thousand casualties. By early afternoon, the number has reached nearly six thousand. The ground is strewn with corpses and the wounded, making the passage even more difficult. And still the senseless carnage continues.

The Second Michigan is lucky. They're posted to guard the lower pontoon bridge in case of a possible retreat. As Poe's orderly, I'm not in such a safe position. Riding up and down the front lines, relaying orders and messages, I have no choice but to rush where the fighting is the worst. Being on horseback, however, I move more quickly and am less of a target. I don't feel as vulnerable as the men who try to advance only to be mowed down in rows. Despite the hail of minié balls, the thud of the cannon all around me, I'm too busy to panic as I feared I would. Instead, I find myself shutting off all thoughts and feelings and just reacting, going where I'm sent, weaving among the dead and wounded, dodging debris kicked up by falling cannonballs. I'm in the saddle for twelve hours, constantly racing around the battlefield.

All around me men fall, hit by cannon or rifle fire. I have to force myself not to act as a nurse. Today I have other duties. I've never before been in such a slaughter, never seen so many fallen men around me, with no one to help them, no one who dares face enemy fire to carry the wounded to safety.

I've never seen a man shoot himself to avoid facing the enemy, either, but that day I watch in horror as an officer is ordered into the line of battle. Instead of advancing, he takes out his pistol and fires a ball into his side, carefully aiming so that the bullet grazes his hip enough to make him unfit for further duty. Watching the waves of blue soldiers fall under the Rebel fire, I can't fault him as a coward. I might have done the same or simply left the field, as so many others have.

I write to Mr. Hurlburt about what happens next, trying to capture the chaos of battle with some semblance of order. By early afternoon it's clear to Burnside's officers that their objections were sound and the general is fatally mistaken. General Darius Couch peers through field glasses, watching in horror from a church steeple in Falmouth. The terrain across the river is covered with men, falling and fallen. He writes that the waves of men dropping before the stone wall at the end of the field are like "snow coming down on a warm ground." Fearing a complete slaughter, he sends a message to Burnside, begging him to call a retreat. "It's only murder now," he insists. Sumner joins his plea, riding over to face Burnside in person. Burnside refuses, demanding that more regiments be sent out. When Sumner tells him there are no more brigades, no more reserves, Burnside still doesn't change his mind. Instead, he sends an order to Franklin to use all his reserves in a final charge up Prospect Hill.

Franklin, supported by General Poe, recognizes the hopelessness of such an action. Like Couch, he considers it murder to send his men on this mission. He refuses, instead holding a defensive position. The decision will cost Franklin his command, but it saves the rest of the Army of the Potomac, including the Second Michigan and me.

Poe no longer trusts Burnside and chooses to follow Franklin's commands instead. As night darkens the bloody field, he and I ride the short distance from our camp to Franklin's headquarters to get orders for the next morning. It's only three miles, but it's as if we were crossing the depths of hell. The agonized moans of the wounded rise up all around us. The bitter cold kills as many men that night as the Confederates have during the day. In the night sky, the northern lights, rarely seen so far south, shimmer. To the Rebels the silvery curtains of light must seem like a sign of the Almighty celebrating their victory. To us they shine over the dead like streamers of fire from heaven, leading the souls of the fallen upward. I don't know yet how many have died, but the numbers must be high—and all for nothing. Not an inch of land has been taken, nor have the Rebels suffered greatly in the battle. My mouth sours with disgust. I try to spit out the acrid taste, to wash it away with water, but all I can taste is blood, all I can smell around me is blood and singed flesh.

Burnside remains intent on renewing the charge the next day, this time with himself personally leading the men, but his generals convince him to at least allow a day's truce to collect the dead and wounded. I've slept very little for the

BURIAL OF UNION DEAD, FREDERICKSBURG, VA.

past three nights, but I spend the truce day delivering messages and carrying the wounded to the hospital set up in a
Southern mansion, Lacy House. Once an elegant home, the
house is now a gory setting, the floors thick with blood, legs
and arms stacked on the veranda like winter firewood.

The extra day gives the generals the time they need to convince Burnside to retreat at last. The full horror of what has happened and his responsibility for it finally sinks in. Antietam has been considered the bloodiest day of the war so far, but there are more casualties for the Union during the Battle of Fredericksburg—fifteen thousand men dead, with only six thousand Confederate losses, and most of those are deserters heading home for Christmas.

The stupidity of the sacrifice galls me. I write in my journal: "When it was clear that it was impossible to take those heights, whose fault was it that the attempt was made time after time until the field was literally piled with dead and ran red with blood?" I blame Burnside. Now not only do I not respect him, a simmering flame of hatred smolders inside me. How can I stay in an army led by such an arrogant, ignorant, pompous ass? What is my true duty? Is it to him or to the Union cause? I'm certainly not serving the Union by obeying Burnside. What is a loyal soldier supposed to do when obeying a superior officer means betraying the army he serves in? How can I follow orders that are obviously suicidal? Does a time always come when the boundaries blur, when what's right, what's practical, and what's demanded don't agree? What is a mere soldier to do at such times? What am I supposed to do?

I wish I had Jerome to talk to, to ask for guidance. I wish he were here to hold and comfort me. My mind is full of ugly images. The moans of the dying echo in my ears. The stench of rotting flesh lingers in my nose. I hug my knees to my chest, curl up in my bedroll, and try to imagine another place and time, the future when I'd share my life with Jerome and everyone would be safe and well. But that's just a dream and I know it.

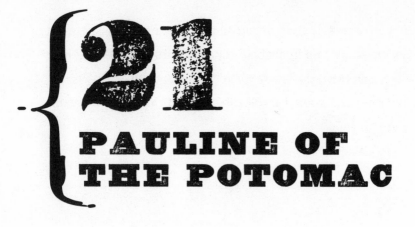

{21}
PAULINE OF
THE POTOMAC

TURNS OUT THAT ON DECEMBER 15, THE SAME NIGHT
when I curled up in the tent dreaming of him, Jerome and
the others were freed from Camp Parole and headed toward Falmouth to rejoin their regiments. Later, Jerome tells
me how they knew nothing of the disastrous battle, but as
they walked south, they passed troops heading north, toward Washington, and got an inkling that something was
wrong.

"I had a bad feeling," Jerome says. "I asked the soldiers if they knew where you were, what had happened to
the Second Michigan. I remember one fellow said there'd
been a disaster. No, the word he used was catastrophe. 'It's
a catastrophe,' he said, 'so many dead, so many.' I didn't
know what he meant, so I asked another soldier. He just
looked at me with big, blank eyes."

That's how Jerome heard about the slaughter at
Fredericksburg. First he saw the hollowed eyes of the men

who survived. Then he heard some of the details—how Lee held the high position and we never had a chance. But when he asked about me, about the Second Michigan, no one could tell him anything except that a lot of men died that day.

Which, of course, only made him frantic to learn more. He describes how he asked each new regiment they passed for news, but no one could tell him anything specific. Instead, he heard the same horrible description of a senseless massacre over and over again.

As the sun set, he could see the church steeples of Falmouth in the distance. This time, when he asked northbound troops about the Second Michigan, they pointed toward the Sixteenth Michigan, which in turn indicated the general area where the Second had settled. Jerome recognized some of the soldiers huddled around the campfire from the Third Michigan.

He stepped into the circle and greeted his old comrades. "Sam, Jed, Marshall." He nodded toward the weary men who looked beaten down with sorrow. "We're looking for the Second Michigan."

"Down that ways, toward the river." Jed pointed.

"You fellows all well?" Jerome asked. "I heard what happened."

"We're alive," said Sam. "Nothing else to say about it. Thought for sure we'd be dead, but here we are."

The men walked the short distance to the camp in

silence, weighed down by the despair that hung in the air around them.

Once they were among their old friends of the Second Michigan, the mood lifted. There were hugs all around, backs clapped, hands firmly shaken, a warm sense of being home again, among brothers. Someone handed Jerome a mug of steaming tea, and at last he heard a detailed description of the previous five days. He tells me how his tea turned cold as he listened in horror to the story of fourteen different charges led against Marye's Heights, fourteen regiments plowed into the earth.

"And no one from here was killed?" he asked. "No one's in the hospital?"

"Just one fellow, George Southworth, but he's down with dysentery," a soldier answered. "We're lucky. General Poe took care of us, he did."

"And where's Frank? I don't see him. Is he in his tent?" Jerome asked.

"He's probably with the general. He's his orderly now, you know. We had a defensive position, but he was on the front lines, riding right into the thick of the fight. You know how he is—nothing scares him. He's got more spine than I don't know what."

I write down this conversation word for word when Jerome repeats it to me, and now I'll always have it, always know what the men thought of me. It gave Jerome hope that I was all right, but he was still worried, wondering if I would be like the other hollow-eyed soldiers he'd met on the road.

He has his answer the next afternoon. I ride into camp on Lucky, my saddlebags full of mail. I'm handing letters out to the soldiers gathered by regimental headquarters when I recognize a familiar silhouette at the back of the crowd, a tall, dark-haired soldier.

I quickly give out the remaining envelopes, then push through the circle of men.

"Jerome!" I yell, running toward him. I throw my arms around him, then catch myself and pull away, but I can't stop grinning. "You're here! And not a day too soon, I must say."

"It's good to see you, Frank," he murmurs. "Your letters brightened my days at Camp Parole. It would have been much harder to bear without them. And thank you for all the money you sent."

"It was a pleasure—as close as I could come to having a real conversation." I'm happy and relieved to have my best friend back. My fingers fumble in my pocket, drawing out the locket. "I've been waiting to give this back to you. It's had quite an adventure—I almost lost it in an ambush."

Jerome takes the locket, fingering it thoughtfully. "I never thought I'd see this again. I never thought I'd see anything again." He pauses. "I guess that was about as close as I've come to dying in this war. But being taken prisoner was nothing compared to what you've been through. It sounds like even this locket's been in more danger than I have." He slips the necklace into his pocket. "You'll have to tell me the story."

"I've had my fair share of scrapes," I admit, and launch into the story of the ambush and Flag's death. I can describe the chaos and my fear, but I can't tell him what Flag meant to me, how much I miss him. It would seem foolish to care about a horse when men are dying.

We spend the rest of the day together, falling back into our easy intimacy, though I notice that Jerome is careful not to touch me. And I have to remind myself constantly not to touch him. I find myself reaching for him, aching to be near him, but I stop myself. Once again I have to wear my careful mask, hold myself as the young, brave soldier, Frank Thompson. But my skin is thinner now, and it's harder than ever to pretend. I want to sink into a warm embrace, to be held by loving arms, I want to cry for Flag and the dead cavalrymen and be comforted in my grief. I want something I can have only in dreams.

When suppertime comes, I introduce Jerome to my tentmate, James.

Jerome shakes the Scot's hand coldly. "You're with the Seventy-ninth New York, the Highlanders? Isn't that the regiment that mutinied in August of 1861? The ones who were sent to the Dry Tortugas as punishment?" He stares at James as if he were one of the guilty soldiers.

"Aye, that's my regiment," James admits.

"James wasn't there then," I explain. "He was taken

prisoner at the first Battle of Bull Run and was in a prisoner-of-war camp outside Richmond for six months."

"I hear you were captured yourself," James says snidely. "Been in Camp Parole all this time. Much more pleasant than a Rebel prison camp, to be sure."

Jerome grunts. "I was lucky."

"And so was I." James smiles. "I didn't die of dysentery. I didn't waste away from cholera. I wasn't even badly wounded in Fredericksburg, just a scratch really. And Frank here took care of me."

James is talking, but Jerome is studying me as if, for the first time, he can see the woman behind the uniform. What is it about James that prods Jerome to look at me so differently? Could he be jealous? Whatever is going through his head, Jerome clearly dislikes the Scotsman. He glares at him all through supper. Here I finally have two good friends, but it seems neither one can stomach the other.

The next few days, the army prepares for a somber Christmas with Lee's troops still dug in on the other side of the river, watching our every move. Jerome works in the hospital and shares a tent with Dr. Evers but snatches as much time as he can with me. It isn't much. There are no more long evenings, walking and talking, no more afternoons helping patients together. I'm too busy as an orderly and postmaster to also serve as a nurse now. When I'm done for the day, Jerome often finds me sitting by the river with James. I can tell that having James around puts him off, but

I don't want to sacrifice one friend for the other. When I'm alone with Jerome, I have to fight the temptation to throw my arms around him. James provides a good buffer, ensuring we all act like comrades. Except that around James, Jerome is petulant, like he's miffed at me for having another friend. James doesn't make things better. He treats Jerome with suspicion and a strange competitive edge. The way they behave, I can't blame them for detesting each other.

Christmas dinner is hardtack, beef soup, and coffee, and every bit as cheerless as it sounds. Rumors race through camp that Burnside will be kicked out of his post and McClellan reinstated. Then we get the depressing news that General Franklin will be removed from duty for disobeying Burnside's orders to attack Prospect Hill.

"He should get a medal for that!" I complain to Jerome. "It took real courage, real guts to defy his commanding officer. He never would have done it if it hadn't been obvious how useless such a tactic would be. It wouldn't have been sending men into battle—it would have been sending them to certain death, like lambs to the slaughter."

"Still," Jerome says, "to disobey a direct order. That's a serious offense."

"You weren't here," I snap. "You don't understand. It wasn't a clear, direct order. It was ambiguous, garbled, the kind of direction Burnside specializes in."

"I've never heard you so bitter," Jerome says. "You usually have such a rosy view of things."

"This war's enough to make pessimists of us all." I shrug. "Is there any possibility we can win? Tell me, is there?"

Jerome is taken aback. "Of course there is."

I snort. "I wish I believed you. We can talk more tomorrow. Right now there's mail to deliver."

"Sure, tomorrow," Jerome agrees. "Maybe we could go for a walk, the way we used to. We've barely had more than ten minutes together since I got here. Your tentmate seems to take up a good deal of your time."

"My duties take up a good deal of my time," I insist. "And yes, tomorrow we'll have more time."

I show up at Jerome's tent the next morning, leading two horses, Lucky and James's palomino mare. "Hey, Jerome," I yell into the canvas flaps. "Want to ride with me on my mail run today? James is sick with a tetchy stomach, so he said you can use his horse."

Jerome jumps out of the tent. "You bet! It'll be a nice change from the hospital." He pats the mare's nose. "She's a fine animal. Sorry to hear about James." He smiles so broadly, he doesn't look the least bit sorry.

The weather is crisp and cold, but at least it's dry and the roads aren't too slushy. It feels good to get out of camp, and we slip into our old, easy camaraderie as we ride side by side.

"I got a sweet letter from Damon. He says he's happy farming, and he sent me a gift for Christmas. Want to guess what it was?" I ask.

"Socks?" Jerome suggests. "A scarf?"

"No!" I laugh. "Nothing like that. He sent me a book—here, take a look."

I pull a small paperback out of my coat pocket, already worn and well thumbed through.

"You've read it, I take it," Jerome says, reaching for the book.

"In one gulp. It's not great writing. I suppose you could call it lowbrow, but I enjoyed it."

Jerome reads the title aloud: "*Pauline of the Potomac, or, General McClellan's Spy,* by Wesley Bradshaw." He skims the first few pages. "You're right about the quality of the writing, but I can see why the story attracted you. I doubt I'd find it as compelling."

"Damon sent it to me because of the spy part, but it's closer to my life than he imagines! It's about a young French girl—that's Pauline—who becomes a daring spy for McClellan. Just like someone you know." I sigh. We haven't talked about my being a woman since that fateful day so long ago, but I'm tired of pretending. Anyway, I'm only alluding to my sex, not baldly stating it. Now that I don't even have Flag to confide in, I need at least one person to know the truth about me. "Do you think my life would make a good story?"

Jerome laughs. "If you wrote about it, nobody would believe it. It would sound far too melodramatic and impossible. Women can't really be soldiers, you know."

I narrow my eyes. Jerome is finally acknowledging who I am, but it isn't a compliment. At least it isn't an accusation. "They can't? I've seen those stories in the newspaper. You must have, too. I'm not the only woman to wear a man's uniform. That nurse, Clara Barton, wrote about a dying soldier at Antietam who turned out to be a woman." There—I've said it. I'm not the only woman—I'm admitting that I am one. Will Jerome turn on me again? Will he push me away as an unnatural creature? Or after all this time, all we've been through, is he finally ready to accept me?

"But those soldiers probably aren't good fighters." Jerome skips over my admission and focuses on the other women, the ones he doesn't know or care about. "They just want to be close to their husbands or brothers. I read the Clara Barton story. That woman joined to be with her sweetheart, who was a Union officer."

I rein in my horse. This is my chance. "Are you saying that I'm not a good fighter? That I'm not as brave as the next man?"

Jerome blushes. "I didn't mean you, of course. Everyone knows how courageous you are. I heard about the risks you took during the Battle of Fredericksburg from several different men. I've seen you in action myself. You're much braver than I am!"

I kick my horse and gallop forward, hunching low over Lucky's neck. "I'm a better horseman, too!" I yell over my shoulder.

Jerome kicks his mare. "We'll see about that!"

The two horses race flat out, finally pulling up in a lather at Aquia Creek Wharf.

Jerome slides off his horse, wiping the sweat from his brow.

"I admit it, you beat me," he pants, leaning over with his hands on his knees.

"Just don't forget it, then," I say, hands on my hips. "A woman is a better rider than you." I let the words sink in. This time I'm not backing off. I've lost too many friends, seen too many men die, to bother with any more lies. It's time for both of us to face the truth of who I am.

Jerome shakes his head, still winded. "Don't worry, Frank. You're unforgettable." But I notice that he can't meet my eyes.

{ 22

A NEW
RECRUIT

THE WEATHER IN VIRGINIA IS AS HARSH IN WINTER AS in summer. Instead of sweltering heat and clouds of flies, freezing winds howl and snow piles high in muddy drifts. In the midst of this bleakness, we hear strange news from a New Jersey regiment camped downriver from the Second Michigan.

A corporal in the regiment has given birth. The woman had disguised herself so well, no one had noticed her pregnancy. But birthing was more difficult to hide, and when the mother went into labor, her secret was soon known to everyone. To my surprise, the response is sympathetic, not critical.

UNION SOLDIER, POSSIBLY PREGNANT.

I thought a woman dressed as a man would be branded as unnatural at best, a lady of loose morals at worst. But this woman has attained the rank of corporal and shared her tent with her husband, so her character draws respect.

Hearing that the mother is recuperating at Lacy House, I can't resist visiting her. I want to see what she looks like, what kind of person she is. I often check in with Jerome and the doctors at the manor-house-turned-hospital, so it won't seem odd for me to be there. In fact, Dr. Bonine greets me as I walk in.

"Ah, Frank, always good to see you. Jerome isn't here right now, but he'll be back this afternoon."

"Actually, I was curious about the new mother," I admit.

"Yes, she's attracted quite a bit of attention." The doctor smiles. "It's wonderful to have a babe among us. Gives one hope, don't you think?" He leads the way upstairs to a small bedroom. "She's in here." He knocks lightly, then opens the door. "You have a visitor, ma'am, our postmaster, Frank Thompson." The doctor ushers me in, then shuts the door behind him with a soft click.

A small, dark-haired woman with large brown eyes sits up in bed, a swaddled baby nestled in the crook of her arm. Its face is wrinkled and red like a dried apple. The eyes are squinted tight shut, the mouth pursed in an O. It's the ugliest baby I've ever seen.

"You've brought me mail?" she asks.

I take an awkward step closer to the head of the bed.

"No, ma'am. I've just come to pay my respects. I think it was very brave of you to do what you did." I examine the young woman's face. The eyes glitter over dark circles, the cheeks are hollow, and the nose and chin are sharp. It isn't a particularly feminine face. She resembles a weasel more than a lady.

"I needed to be with my man, that's all." Her voice is flat and tired, as if she's explained this many times before.

"Was it hard?" I ask. "Keeping that big a secret from so many people?"

The woman glares at me, narrowing her eyes. "What business is it of yours?"

I quickly lower my chin. I can't hold the woman's piercing gaze. "I didn't mean to pry. Forgive me for asking. I wish you well, that's all." I back out of the room, my ears red with embarrassment. I'm not sure what I expected, but this woman isn't it. I suppose I wanted a model of a woman who could disguise herself as a man but still remain womanly enough to have a baby. Except I don't admire her as a model anything. If I hoped for a kindred spirit, I certainly didn't find one.

I leave the house, breathing in deeply the crisp, cold winter air. It felt suffocating to be with the mother, as if I too risked having my life boxed in, narrowed by being female. I stamp my feet, crunching down the snow. That won't be me, I vow. True, Jerome knows I'm a woman, but my secret is safe with him. I belong here, among men, not trapped in the confined world of women.

Heading back to headquarters, I bump into William Macky, a soldier from the new family's regiment, who's collecting money for the new parents to start a home.

"Frank!" he calls, holding out a cap for donations. "What'll you give for this poor Union baby to have a warm home? The proud father has to finish his last six months of enlistment, but the mother and child have to leave, and they need our help."

I pull several bills out of my wallet and add them to the pile. "Did you suspect?" I ask. "Didn't you see her belly swelling?"

William chuckles. "I guess our attention was elsewhere, like on not getting killed." He locks eyes with me. "Maybe you see what you expect to see. I thought the corporal was on the weak side, but not more than some of our younger, slighter soldiers. I did remark on her getting heavier, but that was only in the last month when we were sitting here idle. I thought she was soft from inaction." He shrugs. "She was a corporal—I expected her to be less fit than us privates."

"I wonder if she's the only one." I rub my chin, thoughtfully. If I could share my secret with other women, would I be less lonely? I don't think so. I have good friends in Jerome and James. Years ago, when I was Sarah Emma Edmonds, I was close to my sisters, but I never enjoyed with them the kind of deep conversations I have with my men friends now. Women's interests, their worlds, are so narrow compared to men's. I think of Virginia's letters, how limited they are, nothing like the discussions I have with men. And I like the respect I see in other men's eyes, something I've never seen granted to a woman, something I could never earn if folks think I'm Sarah and not Frank.

"Anyway," I continue, "I doubt there'll be many other babies, even if there are other women in the ranks disguised as men."

William nods. "Since her identity was discovered, we've heard all kinds of stories about women dressed as men in both armies. Wonder how many are wild rumors, how many are true."

The thought flits through my mind that maybe there are rumors about me, but I quickly dismiss it. I've become a master of relieving myself in hidden places, expert at changing my clothes beneath blankets, skilled at using and disposing of bandages for my monthlies. I've proven my bravery many times over. Not just as a soldier but as a postmaster, orderly, nurse, and spy. No one could suspect a woman of having such abilities. That's what I tell myself as I join the clusters of men speculating about the pregnant corporal and the birth of the newest recruit.

Jerome sits next to me during one such discussion that evening. He stares intently at me all through supper, as if the unmasking of the corporal makes my secret more real to him. I catch him watching me hold my plate and fork like a man, chow down like a man, sit with my legs apart like a man. I make my gestures broader and cruder than usual, burping loudly, wiping my mouth with the back of my hand. If Jerome is searching for a hint of femininity, he's not going to find any.

Jerome isn't the only one studying me with a strange new intensity. James sits on my other side that night and looks at me as if he's never seen me before. He chews reflectively, studying my hands, my face, my every movement. Is he putting together small hints, clues about my sex? I've been careful, I'm always careful, but there was the time James went to great trouble to get a hot bath at Lacy House. General Poe granted him special permission, and James offered to let me soak in the warm tub once he was done. Of course, I turned him down, something he was unable to fathom— why not, he'd insisted—but now maybe he suspects why. And there was the time he found some bloody cloths in the tent and, worried that I was hurt, asked if I needed help. I turned bright red and insisted I was fine, explaining that the rags were scraps from the hospital that I'd stuck in my pocket and forgotten about. Now maybe he suspects the truth—that they were menstrual cloths. Since one soldier has turned out to be a woman in disguise, couldn't another? I spit on the ground, trying to show both James and Jerome that I'm as far from a lady as you can get.

I'm relieved when the topic of conversation shifts from the female corporal to President Lincoln. In September, after the victory at Antietam, he issued the Emancipation

Proclamation, which recently took effect, at least in theory, in January 1863. Supposedly all slaves in the Confederacy are free now, though of course Jefferson Davis, the president of the seceding states, insists that the Union president has no authority for such a law or any other.

"I don't understand why he did that," one soldier gripes. "I thought this war was about preserving the Union, not abolishing slavery."

"It was a wise move," James counters. "The French and British can't possibly support the Southerners now. They recognize slavery as morally abhorrent, even if the Union doesn't."

"I think getting rid of slavery is an excellent reason to fight." I toss some kindling into the campfire. "How can we call ourselves Christians when we allow other human beings to be treated like animals? I've seen the contraband camps in Washington, how hard they work and how hungry they are for learning. Seems to me everyone deserves basic respect and freedom."

"You would think that," Jerome says.

"What's that supposed to mean?" I'm taken aback.

"You're a sensitive soul, that's all, a soft heart." After all this time, is Jerome going to give away my secret now, all because of a stupid woman having a baby?

"As are you," I remark lightly. "I've never seen such a gentle, kind nurse as you, Jerome. All the doctors agree."

The conversation shifts again, this time to where the

army will go next, how long we'll sit at Falmouth, and whether Burnside will remain in command.

Jerome holds my gaze and smiles. "Don't worry," his eyes seem to say. "I'll keep your secret."

I lower my eyes, confused. Is Jerome trying to show me how much power he has over me? Is he protecting me or goading me? I not only have to worry about Jerome: I can see James watching the two of us with sharp suspicion. He can tell that Jerome knows something—he just doesn't know what. And so long as I can help it, he never will. How can I prove myself as a man? When James stands up and stretches, I yawn myself, opening my mouth wide with food still in it. There—how's that for male behavior? James just says his good-nights and heads for the tent.

I watch him go, his broad back melting into the darkness, relieved to have his prying eyes off me. Truth is, I've grown too comfortable with my disguise. Even after five years, I can't afford to take it for granted anymore, now that it's a known fact that people like me exist, people who call themselves one thing but are really another.

I glare at Jerome. "May I speak with you?" I hiss, leading him away from the fire, away from other ears.

"Of course," he says, wiping his hands on his pants. "You sound angry. Did I do something wrong?"

"Yes!" I snap. "You did! What were you talking about? Were you trying to hint to everyone that I'm a woman? I need to know right now if you're going to reveal my secret. Tell me!"

"Whoa!" Jerome holds up his hands. "I haven't said anything yet, so what makes you think I will now? You know this isn't a subject I like to think about, much less talk about. I'd rather you would just stay Frank." Jerome stares at the ground. "I wish you'd never told me."

"Same here! So why don't we pretend I didn't, since you can't see me as anything but Frank anyway." For a second I hate him, hate him for making me weak, hate him for making me love him.

"I would if you wouldn't keep shoving my nose in it, talking about Pauline the spy, how you're as good a soldier or rider as a man. How am I supposed to respond to that?" Jerome looks at me now, his eyes flashing anger. "Stop cornering me!"

"I'm the one who's cornered!" I start to cry, hoarse hiccups of exhaustion and sorrow. I'm so tired of being strong, of putting on an act.

"Now, Frank, please don't cry. Please!" Jerome puts his arm around me. He pats my back awkwardly. "Frank, you can trust me. I'll never tell, I promise. Don't worry. There's no reason to be so upset. Everything will be fine."

I lean into his warm body and let myself sniffle. He isn't holding me the way a man holds a woman, but it still feels good. We stand there that way until Jerome pulls himself away.

"You all right, now?" He dabs at my face with his hand-kerchief.

I nod. It isn't true, but I am better, as good as I could be with the man who doesn't love me.

"Can you do something for me, then?" Jerome asks.

I nod again, calm and clear after all the tears.

"Can you be Frank again, the friend I know and love?"

He loves me? I grin, light-headed. "Of course." After all, who else would I be?

{ 23 SPYING AGAIN

THOUGH I DON'T HAVE TO WORRY ABOUT JEROME, I'M careful with James, acting as gruff and manly as I know how. Which means I break wind and belch, spit and scratch, repeat crude jokes I've overheard. James is as friendly as ever, but I can't shake the feeling that he's watching me, waiting for me to do something that will reveal my secret. I keep my tone light as I hand him several letters addressed in his wife's elegant handwriting.

"How's the missus?" I ask. "She must miss you a lot, writing to you so much."

James's nose is already buried in the first letter. "Yes, she misses me, but that's not the only reason she writes. She's ailing and doesn't know what to do. Her family is all in England, where she's from. She has no one to help her there in New York." He sighs, folding up the letter and opening the next one. "If she gets worse, something will have to be done."

"What's the matter with her?" I ask.

James shakes his head. "I dinna know. She isn't clear about that. But she's weak and getting weaker." He pinches the bridge of his nose, his brow furrowed. "What can I do?"

"Ask for a leave so you can take care of her, since she has no one else," I suggest. "I'm sure it would be granted to you."

James looks up from the letter he's holding. "That's a good idea. Thank you. You're a good man, Frank."

I smile, relieved. He's called me a man. "General Poe is most understanding," I add, then leave to deliver the rest of the mail.

As I hand out letters, I hear nuggets of information. We've been sitting at Falmouth for weeks now, and the idleness gives the men time to think up the most preposterous scenarios. Some think we'll retreat back to the coast and ship out on boats for the Virginia Peninsula again. Others argue we'll give up on Richmond entirely and head back to Washington. Still others think we'll be sent on a broad loop, marching all the way around to attack Richmond from the west. No one expects Burnside's next plan.

The general hasn't given up on crossing the Rappahannock. He thinks we should try the same tactics, only this time a few miles above Fredericksburg, crossing into territory where Lee has no fortifications. We would still have to face the

Confederates, but this way we could cross the river without making easy targets of ourselves. At least, that's the theory.

On a wet, blustery day Burnside announces his strategy. The men are eager to move, despite the heavy rain and strong winds. It's always harder to sit and wait than to do something, and the memory of Fredericksburg has faded some. But as soon as the first regiments start out, the problems begin. The mud on the riverbank is so thick and sticky, a dozen horses can't budge one cannon. The men are forced to wade in ankle-deep sludge that grips at their boots, making each step an exhausting effort. The pontoons themselves get stuck in the mire. Luckily the Second Michigan isn't one of the advance regiments, but I'm at the front line with General Poe, organizing the troops.

Standing on an overlook with the general, we watch the horses straining to pull the artillery. "It's like trying to plow through mud," I observe.

Poe shakes his head in disgust. "It's a mud march." The name sticks. After two days of lurching in the muck, the regiments straggle back to camp, defeated and soaked to the bone. Burnside's Mud March means the end of his command over the Army of the Potomac. Instead, he's given temporary command of the Ninth Army Corps, which unfortunately for us includes the Second Michigan. "Mud March" is how I title my dispatch to Mr. Hurlburt. Might as well let the nation know what's happening.

The rest of the army is placed under Joseph Hooker's command. He's a loud, brash ladies' man who keeps so many women of questionable morals around headquarters that his last name comes to be associated with women of ill-repute. I've heard the same rumors everyone else has and don't like the idea of this new general. Still, anyone has to be better than Burnside.

I chafe at the idea of continuing to answer to Burnside, a commander I don't respect in the slightest, even though General Poe remains my direct superior. Worse still, the Ninth Army Corps is sent back to Fort Monroe, confirming the earlier rumors. The idea is to force General Lee to defend Richmond from the southeast as well as from the north. The boat trip there is less complicated this time, since far fewer regiments make the crossing. But once again it's a wasted journey, and we're stationed on the peninsula for only a few weeks before we're ordered to Kentucky as part of the Army of the Cumberland, joining General Ulysses Grant in his attempt to capture Vicksburg, Mississippi, this spring.

In Grant I finally find a commander I can admire. I'd lost faith that the Union could ever win the war, but Grant has an authority and energy that are inspiring. He's no McClellan, but he's far superior to Burnside or Hooker. He's a real soldier.

The Second Michigan is camped in Lebanon, Kentucky, when General Poe orders me on a new spy mission. This time—for the first time—I'm told what disguise to use: I'll be dressed as a Rebel soldier, using clothes and information taken from a Confederate prisoner.

I'm changing in the tent when I hear footsteps. My fingers fumble as I finish buttoning up the brown shirt when James ducks into the tent.

"Seems risky to me," he says, commenting on my disguise. "They'll ask why you aren't with your regiment and where you come from."

I wipe the sweat from my brow. It is risky, all right, but not the way he means.

"Ah'll say that Ah got lost when Ah wuz sent for provisionin'. Don' worruh, Ah know what Ah'm doin'." I smooth my pants, make sure my belt is buckled.

James chuckles at my Southern drawl. "And what was your last battle and which regiment? Who's your commanding officer?"

"Ah've got all those names. Ah took 'em from the same gen'lman who dun give me his uniform." I pick up my gun. "Well, suh, what do yuh think?"

"You've got nerve, Frank, I'll say that for you. And you're the perfect picture of the young Rebel. But I thought their uniforms were gray—you're dressed in brown."

"That's what they wear in the Kentucky cavalry. There's no particular uniform—they just wear as close to a butternut color as they can match. Leastwise, that's what I've been told. I have to trust our intelligence, since

I'm part of it." I head out of the tent, toward the picket line. "How's your wife?" I call back over my shoulder.

"Not good." James shakes his head. "But don't worry about her—you take good care of yourself."

It's been months since my last mission, and I'm eager to get back to spying. I can finally walk without limping badly, and my ribs and arm no longer ache. It feels good to take big strides. I reach the edge of camp, where I recognize the picket and give him the countersign.

"Don't shoot at me when I come back, now," I warn. "I'll still be dressed like this."

"So long as you hold your hands up high and give the countersign, you'll be safe," the sentry assures me. "Just don't get shot by Johnny Reb."

I start down the road from Lebanon, practicing my story. I'm supposed to have gotten lost while looking for supplies for my cavalry unit, going to farmhouses for butter and eggs. Really, I'm assigned to note Confederate positions and where they're moving. As a single Rebel soldier, I assume the people in the countryside will want to help me find my lost unit. They'll let me know about any troops they've seen in their neighborhood.

Toward evening I come to a small village and knock on the door of the closest house. The door opens and I find myself facing a Confederate officer. Behind him swirls a crowd of soldiers, officers, and farm folk, all dressed up and in a festive mood. Strains of music, a fiddle and a squeeze-box, flow over the murmur of conversation. I'm not sure what to say. I want to know where the troops are—not actually run into them.

"Yes?" The officer raises an eyebrow. "Who are you?"

What else can I do but stick to my story? "Ah'm Private Frederick Tate, suh, from the Fifth Kentucky cavalry."

"You mus' be heah for the weddin' then! Come in, boy." The soldier ushers me into a large room filled with people. Taking me firmly by the elbow, the man leads me to a chestnut-haired officer standing by a plump young woman in a bridal dress.

"Captain Logan, the lucky groom, and Bess Winchester, the beautiful bride."

I hold out my hand to the captain. "Congratulations, suh!"

The new wife giggles. "Why, sweetheart, you have even more men under your command than I thought. Won't Daddy be proud!"

I gape. Could I have run into my supposed commanding officer? Of all the damned luck!

"And who are you?" the captain asks.

Sweat trickles down my neck. I force myself to take deep breaths.

"Private Frederick Tate, suh," I repeat. "Fifth Kentucky cavalry."

The groom's eyes narrow. "Why aren't you with your unit, soldier? You're not a yellah-bellied deserter, now are you?"

"Oh." Mrs. Captain pouts. "He's just an ordinary soldier. Not one of yours."

"He might be," growled the captain. "I asked you, Private, are you a deserter?"

I snap to attention, all military seriousness. "No, suh, of course not, suh! Ah was sent for provisions after the last battle and lost mah unit, suh."

"I don't believe you. I'm a recruiting officer, and I think you need to join up with the company we're forming right now. Then, as my dear wife says, you'll be one of my boys. You'll get a bounty for enlisting, and if you don't, we'll shoot you as a deserter."

"But if Ah join yuh, Ah will be desertin'—desertin' mah old unit," I protest.

"Don't you worry about that." The captain smiles, showing even, white teeth. "We'll take good care of you. So what's your choice, boy?"

"Ah'd like to think about it for a couple of days," I say, trying to sound firm.

"I'll give you a couple of hours. Then you ride with us or we shoot you. Enjoy the party while you're thinking." The captain raises an eyebrow, then turns back to his bride, who has been tugging on him impatiently. He tucks her arm under his and leads her toward the table heavy with food and drink while she leans her head into his shoulder, cooing like a setting hen.

I look around the room, searching for a way out. Maybe I can simply walk away. The captain is celebrating his wedding. How closely will he bother watching someone like me? I edge toward the front door, smiling and nodding at people as I pass. I lean forward to grasp the door handle.

"Boy!" a voice bellows. "Where do you think you're going?" The captain lunges behind me and grabs me by the collar. "Put him under guard," he orders, thrusting me at a soldier.

Sitting between two Confederate soldiers, watching the wedding guests dance and drink, I search for a way to escape. Maybe everyone will get drunk and fall asleep and then I can slip away. Or maybe I should pretend to enlist and simply wait until I find a chance to escape. They can't watch me all the time. Surely I could say I was going to the latrine and keep on going. But what if I have to take an oath of allegiance to the Confederate government? I can't do that. I won't. And then they'll know I'm a Union spy and hang me, just like Damon always thought would happen. All I can do is wait and take the opportunity to leave when it comes.

The sun dips lower in the sky and candles are lit. True to his word, Captain Logan takes a break from the festivities to face me.

"I see you've decided to enlist, boy. Good choice. We need to leave before the Union troops get here, so you'll get a horse and we'll all be off at ten tonight."

I stare straight ahead. But at the mention of a horse, my heart lifts. I have good luck with horses—except for the bite from Rebel. If I can avoid taking a loyalty oath until I'm riding, I'll have a chance of bolting away from the rest of the cavalry. I just pray they give me a decent horse, not some old swaybacked nag that can't muster a gallop and not a vicious brute like Rebel.

The guards march me outside and lead me to a saddled mare. She doesn't look too worn out. Her eyes are bright, and her dappled coat shines from having been recently brushed.

"Get on," grunts one guard while the other holds the reins.

I do as ordered. I sit still in the saddle, trying to get a sense of the horse by feeling her flank beneath my legs, studying how she twitches her ears and snorts. I can tell the animal is nervous. Will she balk when I need her most? Edgy as she is, she seems steadier than Rebel, not as skittish. I lean forward in the saddle and pat her neck. She's my only chance.

The guards mount as well, one on either side of me, waiting for the captain. By midnight he still hasn't showed.

"Ah guess the bride had other plans for her groom." One of the guards grins.

"Yup," agrees the other. "We won't be leavin' till morning. Might as well get some sleep."

They pull me off the mare and take turns guarding, one

dozing on the saddle blankets while the other one watches me.

Can this be the moment to escape? I wonder. Most of the guests are probably asleep. Only one soldier guards me. Surely I can take him unawares, knock him out, run away.

I itch to leap up and grab the gun out of the man's hand, but something about the set of his ears, how alert he is to my every move, defeats me. He watches me too closely. Maybe when it's his turn to sleep, the other guard will be less vigilant. I decide to wait and hope for a better opportunity with soldier number two.

When the second guard takes over, he's even worse than the first one. He ties up my hands and feet, "just to be sure."

"It's too uncomfortable," I complain. "Ah can't sleep like this."

"Would yuh rather Ah hog-tied yuh? Ah didn't think so." The soldier leans back, satisfied.

"Ah really do belong with the Fifth Kentucky. Don' yuh believe me?" I wheedle.

"Don' matter whether Ah believe yuh. The captain don', and he gives the orders around heah." The guard opens his tobacco pouch and rolls himself a cigarette. "Yuh might as well git yuhself some sleep. Yuh'll be working hard tomorruh."

I close my eyes. The guard's right. There's no sense staying awake, worrying. I need to rest so I'll have energy to make a break when the time comes. I think of how James must have felt when he was taken prisoner, of how it was for Jerome trapped in Camp Parole. Lying in the dirt, trussed up and guarded by Rebel soldiers, far from the Union camp, I feel closer to my friends. Now I understand what they endured and I can feel them encouraging me, promising me I'll get away, just as each of them did.

In the morning the captain gathers his new company, keeping me close by his side.

"You're a good horseman, boy," he approves. "Believe me, once you've steeped your saber in Yankee blood and the South is free, you'll thank me."

I choke down the grimace that rises to my mouth at his ugly words. "Ah'm a patriot, suh," I finally say. "Ah love my country and Ah've always served it proudly." It seems like the only safe thing I can say.

We trot through small villages, past rolling fields. The countryside is too open to make a dash for cover. Whitewashed fences, low rises, and big farmhouses are all we pass, no place to duck and hide. Where are the thick woods of Virginia I've seen so often?

"Look what we have here!" Captain Logan calls, point-ing to the road ahead. A group of Union cavalry rides toward us. "Fan out, men, across the road in a line," he orders.

I take the chance to edge myself away from the captain, to the end of the line. As the two groups of horsemen near each other, my mare, always anxious, bolts. I wheel her in a tight circle, struggling to gain control. As she frantically flings her head around, the Union riders close in on the Confederates. Bayonets glint in the morning light. The clash of steel on steel rings out. I take advantage of the chaos of battle and force my horse over to the Union side. Their commander, naturally thinking I'm a Rebel soldier, levels his gun at me.

"Thomas, it's me, Frank Thompson!" I yell, praying the Union captain will recognize me. He quickly turns his gun onto the nearest Rebel, squeezes off a shot, and gestures to me to fall in beside him.

I'm now head to head with Captain Logan.

"Boy!" the recruiting officer roars. "Get out of the way! Are you a traitor?"

Without pausing, I take the Rebel pistol they issued me and fire it into the captain's face.

The Rebel horsemen, roaring in rage at the direct hit to their leader, rush toward me. The Union cavalrymen mass around me, driving back the frantic Confederate bayonets. The fighting is tight and pitched, horses wheeling, blades slashing, guns firing, a blur of noise and movement. I thrash around with the saber the captain promised I'd soak in Union blood. I slice at gray and brown uniforms, anything that isn't blue. In the midst of this chaos, the regiment of Union soldiers following the reconnoitering cavalry runs up, throwing the balance of the fight squarely to our side. The Rebels retreat, leaving behind eleven dead, twenty-nine wounded, and seventeen prisoners. Several of our men are also dead and many more wounded.

Captain Logan hasn't been killed, but no longer the handsome bridegroom, he has lost part of his nose and lip. I jump off the mare, stroking her bloody neck where a saber nicked it. "Good thing you're so nervous—your bolting saved the day." I stand over the recruiting officer lying on the ground, his hand over his bleeding face.

"You snake! You lyin' traitor!" the captain spits.

"Just a thank-you for your words about spilling Yankee blood. I told you I was a patriot." I should be sorry for him, but I feel none of my usual nursing instincts. Instead, I'm resolved, determined to fight as best I can until this ugly war is over.

Riding back to camp, I try to push away the image of aiming a gun square into another man's face and firing. I did that, point-blank. And not to a stranger either, but to someone I knew, someone whose wife I met, someone whose death wouldn't be abstract but real. Whenever I've fired my rifle in battle, it's been at a general target, a blur of motion, a uniform. Of course there was the time I shot the Confederate woman cleanly through the hand. But that was different. Then I intended to wound, not to kill. This time I wanted to kill him—a man I knew. What's happening to me? Is the war deadening my soul? Am I turning into someone brutal and cruel like Pa?

"I did what I had to," I mutter. I want to convince

myself, but it's harder when the person you're trying to fool is yourself. Some part of you will always know the truth, no matter how much you try to delude yourself. I consider myself a brave soldier, a compassionate nurse, a daring spy. Am I also a cold-blooded killer?

{ 24 }
A SOLDIER'S JOB

"WAIT A MINUTE!" JEROME SAYS, GLARING AT ME ACROSS the campfire that night. "You watched the man get married and then you shot him? That's coldhearted, Frank."

"I'm a soldier, Jerome. I did my job." I stare into the fire, avoiding Jerome's eyes. I was telling the story of the Confederate wedding. Most of the men are impressed, especially when they hear I shot the Rebel recruiting officer. But Jerome knows I'm a woman, and killing isn't womanly.

Easy for him to criticize—he's never fought in a battle. He's seen the brutality of battle only after the fact, tending to the wounded in a hospital tent. He doesn't know what it's like to face a gun, a bayonet, a saber. He thinks I'm unnatural, unwomanly, because I can stanch the blood pouring from a gash, hold a man down as his leg is sawed off, and worst of all, shoot a man at close quarters. I lift my chin, defiant. I'm no ordinary woman, and Jerome should be proud of that.

"You did right," James says, patting my back. "I would have done the same."

There are grunts and nods all around the campfire.

"You expected Frank to shake the fella's hand?" a grizzled soldier asks. "Wish him well? The Reb was yammering about skewering Yankees, making his sword drip with our blood! Shouldn't we return the favor?"

Jerome shakes his head. "Of course we have to fight back. This is war. But . . ."

"But nothin'!" a jug-eared private clenches his fist in disgust. "There's no niceness to this here business. If you have to shoot the enemy in the face, in the back, in the bloody buttocks, you do it! That means one fewer to shoot at you!"

Lying on my cot, I can't shake off Jerome's disapproving stare. I want him to like me. And now he thinks I'm a heartless beast. I have a heart, but I keep it safely tucked away where no one can bruise it anymore, especially Jerome.

I wonder if living as a man has made me more callous. Not that I've ever been refined. I've acted more boy than girl for most of my life. That's who I am. I never wanted a life confined to the kitchen and garden. But I do want Jerome. Even though he brings out a part of myself I've kept in check for so long, I've forgotten it exists.

And if I am honest with myself, sometimes I like how he has changed me. In those rare moments, my few feminine traits seem my best, my noblest side. When I'm with Jerome, I notice every nuance of his mood. Just the sound of his voice can warm me. I've never felt such delicious anticipation as waiting to see him, never known such happiness as when we're together, such misery as when we're apart. I can be careful to hide my feelings, but I can't pretend I don't have them. Truth is, I don't want to. Still, I can't stop myself from trying to untangle my relationship with Jerome. I toss in bed until James shakes my shoulder.

"Having nightmares?" he asks.

"It's Jerome," I sigh. "I want him to respect me, not think I'm some kind of brute." That much I can admit out loud.

"He does respect you," James says. "He shouldn't have called you coldhearted. Unless . . ." He pauses, staring at me. "Unless there's a particular reason he thinks you shouldn't have shot that man. Maybe he thinks you should be tenderhearted for some reason?"

"Why would he think that?" I snap.

"Maybe"—James reaches over and takes hold of my hand—"maybe he thinks you're a delicate soul. Look at this fine hand you have, such elegant fingers. Almost as nice as a lady's hand." James waits, studying my face.

I pull my hand away, irritated and nervous. James can't possibly be hinting that I'm a woman. I refuse to believe it.

"My hands are no nicer than yours—and I'm no more delicate." I turn away gruffly. "Good night."

"Good night." James settles back under his blanket.
He may suspect that I'm a woman, but he doesn't have any
proof and he's not going to get any.

I've just fallen back to sleep when the ground shakes,
jolting me awake. I stare into the darkness, straining to hear
what's going on, but it's quiet now. James is sitting up, listening, too.

"What was that?" I ask.

"Don't want to know," says James. "A shell probably,
one of ours, one of theirs. We'll find out in the morning."

⊱ ⊰

The next morning we hear the news. As James suspected,
it was a Rebel shell hitting our camp. Six men are dead. If
there's a shred of complacency left in anyone, it's shaken
out of us now. We're close enough to the enemy camp for
their artillery to hit us. The order comes to pack up and
move out. I walk over to the pit where the men were sleeping
in their tents when the shell hit them. Bits of flesh, blood,
and clothes still litter the charred ground. The dead have
already been buried, but I can imagine them there. I've
already seen so many grisly sights, these ghosts should pro-
voke no more than a sad shrug, but suddenly images of all
the brutality, all the carnage that I've shoved deep down

inside me for so long, erupt in my head, and I can't shake off the dreadful memories. As I stare at the gash in the dirt, tears for the many dead and wounded stream from my eyes. My chest heaves with sobs. I pinch my arm, trying to shut off the grief, but the tears keep welling up. I hear hoarse wails of anguish and am startled to realize they're coming from me.

"Frank, are you all right?" Richard, a private from our unit, comes up to me. "We're getting ready to march out, you know."

I drag my sleeve across my face and nod. I have to keep my mouth clamped tight to shut in the sobs. I don't know why I'm crying so much. I just feel worn out—I've been strong for so long and now I can barely hold myself upright. I want to sink into the ground and weep for days, but I force my feet to carry me back to the tent. I pack up everything in a foggy, teary haze.

By the time James comes, I'm set to go. The tent is rolled up, the stakes put in my knapsack, my canteen and rifle slung around my neck.

"Frank, what's the matter? You look terrible." James puts an arm around my rigid shoulders.

I wave him away. "Nothing. It's just . . ." I pause. "This war is getting to me. That's all."

James nods slowly. "The shell last night. It shook me up, too. We've been hit before, but always in battle. It's something else to have the enemy attack you when you think you're safe asleep in your own camp."

"That's it," I say. "I don't feel safe anymore. I'll never feel safe."

I have to talk to Jerome. I desperately need my best friend. He has to understand—he's the only person in the entire world who truly knows me, everything about me. I search him out on the march toward Louisville, the two of us straggling behind the main regiment. I need to talk but I don't know how to start. I can't admit to the attack of tears. Instead, I decide to clear the air about firing my gun at the Rebel captain.

"Jerome, I need to explain about shooting that man." I match my gait to his long paces.

"There's nothing to explain. You did the right thing— for a man." He keeps his eyes forward and quickens his step.

I grab his arm. "That's why you're mad at me. You think I shouldn't be doing the same things men do."

Jerome wrenches his arm out of my grip. "Why would I think that? You're obviously capable of anything."

"Jerome, stop this!" Tears glitter on my lashes.

"Can't you understand how hard this is for me?" he whispers harshly. "If you could just be a man to me, it would all be fine. But how can I ignore that you're a woman?"

"You did fine before," I observe, wiping my eyes.

"That's true," he snorts. "Before I saw you making

goo-goo eyes at that idiot Scotsman, before news broke about other women disguised as men, before you shot a man in the face!"

"So that's what this is about? You're jealous of James? There's nothing to be jealous of."

"I'm not jealous!" Jerome barks. He can't cloak the anger in his voice, a tone that sounds very much like jealousy to me. "I just don't know what to think. You act like a man, then like a woman, then like a man again. It's too hard!"

"I'm acting like myself," I say, keeping my eyes on the ground. I can't bear to look at him.

"Just promise me, please, promise me you won't love that Highlander," Jerome presses.

"You won't let me love you, but I can't love him, either? Are you even my friend anymore?" My voice quavers. "Sometimes it's hard for me to be so strong. You think it's easy, but it's not."

Jerome sighs. He reaches out and tentatively takes my hand. "You are strong, Frank. Crying doesn't change that. And the one thing I'm sure of is that I'm your friend. You can count on that, no matter what."

I squeeze his hand, then tug mine away. "Then that will have to be enough, for both of us." And now I dare to look at him, to lose myself in his warm brown eyes. "I'm sorry there can't be more."

Jerome doesn't answer. We march the rest of the way to

Louisville without another word. I watch his profile out of the corner of my eye. I know he loves me, but not the way I want to be loved. And I love him, but not the way he wants. I shake my head. Maybe someday when this war is long over, we can love each other the way we both want.

{ 25 }

ANOTHER DISGUISE

BY MARCH THE WEATHER HAS WARMED UP, THE SNOW
has melted, and fresh green shoots cover the Kentucky
fields. Stationed in Louisville, the men of the Second
Michigan are restless. We haven't seen combat for months,
but we're surrounded by Confederates—civilians, maybe,
but Confederates all the same.

I'm doing laundry, since there's nothing better to do,
when a soldier tells me to see General Poe about some new
orders.

"Private Frank Thompson, reporting as ordered, sir!" I
salute the general.

"Private Thompson." General Poe nods. "Here's the
situation. Louisville is under Union control, but it's also the
headquarters for Rebel sympathizers. The place is full of
Rebel spies eager to report anything at all useful to the nearby
Confederate troops. We need you to dress as a Southerner,
get a job, and ferret out the agents for the South."

"Get a job where, sir, as what?"

"The general store would be best. That's where everyone comes for everything from tobacco to tooth powder—and most of all, for gossip. If you can't work there, try the saloon. Liquor loosens men's jaws, and you should hear plenty."

There's no time to explain my mission to Jerome or James before I leave, so I send each of them letters assuring them there's no reason to worry. I write to Damon, too, and tell him I hope he's busy planting a new crop, with his girl at his side. I don't tell him about spying, but I do mention that Virginia seems downright cold and disinterested, which is just fine with me. He should tell her not to write to me anymore, since we haven't gotten any closer as friends and she's definitely not my sweetheart. The last person I write to is Mr. Hurlburt, promising him a juicy story if he can wait until I'm back in camp.

I become Charles Mayberry, rooming at the National Hotel. So many men of the town have left for the Rebel army that it's easy to land a job at Harris & Son's Dry Goods Emporium. The place reminds me of the general store back home in Flint, Michigan. Piles of cloth are stacked on shelves next to packets of needles, coffeepots, sheaves of stationery, bottles of ink. On the floor sacks of meal, beans, and crackers crowd out barrels of flour, sugar, and apples. Just about anything you could possibly need is somewhere in that store, but I'm not sure I'll be able to put my hand to it when a customer asks for it. Being a clerk isn't as easy as it seems.

It turns out another Union spy is staying at the same hotel as me. Colonel Moore, the federal provost marshal in charge of the secret service in Louisville, comes to my room after work my first day and asks me if I can give a few tips to the new agent.

"I'd be happy to," I say, though I'm not sure what exactly I can advise. Rely on your horse? Trust your instincts? Learn different accents?

"Good!" The colonel leads me down a hall papered in red flocking, knocks at a room, then opens the door.

"Frank, I want you to meet Miss Pauline Cushman. You may have seen her in the role of Plutella in *The Seven Sisters,* playing in town recently."

I gape at the curvaceous woman with long blond curls perched on a crimson settee. This woman is a spy, like in the book Damon sent me? She looks like someone who plays burlesque, not theater, and certainly not like any kind of spy.

Pauline extends a pinkly dimpled arm. "Delighted to make your acquaintance."

I take the offered fingers, glittering with rings, and raise them to my lips. "You're certainly the most beautiful spy I've ever seen! I can see you'll have no trouble coaxing information out of Confederate officers."

"Well, aren't you the flatterer!" Pauline coos. "Unfortunately, I won't be using my feminine wiles. Your Colonel Moore insists I do my spying dressed as a boy."

I arch an eyebrow. "Isn't that a waste of her talents, Colonel? And how would you hide those curves?"

"I've been told it's possible," the colonel retorts gruffly. "And she'll get a chance to use her gifts in good time. Miss Pauline is a well-known secessionist. She's boldly praised the Confederacy on the stage, acting in front of Union officers. We 'arrested' her last night for toasting Jeff Davis in the closing act of her play, so folks think she's in jail. That's why for the next six months or so, she'll dress as a rough country boy and spy in that guise. Then we'll 'release' her from jail and she can be an even more effective agent as her own charming self. I don't think she'll need advice for that kind of spying. But we don't want to waste the months she's supposedly in jail. I want you to teach her how to walk, talk, eat, and behave like a boy. She needs to be convincing."

I shake my head. "It could take a month to teach her all that. No offense, ma'am, but you're about as far from a boy as a girl can get."

Pauline's full lips curve into a smile. "No offense taken. I've had whole articles in the newspaper written in praise of my looks. I'd rather flaunt them than hide them. Still"— she looks slyly at the provost marshal—"I want to serve my country, so I'll do as I'm told. Remember, I'm an actress. If you give me the role of rube, I'll play it to the hilt."

"I'll leave the two of you to it, then," the colonel says,

bowing out of the room. I want to protest, but the door is shut before I can think of what to say.

I plop down in a chair across from Pauline. Here I am, a woman dressed as a man, expected to teach another woman how to do exactly what I'm doing. You would think I'd be the perfect person for the job. Except I've never had to hide the heaving breasts and curvy hips that Pauline enjoys. My face is square-jawed and boyish, my body thin and wiry, my voice a natural tenor. It's easy for me to look and act like a man. But the woman sitting across from me has a soft, round face, with Cupid's-bow lips, a full womanly figure, and a flutey, high voice.

Is this what Jerome wants in a woman? I wonder with a sharp stab of jealousy. Does Miss

PAULINE CUSHMAN AS A MAN.

Anna have a generous bosom and curvaceous hips? How could my slender hips and teacup breasts compare? No wonder Jerome can't accept me as a woman. If only Pauline could show me how to be more feminine—that's a lesson I desperately need to learn.

I sigh. This isn't about me—it's about Pauline. "You'll have to bind your breasts, of course, but I don't know what we can do about your hips. Maybe if we stuff some cloth down your front, giving you a belly, you'll seem heavyset, not feminine. And you'll have to deepen your voice. Can you do that?"

"Of course." Pauline's voice is husky and dark, lower, yes, but definitely not masculine. In fact it's more alluring than ever. I can't help it—I'm fascinated by how attractive she is in every way, from her voice to her hair to the turn of her wrists.

"Can you try again without sounding so . . . so . . . flirtatious?" I ask. She's such a mistress of womanly wiles, I feel more manly next to her than I ever have fighting in a pitched battle. I'm a stick next to her, with not one ounce of womanly charm. I should be gratified that I'm such a convincing male. Instead, I feel a strange depression at being such a feminine failure.

I try to stop comparing myself with her. My job isn't figuring out how to make myself more like Pauline—it's making Pauline more like me.

It takes an hour just to get her to walk without rolling her hips, another to train her to slurp and chomp rather than sip and nibble. By the end of the day, I'm no longer jealous. I'm exasperated and exhausted.

But Pauline feels she's made enormous progress. "Thank you, Frank—you've been wonderfully patient with me. I do believe I owe you a tremendous debt." She runs a finger along my cheek and down my throat, tracing circles around my collarbones. I inch away, but she leans in even closer. "How can I ever repay you?" Her hand creeps down toward my waist, then lower and lower . . .

I spring up, pushing away Pauline's hand. "No need. I'm doing my job, that's all. We can continue tomorrow." I bolt to the door and rush out.

"That would be lovely!" Pauline calls to my retreating back.

I stumble outside, hungry for fresh air after the long hours in the heavy musk of Pauline's room. I want to tell the colonel that I've done all I can and never see Pauline again. That woman is more likely to discover my secret than any man has been. I should have responded to Pauline's flirting, like any young man, but I could only run away in terror. Her hand was far too close to noticing that I'm missing a crucial piece of male anatomy.

━━ ━━

The next day I steel myself for the task of seeming irrefutably male while I teach a seductive woman how to act like a man. I imagine Jerome laughing at my predicament. "Ha, ha, hilarious," I mutter as I rap on Pauline's door.

"Come in!" a gruff voice calls out.

I walk in, wondering who else is in the lady's room. A cherubic boy sits on the red velvet settee. Blond curls frame a round face that seems too sensitive for the straw hat, rough overalls, and thick boots he wears. He should be a dreamy scholar, I think, not a stableboy.

"Well, can I pass?" The rough voice comes from the sweet-looking boy.

"Pauline?" I ask, peering into the youth's face. "Is that you?"

The boy tips his hat, and the thick blond tresses that have been tucked underneath fall down onto his shoulders. "Born and bred," Pauline purrs.

I grin, impressed and relieved. If she can carry it off, I won't have to give her any more lessons. "Not bad! You make the most angelic-looking boy I've seen. Stand up and walk. Let me see if you move like a boy."

Pauline heaves herself up and clomps around the room. It's a bit of an exaggeration, but at least it isn't a sashaying stroll.

"You're an impressive actress, no question about it."

"Think I'm ready for the curtain to rise?" Pauline bows.

"Definitely! Let's show the colonel. He's down in the front parlor."

Colonel Moore looks up from his newspaper when the stableboy and I walk in. He takes off his reading glasses and stares intently. A slow smile of recognition creeps across his face. He stands up and offers his hand to me.

"Well done, Frank! I knew if anyone could turn a swan into a turkey, it'd be you."

I shake the colonel's hand. "I'll take that as a compliment."

"Wanna see how I eat and drink?" the blond boy asks.

"No need! You're entirely convincing. Now let's map out our strategy. I believe Frank has a store he needs to tend."

I nod. "I'd best be on my way if I don't want to get fired for tardiness. Good luck, Pauline . . . er . . . Paul. You'll do fine, I'm sure."

"Thanks." Pauline tosses away the toothpick she's been chewing on. "I had a good teacher." She reaches out to shake my hand, then leans in for a kiss on the cheek, filling my nose with her perfume. That's one thing she'll have to change to make her costume completely convincing. No fellow smells like lilies of the valley.

I blush a deep crimson and hurry out, touching my cheek where her lips rested. My first kiss—and it's from another woman! Thank the Lord that mission is over! Spying among the Confederates is easy compared to being alone in a room with someone like Pauline.

26

SPYING ON SPIES

I'M MUCH MORE COMFORTABLE IN MY ROLE AS CHARLES, the sales clerk. I lean on the polished wood counter, chatting with the customers. It's a relief going from all-too-close quarters with Pauline to the public propriety of a business. All I have to do is sell goods and probe to see how deeply the customers' sympathies lie with the Confederacy. I don't meet a single person who supports the Union, but most are ordinary citizens. They sell food and goods to Rebel troops on the sly, but don't risk offering more support than that. But Colonel Moore insists there are three Confederate spies who are leaking important information to the Rebels. Those are the agents I'm supposed to find.

After a week of clerking and getting no closer to the spies, I decide to push my boss for a chance to get nearer to the Confederate army.

"Mr. Harris," I ask one morning, "do you think I'm a good salesman?"

"Why, Charles, yuh're one of the best Ah've evah had, almost as good as mah son was."

"What happened to your son, if you don't mind my asking?" I run a cloth along the shelves.

"He's with Gen'l Lee, of course, wheah all fine young men should be." Mr. Harris has been clear from the start whose side of the war he's on, so this bit of information isn't a surprise.

"Does that mean you think I should be in the army, too?" I rub at a stubborn ink stain, avoiding my boss's eyes.

Mr. Harris chuckles. "Mebbe, but Ah'm grateful yuh're not, because Ah need someone to help out heah. But"—he pauses thoughtfully—"if yuh want to do something for the Confederacy and help mah bus'ness as well, yuh could go sell some goods at the Rebel camps neah heah."

My ears perk up. I'm being offered a legitimate reason to walk into the Confederate camps and sniff things out. It's the perfect way to learn who the spies are. If I stay long enough or go back regularly, I'm bound to run into at least one of them.

"I'm not from here, but I'm happy to do my duty, Mr. Harris, to both you and the South. After all, this is my adopted home."

"Wheah are yuh from, anyways, Charles? Ah cain't place yuh accent." The store owner studies me.

"I'm from Canada—New Brunswick." I smile. "I don't have an accent at all. You're the one with an accent."

Mr. Harris guffaws. "That's an accent, boy, but nevah mind, yuh can still be one of us." He bustles around the store, putting together baskets of wares to sell to the Rebel soldiers. He draws maps to three Confederate camps close by, gives me a horse, and sends me out to sell as much as I can. Since I'm Mr. Harris's clerk, none of the Rebel pickets or soldiers questions my loyalty. They welcome me into their camps, offer me coffee and biscuits, and by midafternoon I've sold every comb, pocketknife, handkerchief, and spool of thread that I started out with. I come back with more than money. I've also picked up information about two of the Rebel spies—one is a blacksmith who fits horseshoes on the Union horses. Another is a photographer who sells pictures of the Union generals. I'm sure I can discover the third spy's identity if I get more time in the Rebel camps. After meeting with Colonel Moore and giving him the information I've learned, we come up with a plan for me to take a deeper plunge into the role of Confederate sympathizer.

The next day I thank Mr. Harris for the chance to spend time in the Rebel camps. I tell him that the experience has convinced me to join the Confederate army, but I'm not sure how I can get past the Yankee lines again so soon.

"Won't they be suspicious if they see I'm selling the same goods I sold the other day? They'll either know I'm peddling to the Rebels or think I'm aiming to join them."

Mr. Harris strokes his muttonchop sideburns. "Ah've got it. Ah hate to lose yuh, but Ah know how yuh can get through." There's no one else in the store, but still he lowers his voice conspiratorially. "Ah know a man who the Yanks all think is pro-Union. Really he's a spy and works for Gen'l Lee. He can get yuh 'cross the lines easy as pie 'count of how the Yanks all trust him. Ah'll tell him to meet yuh heah tonight. Pack yuh things an' be ready to go at nine."

I keep my face solemn, but excitement surges through me—this man could be the third spy.

The morning passes quickly. At noon, when Mr. Harris goes home for the midday meal as usual, Colonel Moore comes into the shop. He leans quietly against the counter, waiting his turn to be helped.

I wrap up the penny nails the colonel asked for, slipping a note into the package. I nod as I hand the parcel to him. "I think you'll find these most useful," I say, "for the work you're doing tonight."

"I'm sure I will," the colonel answers. Back at the hotel he can unwrap the package and read my message. I've asked him to capture me and my guide before we reach the Rebel camp tonight. That way we'll get the spy and my real identity won't be discovered.

At ten to nine, I'm back at the store with my clothes in a small cloth satchel, playing the part of an eager recruit. I stare into the darkness, straining my ears for the sound of footsteps. At nine precisely, a shadow emerges from the night. It's a short, chunky man with a mustache too grand for his face. He wears a bowler hat and dark coat and carries a satchel similar to mine. His eyes are round and merry, and his red cheeks show how much he likes his whiskey. He doesn't look at all like a spy. He's the sort of man who seems so ordinary and harmless, he wouldn't attract any attention. Mr. Harris must have made a mistake. Yes, the man might indeed easily get past the Yankee lines, but that could be because he is a complete innocent, because he really is what he seems—a simple fellow.

"You must be Charles Mayberry," the man booms heartily, extending his hand.

I nod and reach out to shake the jolly man's hand.

"You ready to join the ahmy?" he asks. "Ah'm heah to take you."

I narrow my eyes. Should I go with him? The whole thing could be a waste of time.

"You're not changin' your mind now, are you? Don' you want adventure, excitement, glory?" The man doesn't exactly talk like a spy, but he certainly is a secessionist.

"I'm not changing my mind," I decide. "Let's go."

"Atta boy," the bowler-hat man says with approval, leading the way down darkened lanes to the edge of the Union picket line. When we come to the sentry, the man tips his hat, smiles, and keeps on walking. The guard clearly knows him, because he lets the bowler hat pass without a question. I trot at his side, safe by association.

It isn't until we're past the Union soldiers that the man introduces himself.

"Ah didn't mean to be rude, boy, but Ah don't feel free to really talk when Ah'm around Yankees. Now that we're breathin' free Southern air, we can introduce ourselves properly. Mah name is Conrad Morrow and Ah'm an agent in the Confederate secret service. Ah know, Ah know, you thought Ah was a silly clown, but Ah tell you, mah looks are exactly what makes me such a brilliant spy. Who would evah suspect me? Ah can tell you, Ah've had some amazin' adventures. You may have heard of other spies, but they ain't nothin' compared to me."

I grin in the dark. The bowler hat *is* a spy! And it sounds like he's eager to talk. "I have heard of two famous spies. Maybe you're one of them—the blacksmith and the fellow with the photographs. Are you one of them? I can't believe I'm meeting an actual spy! It's so exciting! You must be a brave man!" I lay it on thick.

The bowler hat chuckles. "Those boys haven't gone on half the missions Ah have. Ah'm at Yankee headquarters 'most every day, and you'd be surprised how easily folks tell me things. They think Ah'm selling books and pamphlets, but Ah'm gatherin' information, all kinds of information. Ah can tell you wheah each gen'l sleeps, wheah the pickets are posted, and when they change guard. Ah know which big guns are facing what. Ah know when Gen'l Grant is gonna sneeze afore he knows it hisself!"

"It's truly an honor to meet you, sir!" I gush. "But I've heard that blacksmith, he's done some important work. I'd really like to meet him. Perhaps you could introduce us."

The bowler hat snorts. "Well, if you call countin' hosses important. Sure, he's done that. He's shoein' 'em, so it's no great stretch to count 'em. That kind of work don' take no cleverness. And yeah, he's lamed a few on purpose, but not enough of them to really make a difference. He's afraid to take risks. Not like me!"

The farther we walk from Louisville and the more I express admiration for the farrier's exploits, the louder the bowler hat's boasts grow. I've heard the details of three different spy missions when the thud of hoofbeats interrupt the story of the fourth.

"Stand still, boy!" the bowler hat whispers. "We've got to get off this road!"

Before he can turn, a swirl of movement surrounds us. Horsemen hold us in a tight circle. I recognize Colonel Moore as one of the riders.

"Where are you going?" the colonel demands.

The bowler hat grins impishly and fumbles with his satchel. "Ah'm jus' a peddler man, peddlin' his wares. Ah'm sure y'all seen me in the Yankee camp. Ah sell books to y'all."

The colonel squints down at him. "Yes, I recognize you. I don't mean any offense, but we've heard that spies are taking this road tonight. You don't mind if we search you, now do you?"

The bowler hat blanches. His mustache jiggles in panic. "That's an outrage!" he blusters. "Ah'm an honest workin' man. Y'all cain' tread on my rights like that!"

"No treading at all. We'll just do a little looking." The colonel nods, and the soldier next to him jumps off his horse and rifles through my satchel, then my companion's.

"What's this?" the soldier asks, handing a packet of papers to the colonel.

"You can't have those!" The bowler hat tries to snatch them away. "Those are private and personal! Those are love letters! You give 'em back to me now!"

"I don't think so," says the colonel, unfolding the papers and sorting through them in the moonlight. "These look like plans of headquarters, the layout of the camp, and lists of artillery. Love letters, huh?" He pockets the package and signals to the soldier on the ground. "Arrest the both of them. They're spies!"

I glare at the bowler hat. "This is your fault! I didn't do anything. I'm not a spy! Tell them—I'm not a spy!"

The bowler hat turns away from me. "Listen, Ah'll make you a deal. This boy's a real weasel. I know he has a baby face, but he's done more spyin' than you can imagine. Ah'll tell you all his contacts if'n y'all let me go. He's the real spy— Ah'm jus' his unfortunate uncle, duped into helpin' him."

"We can discuss a deal later. Right now, you're going to jail." The soldier ties our wrists with rope, yanking hard to show he means business.

"Dammit!" It's not that my wrists hurt. Something warm trickles down my leg, and that means the cloth I've stuffed down my pants for my monthly isn't doing its job. At least it's dark and no one can see anything, but I feel totally exposed, as if everyone can plainly see what I so distinctly feel.

"Don't expect no kid-glove treatment," growls the soldier as he prods us back down the road to Louisville. All the way, the bowler hat protests his innocence. I say nothing, focusing on the trail of blood as it runs down the inside of my leg and slowly seeps toward my sock. I pray there'll be no more, just that one slight leak. I walk as stiffly as possible so as not to jar the cloth any farther from where it belongs. It strikes me as ridiculously ironic that I'm a pretend prisoner, but if my true nature were discovered, I'd quickly become a real one. Then the bowler hat would have the last laugh.

When we arrive at camp, the colonel sends the bowler hat in one direction but calls for me to follow him with my soldier guard.

"We've got him, sir, the third spy," I say as soon as the bowler hat is out of sight.

"Yes, indeed! Good work, Private. Come join me in my tent for a drink to celebrate," the colonel offers.

"Thank you, sir, but I need to get back to my room. It's been a long day. I'm tired, and I've some letters to write and some mending to do." I pile on the excuses, desperate to get away before we come close to any light.

The colonel laughs. "If you don't want my company, just say so. No need to darn socks to ward me off."

"That's not it at all, sir. It's just, it's just . . ." And then I know the perfect thing to say, the words that will describe my situation perfectly but not arouse any suspicion. "It's just that my bowels are about to burst and I've got to get to the latrine. It was those buttered grits and greens at supper, I know it."

Now the colonel really laughs. "Well, that explains why you've been walking so funny! Go relieve yourself, Private, and if you're up to it, join me for a drink. If not, I understand completely."

"Yes, sir!" I salute and dash off into the darkness. I pause to quickly secure the cloth in my pants, then run back to my hotel room. I carefully step out of my pants, praying no blood has got on them. I'm lucky. There's a small stain near the crotch, but the rest of the leg is clean. I pour some water into my washbasin and start scrubbing. A little cold water and soap, and the blood will come right out. I just hope the pants will be dry by morning. They're the only pair I have. Naturally, I won't be joining the colonel for a drink. I'm not going anywhere until the bleeding has stopped and I can be a man again.

{27

FAREWELLS

MY MONTHLY NEVER LASTS MORE THAN THREE DAYS, SO I'm not holed up long. Since I've supposedly been arrested along with the bowler hat, I can't go back to clerking at the store anyway. And having found out the spies, there's no need to stay in town, so Colonel Moore sends me to rejoin my regiment camped outside of Louisville. The weeks in the hotel have been a wonderful luxury, but they've also been lonely. And even all that privacy hasn't protected me. Pauline and the cloth-slippage problem remind me that it won't be the thing I'm guarding against that will expose my secret. It will be something completely unexpected. Which means I can't ever relax my vigilance.

As soon as I get to camp, I go straight to the hospital to find Jerome. Of course I don't act like a woman around him, but since he knows my secret, I don't have to worry about slipping up, exposing myself. Instead, I work to control myself in a different way. I have to be careful not to touch him, to lean into his warmth, to graze my fingers on his arm, to rub his back. I can talk honestly with him, the way I used to with Flag, so long as I keep my distance and don't dwell on certain subjects. After the tension of the last mission, I desperately need that comfort. I help him on his rounds, bandaging and dosing with quinine, chatting with him the whole time, savoring the familiar tingling that his presence always gives me.

"Anything new happen while I was gone?" I ask, leaning over to feel a soldier's forehead. It's hot and sweaty, and I press a cool cloth on it to ease the boy's fever.

"Not too much. There was some scrapping between the Union Kentucky regiments and our Michigan boys. The Kentucky soldiers threw some stones at the colored soldiers in the Second U.S. Colored Artillery, and the Michigan soldiers didn't take kindly to it. They insisted soldiers should be treated like soldiers. The Kentucky boys didn't see it that way—they think all colored people should be slaves and that's that. It ended in a fistfight and a couple of broken noses." Jerome shrugs. "The men are restless. What can you expect?"

"Well, I expect if you're fighting for the Union, you're fighting against slavery. I would have punched some of those Kentucky soldiers myself if I'd been there."

"You know that's not how most men see it," Jerome says. "How many white folk really care about slavery?"

"I do! And many others do, too! Why, I heard that even General Bobby Lee himself doesn't own slaves, and he freed the ones his father-in-law left to him. Their own general doesn't believe in slavery!" We're moving down the rows of cots, arguing across the sick soldiers.

"Maybe you're right," Jerome admits. "Anyway, besides that ruckus there's not much to tell except that General Poe's commission has run out and he hasn't been reappointed. Talk is he's being punished for sticking with Franklin at the Battle of Fredericksburg."

"You mean he's leaving? He hasn't said a word to me!"

"He hasn't had the chance, has he? You just got here. Go see him yourself and see what he says."

"I will." I finish changing a dressing and turn to Jerome. "Do you know who's replacing him? Who's our commander now?"

Jerome shrugs again. "I don't know and I don't care. It's all the same to me."

"How can you say that? I don't want another Burnside!" I slump down on a stool, suddenly exhausted. "I'm tired of this war. I've been fighting for so long, I'm not sure there's any fight left in me."

"C'mon, Frank. You've got more grit than anyone I know. You love the army." Jerome pulls up a stool and sits next to me.

I sit up stiffly, keeping my body away from his. "I don't love the army—I love the men in the army." I look at the bandaged men filling every bed. "They're like brothers to me—they're my family. I'd do anything for them."

"I know you would. And they know it, too." He takes my hand and pats it. "But you deserve a rest. Why don't you ask for a leave?"

I let my hand linger in his, the touch a rare gift. My heart pounds as I try to sound casual, normal. "After I've had it so easy, sleeping in a hotel these past few weeks? I don't think so." As if suddenly aware of what he is doing, Jerome pulls his hand away roughly. I've kept the contact a second too long. Now he won't even look at me. I stand up. "I need

SOLDIERS AT REST AFTER DRILL, PETERSBURG, VA. THE SOLDIERS ARE READING LETTERS AND PAPERS AND PLAYING CARDS.

to see General Poe. I have to find out what's happening to him and who's taking his place." I sigh, aware of a second conversation underneath the words, the one where my every fiber turns toward him, asking him to love me, the one where he pulls away and makes it clear that will never happen. So I ask a safer question. "See you at supper?"

Jerome nods stiffly. "I'll save a plate for you."

It's the time of day when drills are over and the men are free to go to prayer meetings, write letters, patch their clothes, or even boil up a pot of laundry. I amble toward headquarters, letting the cozy, domestic feeling of the camp wash over me, relaxing more with every step. The light is low and golden, the air soft with the coming evening. It's my favorite hour, ever since I was little, that time when work is over and a soft, tired feeling spreads through my body.

I knock on the post outside General Poe's tent.

"Enter!" his voice calls out. "Frank!" The general looks up from his table heaped high with the usual papers. "I heard you caught yourself a nest of spies—good work!"

"Thank you, sir. And I heard you're leaving us. Is that true?"

The general nods. "Yes, for once the rumors are right. I've been assigned as chief engineer on General Burnside's staff."

My eyes widen in surprise. "You're being punished, sir, for disobeying General Burnside!"

"It looks that way, yes." He raises an eyebrow. "I'll follow orders and do my best. But I'll miss you, Frank, and this brigade. You're good men, all of you. We've fought well together."

"Thank you, sir." I offer my hand. "It's been a privilege and an honor to serve under you, sir."

General Poe clasps my hand and shakes it warmly. "The honor is all mine."

Walking back through the camp, I realize nothing has changed. It's just as peaceful as before and that's reassuring. The army is bigger than any one man. We've gone on without McClellan. We'll go on without Poe.

I think about Damon, how much I miss his lopsided grin, his complaining, even his crude jokes. He's not the same person in his letters, as if writing down his thoughts changes his voice somehow, makes it more formal. His last letter was all about farming, not a word about Polly, nothing about Virginia.

When I get back to my tent, James is packing his knapsack.

"I just get back and you're going somewhere?" I ask.

"Frank! I didn't know you were back!" James shoves a book into his bag. "But yes, I'm leaving."

"Have you asked for a transfer or been reassigned? Are you following General Poe?"

"No." James sighs. "Nothing like that. You know my wife has been ill for some time, and she's gotten so bad that I've taken your advice and tendered my resignation. I need to take her home to Scotland. I'm leaving tonight."

"I said you should ask for a leave, not resign!" I protest.

"I can't say when I can return. Resigning was the right thing to do."

I sit on my bedroll, head between my hands. "I'll miss you, James," I say. "It won't be the same without you." Though really, I know it will be. Everything will be exactly the same, just lonelier.

James ties up his bag and sets it outside the tent. He sits next to me and puts his arm around me. "I'll miss you, too." My shoulders tremble under his touch. Without a word, he pulls me toward him and kisses me gently on the lips. I freeze, stunned. He presses himself more firmly. I can't help it—I kiss him back.

"Oh, Frank," he murmurs. "Or whoever you really are. Be safe." He kisses me again as the tears run down my cheeks. I close my eyes, not daring to face him. He knows what I am, who I am. When I open my eyes again, he's gone.

I curl up on the bed, shivering, pulling the blanket tight around me. I feel drained and queasy. How could I have let James kiss me? How could I kiss him back? I'm disgusted with myself. My body feels heavy and clumsy, my head thick and cottony, as if I've literally made myself sick by failing to act like a man. I've slipped, let down my guard, and for one minute I've been a woman. The shame is over-whelming.

But it's more than shame that makes me tremble. The familiar fever grips me again. I haven't had a bout of the swamp fever for months, but now it's back fiercer than ever. I welcome the oblivion, the escape from thinking about what's happened.

When I open my eyes again, late-afternoon light slants through the tent flap and Jerome is sitting next to me, pressing a cool wet cloth to my forehead.

"Frank," he murmurs. "You're awake. It's good to see your eyes open. You've been asleep a long time. When you didn't come to supper, I checked on you and found you thrashing around with fever dreams."

"Thanks for taking care of me." My voice is hoarse and weak.

"Of course." Jerome smiles. "But you really should be in the hospital. This is the worst I've seen you. I can bring you quinine, but you really should have a doctor tend to you."

"No," I protest. "I can't do that. You know why."

"It's not like we undress our patients. Your secret will be safe. You know I wouldn't put you at risk! There was an article in the Louisville *Daily Democrat* yesterday about a woman dressed as a man in the Fourteenth Iowa Regiment." Jerome looks like he's sorry he's said it as soon as the words have left his mouth.

"What article? Why didn't you tell me? How did they find out she was a woman? What happened once they did?"

Jerome frowns. "I didn't want to worry you. And I shouldn't have mentioned it just now. I forgot that it's not a pretty story, not something you need to hear about."

"What do you mean?" I press. "You brought it up. Now you have to tell me what the article said."

He sighs, stares at the ground, but doesn't answer me.

"Jerome!" I insist. "You have to tell me!"

He still avoids my gaze, but he at least answers. "The newspaper didn't say how she was discovered. It just said that after the soldiers in her regiment found out, she killed herself."

"You see!" My voice squeaks with panic. "That's why I can't go to the hospital! I've seen doctors unbutton men's shirts to listen to their lungs and heart. I'm not taking that chance." I want to say more, but I can't. My head is heavy and thick, and I can feel the pulse throbbing in my ears. The thin daylight is more than my eyes can bear, and I squeeze my eyelids shut.

"Don't worry, Frank, I'm here with you. You rest now." Jerome's voice is low and reassuring. I follow it in my head into a dark, warm place.

When I wake up again, Jerome is gone, but a bottle of quinine has been left near the bed. I drink some down and fall quickly back to sleep.

When I open my eyes, it's the middle of the night, or early in the morning before sunrise. My clothes are sticky with sweat, my bones achy and brittle. "I've got to see a doctor," I mutter. In the dark, I pack my knapsack and sneak out of camp, my legs wobbly and weak. I'm too sick to worry much about being caught—all I can focus on is moving my feet, planting one step after another in the crisp night air. I scan ahead for guards but don't see any. All I can hear is my own heavy breathing. I've marched miles and miles without much effort, but now I can barely force myself to cross the sleeping town to the train station. I collapse on the bench outside, waiting until morning. When the first train pulls into the station just as the sky turns pink, I clamber onto it, explaining to the conductor that I've been given a week's medical leave from my regiment. I look sick enough, so he doesn't doubt me. After I get out in Oberlin, Ohio, I stop at a dry-goods store and trade my watch for a dress, a gift, I explain, for my sister. Then I stumble into a rented room and sleep. The whole escape has happened in a feverish haze. I can't tell which part I've dreamed and which has really happened. All I know is that I need to see a doctor, and for that I'll have to turn back into a woman.

The next day, I take off the blue uniform I've worn so proudly for the past two years. I fold it up carefully, tracing my fingers around the familiar gold buttons. Then I do the unthinkable—I put on a dress for the first time in five years. As I stand in front of the mirror, I remember the moment when I first took off my dress, how freeing it felt. Now, putting on the heavy skirts, it feels like I'm caging my body and spirit. I've never thought of clothes as a prison before, but now I wonder why women wear dresses in the first place. The bony corset body holds my chest tight, making it hard to breathe, as if being a woman is meant to be suffocating.

The skirts seem intended to drag me down, making any movement unnatural and difficult.

Even in a dress I look like a boy, with my square shoulders, broad forehead, and short hair. I don't know how to lower my eyes modestly, how to giggle instead of guffaw, how to sashay instead of stride. I make an unconvincing lady, but good enough for the part I have to play now, a sick woman who needs medical attention.

I wrap a shawl around my short hair and totter down to the parlor of the rooming house, my legs unsteady though my feet are still sturdily shod in men's boots. My left foot is so misshapen from how it healed after the accident with the mule, it can't fit into a woman's narrow slipper. Besides, I draw the line at women's shoes—they make it too hard to walk or run or ride. The skirts cover my feet enough for me to get away with my old boots.

The owner of the rooming house, Mrs. Brown, a portly woman with a shelf of a bosom, looks up from her embroidery when I stumble in.

"Where did you come from? I don't recall renting a room to you," she wheezes. I brace myself for an interrogation, thinking of how to explain myself. But I can barely stand and my brain feels thick and heavy.

"Are you all right?" Mrs. Brown reaches for my arm. "You look terrible! Should I call a doctor?"

I collapse onto the poufy chair next to her. "I'm sorry to trouble you. My cousin, Frank Thompson, rented the room for me." The words spill out. I hope they sound plausible. "He's on his way back to his regiment, but he brought me here so I could get a doctor's care. Can you please send one to my room?"

"Certainly, my child, of course! And you are?" She peers at me over her half-moon glasses.

I gulp and sigh. "Sarah Emma Edmonds," I say.

There, I've done it. Even if it's only for while I'm getting cured, I'm Sarah again. The name feels almost as binding as the dress.

{ 28 WEARING A DRESS

EACH DAY LIVED AS A WOMAN SEEMS TO PASS TWICE AS slowly as normal. It was work to keep my male mask on, but now it seems much more natural than taking it off. I'm doomed to be neither fish nor fowl. Sometimes as I lie in my sweat-soaked bed, staring out the window at a wedge of sky, I wonder if the fever isn't a good thing, a purging of my errors, my lies, my weaknesses. When it's over, I'll be a finer, purer me. I'll know who I really am.

After the longest month I've ever lived, under the diligent care of Dr. William Bunce, I finally feel strong enough to rejoin my regiment. When I take my first walk outside, the air is fresher, the colors more vibrant, the sounds crisper than I remember. I move on unsteady feet, but I'm moving. The clip-clop of horses, the distant whistle of a train, the trill of birdsong are music to me. I admire the peeling paint on the barbershop sign, the rich black lettering on the window of the telegraph office. The world is new and sharp around me. It's time for me to rejoin the living, to become a man again.

As a woman, I let my hair grow (having told the doctor it was shorn because of lice), but once again I cut it close to my nape and unfold my old uniform. It's a tremendous relief to take off the cumbersome dress and put the familiar shirt and pants back on. I meant to write to Jerome, to tell him where I went, but I didn't want to get him in trouble should any officers ask him about my absence. Besides, it would be better to explain everything in person, now that I'm healthy again.

I repack my old knapsack, hesitating over the dress. Should I keep it, just in case, or get rid of it? I certainly don't plan on wearing it again. Still, leaving it in the room might seem suspicious. So I shove it in and tie up my pack, shouldering it easily and walking downstairs, enjoying the freedom of movement pants allow. It feels good to be back in my old skin again, and I'm eager to get back to my regiment.

I say good-bye to Mrs. Brown and stroll into the street, my limbs loose and easy, and head for the train station. As I near the low wooden building where I disembarked a month earlier, a poster on the station wall catches my eye. "WANTED!" it calls out in large letters. "FOR DESERTION! PRIVATE FRANK THOMPSON, FLED FROM THE SECOND MICHIGAN IN LEBANON, KENTUCKY." A brief description follows, and then the words "SHOOT ON SIGHT!" My stomach drops and the blood drains from my face. I never meant to desert. But how could I ever explain? I hurry back into town, pulling my cap down to hide my face. I run into the boardinghouse in a panic.

"Is something wrong?" Mrs. Brown asks as I rush in.

"I'm afraid I left something in the room. Can I go up and check?"

"Of course—here's the key back." Mrs. Brown hands me the silver key and turns back to her embroidery. "No need to hurry. I don't rent out rooms that quickly," she says, chuckling.

I force myself to walk calmly up the stairs, but my heart races. Do I have to stay a woman? I wrack my brain, but I don't see any other choice. Back in the room, I tear off the uniform and put on the despised dress, wrapping my shorn head in a shawl. Now the clothes are more than a prison— they're another disguise, cloaking me from the identity of a deserter. But how do I explain to Mrs. Brown that a man went up to check the room, yet a woman is leaving it?

Best not to say anything, I decide. I tiptoe down the stairs and lay the key on the parlor desk, sneaking behind Mrs. Brown, bent intently over her needlework. I slip quickly out the door, then stop, dazed in the street.

Where can I go? What can I do? I need time to think, to figure things out. I turn around and walk back into the boardinghouse for the second time this morning.

Mrs. Brown peers over her glasses. "Is that you, dear?

Your cousin was just here, looking for something you left in your room. You can probably still catch him if you go up now."

"Actually"—I push my mouth into a smile—"I've decided I need the room for another month. Is it taken yet?"

"Hardly!" Mrs. Brown says. "As I told your cousin, rooms don't rent that quickly. No need to hurry. It's yours as long as you want it. You can get the key from him."

"Thank you." I pick up the key, still lying unnoticed on the desk, and climb the stairs again. I have an idea of what to do next. I think of my old boss, Mr. Hurlburt. He won't hire me as a book salesman again, not now that I'm a woman, but he liked my army dispatches. He said they were popular with his readers, was always urging me to write more. Maybe it's time I did just that.

For the next few months I sit at my rented desk and write. I'm used to keeping a daily journal, sending out a regular dispatch, but this is different. I write to capture my life in the army, to make Frank Thompson real. I write to explain why I enlisted and what my time in the Second Michigan has meant to me. I write to sort out my feelings for the people I've met: Jerome and James, Colonel Poe and General McClellan; Alice, the Southern widow I captured, and Captain Logan, the confederate officer I shot; Damon, and the woman officer who had the baby, and all the soldiers I tended on the battlefield and in the hospital. I collect a jumble of impressions and work to weave them into a coherent story. I reread my journal for specific dates and battle plans, but mostly I rely on memory, shards of clear images, scents, and sounds.

At first, I spend all day in the room, leaving it only for meals in the boardinghouse dining room. Though I've convinced myself I can be my own kind of woman, I'm uncertain about other people's reactions. But the more I write about my life, the less I care about others' judgments.

After a week cooped up that way, I crave fresh air and enjoy a long stroll along the town's boardwalk, stopping to treat myself to tea and cakes. I feel the way I did so many years ago when I made my first sales call as Frank Thompson and sweated in my stiff collar, anxious that the lady of the house would see through my disguise. Now I sit at a small round table draped with a lacy tablecloth. Around me cutlery clinks and china cups rattle on their gold-rimmed saucers. I thump down the menu and place my order, no dainty gestures, no simpering smile, just simple and direct.

"Yes, miss," the girl in the apron and lace cap says, as if I were a perfectly normal customer, not the bull in a china shop that I feel myself to be.

When the steaming tea arrives with the gingery cakes, it feels like a minor triumph. I can do this. I'm a woman at last, my own kind of woman. I drink the tea the way I did in the army, noting how the other ladies favor small sips. I munch the pastry like the private I was, wiping crumbs off my mouth with the back of my hand, not dabbing delicately with a napkin like the women around me. And nothing happens. No heads turn to gawk. No fingers point accusingly. Instead, the aproned girl comes back to ask if I want anything else.

"No." I smile. "That will be all, thank you."

It's like that each time. No one considers me at all noteworthy. I stroll, run errands, buy things in shops. The more I write about my life, the bolder I become, starting up small conversations with clerks, chatting with the other guests in the boardinghouse. I miss the army, but in my pages I'm with the Second Michigan all over again, and their company gives me the encouragement to be the Sarah I wanted to be before Pa crushed my dreams.

When I'm finished, I have a slim manuscript, a memoir of my two years in the Army of the Potomac, dedicated to the sick and wounded Union soldiers. Nothing in the memoir describes my disguise or my need for secrecy. It's the story of a Union nurse and spy and the battles I experienced. I don't write about Jerome except as a fine fellow nurse. I barely mention James. I describe courageous soldiers and cowards, bloody battle scenes, and exhausting marches. I write about the contraband slaves who freed themselves, and I call for the end of injustice toward Africans. I write of my admiration for General McClellan and my disdain for General Burnside. I write about some of my spying missions and admit, after crossing out the paragraph several times, to shooting the surrendering Southern widow in the hand. I don't tell about being accused of desertion but instead write that I've taken a medical leave. I call myself Sarah now, but I can't write about myself that way. In the army I was Frank Thompson, a passionately patriotic young man, eager for adventure, and that's the character I play. Being a woman has nothing to do with my wartime story.

Now I just have to convince my old employer that Sarah Emma Edmonds was Frank Thompson, his best salesman and the author of the popular dispatches for his newsletter. Then I'll offer him my thrilling new book to publish.

Using my army pay tucked neatly into my new lady's reticule, I buy a train ticket to Connecticut, where my old boss still has his publishing office. Carrying my flower-print satchel instead of my old soldier's knapsack, I nearly trip over my skirts as I clamber into the carriage. A man in a bowler hat swoops up my bag with a gentlemanly smile before I can protest and heaves it onto the rack over the seat. I have no choice but to thank him, though really I want to scowl and bark at him to keep his hands off my things. Worse yet, he sits next to me and introduces himself, beaming at me with a smile that's both toothy and oily. It's a very long train ride.

Even with my hair grown out and wearing a dress, I figure there will be something familiar about the slim young woman who marches into Mr. Hurlburt's office at W. S. Williams & Co., Booksellers, in Hartford. I can tell that Mr. Hurlburt recognizes me as someone he's met before, but he can't quite place where. I smile, wondering if I should tease him about forgetting my name. He'll be flustered, sure it's on the tip of his tongue, but he'll never guess it.

"What can I do for you, miss?" he asks.

"I'm hoping you'll publish my memoir," I say, lifting a sheaf of papers from my satchel and setting it down on the counter between us.

"You look too young to be writing a memoir!" Mr. Hurlburt chortles. "Have you had a particularly interesting life so far?"

"You might say that." I lean forward across the counter. "Don't you recognize me?"

As I expected, his cheeks turn bright pink. "I'm terrible with names. Pardon me for not remembering yours, though I'm sure we've met." Mr. Hurlburt mumbles nervous excuses, saying he must be getting older, forgetting simple things like that.

"It's quite all right," I say. "After all, it's been more than two years since we last saw each other. I'm Sarah Emma Edmonds."

Mr. Hurlburt shakes his head, wobbling his jowls. "Doesn't ring a bell, I'm afraid."

"It wouldn't. When you knew me, I was Frank Thompson, your top salesman and army news writer. Now do you remember?"

"Frank?" My old boss stares at me, mouth open. "My God, Frank; is that really you? You were a woman all along?

I don't believe it!" His eyes boggle as the truth sinks in. "You were in the army? No, that can't be. It all sounded so real."

I grin. "It sounded real because it was. I wrote about what really happened. I was there."

Mr. Hurlburt takes off his glasses, wipes the lenses with a kerchief, and perches them back on his nose. He peers at me intently for a long minute.

"You were a handsome lad, but you're a much nicer-looking lady! You sure had me fooled! I would've sworn on a stack of Bibles that you were a boy—you were my best salesman! The most popular author in the newsletter! We got more mail about you than anyone else!"

"And now I've written you a book," I say. "You know I left your employ to enlist, and I've just spent two years in the Army of the Potomac, working as a nurse and a spy. There are lots of things I didn't write about for your news-letter, but it's all here. I've had more adventures than some of your wildest serials."

Mr. Hurlburt gapes again. "Well, that *is* a story!" He scans the first few paragraphs. "Hmmm, now, you seem to have left out something vital. Reading this, anyone would think you're a man."

"Everyone thought I was. That's the way I lived it, so that's the way I wrote it," I explain. "It worked for the dis-patches. It'll work for the book."

"The newspapers are full of stories these days about

women dressed as men fighting in this war, on both sides. There's a lot of interest in a story like yours."

My shoulders tense. It feels like Mr. Hurlburt is trying to take something away from me, the truth as I lived it. No one in the Second Michigan knew I was a woman, except for Jerome—and at the very last minute James. My sex shouldn't matter in terms of the story I'm telling. Isn't being a spy exciting enough? Do I have to appeal to prurient interest, to those wondering what kind of unnatural woman would disguise herself as a soldier? I want to publish a solid book, not sensationalist scandal-mongering.

Mr. Hurlburt strokes his chin, thinking. "I can see you're set on this, but I have an idea that could please us both. I'll publish your story, just as it is, but we'll give it a title that tells the readers what they should know to fully understand the import of your experiences. Let's call it *Unsexed, or The Female Soldier.* Now let me read this. Come back tomorrow. We can discuss terms then."

I hesitate, then nod. "I'll see you in the morning." I turn to go.

"Sarah!" the bookseller calls after me.

"Yes?" I pause in the doorway.

"You still walk like a fellow, you know."

"I know!" I bellow back over my shoulder. "And I still wear men's boots!" I smile all the way back to the hotel. If I can be a published writer, maybe it won't be so bad being a woman after all. I've learned that if I wear the simplest dresses, the ones without corsets and bustles, they aren't horribly confining. They still aren't easy for riding, but I keep a pair of trousers for that. I've faced rifles, cannon, sabers, and bayonets—damned if I'm going to let anyone tell me I can't wear pants on a horse.

The next day, Mr. Hurlburt offers to publish my book. I accept some money but ask that all the proceeds from the sales be given to the Sanitary and Christian Commissions for the care of disabled Union veterans. I remember the time at Malvern Hill when I brought food to the hungry troops, how satisfying that was. If the money from my book can feed and house my fellow soldiers, I feel that my deception will be forgiven.

I pause over the contract, the pen poised in my hand. The last time I signed a legal document was when I enlisted in the Army of the Potomac. I recall vividly that first time I put my name in ink on a page—writing it down made it real, made me Frank Thompson. Now I sign "Sarah Emma Edmonds" with the same flourish. That's who I am now, I think, that's me. It isn't a bad feeling.

Unsexed, or the Female Soldier becomes an overnight sensation and grows into the national seller I promised, selling more than 175,000 copies. My story is featured in newspapers. Photos of me in uniform are printed next to ones of me in a dress with my hair grown long and tucked into a bun. Other women's stories appear in the press, as more female soldiers in disguise are discovered, but as far as I know, I'm the only one who has been more than a soldier—I've been a nurse, a spy, a postmaster, and an orderly. I'm proud of the risks I've taken, honored to have served with the men of the Second Michigan. Even in a dress, I hold myself with dignity and pride—no sweet modesty for me. I'm Sarah Emma Edmonds, the woman who dressed as a man and fought bravely for the Union, and that is something no one can take away from me, something I will always be proud of.

{EPILOGUE
A SOLDIER'S
REUNION

MANY YEARS AFTER THE UNION WINS THE WAR, I WALK into Damon Stewart's dry-goods store in Flint, Michigan. Like Mr. Hurlburt, he doesn't recognize me, but I can see in his eyes that something about my worn face nags at him, familiar despite the gray hair and wrinkles. Of course, his hair is thinner and gray, too, and deep creases fan out from the corners of his eyes, but he looks as good-natured as ever.

"Can I help you, ma'am?" Damon asks.

"I believe you can." I smile. "Damon, you haven't changed a bit! It's good to see you—and you're doing so well, with your own store and everything!"

Damon scratches his head, puzzled. "I can see that you know me, ma'am, but I can't say I know you. Remind me where we met. And when."

"Well, it was nineteen years ago, so you can be forgiven for not remembering, but we spent a lot of time together then. In fact, we shared a tent for near two years." I pause. "I was Frank Thompson."

"Frank!" Damon goggles. "You're really Frank? I mean, you were Frank? I mean, he was you? Frank was a woman?"

"Didn't you call me your little woman?" I tease.

"But we didn't mean it!" Damon's mouth opens and shuts like a fish gasping for air, trying to make sense out of the incomprehensible.

"You always wondered why I didn't have a sweetheart. Now do you understand?"

Damon plops down heavily on the stool behind the counter and wipes his brow. "Just give me a minute, now. This is a lot to reckon with. If you were really Frank, you've got to prove it to me somehow."

"I could tell the story about how your leg wasn't amputated. Or the one about the nasty Rebel horse I gave to the chaplain. Or when General Kearney presented me with a Confederate sword."

"Glory be!" Damon holds up a hand. "I believe you— you must be Frank. You sure look like him—or at any road, his sister! What happened to you? I heard you deserted. I couldn't believe it."

"I didn't mean to. Do you have time for a visit now? I'll explain everything."

Damon nods. "Of course, sit down." He blushes just the way I remember him doing so many years ago. "You know I got married. To Virginia. I felt so bad about it, I couldn't tell you."

"To Virginia?" I hoot. "No wonder her letters got so cold and boring after you went home! I should have figured it out."

"It wasn't like that, really—I wouldn't have stolen her from you." Damon's cheeks are even pinker. "She said that things just weren't that way with you."

"Of course not," I agree. "But what about Polly? I thought she was your true love."

"I thought so too, but she up and married some other feller. Didn't even have the decency to send me a 'Sorry, Sweetheart' letter! That left me commiserating with her cousin, Virginia, and well . . ."

I reach over and put my hand on Damon's arm. "It's fine. I'm happy you two found each other. Obviously nothing could ever have happened between Virginia and me."

"Now I see that, but I felt so guilty about it, I could barely write you. Nor could she."

That explains all the talk of farming in Damon's letters and not much else. I thought he was just a poor writer, not someone hiding his own secret.

"Any children?" I ask.

Damon nods. "I have three strapping sons and one sweet daughter."

"I'm delighted to hear it, Damon. You deserve a fine family. And so does Virginia."

We pass the rest of the afternoon catching up on the last nineteen years. Damon left the farm after his marriage, taking over his father-in-law's store. It's a good, simple life. Whenever it rains, his leg and arm ache, reminding him of the old wounds, but the war seems like something that happened a lifetime ago. He knows he's one of the lucky ones, coming home with all his hands and legs, both eyes, no horrific scars.

I in turn explain why I left camp, how I tried to return but had already been branded a deserter. I sketch in the next years: writing the memoir, then the last years of the war working as a battlefield nurse—a woman this time—then going to college. After peace was declared, I moved to Louisiana to manage a home for the children of slaves whose parents had been killed in the Civil War, but the climate there was too hard on me—the old bouts of swamp fever grew more and more frequent until I had to move away. I finally settled in Kansas, where I live now, working on my old dream of building a home for disabled veterans.

"What about a family?" asks Damon. "Did you ever find that sweetheart you were looking for? I mean, a feller." He blushes again.

I smile sadly. "I did. I married a kind, good man who knew me when I was a girl back in Canada. Linus Seelye didn't mind that I wore men's boots and was better with a gun than he was. We had three children." I sigh. "The two boys didn't make it to a year. The girl died before she was six. The sorrow killed my husband."

"That's a heap of grieving," Damon says. We're both quiet, remembering all the people we've known who have died. Damon gently cups his hand over mine. "What brings you here now? Are you moving back to Flint?"

"No." I straighten my back and look levelly at my old tentmate. "I'm here because I need your help."

"For the feller who saved my leg, anything!"

"As far as the U.S. government is concerned, Frank Thompson deserted. I want to clear my name. It's been eating at me all this time that people think I was a coward. I'm applying for an honorable discharge and a pension as a legitimate veteran. For that I need affidavits from the soldiers who fought with me, attesting to my bravery and that Frank Thompson and Sarah Emma Edmonds are the same person."

Damon grins. "You deserve that, Frank, I mean, Miss Edmonds. I mean, Mrs. Seelye. I'll write to everyone I know—we'll get you that honorable discharge and the pension, too."

Damon is as good as his word. In my clapboard Kansas farmhouse I receive copies of the letters pouring into Congress from men in the Second Michigan. Doctors, nurses, General Poe, even James Reid sends an affidavit from Scotland, though he doesn't admit to ever knowing that Frank Thompson was a woman, a consideration I deeply appreciate. Other soldiers write that they heard rumors that Frank was really a female after I deserted. In fact, my abrupt departure was explained as a love story—supposedly I was following my tentmate, James Reid. We were said to be lovers, and when he left, I naturally followed. Reading those letters alone at the kitchen table, my cheeks flame red. I had no idea I was the subject of such vile gossip. I remember that last parting kiss with James and feel as horribly ashamed as I did when it happened. I never wanted to kiss him. We were friends, no more. How could people believe otherwise?

"It was idle talk, that's all, Sarah," Damon reassures me. We've rekindled our friendship, and I often go to see him. It's a long train trip and every penny matters, but I can't stay away long. It means a lot to have someone to talk with about those years. It keeps them alive for me, reminding me of who I'd been and what I'd done.

Of all the men who write in my support, testifying to my bravery, the one who matters most is silent. Damon says he doesn't know where Jerome ended up—the veterans of the Army of the Potomac have lost track of him.

The overwhelming goodwill behind the letters convinces Congress and President Chester Alan Arthur. It takes two years, but in the spring of 1884 two different congressional acts are passed, the first recognizing Sarah Emma Edmonds Seelye as Frank Thompson of the Second Michigan and granting me an honorable discharge and back pay. The second act grants me a pension as the only recognized female veteran of the War Between the States.

That bill reads in part:

Truth is ofttimes stranger than fiction, and now comes the sequel. Sarah E. E. Seelye, alias Franklin Thompson, is now asking this Congress to grant her relief by way of a pension on account of fading health, which she avers had its incurrence and is the consequence of the days and nights she spent in the swamps of the Chickahominy in the days she spent soldiering.

That Franklin Thompson and Sarah E. E. Seelye are one and the same person is established by abundance of proof and beyond a doubt.

When I get the news in an official telegram, I rush to take the first train to Flint, eager to share my triumph with Damon. I spend my last twenty dollars on the round-trip ticket, but now that I have a pension coming, I don't care.

"We did it!" I call, waving the telegram as I run into the store. "I'm official now!"

"Congratulations!" Damon cheers. "That means you can come to the reunion next month."

"What reunion?" I ask.

"A reunion for our old regiment. Here, in Flint. You

need to be a member of the G.A.R., the Grand Army of the
Republic, but now that you have an honorable discharge, all
you have to do is apply and they'll let you in."

"Are you sure? Maybe they won't want me because I'm
a woman." I've put so much time and effort—two years of
steady work tracking down comrades and sending materi-
als to Congress—that I'm not ready to face another bureau-
cratic ordeal.

"Let me take care of it," Damon insists. "You'll be at
that reunion."

Many women veterans have applied to the G.A.R., but
none have been admitted until my case reaches their office.
The piles of papers testifying to my service along with my
honorable discharge push them to give me a quick answer—
yes, they would be proud to muster me into their association.

That July I walk into the reunion, Damon at my side. The
talk in the hall all swirls around the name Frank Thompson.
"He's here!" "He's really a she!" "She's here!"

Richard Halsted, a private from our regiment, comes
up to me first, then General Poe, then Dr. Bonine. My old
friends crowd around, all eager to share some memory of
how I helped them, how grateful they are to me.

"You were the best orderly I had," General Poe says, his
voice thick with emotion. "I had no idea you were a woman,
Frank, none at all."

I grin. It's good to be called Frank again, and Poe isn't

the only one to lapse into using my old name. I don't correct them. In some ways, I'll always be Frank.

The crowd quiets down for the keynote speech by Colonel Handy. His remarks are the traditional sort of thing said at these reunions until he comes to the end of his talk. "I know you've all heard the story of the remarkable Frank Thompson," the colonel says. "He was a brave soldier who distinguished himself with uncommon daring as a postmaster, nurse, orderly, and even, I'm told, a member of the secret service. We all know now that 'he' was really a she. I'm proud and honored to introduce to you Sarah Emma Edmonds Seelye, alias Frank Thompson, your old friend and mine!"

Applause thunders through the hall. I'm swept up by my old comrades' support, buoyed by their affection. I stride to the dais, wearing men's boots as usual. I wave and wait for the roar to hush.

"My dear comrades," I begin, my voice breaking. I take a deep breath and start again. "I am proud and honored to be part of your company, this brave brotherhood. I've never met better men than those of the Second Michigan. You taught me what it means to be loyal, courageous, and compassionate. Without you, I never would have become the person I am today. Strange to say, but living among you, surrounded by men, I learned to become a strong, independent, proud woman."

"Frank! Frank! Frank!" The crowd chants and claps. I wave again, then turn and shake hands with Colonel Handy.

I step down into the crowd surging around me. Men thrust out hands to shake or simply smile and nod. It feels like I've truly come home. I'm back with the family that has always mattered most to me.

Out of the mass of people, a tall, dark-haired man approaches me. My stomach drops. I know without a doubt.

"Jerome," I say.

"Sarah." He smiles.

"I didn't know you'd be here. Damon said the veterans had lost track of you. And I never heard from you." I don't know what to say, where to begin. I run my eyes over his familiar face. He's older, yes—his dark hair is streaked with gray and the years have carved wrinkles on his face—but he's as handsome as ever. It's been two decades since I felt that familiar throb in my throat, that tingling warmth that being near Jerome has always sparked. So many years and the feeling is as strong as ever.

"It's good to see you, Sarah. I wanted to write to you when I saw your story in the newspaper, but I have to admit I was jealous like you thought. I was too hurt and angry to say anything for years." Jerome pauses, lowering his eyes. "I'm sorry."

"Sorry for what? I didn't write to you either. I was afraid you'd get in trouble if you knew where I'd gone when I left camp. I thought it was better to leave you out of it, but maybe I was wrong." I take Jerome's hand and press it warmly. "I've missed you all these years."

Jerome raises his eyes and pulls back his hand. "You don't understand. I'm sorry for the rumors. I'm the one who started them. When you left so soon after James Reid, I . . . I mean, I thought . . . Well, I knew you were a woman sharing his tent, so I assumed that you were lovers. I'm so sorry— I'm the one who told people you were a woman and had left to follow your lover. It was me."

"You!" I gape. And then from deep in my chest, laughter rumbles. I throw back my head and roar. Jerome watches, perplexed.

"I'm sorry," I gasp. "It's just so funny! You kept my secret for so long, and when you finally told people, you got it all wrong. Jerome, there was only one man I fell in love with in the army."

Jerome takes back my hand. "I know. I think I always knew." He stares at the floor, avoiding my eyes. "And I read your book, I saw what you said about me."

"You were a good nurse, a true friend, so that's what I wrote." But my head is buzzing. I hadn't imagined Jerome would read my words, that he would see me in all my faults, from the time I shot the Southern woman's hand to the time I fell off the mule. All the many mistakes I made. And all the things I did right. Getting food for the men at Malvern Hill. Helping the wounded off the troop train that had been ambushed. And of course all my spy missions.

I'm proud of who I was, who I am. I look Jerome in the

eye. "How have you been?" I ask. "How is Anna? Any children?" My hand is warm in my old friend's.

"Anna died, years ago, in childbirth. It was our first child, and the baby died, too."

"I'm so sorry." I read the lines of grief etched on Jerome's face. They mirror my own. "I lost three children myself. I guess I wasn't meant to have a family."

"Don't say that," Jerome says, raising my hand to his lips and kissing it, like I'm a real lady to him. Finally.

I smile slowly. I've waited so long for this moment and I want to savor it. All the fragments are coming together; the parts of myself I've closed off or shoved down are free now. It's taken many years, but I can be both Sarah Emma Edmonds and Frank Thompson. No more disguises for me. And no more secrets. Ever.

(TOP) SARAH EDMONDS, WITH HER HAIR CUT SHORT, DRESSED AS FRANK THOMPSON. SHE IS WEARING A MAN'S SUIT AND A BOW TIE. (BOTTOM) SARAH DRESSED AS A WOMAN, WEARING A DRESS, WITH HER LONG HAIR SWEPT BACK IN A BUN. (DATES OF PHOTOGRAPHS UNKNOWN.)

SARAH EMMA EDMONDS REALLY EXISTED, AND THE
bones of the story told here are all true, from disguising herself as a man to flee an arranged marriage to serving with
distinction in the Army of the Potomac. All the names used
here, from Damon Stewart to Jerome Robbins to James Reid,
belonged to actual soldiers who served with Sarah, and the
lines of their stories are all based in fact. I've used Jerome's
diary as a source, along with letters and journals of other
soldiers who served with Frank Thompson. The quotes from
Frank's diary and about her service and the congressional
acts are real. Some of the events, places, names, and statis-
tics that Sarah presents in her own writing have since been
proved to be inaccurate (granted, she couldn't be everywhere
at once, and she was in the middle of a war!), so I have taken
the liberty to stick to Sarah's version. However, the timeline
that follows is accurate.

Although more than four hundred women are known to

have dressed as men to fight in the Civil War, most of them were joining husbands, brothers, fathers, or fiancés. They had someone to help with their disguise and share the burden of their secret. Sarah Emma Edmonds was the only one known to have lived as a man before enlisting. Jennie Hodgers (or Hodgens), who also fought with the Union, lived her entire life as a man, which is a different kind of story. Sarah was the only woman to be recognized by acts of Congress as an honorably discharged soldier, with rights to back pay and a pension, and the only woman allowed to join the Grand Army of the Republic, the association for Civil War veterans.

In her memoir, she summed up what sustained her during the difficult battles and spy missions in the army:

> I am naturally fond of adventure, a little ambitious
> and a good deal romantic, and this together with
> my devotion to the Federal cause and determination
> to assist to the utmost of my ability in crushing
> the rebellion, made me forget the unpleasant items
> and not only endure, but really enjoy, the privations
> connected with my perilous positions. Perhaps a spirit
> of adventure was important—but patriotism was the
> grand secret of my success.

Among the letters written to Congress urging that she be given an honorable discharge, one, written by Major Byron Cutcheon of the 20th Michigan, described Sarah's bravery during the harrowing Battle of Fredericksburg, saying that she "rode with a fearlessness that attracted the attention and secured the commendation of field and general officers."

After leaving the army, Sarah married Linus Seelye. Although her children died as told in this book, her husband outlived her, as did two adopted sons. During their years together, she was said to wear the pants in the family, both literally and figuratively. Together they built the home for Civil War veterans that Sarah had dreamed of.

Sarah really went to the reunion for the Second Michigan and received a moving tribute, but there is no record of Jerome Robbins being there to hear it. She was mustered into the Grand Army of the Republic, the organization for Civil War veterans, after the second act of Congress and went to that reunion as well. I've conflated the two reunions here for dramatic purposes. The only part I've taken the liberty to invent completely is the final meeting between Jerome and Sarah. It seemed like something that should have happened, and the advantage of fiction is that you can choose the shape of the story.

The malaria that plagued Sarah ever since the Virginia Peninsula campaign caused her death in 1898 at the age of fifty-six. She was the only woman of her era granted a military funeral and is buried in a cemetery for Civil War veterans in Houston. Her headstone simply describes her as NURSE, the role she was proudest of.

UNION ARMY OFFICER BIOGRAPHIES

GENERAL AMBROSE E. BURNSIDE

A career military officer, Burnside took part in the Mexican-American War, although he arrived in Mexico after hostilities had ceased. He resigned his commission in 1853, turning his attention instead to manufacturing rifles, the Burnside carbine. He was named a brigadier general in the Rhode Island Militia at the outbreak of the Civil War. Because of his experience, he led a brigade in the Department of Northern Virginia, in the first Battle of Bull Run. After his initial ninety-day term of enlistment ran out, he was named brigadier general of volunteers and assigned to training the Army of the Potomac. He commanded the Coast Division in the early years of the war and did so well in his coastal campaign that he was promoted to major general. His forces were then moved to Virginia and became the IX Corps of the Army of the Potomac. When McClellan was removed from command of the Army of the Potomac, Burnside took over from him. Ordered by President Lincoln to take aggressive action after all of McClellan's wavering, Burnside led the Army of the Potomac at the catastrophic Battle of Fredericksburg. When he failed again with his "Mud March," the president replaced him with General Joseph Hooker, sending Burnside back to command the Department of the Ohio and his old troops in the IX Corps. Toward the end of the war, Burnside was blamed for the Confederate massacre of Union troops at the Battle of the Crater, near Petersburg, Virginia. Relieved of command, Burnside subsequently resigned his commission in 1865. He was later elected governor of Rhode Island, then U.S. senator. Besides giving the name "sideburns" to our lexicon in honor of his signature facial hair, Burnside served as the first president of the National Rifle Association.

GENERAL DARIUS COUCH

A graduate of West Point, Couch fought in the Mexican-American War and the Seminole Wars. He was appointed to garrison command after the wars and subsequently took a short leave to do scientific research in Mexico. When the Civil War broke out, he was named commander of the Seventh Massachusetts Infantry, first as a colonel, then a few months later as a brigadier general. He commanded a brigade in the Army of the Potomac, then was given divisional command in the VI Corps, working and training around the capital. He led his troops in the Peninsula Campaign and the Maryland Campaign, and was then put in charge of the II Corps for the Battle of Fredericksburg. His men supported the engineers who built the pontoon bridges across the Rappahannock River. Once over the river, his troops incurred very heavy casualties attacking the fortified Confederate positions on Marye's Heights and were forced to withdraw. After General Burnside was replaced by General Hooker, Couch continued to lead the II Corps in the Chancellorsville Campaign in Virginia. Unhappy with Hooker's failures in that battle, Couch requested reassignment and was moved to command of the Department of the Susquehanna. He then fought in the Western Theater as commander of a division in the XXIII Corps of the Army of the Ohio for the rest of the war.

MAJOR GENERAL WILLIAM B. FRANKLIN

A graduate of the United States Military Academy, Franklin served under General Philip Kearny in the Mexican-American War. Before the Civil War he worked as the engineer in charge of building the United States Capitol dome. With the declaration of war, he was named colonel of the 12th U.S. Infantry. Only a few days later he was promoted to brigadier general of volunteers. He subsequently became a corps commander in the Army of the Potomac, leading troops in the Peninsula Campaign, the Battle of Antietam (Maryland), and the Battle of Fredericksburg. General Burnside blamed Franklin personally for the disastrous defeat at Fredericksburg and suspected the major general of working to dismiss him from command. In retaliation, he had Franklin removed from field duty for months until he was reassigned to corps command in the Department of the Gulf. There Franklin led his men in the unsuccessful Red River Campaign and was wounded in the Battle of Mansfield, both in Louisiana. Put on a troop train with other injured soldiers, he was captured by Confederate partisans in a train ambush but managed to escape the next day, though his injury prevented him from returning to active duty.

GENERAL ULYSSES S. GRANT

A West Point graduate who fought in the Mexican-American War, Grant quickly earned a reputation as an effective commander, gaining control of most of Kentucky and Tennessee and commanding the Union forces at the pivotal Battle of Shiloh. While Generals McClellan, Pope, Burnside, and Hooker were largely meeting with failure in the east, Grant defeated five Confederate armies and led his troops to an impressive victory at Vicksburg, Mississippi. After his success in the Battle of Chattanooga, Tennessee, President Lincoln promoted him to lieutenant general, in charge of all the Union armies. In that position Grant fought the Confederate general, Robert E. Lee, in the spring of 1864 for control of Virginia in a series of bloody battles leading up to the long siege of Petersburg, Virginia. Finally, in April 1865, Grant broke the siege, capturing Petersburg and Richmond, Virginia, and running the remnants of Lee's army to ground at Appomattox Court House, effectively ending the Civil War after four bloody years. Grant was elected president in 1868 and served two terms.

GENERAL SAMUEL HEINTZELMAN

At the start of the war, Heintzelman enlisted in the 17th Pennsylvania Infantry and quickly became a division commander in the Army of Northeastern Virginia. Wounded in the first Battle of Bull Run, Heintzelman recovered and subsequently had command of units that included the Second Michigan Infantry. He went on to command the III Corps of the Army of the Potomac during the Peninsula Campaign and the second Battle of Bull Run. Afterward, he commanded the XXII Corps, which had partial responsibility for the defense of Washington, D.C.

GENERAL JOSEPH HOOKER

A career military officer, Hooker fought in the Seminole Wars and the Mexican-American War. After resigning from the regular army, he served as a colonel in the California militia. He had to borrow money to head east at the start of the Civil War; once there he requested a commission and was appointed brigadier general of volunteers. He commanded a brigade and then a division in Washington, D.C., under General McClellan, as the Army of the Potomac was being trained for battle. Hooker led the Second Division of the III Corps in the Peninsula Campaign, earning a reputation as a solid combat commander. When McClellan retreated at the end of the campaign, Hooker was transferred to Major General John Pope's Army of Virginia, where he led a division in the III Corps under Major General Heintzelman. Hooker took over command of the III Corps of the Army of Virginia after the Northern Virginia Campaign and the second Battle of Bull Run. His troops were renamed the I Corps and transferred back to the Army of the Potomac to face the Confederate troops in Maryland. Hooker pushed hard at Antietam, and his troops continued the assault even after he left the field, wounded in the foot. Once he had recovered, he was named commander of the V Corps for a short time, then promoted to lead both the III and the V Corps. Despite his protests at Burnside's suicidal decisions, he lost many men at the Battle of Fredericksburg. When Burnside was removed after the debacle, Hooker replaced him. He worked hard to restore the morale that had plummeted under Burnside's disastrous command but suffered a major defeat in the Battle of Chancellorsville, routed by the smaller Rebel army. Having lost confidence in the general's abilities, Lincoln replaced him with General Meade a few days before the Battle of Gettysburg in Pennsylvania. Hooker kept on fighting as a corps commander in the battles of Chattanooga and in the Atlanta Campaign. After Atlanta, Hooker spent the remainder of the war in command of the Northern Department, headquartered in Cincinnati, Ohio. Because of the ribald atmosphere of his headquarters, rumors spread that his name had become a slang term for a prostitute.

GENERAL PHILIP KEARNY

A captain in the Mexican-American War, Kearny was shot in the arm during a daring cavalry charge, and his arm had to be amputated. After leaving the army, he spent time fighting in Europe, with the Austrians against Italy and then with Napoleon III's Imperial Guard. He returned to the United States at the outbreak of the Civil War and was named brigadier general in command of the First New Jersey Brigade. Despite his disability, his troops performed strongly and he was given command of the Third Division of the III Corps, leading the men in the battles of Williamsburg and Fair Oaks. Kearny disagreed with McClellan's overcautious approach in the Peninsula Campaign. Nevertheless, Kearny continued to perform with distinction and was promoted to major general on July 4, 1862. Two months later he was killed in the Battle of Chantilly, Virginia. Courageous to the end, (he plunged into heavy fighting after telling his troops that "the Rebel bullet that can kill me has not yet been molded"), he refused Confederate demands that he surrender. Kearny was killed while trying to break through superior Confederate forces, having led his men from the front rather than from the rear.

GENERAL GEORGE McCLELLAN

A major general in the Civil War, McClellan organized the Army of the Potomac and acted as general-in-chief of the Union army. Although he managed to train and organize an army from scratch, his Peninsula Campaign was a complete failure. While he blunted General Lee's advance north in the Battle of Antietam, his careful approach and indecisiveness allowed Lee to retreat to Virginia when more aggressive action might have led to the destruction of Lee's army. Although he was deeply popular with the troops, President Lincoln no longer trusted him as a battlefield general. After being relieved of his command, he ran unsuccessfully against Lincoln in the 1864 presidential election on an antiwar platform.

GENERAL GEORGE MEADE

A career army officer and civil engineer, Meade served in the Second Seminole War and the Mexican-American War. In the Civil War he started as a brigade commander in the Peninsula Campaign and the Seven Days Battles. In the horrible Union defeat at the Battle of Fredericksburg, his division was the most successful. He was appointed to command the Army of the Potomac three days before Gettysburg. Although he won the battle, his hesitation allowed General Lee and the Rebels to escape back across the Potomac River into Virginia. He continued to lead the Army of the Potomac, but only under direct supervision of the general-in-chief, Lieutenant General Ulysses S. Grant.

COLONEL ORLANDO POE

L ike General Meade, Poe was a civil engineer. He organized volunteer soldiers from Ohio at the start of the Civil War and quickly joined Major General McClellan's staff in western Virginia. He was promoted to colonel and given charge of the Second Michigan Volunteer Infantry, leading them in the Battle of Yorktown and through the Peninsula Campaign. Right before the Battle of Fredericksburg, Poe was promoted to brigadier general, but the promotion was taken away the following spring, possibly as punishment for following General Franklin in that calamitous battle. He was demoted to lieutenant, then was quickly promoted to captain and transferred to the Western Theater as General Sherman's chief engineer of the XXIII Corps. He continued to serve as chief engineer for the rest of the war and oversaw the burning of Atlanta. After the war, he built many of the lighthouses on the Great Lakes.

MAJOR GENERAL JOHN POPE

A career army officer, Pope was named brigadier general of volunteers at the start of the war. He was given command of the District of North and Central Missouri under Major General John Fremont. Fremont suspected Pope of treachery, but incompetence was more likely the issue. Through his ability to manipulate press coverage, he impressed Fremont's replacement, Major General Henry Halleck, who appointed Pope commander of the Army of the Mississippi. His success in battles in Missouri and along the Mississippi River led to a promotion to major general. After McClellan's dismissal following the disastrous Peninsula Campaign, Pope was named commander of the Army of Virginia. After his own terrible failures in the second Battle of Bull Run, Pope was relieved of command.

GENERAL EDWIN SUMNER

A career army officer, Sumner was the oldest field commander on either side of the Civil War. He served with distinction on the western frontier in several Indian campaigns and in the Mexican-American War. With his booming voice and the legend that even cannonballs bounced off him (earning him the nickname "Bull Head"), he was the first general created for the new Union army. Despite that honor, he was immediately sent to California to replace Brigadier General Albert Johnston as commander of the Department of the Pacific for the first year of the war. Chosen to command the II Corps by President Lincoln himself, Sumner fought in the Peninsula Campaign and the Seven Days Battles. He did well in Virginia in the Battle of Seven Pines but was savagely criticized for his part in the Battle of Antietam. His divisions were among those massacred in the Battle of Fredericksburg. After General Hooker took over for General Burnside, Sumner asked to be relieved of duty. He died of a heart attack not long after.

A BRIEF CIVIL WAR TIMELINE

** Denotes battles and events in which Frank Thompson and/or
her regiment participated.*

► **DECEMBER 1860–FEBRUARY 1861:** Spurred by the election of
Abraham Lincoln as president, seven Southern states
secede from the Union—South Carolina, Mississippi,
Georgia, Texas, Florida, Alabama, and Louisiana.

► **FEBRUARY–MARCH 1861:** The seceding states form the Confederate
States of America, with Jefferson Davis as provisional
president, and begin seizing Union forts, customs houses,
and mints.

► **MARCH 4, 1861:** Abraham Lincoln inaugurated as president of
the United States.

► **APRIL 12, 1861:** Battle of Fort Sumter, Charleston Harbor,
South Carolina. The opening shots mark the military
start of what would come to be known as the War
Between the States.

► **APRIL–MAY 1861:** Inspired by the attack on Fort Sumter, four
more states join the Confederacy—Virginia, Arkansas,
Tennessee, and North Carolina.

► **MAY 1861:** Private Frank Thompson enlists in the Second
Michigan Infantry, Army of the Potomac.

► **JUNE 1861–MAY 1862:** West Virginia is created when the western
part of the state decides not to secede with the rest
of Virginia and is admitted into the Union as its own
separate state on June 20, 1863.

- **JUNE 1861:** Union navy sets up a blockade along the Southern coast.

- **JULY 21, 1861:** First Battle of Bull Run*, Manassas, Virginia (called the Battle of Manassas by the Rebels). Frank's first battle.

- **JULY 1861:** General George B. McClellan replaces General Irvin McDowell as commander of the Army of the Potomac following defeat at Bull Run.

- **FEBRUARY 6 AND FEBRUARY 11–16, 1862:** Union forces, led by Brigadier General Ulysses S. Grant, capture Fort Henry and Fort Donelson along the Tennessee and Cumberland Rivers in Tennessee.

- **MARCH 8–9, 1862:** In the first battle involving ironclad (armored) ships, the Union ship *Monitor* and the Confederate ship *Virginia* (originally a captured Union wooden ship called the *Merrimac*, which the Confederates had armored) fight to a draw at Hampton Roads in Virginia.

- **MARCH–JULY 1862:** General McClellan leads the Army of the Potomac on the Peninsula Campaign*, trying unsuccessfully to reach the Confederate government in Richmond and end the war quickly.

- **APRIL 1862:** Frank forages for provisions and takes a Southern woman prisoner after being shot at. Frank becomes a spy and goes on her first mission, infiltrating a Confederate camp at Yorktown.

- **APRIL 6–7, 1862:** Battle of Shiloh in southwestern Tennessee is the first major battle of the war, causing heavy casualties on both sides.

▸ **APRIL 1862:** Union navy captures New Orleans.

▸ **MAY 5, 1862:** Battle of Williamsburg*, Virginia, first heavy fighting in Peninsula Campaign.

▸ **MAY 1862:** Frank's second spy mission, disguised as an Irish peddler.

▸ **MAY 31–JUNE 1, 1862:** Battle of Fair Oaks*, Virginia. Confederate General Joseph E. Johnston is badly wounded. General Robert E. Lee takes over command of Confederate army. Frank acts as orderly for Brigadier General Philip Kearny and is bitten savagely by her horse. Kearny awards Frank a Confederate sword for her valor.

▸ **JUNE 12–16, 1862:** General J. E. B. Stuart's cavalry raid around entire Union army. Frank's train chases hijacked train.

▸ **JUNE 25–JULY 1, 1862:** Seven Days Battles*—Six major battles (and a couple of minor ones) fought over seven days near Richmond, Virginia, as part of General McClellan's Peninsula Campaign. Frank's friend Jerome is captured and paroled. Frank captures colt and almost rides into the enemy. Battle of Oak Grove; Battle of Mechanicsville; Battle of Gaines' Mill; Battle of Garrett's and Golding's Farms; Battle of Savage's Station; Battle of White Oak Swamp; Battle of Glendale; Battle of Malvern Hill

▸ **AUGUST 1862:** Army of the Potomac is ordered to assist General John Pope's Army of Virginia, leaving General McClellan without a command.

▸ **AUGUST 28–30, 1862:** Second Battle of Bull Run*, Virginia. Horrible Union defeat leads to General Pope being relieved of command, with General McClellan reinstated. Frank goes on a spy mission.

▸ **SEPTEMBER 1, 1862:** Battle of Chantilly*, Fairfax County, Virginia. Frank's regiment is in battle, but she misses it because of an accident with a mule. General Kearny is killed in battle. Frank goes on another spy mission.

▸ **SEPTEMBER 14, 1862:** Battle of South Mountain, Turner's Gap, Maryland.

▸ **SEPTEMBER 15, 1862:** Battle of Harpers Ferry*, West Virginia.

▸ **SEPTEMBER 17, 1862:** Battle of Antietem, Sharpsburg, Maryland. Frank goes on a spy mission, misses the battle.

▸ **SEPTEMBER 1862:** Frank is caught in an ambush. Her horse is shot from under her and she is left for dead.

▸ **NOVEMBER 7, 1862:** Due to his failure to pursue General Lee's army following the victory at Antietam, General McClellan is replaced by General Ambrose E. Burnside.

▸ **DECEMBER 11–15, 1862:** Battle of Fredericksburg*, Virginia.

▸ **JANUARY 1, 1863:** President Lincoln's Emancipation Proclamation goes into effect, freeing slaves in Confederate states not occupied by forces of the United States.

▸ **JANUARY 25, 1863:** After disaster at Fredericksburg and "Mud March," General Joseph Hooker replaces General Burnside as Commander of Army of the Potomac.

▸ **FEBRUARY 1863:** Frank goes undercover as a Southern cavalryman, stumbles onto a Confederate officer's wedding, and is forcibly recruited into his newly formed regiment.

- **MARCH 1863:** Frank works at a merchant's shop in Louisville, spying on Confederate spies. She helps train another Union spy in undercover techniques.

- **MARCH 3, 1863:** First Conscription Act is passed, calling for a general draft of all men aged twenty to forty-five, unless they can pay three hundred dollars or provide a substitute.

- **APRIL 20, 1863:** Frank falls ill and sneaks out of camp to recover under a doctor's care.

- **APRIL 30–MAY 4, 1863:** Battle of Chancellorsville, Virginia. Stonewall Jackson is mortally wounded by his own soldiers and dies on May 10, 1863.

- **MAY 19–JULY 4, 1863:** Siege and capture of Vicksburg, Mississippi.

- **JUNE 28, 1863:** General George Meade is named Commander of the Army of the Potomac, replacing General Hooker after his defeat at Chancellorsville.

- **JULY 1–3, 1863:** Battle of Gettysburg, Pennsylvania. The Army of the Potomac defeats General Lee, forcing his retreat to Virginia; combined with the fall of Vicksburg at the same time, the tide of war turns in favor of the Union.

- **SEPTEMBER 19–20, 1863:** Battle of Chickamauga, Georgia.

- **OCTOBER 16, 1863:** General Ulysses S. Grant is given command of all operations in the Western Theater.

- **NOVEMBER 19, 1863:** President Lincoln delivers the Gettysburg Address, dedicating a portion of the Pennsylvania battlefield as a national cemetery.

- **NOVEMBER 23–25, 1863:** Battle of Chattanooga, Tennessee.

- ▸ **1864:** *Unsexed, or the Female Soldier* by Sarah Emma Edmonds becomes an instant bestseller, selling over 175,000 copies. Later reprinted as *Nurse and Spy in the Union Army: comprising the adventures and experiences of a woman in hospitals, camps, and battlefields.*

- ▸ **MARCH 9, 1864:** General Grant is made commander of all Union armies. William Tecumseh Sherman takes over the western command.

- ▸ **MAY 5–6, 1864:** Battle of the Wilderness, Virginia.

- ▸ **MAY 10–12, 1864:** Battle of Spotsylvania Courthouse, Virginia.

- ▸ **JUNE 1864–APRIL 1865:** Battle and Siege of Petersburg, Virginia.

- ▸ **AUGUST 5, 1864:** Battle of Mobile Bay, Alabama.

- ▸ **SEPTEMBER 2, 1864:** Atlanta is captured by General Sherman after a month-long siege.

- ▸ **NOVEMBER 8, 1864:** President Lincoln is reelected, defeating General McClellan.

- ▸ **NOVEMBER 15–DECEMBER 21, 1864:** Sherman's March to the Sea, resulting in the capture of Savannah, Georgia.

- ▸ **DECEMBER 15–16, 1864:** Battle of Nashville, Tennessee.

- ▸ **JANUARY 31, 1865:** U.S. Congress approves the Thirteenth Amendment, abolishing slavery.

- ▸ **MARCH 4, 1865:** President Lincoln is inaugurated for his second term.

- ▸ **APRIL 1, 1865:** Battle of Five Forks, southwest of Petersburg, Virginia.

- ▸ **APRIL 2, 1865:** Confederate government abandons Richmond.

- **APRIL 4, 1865:** President Lincoln tours Richmond.

- **APRIL 9, 1865:** General Lee surrenders the Army of Northern Virginia at Appomattox Court House, Virginia.

- **APRIL 14, 1865:** President Lincoln is shot at Ford's Theatre.

- **APRIL 15, 1865:** President Lincoln dies. Vice President Andrew Johnson is sworn in as president.

- **APRIL 26, 1865:** General Johnston surrenders last major Confederate army in the east to General Sherman near Durham, North Carolina. John Wilkes Booth, Lincoln's assassin, is tracked down and killed after an eleven-day manhunt.

- **MAY 1865:** Remaining Confederate soldiers surrender. Over 620,000 men died during the four years of war, and over 50,000 survivors returned home as amputees.

- **JULY 1884:** Sarah Emma Edmonds Seelye, a.k.a. Frank Thompson, attends veterans' reunion in Flint, Michigan.

- **JULY 3, 1884:** Sarah Emma Edmonds Seelye is granted by an act of Congress an honorable discharge and any back pay due her as a private of Company F, Second Michigan. All charges of desertion are dropped from her record.

- **JULY 5, 1884:** Sarah Emma Edmonds Seelye is granted by an act of Congress a military pension of $12 a month as a war veteran.

- **APRIL 1897:** Sarah Emma Edmonds Seelye is mustered into the Grand Army of the Republic (G.A.R.), the veterans' organization for Civil War soldiers. She is the only woman to be so honored.

▸ **SEPTEMBER 5, 1898:** Sarah Emma Edmonds Seelye dies from malaria, the swamp fever that plagued her since the start of the Peninsula Campaign.

▸ **MEMORIAL DAY, 1901:** Sarah Emma Edmonds Seelye is reburied in the G.A.R. section of a cemetery in Houston, Texas, the only woman of the Civil War era to be given such an honor as a soldier and veteran.

SELECTED BIBLIOGRAPHY

FOR SARAH EMMA EDMONDS'S LIFE STORY, I RELIED ON her own memoir, *Unsexed, or the Female Soldier*, published first in 1864, reprinted as *Nurse and Spy* in 1865, as well as Sylvia G. L. Dannett's *She Rode with the Generals: The True and Incredible Story of Sarah Emma Seelye, alias Franklin Thompson*, Thomas Nelson & Sons, 1960; *The Mysterious Private Thompson: The Double Life of Sarah Emma Edmonds, Civil War Soldier* by Laura Leedy Gansler, Bison Books, 1970; *Where Duty Calls: The Story of Sarah Emma Edmonds, Soldier and Spy in the Union Army* by Marilyn Seguin, Branden Books, 1999; and numerous books on women in the Civil War as well as on the Civil War in general. The ones I drew on most were: *She Went to the Field: Women Soldiers of the Civil War* by Bonnie Tsui, TwoDot, 2006; *Women on the Civil War Battlefront* by Richard Hall, University Press of Kansas, 2006; *Women in the Civil War* by Mary Elizabeth Massy, introduction by Jean Berlin, University of Nebraska Press, 1994; *They Fought Like Demons: Women Soldiers in the American Civil War* by DeAnne Blanton and Lauren Cook, Vintage, 2003; *Women at the Front: Hospital Workers in Civil War America*, Jane E. Schultz, University of North Carolina Press, 2004; *Women in the Civil War: Warriors, Patriots, Nurses, and Spies*, edited by Phyllis Raybin Emert, History Compass, 2007; *Honor Unbound* by Diane L. Abbott and

Kristoffer Gair, Hamilton Books, 2004; *Spies and Spymasters of the Civil War*, Donald Markle, Hippocrene Books, 2004; *South After Gettysburg: Letters of Cornelia Hancock from the Army of the Potomac, 1863–1865*, Books for Libraries Press, 1971; *Letters of a Civil War Nurse: Cornelia Hancock, 1863–1865*, Bison Books, 1998; *Women During the Civil War: An Encyclopedia* by Judith Harper, Routledge, 2004.

ACKNOWLEDGMENTS

THERE ARE MANY PEOPLE WHO HELPED SHAPE THIS book and have earned my thanks and appreciation: Paul Kleven, for historical issues; Elias Stahl, for describing battle scenes; Diane Fraser, Penny Kramer, Danielle Sunshine, Eleanor Vincent, Joan Lester, Elisa Kleven, Thacher Hurd, Asa Stahl, Adrienne Boutang, Martine Boutang, and Rob Scheifer for storytelling in general. And most of all Sarah Emma Edmonds, an inspiring force to me still.

{READING GROUP GUIDE

1 *A Soldier's Secret* is the fictionalized account of an actual person's life. Do you prefer reading about history this way? Why or why not?

2 Sarah has several different jobs while serving in the Union army—nurse, postmaster, and spy. What qualities does she possess that make her well suited for these roles?

3 Early in her service, Sarah becomes close to her fellow nurse, Jerome. What does their friendship mean to Sarah, and how does it change her view of herself? Why doesn't Jerome betray her secret?

4 Some of the best relationships Sarah has throughout her life are with animals. Why do you think she makes such strong connections with her horses?

5 When Ambrose Burnside takes control of the Union army, his strategy leads to heavy casualties at the Battle of Fredericksburg. Later, General William Franklin and General Orlando Poe are both punished for refusing to advance in order to protect their men. Do you think the two generals were right to do what they did, or should they have followed the orders of their commanding officer?

6 During one Independence Day, Union and Confederate soldiers meet during a planned ceasefire to celebrate. Why was it important to have rules of civil warfare, like parole for prisoners and brief truces to bury the dead? How do you think these practices affected Sarah's choice to treat wounded enemy soldiers?

7 Several times during her career as "Frank Thompson," Sarah has to requisition food and medical supplies from Confederate townsfolk who don't support the Union cause. Do you think this is fair, even if Frank paid them for their goods?

8 On one of her requisition missions, Sarah shoots a woman in the hand, and, later, she regrets it. Was she right to fire in retaliation? Give examples from the text that argue both sides.

9 Author Marissa Moss uses tangible details to make the war more immediate. Think of some examples of her sensory writing—dealing with sight, sound, scent, touch, and taste—and list them. What made the biggest impression on you?

10 As Frank, Sarah could do many things that a lady of the time was not allowed to do. Are there things today that a woman can't do but a man can, and vice versa? If you could pass as the opposite gender, what would you do?

11 How does Sarah's position as a woman—from her life at home to her disguised army days—make her more sympathetic to the slaves she encounters? What experiences motivate her to fight for their freedom?

12 This book is pieced together using Sarah Edmonds's real journal entries and other primary-source documents. Did this book inspire you to look up these original sources? Are you curious to do research on your own about other female war heroes, like the Union nurse Clara Barton?

13 Throughout the book, soldiers have conversations with each other about their motivation for enlisting. What were soldiers from the North fighting for? What about soldiers from the South? Do their reasons change as the war goes on? How did slavery factor into their respective causes?

14 Sarah mentions that escaped slaves are called "contrabands," which is a word normally used to describe stolen or illegal goods. Based on what you know of the United States at that time, why were slaves seen as property and not as people? How could vocabulary contribute to their dehumanization?

15 Both sides—Union and Confederate—underestimated the time and effort needed to fight the Civil War. What were some of the consequences of this thinking? Were soldiers right to desert, given the conditions?

16 Sarah tells her story in the first person—meaning that the reader sees the war through her eyes. Do you think she is a reliable narrator? What biases might she have that separate this book from a strictly factual account?

{ABOUT THE AUTHOR

MARISSA MOSS HAS WRITTEN AND ILLUSTRATED MANY books for children, including the popular Amelia's Notebook series; the picture book *Nurse, Soldier, Spy*; and a middle-grade novel, *The Pharaoh's Secret*. She lives in Berkeley, California.